**Kate Eberlen** is the author of *Miss You*, which was a Radio 2 Book Club choice 2016 and a Richard and Judy Book Club choice 2017, *Only You* and *Ever After*. Her novels have been published in thirty languages worldwide. She lives in London.

*Also by Kate Eberlen*

Miss You
Only You
Ever After

# Life Begins

## Kate Eberlen

ORION

An Orion paperback

First published in Great Britain in 2025
by Orion Fiction, an imprint of The Orion Publishing Group Ltd
Carmelite House, 50 Victoria Embankment
London EC4Y 0DZ

An Hachette UK Company

The authorised representative in the EEA is Hachette Ireland,
8 Castlecourt Centre, Dublin 15, D15 XTP3, Ireland (email: info@hbgi.ie)

1 3 5 7 9 10 8 6 4 2

A CIP catalogue record for this book is
available from the British Library.

ISBN (Mass Market Paperback) 9781 3987 1216 4
ISBN (Ebook) 9781 3987 1217 1
ISBN (Audio) 9781 3987 1218 8

Typeset at The Spartan Press Ltd,
Lymington, Hants

Printed in Great Britain by Clays Ltd,
Elcograf S.p.A.

MIX
Paper | Supporting
responsible forestry
FSC® C104740
www.fsc.org

www.orionbooks.co.uk

For Rod McNeil,
who introduced me to Umbria

# Prologue

## Saturday 29 October 2022

There was an empty seat on the plane.

Fastening their seat belts, they all kept glancing at it, unable to believe that one of the party was no longer with them.

It was still early in the morning for conversation. Most of them were too hungover to understand what had happened. How could everything have changed so much in just one week?

# Chapter One

## *Jessica*

## Friday 21 October 2022

The crimson leaves of the cherry tree, luminescent in the thin autumnal sunshine, gave Jessica a shot of joyful optimism, just as its froth of pink blossom always did in spring.

As she started walking up the street, she felt her phone vibrate in her pocket, but hesitated before answering it as Mandy's name appeared on the screen.

'Are you doing anything this weekend? Kids are missing you . . .'

'Bless!' She loved Mandy's kids, sometimes more than Mandy appeared to.

'Thing is, it's Keith's work do and the babysitter has—'

'I would if I could, but I can't,' Jessica interrupted her. 'Off to Italy tomorrow for a week.'

'You never said. Is it work? Are things picking up?'

Mandy was like a big sister to her. In a good way, mostly. But there were times Jessica didn't like the fact that she knew her so well, because she found it impossible to lie to her.

'Just trying out a new place on the border of Umbria and Tuscany. Might be a venue for small weddings.' That was all true. Perhaps she would get away with it.

'Trying it out with who?'

It was as if Mandy could see right into her brain even though she was miles away in Milton Keynes.

'A few friends.'

'Robin?'

'Yes, he'll be there. I'm actually just on my way to meet him to finalise arrangements.'

She always said *actually* when she was nervous.

'Well, actually, I won't keep you then,' said Mandy.

It wasn't just about the babysitting. Mandy did not approve of Robin. Jessica knew she was only trying to protect her, but Mandy didn't understand their bond. If she knew him, she would, but Jessica had never quite had the courage to put it to the test by introducing the two of them.

The four faces of the Victorian clock tower at the top of Highbury Hill were each showing different times, only one corresponding approximately to her watch. Usually she enjoyed the momentary kick of thinking she was running late, followed by the relief of realising she wasn't. Just recently though, these fluctuations of adrenaline had begun to feel like regret for minutes not properly lived. The clocks were about to go back. There was a musty chill on the air. In a couple of weeks, it would be too dark to go for a walk at this time. She couldn't quite shake off the jarring sensation the conversation had left her with. Deliberately lifting and releasing her shoulders, she reminded herself that tomorrow she was going to be jetting off to Italy with her love.

For once, an event she had organised was going to be purely for pleasure, not business, although if the house was as good as it appeared on the website, it might well work for weddings as there was a deconsecrated church attached.

Italy was where everyone wanted to go now. Before the pandemic, her high-end clients were tending to favour a cool Scandi experience, but then there was Stanley Tucci's series and nobody had to pretend to like moss or sea lettuce anymore. Tuscany was already one of the most popular destinations for weddings, and she was discovering the appealing possibilities of other regions too. Recently she'd organised glamping on a Prosecco vineyard for the hen party of an influencer, with a Ferrari festival on Capri for the stag. She was currently costing a corporate team builder involving rowing the Vogalonga in Venice. Hopefully, Umbria would inspire some art-themed activities. Who didn't want to set up an easel with a spectacular view after *Landscape Artist of the Year*?

Bus or walk? It was mad to be worried about the fare compared to the restaurant bill she would be paying later, but she was trying to cut down in any way she could. Since going it alone with her events planning business, she missed the cushion of an expense account, and she was still paying off the debts she'd incurred during lockdown. The only inflation she'd known before was house price inflation, which had made her feel rich, not poor. She'd never really believed warnings about high interest rates, which seemed to belong to a long-ago era, as out of date as faxing and landlines. Now the cost-of-living crisis was at the top of every news bulletin. While she claimed to love working from home, she was already missing an office environment that was heated in the physical sense. It wasn't yet the end of October but her flat already felt cold when sitting at a computer for long periods. She'd spent most of the day preparing for any upcoming power cuts by researching torches and oversize fleecy poncho things, adding and removing from her online basket as she weighed the comfort of cosiness against the potential horror of accidentally answering the door in the sort of garment worn by people who watched too much daytime television, eating snacks and never rising from the sofa. Aside from her online Italian lesson, the only real buzz of achievement she'd got was when she'd passed the test to prove she wasn't a robot.

Jessica decided to walk. Her step count was nowhere near ten thousand and exercise would be a good way of releasing the pent-up tension, although recently she'd read that there was something called stresslaxing which meant relaxing that stressed you more because you weren't working on what made you stressed. Like so many of the newly diagnosed conditions she'd clicked on, she hadn't known it was a thing, but it exactly fitted what she was feeling.

On Upper Street, she deliberately avoided glancing at the exquisitely understated rings in the window of Dinny Hall. She couldn't imagine him going down on one knee to propose, but perhaps the moment might be finally approaching when it would become obvious that they ought to spend the rest of their lives together. She crossed the fingers on both hands, trying to shoo away the thought from her mind for fear of jinxing it.

There was a perfume advert on television that asked, 'What would you do for love?' In it, the actress was prepared to put on a couture dress, drive a car filled with artificial flowers, wear a headscarf and lie in a sunny meadow. It didn't seem like that much of a sacrifice compared to all the hours and money Jessica had invested in organising the perfect birthday treat for Robin.

Their place was a brasserie about as close as you got to Paris in London. Robin was a man of habit, which she put down to him to being at boarding school from a cruelly young age. An interior designer friend of his had overseen the redesign a few years ago, so he'd been invited to the opening and taken Jessica as his plus one. They'd been coming every Friday evening since, except for the month he'd been in a play in a south London pub. During the early weeks of lockdown, they'd sometimes met there illegally while Robin walked Lammie, sitting at either end of a bench in the small park opposite, a screw-top bottle of wine between them, staring at the empty windows like three pining, faithful dogs.

Jessica was among the first to book an outside table when restaurants reopened, but as soon as they were fully vaccinated, they'd returned to their usual booth near the bar. Despite perusing the menu every time, remarking on any new dishes and wavering over the plat du jour, they always chose the same thing. Steak frites for him, a salad for her because she knew she should eat more vegetables but couldn't be doing with the faff of preparing them at home. She always stole most of his perfectly salted French fries. Usually one bottle of Côtes du Rhône became two. There had been occasions when a third had appeared on the bill that neither of them could remember ordering.

Friday evenings were what she lived for.

Jessica had loved Robin from the moment their eyes met across a crowded room at the freshers event on her first evening of university when she'd spotted him picking up two glasses of free wine, indicating with a little entitled gesture to the bartender that he was taking one for a friend. Surveying the crowd, he'd suddenly smiled at her and she'd felt a giddy rush of privilege at being chosen. He'd downed the first glass and half of the second by the time he reached her. Flummoxed by his astonishing good looks, she had found his greed more than reasonably hilarious.

'You've got a great laugh,' he'd said. Then, looking around the room, 'Anyone else here you want to meet?'

She hadn't been sure whether he was offering to introduce her, or finding the crowd as underwhelming as she did.

'Scram?' he said, before she'd decided on an answer.

They'd bought a couple of bottles from a supermarket and taken them back to her room, where they'd sat at either end of her single bed exchanging the versions of themselves they'd like to be. She'd never met anyone as posh as him before, but he had such a mischievous quality he didn't seem threatening at all. They'd both spent some of their childhood in institutions and were used to inventing games to pass the time. So when he asked her what she would be if she were a fruit, she immediately replied a pomegranate, because although it didn't look much from the outside, it opened to reveal a complex range of exotic flavours inside. He'd claimed to be a strawberry – superficially pretty, but with nothing in its core. They'd laughed a lot.

In the middle of the night, she had woken to find his foot in her face. His sock had a pattern of Bart Simpson faces that didn't quite compute but made her feel less awestruck. The next morning, she opened her eyes and found herself alone, wondering if she had dreamt him until she saw the two bottles in the wastepaper bin, the glasses washed and placed upside down on a tissue beside the sink alongside a note with a mobile phone number. It was 1999. Not everyone had mobile phones then. She bought her first one that day, a pay-as-you-go Nokia. His was the only number in it for ages, so every time it rang she had the same leap of excitement as when she'd first seen him.

They lived in each other's pockets, laughing at the same things, renting the movies they loved so often they knew the lines off by heart, linking arms on the way back from the pub, often sharing a bed, but always when they were too drunk to do anything other than sleep. After a few weeks, she worried that they had passed that crucial moment of becoming too close to want to risk the friendship with sex. It was an excuse men had given her occasionally before, but raising the idea of sex seemed to have finished off the relationship anyway. She wasn't going to make that mistake again. In her worst moments, she told herself that someone as beautiful as Robin couldn't possibly find her attractive. It crossed her mind that he might be asexual or even gay, but then he snogged a woman at a Halloween party and disappeared without saying goodbye. A gaping void of devastation kept Jessica awake all night, but was instantly replaced with joy when he knocked on the door early the following morning.

'Can you hide me from the witch?'

'Why?' she'd asked.

'It was like waking up with Santa Claus,' he'd said, describing the close-up view of the girl's downy facial hair.

Jessica knew she shouldn't laugh. She wondered if she should even like someone with such a questionable attitude to women. But she took the first opportunity to excuse herself and have a very close look at her upper lip in the bright light of the communal bathroom down the hall. When she returned his smile was incredibly winning.

'Sorry,' he said.

'What for?'

For a moment, she'd thought he was going to kiss her.

'Abandoning you to all those rugby players! Bet you had more fun than me, though.'

Had she inadvertently given him the wrong signals?

He'd thrust a brown paper bag at her. It contained two croissants.

'Put the kettle on, Coco!'

They were so close they'd even developed their own pet names, as couples do.

When she was a little girl, Jessica's mother had scraped her unruly hair into a topknot, which had led to the nickname Coconut. That had quickly been shortened to Coco, which she had hated. It had been a relief to go to a senior school where nobody knew her and she could recreate herself as Jessica. Unfortunately, there were several Jessicas in her class and, as she was tall, she became known as Big Jessica. By then it was too late to revert to Coco, which seemed much cooler to a fashion-conscious teenager than it had for a serious six-year-old. She had revealed all this to Robin after he had confessed that he hated Robin and always secretly hoped that someone would shorten it to Beau.

'My brothers always called me Robbo, and my nickname at school was Beauty. Only because my best friend Tim was, I'm afraid, well, not the best-looking . . . so we were always known as Beauty and the Beast.'

'Gosh! Beau!' The name suited him perfectly.

Three thousand seven hundred and twenty-two steps.

He was already in the restaurant scrolling through his WhatsApp messages. Mandy said that there were some men who were too handsome for their own good. Apparently it made them lazy emotionally. Like a lot of Mandy's opinions, the warning was categoric, as if based on long experience, although it clearly wasn't something she'd had to worry about with her own husband Keith.

From a distance, Robin looked as boyishly beautiful as he had at eighteen. When she had first known him, people would literally turn in the street, assuming he must be someone famous, which he had actually been for a few months at the beginning of the third year. Closer up, there were a few lines. How could there not be, with someone who laughed so much? He was no longer able to get into skinny black jeans, but he wasn't overweight despite the quantities of food and alcohol he consumed. The hairline was a little further back when he raked a hand through his floppy Hugh Grant-style hair, but his eyes were still that endless blue that seemed to draw her in. He was just gorgeous, despite the uneven stubble around his chin. His inability to grow a beard when absolutely every other man his age had one had become a bit of an obsession for him, the reason he gave himself for not getting work. Privately Jessica thought it was more about poor choices and – Mandy was probably right – laziness. Ascribing his lack of success to a sparsity of facial hair was probably easier than the preparation and organisation it took to get to auditions, especially when you'd lost confidence. What Robin really needed was someone who believed in him. If they were together, she would enable him to capitalise on the gifts and opportunities life had given him. Enabling was what she was good at.

As she approached the table, he suddenly looked up, awarding her that sparkling focus that made her feel like she was the only person in the world, then stood and gave her such a close hug it made her heart beat faster.

'Thank god you're here!' he said, finally releasing her. 'You're the only person speaking to me. I've no idea what I've done wrong.'

'What do you mean?'

'I sent everyone a WhatsApp about getting together for my birthday and not a single person has replied.'

Inwardly, Jessica smiled.

'Oh dear,' she said. 'Perhaps they're busy.'

'I offered to cook, and everything . . .'

Unable to bear his disappointment any longer, she delved into her bag and produced an envelope with 'Beau' written in large bubble letters she'd spent an afternoon filling in with little symbols of their friendship.

'What's this?'

He ripped it open without even glancing at her illustration.

'Surprise!' she said.

She'd tried to devise a way of getting him to the venue un-awares, but the feat of organising a surprise party in a different country involved so many variables it was beyond even her. However, in her determination to keep ownership of the reveal, she'd employed all her powers of persuasion to cajole and threaten the other participants into keeping the secret until the last possible moment.

He stared at the card she'd had custom-made with the view from the house featured on the website, then opened it.

'Dearest Beau,' he read. 'Happy Birthday! Life begins at forty . . .'

'It was delayed by Covid . . .' she said, in answer to his raised eyebrow. She'd been planning it for two years. Originally for his actual fortieth birthday, but that had been cancelled because of the pandemic, and things were still dodgy with travel a year later. The virus had surged again recently, which had worried her, but they were all vaccinated and the curve of the graph seemed to be descending from a much lower peak than had been the case the year before.

'To celebrate the beginning of your life,' he continued, 'you are invited to Italy for a week of partying with your favourite people. In a region known for its produce, you will wine, dine and dance the week away. Timetable: Saturday 6 a.m. Meet Stansted Airport for 8.20 flight . . . Oh my god, Coco, I don't think I can . . .'

'Don't worry, your passport's renewed.'

'What, how did you know?'

'It's my job to know . . .'

'So this is why none of them have got back to me?'

'Yup. Sorry!'

She watched his frown turn to relief as his brain clicked through a series of things that hadn't quite made sense at the time but now did.

'Bloody hell!'

It wasn't quite the reaction she'd hoped for.

'You are pleased?'

'Of course! Just trying to work out how you did it!'

'I thought about all the things you love most, and it was obvious . . .'

Now, she scrolled through the photos of the villa saved to her phone, wondering which to win him over with first: the beautifully appointed kitchen with a huge island work surface with strings of garlic bulbs and chilli peppers drying above, a long wooden dining table seating twelve. The slate-grey infinity pool with its view of the surrounding mountains. Eventually, she tapped the interior of the deconsecrated church with original frescoes, now the perfect party room, with a piano, sound system, loads of space to dance and play games.

'Wow!' he said.

It still wasn't the reaction she'd anticipated. Her selling skills clicked automatically into action.

'The pool's heated. They usually turn it off at the end of September, but I've persuaded the caretakers to keep it on. There's a huge lawn with a five-a-side net for George. It's just been the grape harvest, so we can taste the local wine, and it's truffle season, so I've organised a foraging trip. A cookery lesson with a local chef. There couldn't be more fresh produce – there's a market in Città di Castello, where there are actually vans selling hot porchetta panini . . .'

She felt strangely like she was pedalling fast on a stationary bike.

'Speaking of which . . .' Robin picked up the menu, as the waiter arrived to take their order, perusing it for a few seconds as if there was a decision to be made.

'I think I'll have the steak frites,' he told the waiter.

'The superfood salad. For a change,' she added.

'Côtes du Rhône OK for you?' he asked her.

Occasionally she wondered if they did see things in exactly the same way.

Then Robin suddenly gave her his most sparkling smile and

13

repeated, as if he'd only just heard the words, 'Hot porchetta panini! Yummo! Who's coming?'

'Ellis, George and Laura, obviously. And Tim. And Jonny . . .'

'Who's Jonny?'

'His new boyfriend, apparently.'

'He never told me he had a new boyfriend.' Robin frowned.

'I think it's only recent. American . . . obviously I couldn't check with you . . .'

It hadn't occurred to her that Robin wouldn't have known. She wondered if she'd agreed too readily to Tim's request.

'And the brothers?' he asked.

'Of course.'

They had to be included on the list of invitees because it was a tradition in his family, probably left over from the days they were all at school and their parents were in some distant foreign country. They were going to be in a separate wing with their wives. She had made it quite clear to them that the two sections of the house were rented as independent entities.

'So it will be eleven of us?' Robin scrolled through the photos. 'Unless you're bringing someone?' Robin asked her.

'No!'

'No random stone carvers?'

Why had she ever told him about Jake? He was just someone she'd met through work. She'd thought there was a spark, but that hadn't turned out to be the case when he came to London. Robin had found the whole episode unduly hilarious.

'What an amazingly generous gift, Coco!' he said, but her delight at this delayed response was slightly tarnished by worry that he'd got the impression she was shelling out for the whole thing.

'Actually, I'm paying for you and me, but I'm expecting Tim to cough up his share . . .'

Now it sounded perversely as if she was being mean. His

14

perplexed frown told her that he hadn't registered any of her struggles with the business. Robin really had no idea about the restrictions that having to earn your living put on your life. He wasn't excessively rich, as his brothers were, but none of them had ever had to worry. It didn't occur to them that other people might not be in the same position.

In her opinion – not that she'd ever voiced it – the trust fund had held Robin back, and landing a role in a film that became a minor cult success at the smaller festivals when he was still a student had reinforced his assumption that everything in life would be given to him with no need to work at his craft. There had been a moment around the millennium when he had been everyone's pin-up, appearing on *Graham Norton* and in fashion shoots in the Sunday supplements. At the age of twenty, he'd abandoned university and flown to LA, where, courted by agents and directors, he'd been persuaded to star in a sci-fi movie with a mega budget. He had often called her in the middle of the night not realising, or caring, what time it was, regaling her with hilarious anecdotes about parties he'd been to. Then the film had been cancelled amid a flurry of caustic comments about his lateness and incompetence. Like a shooting star, he had shone brightly for a very short time and vanished. When she'd next seen him, his circumstances had changed dramatically.

Robin poured the rest of the bottle equally between their glasses.

'I don't suppose we should have another, should we?' he said. 'Or we'll never be up in time. I'll need to pack . . .'

'That's unbelievably sensible of you.'

'We are forty-two, Coco! God, that sounds so old! I still feel exactly the same as I did when I was twenty . . .'

'Do you?'

'Absolutely! Don't you?'

15

'Of course I do!' She stared into his eyes, trying to fathom if he was implying that he remembered their conversation on New Year's Eve, 1999.

He'd been just about to depart for Los Angeles.

They'd gone down to the Thames to see the fireworks. The Millennium Wheel had only just taken its place on the London skyline. The crowds were buzzing with excitement as the seconds to midnight ticked down. Then Big Ben began to strike the hour and there was cheering all around them. They'd had to shout to hear each other.

'Happy New Year, Coco!'

'Happy New Life in LA!'

'I don't know what I'm going to do without you!'

'You'll meet amazing people!'

'No one like you. I honestly don't know how I'll survive. I love you so much. I know, let's get married!'

'Married?'

'When we're forty or something, if neither of us has found anyone suitable,' he shouted. 'Deal?'

'Deal!' she'd screamed back.

Then the chorus of 'Auld Lang Syne' had started and they'd grabbed each other's hands, bobbing up and down with the people next to them while gazing up at the fireworks, which weren't nearly as spectacular as everyone had hoped because of the low covering of cloud, but she'd been so happy it had felt as if the bursts of light were fizzing and popping inside her.

'See you tomorrow, then!' he said, as they came out of the brasserie onto the pavement, grasping her shoulders as if to look at her properly, his head slightly inclined, his eyes holding hers for so long it felt as if he was gazing into her soul, before eventually drawing her into a brief hug. She watched him walking away, cupping the air beside her ear as if to keep his kiss there, then let out a long sigh as if she'd been holding her breath the entire evening.

Walking home would take her beyond seven thousand steps, but there was going to be plenty of walking in Italy, she thought as she waited for the number 19, resisting the temptation to shake up her step count.

There was a seat right at the front of the upper deck. She loved being up there, especially at night, glimpsing other people's lives through illuminated windows, like scenes from a soap opera fast-forwarded. Maybe, just maybe, drama was about to happen in her own life. A week together in a romantic setting. Anything could happen.

She tried to stop herself thinking about how Mandy had ended their call.

'You'd be a useless lab rat.'

It was a comment that had felt hurtful on a number of levels, but Jessica had still asked, 'Why's that then?'

'You never bloody learn, do you?'

# Chapter Two

## *Laura*

The hollow acoustics of the empty school after everyone had left made Laura's footsteps echo. She imagined a close-up of her shoes walking down the corridor, like the beginning of a crime drama. Heels were always a mistake at work, especially the shiny black stilettos. There had been more teaching than she'd expected because several of the younger staff had called in with Covid. She hoped for everyone's sake that it was an excuse to allow them to get cheaper flights rather than the beginning of another alarming upsurge. None of the kids had dared say anything to her face, but she'd been in the profession long enough to have 360-degree hearing and did not relish being described as fit by adolescent boys.

Laura stopped walking, aware of Rachmaninov coming from the hall. She'd thought she was the last one in the school. She got out her mobile phone, then put it back in her handbag. There were CCTV cameras everywhere. Pretending that she had just remembered something, Laura did an about-turn and walked quickly in the opposite direction, her heart beating faster at the thought of the two of them alone in the building.

There was a blind spot at the back of the stage. They'd had to put a lock on the stage door when the kids had worked that out. Fortunately, she was one of the keyholders. It smelt of paint. The school's production of *Guys and Dolls* was opening four weeks after half-term and the A level design students had been painting a giant replica of Edward Hopper's *Nighthawks* that afternoon on hardboard nailed to the back wall. She stood in the dark tapping out a text. The piano-playing suddenly stopped. She imagined him looking at the message, smiling. Heard him push back the piano stool, close the lid. Her heart rate began to quicken as she realised that though she was invisible, anyone watching a playback of footage from the hall would see him walking up the steps to the stage and slipping behind the curtain, and might wonder what he was up to. Why would they though? As long as nobody saw them together.

She could sense him weaving through the unlit forest of chairs towards her. Then a tinny thud, the unmistakable slop of liquid.

'Shit!'

'What?' she asked.

'I've kicked something over.'

'What?'

The torch of his mobile phone illuminated the floor between them.

'It's OK. Lid's on,' he said, righting the can of paint.

He shone the torch at her.

'If you must insist on meeting in dark corners . . .'

She felt childishly naughty and shamelessly grown up at the same time.

He turned the torch off.

'You're wearing your fuck-me shoes,' he said, so close now she could smell toothpaste, which was more of a turn-on for her than any expensive cologne. She remembered the first time they'd ever kissed, the melting sensation of her body against his and the delightful realisation that he used Woolite to wash his jumpers.

'Would it not have been easier to casually bump into each other in the corridor and leave the building together?' he said, landing a quick kiss on her lips. 'Would it even constitute unprofessional behaviour to go for a drink with a colleague at the end of term?'

She put her arms around him, but he resisted being pulled into a deeper kiss.

'What's wrong?' she asked.

'Not sure I can go on like this, Law.'

Her heart stopped. The moment she had been dreading had come. She had always been sure that he would be the one to end it and that had almost been a comfort to her, allowing her to rationalise the relationship and absolving her of responsibility. But now it was real, it felt like the most terrible shock, an almost out-of-body experience like an unexpected bereavement. She could hear herself saying, 'It's fine. It's OK,' while feeling as if her life had just ended.

'Do you want us to stop?' He sounded surprised.

'Of course I don't.' In her numbness, her voice sounded flat and emotionless, almost professional. 'But I know it's not fair on you.'

'I've been offered another job.'

'I wasn't aware you were looking.'

'I wasn't. I don't want to take it. I'm happy here. Not just because of you. Although, a lot because of you . . .'

He had a straightforward honesty that was unusual to find in a grown man.

'We could forget this ever happened,' she said, not wanting to lose him as a teacher either. The gigantic leaps the school had taken in music and drama in just two terms were entirely due to him. The senior management team were even discussing the idea of expanding the school's specialisation into performing arts as well as art and design, and his involvement was crucial to their bid for funding.

'I don't think I could do that,' he said. 'Could you?'

'I seem to be better than I thought at pretending.'

'I don't want to pretend, though.' He switched his torch back on again so that she could see his face. 'I love you, Law . . .'

'I love you.'

Whenever she said the words she felt a strangely calm euphoria, like the eye of a storm, as all her inner turmoil settled for a moment.

Now, he was kissing her, his hands in her hair. She kissed him back, grappling with his zip as he hoisted up her skirt, and, stepping out of her shoes, she jumped her legs around him as they toppled back against the counter of the café in the Hopper.

Afterwards, they sank to the floor and sat holding hands, their eyes now accustomed to the dark, with just enough light coming from under the stage door to see each other's faces.

'So what do you want to do?' She finally broke the silence.

'I want to be with you, live with you . . .'

'But I'm the deputy head!'

'Is that your first concern? I often wonder if you like it in the dark because it means you can pretend you're not doing it.' He was the grown-up in the relationship, who knew her better than she knew herself

'What's the other job?' she asked.

'A tour of the States . . .'

The band he had played keyboards with when he was at university now filled stadiums.

'Are you sure you don't want to go?' she asked.

'Been there, done that,' he said.

She'd seen videos, but had never quite been able to imagine his life on the road.

'Before they were rock stars, they were students in the engineering faculty,' he'd told her.

'I know what I want,' he said now, stroking her hair.

With his arms wrapped around her, she felt totally secure, but how could she even think of uprooting her whole life just for love?

'Maybe your holiday will give you some space to think,' he said.

'Space? It's wall-to-wall activities for a week.'

'Couldn't you go for walks by yourself? We can still talk . . .'

'If there's a signal. It's up a mountain.'

She sensed him tense at her evasion.

'I need to know whether to give my notice after half-term,' he said, matter-of-factly.

'No. I get that,' she said, standing up, smoothing her skirt, slipping her feet back into the shoes. 'I will think about it. I'll think about nothing else . . .' she offered, trying to make him smile again. 'Now, how are we going to do this?'

'I'll go back to the piano, play a sonata, while you make your escape,' he said, with a sigh.

'How do I look?' she asked.

'Lovely,' he said, pushing a lock of her hair that had escaped from her chignon behind her ear, the brush of his fingertip against her skin so careful and gentle it turned her on again.

Her head ready to explode with all the variables and the guilt, Laura missed her exit from the North Circular and found herself driving round an industrial estate of carpet and car part warehouses in her attempt to get back onto the carriageway heading into the city. It was counterintuitive to live in Hackney and work in the suburbs of London, but it usually meant she avoided most of the heavy traffic that was going in the opposite direction. Now, it was getting dark and she had no idea where she was and couldn't reach her bag to plug in her phone. A car following close behind her slammed on its horn as she took a wrong exit from a mini-roundabout and attempted to reverse without looking in her mirrors. Swerving into the next left turning, she parked up and tried to moderate her breathing. This anonymous wasteland was probably as good a place as any to compose herself; with the noise of the nearby road and lack of any visible humans around, she could scream and no one would hear her.

Sitting at the wheel of a car, lost and terrified, felt oddly similar to the day she'd first fallen in love with Alex.

Then, she'd had an ancient Peugeot 205 with a broken passenger door, not the sturdy, sensible hybrid SUV that befitted her status now. Then, she had been thirty-one and had just been made senior teacher at a huge inner London comprehensive. He was twenty-three, an NQT.

She was supposed to be mentoring him, but he had mentored her with his energy and creativity. He came from a family of musicians, which had given him a winning combination of confidence and humility. He was an accomplished pianist and guitar player, but his itinerant life as a child had demonstrated that being talented wasn't always enough to make a living. His enthusiasm for teaching had given her back her optimism. With the new exam-focused limits of the curriculum it was all too easy to question why one would choose long hours and poor pay. The prevailing mood among teachers was resentment. Whenever she'd had to visit the staffroom when she was a pupil, she remembered an acrid cloud pouring out. Now the atmosphere was just as toxic when she opened the door, but with moaning rather than cigarette smoke. Observing Alex's lessons, she'd seen the faces of teenagers as they suddenly got the transformative power of art. It was a gift she didn't think any other profession truly provided. A writer could inspire a reader, a performer could move an audience, but they never had the privilege of witnessing the moment a young life opened up to new possibility. In her subject, it was often a line of poetry that resonated; in his, the resolution of a harmony or the synthesis of lyrics and melody in a song. She started looking forward to going into work each day, even found herself singing in the car on the way.

They'd taken to eating their lunch together, and at the end of the day, they were always the last in the staffroom, chatting as they did their marking. It had felt entirely natural to offer him a lift when she'd seen him standing at the bus stop one stormy April evening. The flat he shared with some mates from uni wasn't far off her route. They'd sat outside for ages talking as the rain hammered down on the car roof.

He'd taken the opportunity to suggest putting on a musical rather than the usual Shakespeare play she always directed. She'd thought it was a great idea, had even revealed that she had played Nancy in *Oliver* when she was at school. When the rain had finally let up, he'd asked if she had time for a coffee. She'd said no, she had to be getting back and immediately switched on the ignition, her flustered reaction turning a polite offer into something much more freighted. Then the passenger door stuck and she'd had to get out and open it from the outside. When he'd stood up, physically closer than they'd ever been, she'd stepped back into a puddle which had flooded over the top of her suede ankle boot. She'd stalled the car in her haste to get away, then, as soon as she was out of sight, pulled into a cul-de-sac, unbalanced by one freezing wet foot and the strange giddy rush of longing in her bloodstream. She'd taken a long, hot shower when she got in, hoping to wash the feeling away, then spent a wakeful night interspersed with snatches of 'As Long As He Needs Me' whirring in her brain before realising, astonished, as dawn broke, that she was in love for the first time in her life.

She hadn't offered him a lift again. The only way to deal with the trembling when she was around him was by not speaking unless it was absolutely necessary for work. She'd taken up early morning swimming and yoga classes in the evening to try to drive desire from her body. During a feedback session, he'd asked if he'd done something to offend her, and she hadn't been able to dissemble.

'I thought you might understand.'

He'd put his hand over hers.

'I do, and I feel the same . . .'

'But it's impossible . . .'

The school offered him a permanent job at the end of his NQT year but he surprised everyone by announcing that he'd decided to quit teaching and join his flatmates, who had just had a hit single, on a tour of Eastern Europe. She'd rushed to the loo, then thrown a sickie, something she had never done before. She'd spent the afternoon walking round a scrubby park with tears pouring down her face until it felt like there was no more liquid inside her.

The new school in a suburban town in Essex was a fresh start for her. She'd risen rapidly through the hierarchy to deputy head, done such a good job during the pandemic that she was now in a position to apply for head teacher if a suitable vacancy arose. For thirteen years, she had forced herself not to think about him. She was good at compartmentalising. When she'd spotted him once in the background of a photo of the band in one of her daughter's pop magazines, she'd thought how very unlike her the entire episode had been.

Then, just as everything was returning to normal after the pandemic, he had reappeared. She was on the interviewing panel but she'd been so busy she hadn't had a chance to look at the applicants beforehand. It wasn't like her not to be meticulous, but she'd done so many now, she knew what questions to ask. She'd come in late, had been in the midst of apologising when she realised who it was sitting on the other side of the table.

The other members of the senior management team couldn't understand why she had given him such a hard time. Yes, there was a huge gap in his teaching career and it was unusual for someone with an exciting life to return to teaching, but shouldn't they applaud him for wanting to make a difference? He was qualified, had taught an excellent lesson under observation and offered to start a choir. He was eager to develop music for children with learning disabilities. Even the most reluctant kids were going to think it was cool to be taught by a member of a famous band. Frankly, they were incredibly lucky he'd rocked up, the head of HR had reminded her, with a smirk at the pun.

Laura had been outvoted. She'd worried in case she'd gone too far in her objections. Would they look up his references from previous employment and find her name somewhere in the documentation? Why would that matter, though? They hadn't had an affair. Her behaviour had never been unprofessional.

'Did you know I was here?' she'd hissed, as she passed him waiting outside the head teacher's office about to be offered the job.

'Of course I didn't. If it's a problem, I can turn it down.'

'You're very confident,' she'd said in her best clipped deputy head voice.

He shrugged, smiling at her.

'I am the only applicant . . .' he said, indicating the row of empty chairs beside him.

Unlike anyone else she'd ever met, he'd never been intimidated by her steely exterior.

She hadn't seen him for thirteen years, and she suddenly didn't understand how she could have lived such an incomplete life. This time when she offered him a lift, they'd been silent on the drive to his new Docklands apartment and had gone straight up together in the lift. There was a view all over London and the bed had newly washed sheets. His lovemaking took her to places she had never even fantasised about. It was as addictive as she imagined heroin must be. She craved him so much, she began to take risks at work, finding hideouts in the stationery cupboard, the back of the stage in the hall, even the disabled toilet during the first act of *King Lear* at the Globe Theatre where they'd taken a party of sixth formers a couple of weeks before.

It was dark now, the rumble of traffic not as constant as it had been. Laura wondered whether the decision she was facing had always been inevitable. She thought of herself as a person who did the right thing, but perhaps she was a liar, just as her mother had said.

She started the engine and drove off before realising that she hadn't switched the lights on. Shifting her bum on the seat, she made a concerted effort to pull herself together. At this rate, she'd crash the car before she'd even been able to think through the biggest decision of her life.

# Chapter Three

## *Robin*

It was a big surprise to be going away, but he wasn't that keen on surprises and thought Jessica would know that. In fairness he'd probably never told her because he'd learned at a very young age not to share personal information.

Surprises were generally unwelcome. He'd never discovered whether the rat on his pillow his first night at prep school had been murdered deliberately, or just died there, the victim of routine baiting. There were no visible marks on its cold body. He hadn't known what to do with it. Feared he would be held somehow responsible. Put it under his bed where it had lain until the smell was so awful the cleaners must finally have dealt with it. Neither he, nor any of the boys, nor staff, had ever mentioned it, so he assumed that it must have been the non-specific initiation his brothers had warned him might happen in the first few days.

The first audition where he hadn't got the part. The producer and director had laughed out loud, not in a good way, about his reading for Mr Bingley. The realisation that he should have read the book.

The next audition after that, where it had begun to dawn on him that the first audition wasn't a one-off.

Almost all subsequent auditions.

The arrival of George. Not the chap himself obviously, but the awkwardness of the timing. Still, he hoped he had been a good enough actor to disguise his feelings.

Robin's irritation grew in direct proportion to the wait for the number 73 bus which had been indicating 'due' on the revolving LED display for at least five minutes. He wasn't sure how he felt about his own family speaking about him behind his back, especially as none of them apart from Eliza even liked Jessica very much. They'd all assumed he would be available for a week mid-October, which was actually a busy time with the Christmas adverts getting their final touches. No one realised the work involved in doing voice-overs. They thought you went to the studio, spoke the line into a microphone and left, with no idea of the effort it took to get exactly the right balance of levity and seriousness into an advert for house insurance, for instance. As it happened, his diary was clear, but that wasn't the point. Maybe Jessica had checked with his agent? If so, how had she managed to get hold of her? The last he'd heard was an out-of-office reply in the summer saying she was away for a couple of weeks.

On the other hand, he could do with a holiday. He'd said so only the other day.

'As if your whole life isn't a holiday,' Eliza had remarked.

Robin's discomfort subsided as the 73 finally hove into view. The one good thing about getting older was being able to read numbers from a distance.

Upstairs, he was disappointed to find people already occupying his favourite seats at the front of the bus – he liked pretending he was driving.

Getting out his phone, he tapped the link Jessica had sent him and scrolled through the photos of the house. Grander than a farmhouse, but not quite a palazzo, the back of the property had converted outbuildings, possibly stable blocks, around a gravel courtyard with room for several cars. The two-storey frontage of the building had a terrace with terracotta pots and steps down on to a large lawn. There was a pool to one side of the building with another terraced area with a rose-covered pergola and a firepit. In the long-distance shot, the property was surrounded by forests of soft dark conifers and oak trees beginning to turn gold. To be fair, it looked idyllic.

Foraging, truffle hunting, wine tasting. Planning was Jessica's job, so she probably got freebies, but it was still thoughtful to tailor the holiday to his tastes. He pictured himself in a Barbour, sturdy boots, with a gnarled stick, the crunch of leaves underfoot, then swapped the costume for a chef's apron and Crocs, cooking in that stunning kitchen with utensils and dried chillies hanging over the island worktop. Fresh porcini mushrooms would be in season, their slippery deliciousness enhanced with just a little virgin olive oil, garlic and parsley. With home-made pappardelle, perhaps.

The bus stopped at the lights before his stop. The group of clubbers in front of him leapt up to get off, then stopped politely, to allow him to go first down the stairs.

Surely he didn't look that old?

He watched them bowling along the street in the opposite direction in a chaotic tumble of energy and laughter.

He was off to Italy in the morning, he reminded himself. Was it churlish of him to slightly wish that Jessica had chosen Ibiza? Wild dancing. Recreational drugs. It had sounded so much fun when Tim had told him about his trip in the summer.

'Reclaiming my lost youth!' he'd said, by which Robin had assumed he meant a lot of sex.

Strange that Tim hadn't mentioned a new boyfriend. No doubt another one in his twenties. Apparently there were websites for young men who liked older men. Robin hoped he would be game for a laugh. It might be fun with someone to bridge the gap between the adults and the children. Robin finally started feeling excited about a whole week of spending quality time with the people he loved.

They could play charades! He and Jessica were a demon team, as long as she didn't have one of her lame boyfriends in tow. God knows what algorithm matched her with the men she dated but they were always completely unsuitable. Even worse were those she met when sampling 'experiences' for her work. Corporate parties and various types of 'shower', which used to involve some nice food and a spa, now demanded activities like blade surfing, gin distilling, dyeing natural wools.

Jessica always tested new activities before committing, which was also a convenient way of getting away for the weekend and charging it to expenses. She used to invite him along. They'd been surprisingly good at the Argentine tango, even talked about finding a regular class in London, but never got round to it. Ziplining in a former coal mine had also been a blast. But after the incident in the zorbing sphere her invitations to him had stopped. Perhaps she found he was cramping her style? These days, more often than not, the experiences she tried seemed to involve sex. The liaison with the tantric yoga teacher from a retreat on a Greek island was pretty much inevitable, however she later discovered that he found 'a special energy' in almost every woman who participated. Her recent crush on the stone cutter from Dorset was doomed from the start.

The trouble with Jessica, Robin thought, as he fumbled for his front door key, was that her desperation to be in a relationship made her big up men almost in inverse proportion to their interest in her. Jake hadn't been Dorset's answer to Michelangelo, nor was he Gabriel Oak, he was just a bloke with a quarry and stone carving was one of the few creative outdoor experiences she could find in the UK when travel abroad was restricted. He may have been intrigued, even turned on, by

Jessica's metropolitan gushing, and the potential to cash in on a team-building weekend for investment bankers, but he was only ever going to disappoint when she managed to inveigle him to London for the weekend.

Recalling her description of his visit, Robin coughed back a laugh. Jessica was so funny and outrageous that other people found her a bit full-on, but that was the whole point of her. She had the best anecdotes and she could drink anyone under the table. Unlike almost everyone else in his life, he didn't have to watch what he said around her. In fact, he half wished it was going to be just the two of them in Umbria, generally misbehaving like when they first met at uni.

He'd spotted her across a crowded room at the freshers' welcome do. While everyone else was wearing jeans and T-shirts that had been washed too often, she stood out in camouflage cargo pants with a neon-pink stripe and a matching neon-pink crop top. He'd only ever seen a woman's bare skin on the beach and this was October. With her frizz of curls, toned muscles and bright pink lipstick, she looked powerful. Quite unlike any woman he had ever met. Not that he had met many. His mother had been middle-aged all the time he'd known her. The stream of au pairs had come to a halt after his eldest brother was discovered in bed with one of the Austrian ones. Matron. Before university, Robin's only significant contact with the opposite sex had been in the annual school play. At his prep school, he'd always been cast as the girl, which was authentically Shakespearean but led to endless teasing. When he'd finally been given a masculine role – if Puck was actually masculine; he wasn't sure that fairies were gendered, not that it would matter nowadays as it had then – and had to do scenes with an actual female Titania from the sister school, he'd realised how camp his previous characterisations had been. Girls turned out to be much cooler than he'd imagined. Or at least,

Titania was. She had been bone-chilling as Lady Macbeth the following year.

So when Jessica had smiled at him as if she had a secret she wanted to share only with him, he'd made a beeline for her, drinking both glasses of wine he'd picked up in his nervousness. When she'd laughed it wasn't like mockery; more like being drawn into a delicious conspiracy. She swore, she drank, she made jokes. It was like being with a boy, not a girl. Jessica was fun and full-on, both with capital Fs. She wasn't pretty exactly, but she was sexy, intimidatingly so, and so clearly experienced, he had never dared try anything. She was still playing the field now, despite professing a wish to settle down. Her relationships never seemed to go anywhere. He had some sympathy with the constant stream of guys who let her down because she would be exhausting to live with, but for a week of partying, there was no one better.

Pushing through the wodge of coats piled onto the hooks behind the front door, he found the tiled hall strangely noiseless.

In the living room, Bob was asleep on the sofa and George barely looked up from the Fifa game.

'Where's Lammie?' Robin asked, missing the cockerpoo's usual enthusiastic greeting.

'He's staying with Hetty for the week.'

More deceit. He would have liked the chance to explain to Lammie – he was increasingly sure that the dog understood every word he said to him – because he didn't want him getting scared he was being abandoned again. It was amazing how attached you could get. He'd never felt the same way about Bobtail, the cat, so-called because he'd lost his tail in a fight, and now always shortened to Bob. He'd been part of the family for longer, but cats were far more inscrutable than dogs. They'd got Lammie when Eliza was eleven. She'd been in a phase of deciding to be a vet and stamping a lot when she didn't get what she wanted. Lammie wasn't much more than a puppy, painfully thin with coal-black woolly curls that made him look more like a lamb than a dog, which is how he'd got his name. His big eyes were so sad, his face so cute, he could have starred in a dog calendar. Some dogs who had been badly treated reacted with aggression, they were told at the rescue centre. Lammie had obviously worked out that being adorable was more effective if you wanted people to stick with you. Robin had felt a sort of kinship with him from the start. Lammie even managed to win Bob round once he'd understood that the sofa was Bob's territory.

Eliza's passion had rapidly transferred to horses – thankfully they had resisted her pleas to buy one of those – then to bands featuring androgynous young men, before settling, for the moment at least, on veganism and identity politics. Care of Lammie had been Robin's responsibility, since he was the one who didn't really have a 'proper job', as he'd once overheard his daughter describing self-employment.

Robin had never been allowed a pet as a child because the family moved around a lot. When they were in Malaysia, he'd adopted a mouse, bringing it titbits from dinner that he'd snaffled into his pockets and leaving them outside the mousehole he had discovered behind his bedside table. He was sure the creature sometimes paused and looked up at him in gratitude, but it always dashed back into the skirting board when Robin tried to stroke it. One of his brothers probably told on him. How else would Mummy have known? She'd ordered the maid to set a trap, one of the old-fashioned sort with a spring, rather than the humane boxes preferred in the UK. Turned out that the mouse had family and friends. Robin had been woken each night by the snap of another execution. When he'd tried to disarm the mechanism, he'd caught his own fingers. After he returned from hospital, he'd been ordered to sleep in the guest suite until the infestation was eradicated. He'd longed for a pet ever since.

At first he'd found all the time involved in walking a dog and cleaning up after him rather a chore, but Lammie was so obliging and sweet-natured, you couldn't not be friends. During lockdown it had been great to have a reason to go out more than once a day, although he wasn't sure that it was technically allowed.

If he'd known they were going away, he would have prepared some decent food for him to eat, Robin thought. Hetty, their neighbour, was lovely, but her idea of dog food was a bag of dried biscuits and a bowl of water.

'Is Mum back?' Robin asked George.

'No.'

'Have you eaten? Shall I make you some pasta?'

George finally awarded him a smile.

'Thanks, Dad. Bit early for you on a Friday, isn't it?'

'Apparently, I need to pack . . .'

George looked shifty. He was terrible at keeping secrets. It finally explained why he had been a bit arsey over the past few weeks, doing anything to avoid spending time with Robin. Now, he could almost see his son's brain trying to work out whether he was allowed to fess up.

Robin looked at the screen.

Belgium against Brazil. The two top-rated teams globally. George was clearly preparing for the World Cup.

'I'll do you a carbonara if I can be Brazil . . .' Robin infinitely preferred Fifa to the real game. 'Is Eliza home?'

'It's Ellis now, Dad. Yes, they are in their room with Jaz.'

As Robin walked back out into the hall, his daughter emerged onto the landing.

'Oh, it's you,' she said.

35

She had never been the easiest person to deal with. The terrible twos had lasted well into primary school and were rapidly followed by the smart-arse remarks. Now she thought she was the only person in the world, or certainly in their family, who had identified injustice. Which was fairly normal for a teenager, apparently. Actually, it made a lot of sense. He didn't know why Gen Z weren't angrier about the shitshow boomers had left them to deal with, but it made it all a bit eggshells at home.

'I'm making pasta. Do you want some?'

'We've eaten.'

'How was school?'

She glowered at him. She was at a stage where every question appeared to be an imposition. He noticed she was wearing one of his shirts. Cornflower blue from Barneys. A gift from Tim. He'd never had an occasion to wear it. It suited her fair colouring, he thought, but knew better than to say so. Compliments were risky territory.

She'd recently announced herself as non-binary and demanded to be called Ellis because she didn't want to be defined as one gender or another. Though he kept forgetting to refer to her by her new name and the pronoun 'they', it seemed very sensible to Robin. He wished he'd had the independence of thought about such fundamental issues when he was their age. Or even now.

'So the secret is out?' they said.

'The holiday.'

'Yes!'

He was somewhat surprised Ellis had agreed to participate in the deception, given their usual impatience with the lies told by their parents' generation. But they had always had a special closeness to Jessica, who tended to indulge them. The last time she had come to Sunday lunch, she'd produced the latest mobile phone with a high-spec camera because Ellis had expressed an interest in photography. He'd thought at the time it was especially generous as it was nowhere near Ellis's birthday, or Christmas.

'Why do I have to have a reason to treat my godchild?' Jessica had said, handing it over. She'd awarded herself the title when Eliza was born although none of them believed in that sort of thing, and the fact that he hadn't put a stop to it was still a cause of friction with his wife. The gift had elicited a rare smile on Ellis's face. It now made more sense as a bribe.

'Not as drunk as you usually are on Fridays,' Ellis remarked.

'I've got to pack. Are you guys ready?'

'We're not coming until Sunday.'

'Why?'

'Tim's going to watch George's match then bring him on to Barty's birthday party, so it's just you and Mum going with Jessica.'

Robin was simultaneously relieved and slightly alarmed to learn he was not being roped in to supervise at his youngest nephew's party. Barty had few redeeming features other than the fact that he was family. He must be fifteen now, a year older than George, and he wasn't improving with age.

'Where's the party?' Robin asked.

'Floodlit paintballing.'

The thought of his daughter being shot at by her cousin and his oafish friends filled him with horror, although he knew Ellis wouldn't take any shit and hopefully Tim would have George's back.

'Has Mum sanctioned this?' he asked. Hopefully she'd have carried out some sort of risk analysis, as she had to for every school trip.

At that moment, he heard a key in the front door behind him.

'We were just talking about you!' he said.

Laura looked uncharacteristically flustered.

'Barty's party . . .' he explained.

'I rang the venue. They seem pretty switched on. They're used to dealing with marauding stag parties, so teenagers shouldn't be a problem. Camilla has booked a restaurant for after so they can't trash the house this time.'

'Watch they don't slip anything into your drink,' Robin said to Ellis, who lifted her eyes to the heavens and returned to her room.

'They don't drink,' Laura said.

The use of the plural still confused him.

'What's that on your jacket?' he asked his wife.

Laura craned her neck to look in the hall mirror at the back of her jacket where there was quite a large uneven patch of yellow.

'Oh god! Must have stumbled into the backcloth. *Nighthawks*. The Hopper,' she added impatiently, as if he were the one who was being obtuse.

Laura wasn't a stumbling kind of person.

As if she heard what he was thinking, she said, 'These bloody shoes! I must be having a midlife crisis.'

Was it supposed to be a joke? You could never quite tell with Laura, but the shoes did seem rather impractical for her work.

'I need a shower,' said Laura. 'It's been a long day.'

'I gather we're off to Italy in the morning,' he called as she reached the top of the stairs.

'Excited?'

'Of course!'

'Well, that makes one of us,' she said.

# Chapter Four

## *Jessica*

## Saturday

It was still dark when Jessica opened the front door, and the street was silent apart from a jogger on the other side of the road whose steps echoed long after he'd disappeared down the hill. Jessica tried to visualise the checklist she had left on her desk in her second-floor flat.

- Large suitcase with costumes, games, clothes and toiletries.
- Hand luggage suitcase containing easily accessible miniature toiletries in plastic bag, laptop and enough clothes and essential props in case the large suitcase failed to turn up. It had happened to her before.
- Cross-body bag small enough not to count as a bag, containing passport, phone and essential information printed on a sheet of paper just in case her phone died. She had learned not to take risks.
- Down jacket because apparently it could get very chilly at night at altitude. Slight panic until she remembered she was wearing it, though it was far too warm for the current weather. She hoped the others had taken note of this on the list of instructions she had sent because she planned to spend at least one evening around the firepit.

She'd forgotten her glasses. All the staring at a computer screen during lockdown had given her a mild astigmatism, the optometrist she'd visited recently had told her. She only really needed glasses for working and driving at night, and she hadn't yet worn them in public, but the world seemed far clearer and the headaches disappeared whenever she put them on at home. It would be ridiculous not to be able to drive in Italy or see the starlit dome of the sky with no light pollution. Robin would probably tease her, but she'd noticed him holding the menu as far as his arm could reach, so it probably wouldn't be too long before there would be a trip to the optician for him too.

Another quick check of the flat. This time, Jessica snatched the list from the table. One of the best bits of advice Mandy had ever given her was that you had to keep a grip on things because no one was going to do that for you. After turning the key in the deadlock, Jessica pinched herself hard enough on the arm for it still to hurt in a few minutes' time when she inevitably asked herself whether she had, then ran down the stairs and breathed a sigh of relief that the suitcases were still there and Laura's car was pulling up.

Robin jumped out to give her a hand getting everything into the boot.

'Do you want to sit in the front?' he asked.

'No, no, it's fine,' Jessica said, sliding into the back seat.

'I didn't know about the new traffic restrictions,' Laura said, looking at her in the rear-view mirror.

It could have been a simple statement of fact, but it sounded like an accusation. Jessica had promised herself that she was not going to let Laura get to her. Now she wished she'd never agreed to her driving them to the airport, but there was no way she could afford an Uber these days and it was such a hassle getting a bus, then a tube, then the Stansted Express, and if Laura was taking Robin anyway, it seemed perverse to refuse.

'This is so kind of you,' she said.

'Not a problem,' said Laura.

Jessica stared out of the window as the first rays of sunlight began to filter through the dawn, only to find herself face to face with a single magpie sitting on top of the postbox at the top of the street.

'Good morning, Mr Magpie, where's your lady friend?' she said automatically.

'I'm sorry?' said Robin, turning round.

'Single magpies are unlucky unless you salute them. I think it has to be out loud to count.'

Aware that Laura was squinting at her in the rear-view mirror with that perplexed expression she always had that made her feel like a naughty child, Jessica got out her phone as if she had just received a notification. Seven hundred and eleven steps. How was that even possible?

'You don't really believe that, do you, Coco?' Robin asked.

'Better safe than sorry.' She tried to sound breezy and ignore the exchange of glances in the front.

'Why is a single magpie unlucky anyway?' Laura asked, making Jessica feel even more of an idiot than she normally did because she didn't know the answer.

Jessica had never thought to ask the origin of all the sayings and superstitions that were drummed into her by her mother from the earliest age. She still hadn't forgiven herself for breaking a mirror when she was ten and causing the two years' bad luck that followed, although every cloud had a bit of a silver lining because that was when she'd met Mandy. It was supposed to be seven years of bad luck, but she didn't think they had to run consecutively because there had been five lucky years from twelve to seventeen before disaster had struck again.

'There are so many bird superstitions, I think poultry must have played a far more important societal role in the past . . .'

she offered, wondering why she always felt the need to sound intelligent around Laura. Maybe because she was a teacher.

'God yes, all those bloody birds in "The Twelve Days of Christmas"!' said Robin.

'Twenty-three,' said Jessica. 'Though, oddly, no turkey!'

They both laughed.

Laura was frowning at her.

'It was the answer in a pub quiz,' Jessica explained.

'Except we got it wrong,' said Robin.

'You were supposed to calculate the number if you sang the whole song with all the repetitions...'

'Which the quizmaster did not actually make clear...' said Robin, still peeved at the injustice, although the incident had happened years ago.

'Except to the bloody Real Ale Pythagoreans,' said Jessica.

'Those bloody Pythagoreans,' sighed Robin.

The only time they'd won that quiz was when the RAPpers were on a charity hike between the microbreweries of southern England.

The conversation had run out of steam. The atmosphere inside the car was tense with Laura's disapproval.

'Is Hetty going to feed Bob, too?' Robin asked Laura, initiating a conversation about domestic arrangements that made Jessica feel as if she was a child sitting in the back while the adults discussed grown-up things that didn't concern her.

She googled *Why are there superstitions about magpies?* There was enough information to fill a programme on Radio 4. She thought there must be a huge overlap in the Venn diagram of their listeners and twitchers because there were often programmes about birds. How many people would actually recognise an egret or an osprey? Yet every time she left the radio on, she seemed to find herself listening to another instalment about them flying from some remote place in the UK to some ever more obscure spot in Africa. It had proven useful unconscious research when she went on a date with a wildlife photographer, though once he'd got started on the reintroduction of the great bustard, her concentration had wandered onto how his bird migration-driven schedule might fit around her life. Would she even be able to exist in the countryside? One of those beautifully preserved golden villages in Oxfordshire, in easy reach of the mainline into Paddington, perhaps. It wasn't that far from Mandy in Milton Keynes, so they'd get to spend more time together. But house prices there were ridiculous, and how much did a wildlife photographer earn? Would their combined salaries be enough? When she'd become aware of him asking if she had ever been to Scotland, she'd pictured an isolated croft, which was why she'd replied, 'I'm sorry, I just don't think I could live so far away from London even with a sufficiently high broadband speed.' He'd been a bit too beardy for her anyway.

Amazingly, the brain to body mass ratio of a magpie was the same as a primate. Some cultures revered them; others associated them with death. They mated for life, which was surprising, given that they otherwise seemed like opportunists, but that was why if you saw a lone one it meant that its partner had died. Hence the bad luck.

Jessica's faint feeling of dread lingered until they were out on the motorway when she spotted a flash of black and white in a newly ploughed field and, putting on her glasses, saw not one but two magpies. She wondered if seeing one, then a pair, meant that technically she could count two for joy, which would be a good result at the beginning of such an important week, or, even better, a total of three, for a girl? Could three magpies mean that the holiday was actually going to be the beginning of a baby, as she desperately hoped?

Obviously, they wouldn't get as far as conception this week.

But the idea was that seeing her in a domestic environment, Robin would realise that, unlike Laura, she was both a good time and a homemaker. Granted it was a fully furnished and equipped luxury rental, but it had taken her ages to find just the right place. All the activities she'd arranged were designed to show him that she genuinely cared about him and wanted to nurture his talent and make his life more fulfilled. Perhaps the revelation would come as he looked across at her in the flickering glow of the firepit, a glass of Vin Santo in one hand, a cantuccini dipping biscuit in the other; or as they stood in front of a painting and she explained about the mystical qualities of Piero della Francesca or the multiplicity of Raphael's talents. She'd done an online course about Renaissance art during lockdown.

'So what can you tell us about Umbria, Coco?' asked Robin, as if suddenly aware that they had been ignoring her.

'Wasn't there a huge earthquake there recently?' said Laura.

'Twenty sixteen. The epicentre was further south than where we will be. It destroyed the town of Amatrice,' said Jessica.

'Isn't that where penne all'amatriciana comes from?' said Robin.

'So typical of him to remember a major disaster by a pasta dish,' said Laura, smiling at Jessica in the mirror.

Laura often made casually disparaging comments about her husband, and every time she did, the song in Jessica's head grew so loud it blotted out all her other thoughts. *It should have been me!*

'It probably helped him to relate to the people, which is more than most of us do when there's a disaster in a foreign country,' said Jessica.

'Exactly,' said Robin. 'I think I gave a donation . . .'

'Did you, though? Did you really?' asked Laura.

How mean Laura was to him.

Not long now until they would be alone, she thought, her heart beating a little quicker as she spotted the exit for the airport. Then Laura took the wrong turning.

'Er, you're heading to long-stay instead of drop-off . . .' she pointed out.

'Oh, didn't I say? I'm on your flight now,' Laura said.

'Really?' Jessica's attempt to sound delighted came out more strangled. She'd been counting on at least one evening alone with Robin.

'Originally,' Laura explained for Robin's benefit, 'I was going to bring the children and Tim was flying to Italy direct from New York, but he split up with Jonny, so was in London earlier, and he wanted to see George play, and with Jaz coming too there were no seats left on tomorrow's flight, so I got one on yours.'

'Jaz?' Jessica asked.

'Ellis said they wouldn't come unless they could bring a friend!'

'Why didn't you inform me?' Jessica said.

'To be honest, I've been pretty busy, and you've done so much of the organisation, I didn't want you having any more hassle.'

'It's just, well, I like to know what's going on . . .' Jessica tried to suppress the fury inside her. It wasn't just a matter of who was coming, it was allocating rooms, booking restaurants. Planning an event required a great deal of thought about the dynamic, although she couldn't immediately think how the new arrangements would change anything except for this evening.

'Don't worry, Coco, nobody tells me anything . . . I didn't even know Tim had a new boyfriend, let alone that they'd split up,' said Robin.

'That's because Jessica made us all swear a vow of omerta!'

'Here we are!'

45

As Laura pulled into the parking place and switched off the engine, both of them turned round with big smiles on their faces.

'Like the glasses,' said Laura.

'They make you look almost like a serious person!' said Robin.

'Serious, *moi*?'

It didn't work as well as pretentious, *moi*, but Jessica hoped that at least she'd managed to mask her distress.

# Chapter Five

## *Laura*

The seats Jessica had booked were at the front of the plane because she liked to be first off. Laura's was right at the back.

'We could ask someone if they'd move.'

Jessica's suggestion couldn't have sounded more half-hearted.

'No, it's fine, Robin and I see quite enough of each other,' said Laura, somehow making what she'd intended as a generous gesture sound resentful.

Robin looked slightly crestfallen. These days, they didn't actually see very much of each other at all.

'Will you be OK?' he asked, aware of her dislike of flying.

'Of course!' she said, adding, 'Sorry!' to the queue that was building up behind them and making her way as quickly as she could to her aisle seat at the back.

She sat down and breathed a sigh of relief to have got away from Jessica for at least a couple of hours. There were so many things to admire about Jessica. She was bright, often funny and she had a good heart, but she was so extreme in her enthusiasms, particularly for Robin, that Laura always ended up feeling negative in comparison. She knew Robin would have loved the two of them to be friends, but the only common ground they shared was him. The usual dynamic between two people who knew each other through someone else was to tease, but any attempt she made to enlist Jessica's support in calling out Robin's foibles was always met with staunch defence, making Laura feel unreasonable or downright nasty.

As the plane began to taxi, Laura gripped the armrest, wishing that she had George's hand to hold. They'd always sat next to each other on planes. When he was a little chap she could pretend to herself that she was the one offering the comforting squeeze as the plane hurtled down the runway, accelerating towards that moment of curious relief that you were airborne and there was nothing you could do to change it. Now that her son was older, she thought they were both aware that he was the one providing the reassurance. Would he have held her hand if he'd been with them today? In the past few weeks, he'd suddenly become awkward about any kind of physical contact and had stopped allowing anyone else to use the bathroom when he was showering. Last night, when she'd hugged him goodbye, knowing there was no way either of her children would be up to see them off that early in the morning, his newly lanky form had rigidly endured her embrace instead of returning it. She'd clung on for far too long, overwhelmed by a presentiment that she would never see him again, then lain awake in bed for most of the night trying to chase the thought from her mind.

'Don't put that out into the Universe,' was something that her students had taken to saying to almost any warning, however mild, about needing to work for exams, or protecting themselves from STDs. It was as if they believed that mentioning something, or even thinking it, would cause it to happen. It was easier than taking responsibility for their own well-being. She considered it the Gen Z equivalent of Jessica's superstitions and just as illogical, but right now, she was so discombobulated by the flux in her life, she seemed to have temporarily lost all confidence in her rationality.

'Not keen on flying?' the woman in the middle seat next to her asked. She had an American accent and was smartly dressed in a black and white checked jacket and sported a red beret.

Laura had sensed her glancing at the side of her face and had deliberately not made eye contact, hoping not to have to engage in conversation. Now she wished she had closed her eyes and pretended to be asleep, although the tension in her body would probably have given her away.

'That obvious, eh?' she said with what she hoped was lightness rather than irritation.

'Me too!' Gratifyingly, the woman smiled, the skin around her eyes remaining curiously smooth. She'd clearly had work. Perhaps she was a client of Tim's? As the woman continued to stare at her, Laura wished she had a book, or that airlines still produced magazines or even menus that she could pretend to be perusing.

'Your face looks kinda familiar, I'm wondering whether we've met before?'

Laura had heard this often enough to guess what was coming.

'No, I've got it! It's because you look just like a young Catherine Deneuve.'

'You're not the first person to say that . . .'

It was a statement of fact, but somehow Laura felt she had made it sound both arrogant and rude, as if she was accusing the woman of being unoriginal.

'Are you an actress?'

'No. I'm a teacher.'

The dismissiveness most people showed towards teachers generally made Laura avoid mentioning it, but on this occasion she hoped it would close down the conversation.

'I represent models. Always on the lookout for undiscovered beauty . . .' The woman was holding out a card.

'I'm a deputy head teacher with two teenage children, so I've got quite enough on my plate,' Laura said. If the proposition had come at the end of the flight, she might have declined the card outright, but she didn't want to make a big deal of it with two hours still to go, so she took it, adding, 'I was actually looking forward to catching up on a bit of sleep.'

Laura always felt herself relax when the seat belt lights went off, though that was illogical, because if something went wrong at the highest altitude, no amount of bracing or taking off shoes with heels would help.

She had read about models being discovered at airports. She'd assumed it was something that happened only to young people. Most women of forty-five would probably be flattered at the approach, so why did she regard it as an imposition? She had always thought of her looks as a burden, not a gift, as they encouraged expectations that she couldn't satisfy. The most frequent comparison was Catherine Deneuve, or occasionally the blonde one from ABBA. At school she'd been known as the Ice Queen and not just because of her Nordic looks. Robin's brother Piers, who was in the same year as her at the neighbouring boys' public school, still called her that. She'd done nothing then to try to warm her image up, because it was easier to look as if she was in control than reveal the turmoil of doubt inside.

Closing her eyes, she tried to relax each part of her body as Alex had taught her. Each arm in turn, each leg in turn, her shoulders, her solar plexus, gradually releasing the stiffness of anxiety and allowing the pleasant thoughts to float into her mind, like the memory of lying against Alex's chest in the backstage darkness the previous evening.

'I love this job,' he'd said, gently stroking her cheek. 'What I don't like is going home separately.'

She imagined them waking up each morning in his Docklands apartment, looking at the view from on high where nobody could see them. Having breakfast together perched at the bar in the pristine kitchen with its wooden floors and granite surfaces uncluttered by anything except the duck-egg blue Dualit toaster and matching kettle. It was a bachelor pad with none of the chaos of a family home. It would be like being on holiday all the time, free from all the baggage of the past. He made her happy. She hadn't really known what that felt like before him.

But would her family ever forgive her? Ellis didn't seem to like her much anyway. They'd never been close. They'd be leaving home for university soon, so what difference would it make? But George! He'd always been so easy-going, but she couldn't simply assume he would understand, especially now with all the changes of adolescence to cope with. She couldn't bear to lose him. Perhaps that was the reason she had clung to him so desperately the previous evening.

How would she even begin the conversation with Robin? He hadn't done anything to deserve it. He was a good father, although now the kids were more independent, Laura wasn't sure what he did all day, apart from walking Lammie and making supper. If she did find a way of talking to him, how would he react? Surprise, she thought, initially, because he was usually a step behind everyone else. Perhaps a shrug. One of his appealing characteristics was that he didn't bear grudges. Grudges required a good memory and quite a lot of energy, neither of which he had in abundance. That was unfair. Whatever spin you wanted to put on it, relaxed, chilled, idle, disengaged, Robin was easy to live with. From the conversations she'd overheard in the staffroom between her female colleagues, a lot of men weren't and she mustn't forget that.

Committing to a relationship was so different from having an affair, which had found relatively easy because if it was just about sex, she didn't think Robin would mind. She couldn't remember the last time they'd done it. Long before Alex came

51

back into her life. Their marriage had never been particularly physical. Which probably would have surprised people, because they had both been so desired when they were young. It had always felt like an intimate secret they shared, somehow bringing them as close if not closer than other couples. Although just how much sex was normal she'd never been able to work out. Did Crispin and Cassandra still do it? Did Camilla and Piers? And if so, with each other, or with other people?

Did Robin? Her heart leapt at the scenario of them each confessing a secret lover. How convenient that would be. She thought not. All the secrecy involved more rigour than he was capable of.

Jessica and Tim probably had more sex than any of them, which was ironic because they were single but then you usually did at the beginning and they each had a lot of beginnings. Neither of them was lucky in love. She wasn't close enough to Tim to know whether his nonchalance when a relationship ended masked deeper disappointment. With Jessica, there was no doubt. God knows what had happened in her past to make her so pathologically keen to be coupled up. It wasn't that she was unattractive, but there was an element of desperation that had only increased during the isolation of lockdown. Jessica could convince herself she'd fallen in love with almost anyone, from the owner of the local dry cleaner who offered her a discount for quantity, to a canvasser from the Labour Party who'd asked through her entryphone whether she would be putting a tick in his box. The interior designer she'd Hinged with hadn't been asking her to form a bubble when he'd complimented her on her curtains. Everyone was still learning the language of Zoom backdrops then. And who could blame the stone carver for fleeing before she'd even got him into her building? They'd only met once, and yet she had felt the need to assure him that she would be prepared to sell her second-floor flat in order to buy a basement so there'd be no problem about the floor supporting the weight of his materials.

To her credit, she'd turned her many disappointments into funny anecdotes for Robin's benefit.

'You're the living embodiment of the triumph of hope over experience,' he always said.

'You can say that again!'

'You're the living embodiment...'

Gales of near-hysterical laughter.

'Robin wants to know if you'll drive.' Laura opened her eyes to find Jessica looking down at her, as if she had manifested her. 'I needed the loo, so I said I'd ask.'

'Does he really want a drink at this time in the morning?'

'It is his birthday,' said Jessica.

Laura wanted to say, It's not his birthday until Thursday. Why do you infantilise him? All the private jokes, calling each other Coco and Beau, giggling together like teenagers. It must be gratifying to have someone who constantly laughed at your wit and told you you were marvellous, but Laura found it infuriating. She didn't think Robin was even aware that Jessica adored him and no doubt thought she would make the better wife.

Perhaps she would. Perhaps she should regard her as an ally.

'Tell him I'll be happy to drive,' Laura said, trying to smile in a friendly way.

'Not only do you look like an angel, you actually are one!' said Jessica.

Jessica lived her life in superlatives, Laura thought as she watched her skipping down the aisle back to Robin. Everything always had to be brilliant, fantastic, legendary. When she'd arrived for Sunday lunch a couple of months back – a visit thankfully not as frequent as it used to be, now that Ellis was older – Robin had forgotten he'd invited her. He'd thrown together a hasty courgette soup.

'Oh my god! That smells divine!' said Jessica as he ladled it out.

'It just needs a swirl of . . .' Robin put a dollop of Greek yoghurt, then a sprinkle of chilli, on top. 'It's very easy to make.'

'I don't know how I've lived without this sheer deliciousness!'

If it had been fake, it would have been intolerable, but over the years Laura had come to realise that it wasn't. Jessica genuinely wanted to share her enthusiasms in order to improve people's lives. It was an admirable quality, really, and Laura supposed she should make an effort to join in and be more tolerant. A week wasn't very long and they were returning the following Saturday so she would have Sunday to tell Robin her plans, if she'd managed to work out what they were.

As the timbre of the engine noise changed, signalling the plane had started on its descent, Laura clasped her own hands together as tightly as she usually gripped George's next to her and Robin's across the aisle. How could she even think about leaving, she wondered, if she missed the security of him when he was only the length of a plane away?

# Chapter Six

## *Robin*

As soon as the doors were open, Jessica left him to deal with the hand luggage and was off down the steps in order to be first through security and avoid queuing at the car rental. He let the rest of the queue go in front of him while he waited for Laura. They were last off the plane.

Italy's October sunshine had a warmth that felt benign compared to the scorching heat of July and August when they usually holidayed there. He was pleased to see that unlike Pisa, where they normally landed, Perugia airport was one of those modest little terminals where you didn't need to take a shuttle bus.

'How was your flight?' he asked Laura as they walked down the steps together.

'Uneventful. Oh, except for being offered a new career!'

As she pointed out the woman in the beret ahead of them on the tarmac, he felt simultaneously proud of having such a beautiful wife and somewhat resentful that he hadn't been sitting in her row. Catching a reflection in the plate glass window of the terminal building, with the backdrop of the plane and distant hills, he thought the two of them could be cast in an advert for an upmarket holiday company. He could do with the work. Since his last disastrous television appearance, he'd become one of those actors with a great face for radio, which wasn't nearly as funny a soubriquet when other people said it as when he'd offered it himself.

Reaching for Laura's hand, he half hoped that the agent would turn around and see them. The gesture of affection seemed to startle his wife, disproportionately. He knew the holiday was her idea of hell, especially since his brothers and their wives were going to be joining them, as if it wasn't bad enough for her spending a week with Jessica. In an ideal world, their different personalities would complement each other. Emotionally volatile Jessica who wore her heart on her sleeve; Laura all seriousness and composure, outwardly at least. His wife kept the inner seething well hidden, but after knowing her so long, he could sense it.

The one real bit of luck in his life had been marrying Laura. It was something nobody would have predicted, least of all the two of them. When they'd met she'd seemed already a woman, meanwhile his voice hadn't yet broken. He'd been cast as *Oliver* in the Christmas musical. It was his first term at school. She was at the sister school, in her GCSE year like his brother Piers, who'd punched Robin's arm with more viciousness than usual when he had announced he was acting opposite her.

They'd called her the Ice Queen because she appeared immune to any number of compliments, gifts or sonnets that the boys heaped upon her. Off stage, Robin's interactions with her had been non-existent. The following summer, when he'd taken the role of Puck in *A Midsummer Night's Dream*, she hadn't appeared to recognise him. Nor when he'd played Macbeth the next year, by which time he'd grown ten inches, sprouted underarm hair and developed body odour, which he hadn't been aware of until seeing her recoil in one of their closer moments. In her final term, he'd completed his metamorphosis from adolescent youth to beautiful young man and discovered deodorant, which was just as well as he was playing Romeo to her Juliet. She was the first woman he ever kissed.

'Let's get it over with,' he remembered her saying. 'And don't even think about putting your tongue in my mouth.'

Knowing that he was the envy of every single boy in the school apart from Tim had made him even more nervous. The kiss had been very tentative, which had actually worked rather well for the role.

*Saints have hands that pilgrims' hands do touch and palm to palm is holy palmers' kiss.*

At the wrap party, emboldened by a slug of vodka from the bottle that Tybalt smuggled in, he'd asked her.

'Are you going to drama college?'

'Certainly not. Far too precarious a life.'

'Quite!' he'd said, which he'd found a useful word when you didn't have a clue what to say next.

The trace of a smile passed across her lips.

'Well, parting is such sweet sorrow, etcetera,' she said, as his brother approached.

'Quite.'

He could almost feel the heat of Piers's wrath on the back of his neck. His brother wasn't even in the Dramatic Society, but he was Head Boy and he claimed that entitled him to come to any school event he wished.

'Playing hard to get, as usual,' Piers said, as they watched her leave. 'She's the mistress of it. Cold bitch.'

'She seems very nice to me!'

'God, you are such a loser!' said Piers.

'Loser!' the rest of the boys chorused around him.

Which was odd when he was the one who'd just been on stage lying in bed with the woman they all craved.

Ironically, it was at Piers's wedding seven years later where Robin had encountered her again. By then, he was used to women hitting on him, but he'd still felt flattered when she waved and started walking across the crowded marquee towards him. She was wearing a belted black linen shift dress, no hat, just her platinum-blonde hair swept up into a ponytail. No discernible make-up apart from a slick of coral lipstick. In a tent full of fascinators, flounces and florals, it was as if she had been teleported in from the monochrome cover of a nineteen-sixties edition of *Vogue* and the rest of them were at a tea party in *Homes & Gardens*.

Turned out she had been Camilla's doubles partner in tennis at school.

'I could never understand how you were Piers's brother,' she said.

He was suddenly fifteen years old again.

'Quite!'

'And now you're a famous actor.'

'Not such a precarious life!' he'd said, quoting her words then realising she didn't remember the conversation.

Whenever he thought about that exchange, the pleasure of her appearance in his life was tempered by the memory of his hubris. It wasn't the exact moment his fortunes had changed, but he had been arrogant enough then to think they never would. Sometimes he'd asked himself would it have been too much to have fame, untold riches and the girl? Not that it was ever a choice between them. But if Hollywood had wanted him, he couldn't imagine that he and Laura would have built a life together there. She had no time for all the nonsense surrounding fame. Which was just as well given that it proved so ephemeral.

Theirs wasn't a perfect marriage, but it seemed to work. His lack of consistent employment had enabled her to progress in her career. He hadn't planned on being a househusband, but he found it rather enjoyable having never had a home life when he was growing up. The house wasn't perhaps as clean as it should be, but he was great at cooking. As parents, he thought they made quite a decent team, with one good at admin, the other at nurturing. It wasn't the most traditional division of labour. Crispin and Piers never let him forget that. Nor did they approve of him sending the children to state schools. Not that there'd been a choice, but Ellis and George seemed to be doing OK and at least neither of them had a police warning for shoplifting, like Barty. He'd always enjoyed taking the kids to school, being creative with their packed lunches, the camaraderie and, frankly, adoration he and Lammie received at the school gate. Now they were reaching an age where the children no longer required nor welcomed so much attention, he wasn't sure what his function would be once they no longer needed rousing in the morning and nourishing food to come home to. An offer of modelling work would have been gratefully received, and he wished Laura had considered that before being quite so blasé.

Industrial estates and out-of-town superstores, which were just part of the English suburban landscape, looked incongruous when plonked adjacent to vineyards in the road systems surrounding Italian towns whose centres had remained unchanged since medieval times. Robin had forgotten how difficult it was to negotiate roundabouts the wrong way round with no advance warning about directions. Laura's knuckles were white from gripping the steering wheel.

'Which road is it?' she asked, amid the beeping of horns all around them.

'Sorry, the signal's a bit erratic,' said Jessica.

'Shall I try yours?' Robin offered, picking up Laura's handbag from beside his feet.

59

'No time!' she screeched, as he pulled back the zipper. 'Just choose an exit now!'

The interior of the car felt like a balloon overfilled with anger. It wasn't fair to expect her to drive again. He blamed Jessica because she'd practically forced him to have a gin and tonic, the relaxing effect of which had now turned into a sour taste in his mouth and a jangly headache.

'Take the third exit!' He'd never been so glad to hear the disembodied, and in his view slightly smug, female voice of Google Maps.

The balloon deflated, but he and Jessica remained silently chastened. It was easy to see how Laura maintained discipline among unruly students. Scary enough negotiating a glacier, but worse when you knew there was a volcano underneath that might erupt without warning.

'At the roundabout, take the first exit.'

Finally they were on a country road, bumping along past olive groves, then up along a forested valley, occasionally glimpsing the silvery glint of a rushing river between trunks of deciduous trees, their golden foliage among dark green conifers making the hills look like a richly embroidered tapestry. Google continued directing them up winding potholed lanes until their ears started popping and finally, when they were just beginning to doubt whether they were on the right track, they spotted a pair of gates and the voice told them they had reached their destination.

At the top of the long driveway, in a kind of courtyard at the back of the house, between two single-storey buildings that might once have been stables, Laura parked the car next to a battered white Fiat Panda.

'Well done, darling!' said Robin. 'Promise I'll do all the rest of the driving this week.'

'If you're allowed to,' Laura said, crisply.

The air outside had the chill of altitude.

'How high are we?' Robin asked.

'I think about eight hundred metres,' Jessica replied. 'It gets cold at night. You did bring warm things, like I said on the instructions?'

'Down jackets, tick!' said Laura.

An awkward impasse was interrupted by a very attractive woman, and a man who looked like an Italian romantic hero from central casting who was holding the hand of a shy little girl.

'Vittoria? *Sono* Jessica! *Buon giorno!* Or is it *buona sera*? They look after the house for the owners,' she explained.

The man's name was Enzo, the child Gaia. After the introductions, they reverted to English.

'I show you the house,' said Vittoria.

'*Si, grazie!*' said Jessica. Robin followed her in, only realising when they were in the hallway that Laura was still outside.

'Darling?'

'Enzo's going to show me the pool area!'

Typical Italian, Robin thought, hitting on the blonde. He followed the sound of Jessica's enthusiastic cooing through an ancient wooden door into a space with a vaulted ceiling that had the cool stillness of a chapel and conjured the uncomfortable memory of school assembly. Fragments of fresco were still visible on the walls, but he was relieved to see that where the altar might have been there was now a raised platform with a baby grand piano, and instead of pews there were comfy-looking sofas, a long table and a smaller one with an inlaid chessboard.

'The party room!' said Jessica.

Vittoria opened one of the ornately carved wooden cupboards which were probably designed to hold the communion silverware, but now contained stacks of board games.

'Everything you need for fun and frolics,' said Vittoria, sounding as if she'd learned her English from The Famous Five series. He avoided catching Jessica's eye, but he knew that she'd registered the words and that it would become one of their catchphrases.

'What do you think?' Jessica asked. There was a gleam of triumph in her eyes.

'Awesome!' he said, rather pleased with himself for finding a word that sounded suitably enthusiastic while also expressing his faint sense of dread.

'Come and look at the kitchen.'

They walked back across the hall through another wooden door into another huge room. It was one of those rare occasions where the reality was better than the promotional photo. The flagstone floor, beams and fireplace complete with original oven had been retained. There was an enormous wooden refectory table and chairs to seat twelve. The rest of the kitchen-diner had been kitted out with state-of-the-art steel hob, ovens, fridges and freezers. On a central island with a polished black marble surface sat a giant bowl of fruit, a large round loaf of bread and platters of salumi and cheese. Above hung a frame garlanded with strings of chillis, garlic, onions and every type of kitchen utensil he could imagine.

'Coco, you absolute legend!'

Vittoria waved her hand over the platters of antipasti.

'I prepare *aperitivi*, so you can relax, drink wine, enjoy, how you say, settle in the climate.'

She opened the cupboards to reveal packets of pasta, bottles of olive oil and passata alongside an array of dried herbs and condiments.

'Fantastic!' he said. '*Fantastico*?'

'Some salad . . .' She pulled open the door to a huge fridge and showed them the bottom drawer. 'Now is time for Gaia to sleep. You have any questions?'

'This is all *perfetto,*' said Jessica.

'Just one thing,' said Robin, lowering his voice. 'The mouse-trap in the fireplace . . .'

'You are in the country! The mouses are very tiny, very sweet . . .'

'Could we put the trap somewhere less visible?'

'We put it here,' said Vittoria, opening one of the cupboards under the sinks, which he couldn't help noticing contained at least a dozen further traps.

'Now we leave you.'

Through a utility room that was as big as most kitchens, and a well-stocked wine store, they came out onto the paved area around the pool. While Vittoria opened another door to show Jessica the pump room, Robin wandered round to the front of the house where Laura was sitting on a stone bench on the formal terrace, looking out over a breathtaking panorama. In the foreground, the balustrade was topped with four urns planted with small lemon trees, their fruit just beginning to turn from green to yellow. Steps led down to a large, gently sloping lawn edged with shrubs. There was a five-a-side football net at the side that looked incongruously man-made against the vast natural panorama of mountains. In the far distance, a scatter-ing of farmhouses and a tiny hilltop town with a campanile, pale ochre in the fading light, were the only other signs of human habitation.

'Wow!'

'You like?' Jessica and Vittoria joined him on the terrace.

'It's paradise!' he said.

The little girl was kicking a football around with her father.

'*Vieni* Gaia!' Vittoria called, her hand outstretched.

Enzo turned. He really was Dolce and Gabbana advert-level handsome.

The little girl came hurtling over. She was as beautiful as her parents, with the same black wavy hair and large brown eyes that shone like polished stone.

'Gaia! What a lovely name!' said Jessica, crouching down to the child's level. '*Che bella ragazza!*'

Gaia was suddenly all shy again, hiding behind her father's legs.

'*In Italia, le ragazze giocano a calcio*, Gaia?'

The little girl peeped out from behind his thigh.

'*Si, certo!*'

'*Inghilterra, molto populare*,' Jessica said. 'The Lionesses! What would that be in Italian?'

To the delight of the child, Jessica got down on all fours, prowling and roaring. It reminded Robin of how good she'd been at playing with Eliza. He felt a stab of shame, knowing how much she longed for a child. A couple of years before, one Friday night, well down their second bottle, she'd told him she was thinking of trying IVF. He'd assumed she was joking when she'd asked him to be the donor, then felt flustered when she'd started crying. He'd told her that he'd have to ask Laura, who had pointed out that it might get very complicated. So the following Friday, he'd straightaway informed Jessica, before wine could exaggerate emotions, that it was impossible. When she'd laughed and protested that it hadn't been a serious suggestion, even he could see she was lying.

'*Le leonesse*,' Enzo translated. 'Here we have *Le Azzurre.*'

'The Blue Women,' Jessica translated.

'You speak Italian very well!' said Enzo.

Robin was almost certain that wasn't true.

'Not really,' Jessica said. 'I'm trying to learn, though.'

'*Allora, andiamo*,' said Vittoria impatiently.

It must be boring when your husband flirted with every woman who crossed his path.

'You have number if any problems...'

The family disappeared around the side of the house, leaving the three of them staring for a second at the space they'd vacated.

'Well,' said Jessica as the sound of tyres on gravel faded to silence. 'We need to allocate the bedrooms. Do you want to help me, Laura?'

'I'm sure you'll be happier doing it yourself.'

Robin knew that his wife didn't mean to be rude. It was just how she was, although sometimes he wished she could be more diplomatic.

'I'll come,' he said quickly, following Jessica back into the house and up the staircase.

'There's two smaller bedrooms at the front of the house downstairs, one with bunk beds, so perhaps Ellis and Jaz in there? They share a Jack and Jill shower room. All the doubles are en suite,' Jessica said, as they went upstairs. 'So there's one for me, one for Tim. You and Laura are in the master.'

The rooms were all beautifully appointed with luxurious soft furnishings. The master had a sunken bath with mosaic tiles as well as an enormous shower cubicle.

'The brothers? Where do they go?' Robin asked.

'The stable block. It's an entirely self-contained unit with two doubles. It's rented separately from the house.'

'What about Barty?'

'Barty's not coming, is he? Camilla said he was staying with a friend.'

'Thank god for that!'

The nagging fear at the back of his mind since he'd seen the quality of the soft furnishings lifted. Trouble seemed to follow Barty around, although it was always someone else's fault. He was the type of boy who had terrorised him at school and from the earliest age, Barty seemed to sense that power. 'Brave Barty, Wussy Uncle Robbo!' How had it even been possible to be intimidated by a toddler?

'Wine o'clock?' Jessica asked.

'I thought you'd never ask,' said Robin. 'Just one thing, Coco . . .' He lowered his voice to a whisper. 'Best not to mention the mousetrap, and if you see a mouse, for god's sake, don't tell Laura.'

'Why?'

'She's seriously phobic.'

'I can't imagine Laura being phobic about anything,' said Jessica.

'Well, she is. I'm serious, Coco. Omerta?'

'Omerta,' she said solemnly.

'What are you two conspiring about?'

'Nothing!' They spun round simultaneously.

# Chapter Seven

## *Laura*

It was obvious they were talking about her. Were they saying that she had been a bitch in the car or that she had been flirting with the caretaker? Not that she had, although he was extremely good-looking in a movie star way so that when he smiled you almost had to look away for fear of blushing. He'd shown Laura the pool, which was a decent size for doing proper lengths. There was a football net for George. The views were magnificent. Inside, the house was big enough for everyone not to feel on top of one another. For the first time, she began to feel like she might be able to enjoy a relaxing break. Maybe she could find a quiet room to practise yoga, gain some perspective and return to London knowing she had made the right decision. Whatever that was.

'We're just sorting out the sleeping arrangements,' said Jessica, ushering her into a bedroom furnished with brocades and silks in shades of crimson, rust and gold.

'You and I are in here,' said Robin.

'How beautiful this place is!' Laura said, trailing her hand across the quilt on the bed. 'I really don't know how you do it, Jessica, but we are very lucky you do!'

Paying compliments didn't come naturally to her. It was rarely appropriate at work, and at home everything always seemed to be such a rush – have you got your homework/shin pads/Oyster card? – there was never the time. Was that too much? Did she sound like she was handing out an award on Leavers' Day? Robin was still looking anxious; Jessica almost suspicious.

'Don't know about anyone else,' said Robin, 'but I'm starving.'

Laura's watch said three o'clock, but Italy was an hour ahead. By the time they'd demolished the antipasti laid out for them, the sun had set and it was dark outside. The bottle of wine Jessica produced from the wine store was delicious. Laura wasn't normally keen on red wine, especially the full-bodied stuff Robin's family served, which tasted like sucking on a piece of timber, but this slipped down as easily as warm Ribena, melting away the tension in her body.

Robin filled a huge saucepan with water and put it on to boil.

'Hope everyone's OK with spaghetti al pomodoro, because that's really all there is.'

'Perfect!' said Jessica.

Robin could make the simplest dishes taste delicious. Watching him tying an apron round his waist in the way professional chefs did on television, Laura felt suddenly, tearily, fond of her husband. As a grown-up, now that acting roles were rare, cooking gave him his identity. It always amazed Laura how a man who seemed like the laziest person on earth switched into action whenever cooking was involved. She attributed it to the fact that the only praise he'd had as a little boy was when he sneaked down to the kitchen to be with the staff.

If Laura was ice, Robin's mother was liquid nitrogen. She was fond of remarking that Robin's arrival in the world had been accidental.

How cruel it was to repeatedly tell a boy that he was surplus to requirements. It was hardly surprising that Robin had spent most of his childhood pretending to be someone else. Peter Pan, mostly, if the photographs were anything to go by, although he had once joked that all records of him playing Tinker Bell had been destroyed.

'Do you need any help?' Laura asked, in the absolute certainty of receiving a negative answer.

This was his domain. The only thing that would blunt his contentment would be someone slicing the garlic the wrong way, or adding a can of tomatoes before it was sufficiently softened. The island was his stage, and he enjoyed having an admiring audience.

Laura recalled the first time she'd gone to the house in Hackney. When she'd told Robin at Piers's wedding that she was moving to a job in London, he'd immediately invited her over for brunch the following weekend. She hadn't realised that it was going to be an interviewing panel with both brothers and their wives sitting at the table. Crispin and Cassandra were already living in a house they'd bought in Islington. Piers and Camilla had just returned from honeymoon and were waiting for a new-build canal-side flat to be ready for them to move into.

'Long story short,' said Crispin, 'Piers and I own this house. Obviously, as long as it's silly prices in London, it's a good investment. But we don't want the hassle of dealing with disgusting tenants, letting agents, etcetera . . .'

'And I live here,' said Robin.

'But you can't even pay the bills,' said Piers.

'So we're looking for tenants for a house share,' Crispin said.

'And Robin tells us you're moving to London,' Piers added.

'He says you're a teacher.'

Crispin made it sound like an accusation rather than a job description.

'Clever you!' said Camilla.

'That must be such fun!' said Cassandra.

Laura didn't know whether she wanted to be indebted to these people, especially Piers, whose gaze she'd always found disturbing.

'I'm not sure I could afford . . .'

'We're not unreasonable people,' Crispin said.

'As long as the bills are paid, the place is kept clean, council tax, etc, we're happy for you to pay the market rate for a room, whereas you'd have the benefit of a whole house, with someone you know . . .'

Piers was shrewder than she'd given him credit for. It was almost as if he'd sensed her dread of sharing a flat with strangers.

'You'd be doing me a favour,' Robin smiled at Laura. 'Eggs Florentine OK for everyone?'

She told herself that it was his sweet character rather than his perfectly emulsified hollandaise that had sealed the deal. Occasionally she wondered whether, if she hadn't decided to move in, they would ever have seen each other again. They weren't in love then. Had they ever really been?

The arrangement had given them a home they couldn't otherwise afford. After a couple of years, when his brothers had wanted to sell the property, she'd been the one with a regular salary so was able to get a mortgage to buy them out. The friendship between her and Robin had been entirely platonic. They were both from expat families, which had given them a degree of self-sufficiency. She was working very hard. His life was chaotic, but he was house-trained. If he was there, he cooked for them both. Various girlfriends came and went. If she ever asked what had happened, he'd say he didn't like it when women parked their tanks on his lawn.

One Sunday evening when they were both unexpectedly at

home together, they rented a rom com which had a line about men not being able to have women as friends.

'Is that true?' she'd asked.

'Maybe for some guys, my brothers, for instance,' he'd replied. 'For me, it's the friendship bit I like. When you're the object of people's fantasies, you're never going to live up to expectations as a lover, are you? Women always think I'm the answer to their dreams. But I'm about the last person they need...'

That statement would probably have sounded preposterously arrogant to most people, but to Laura it made complete sense.

'It's what I like about living with you,' he'd said. 'You don't expect me to be anything.'

Nor you me, she thought.

Neither of them had intended it as a flirtation, but somehow they'd ended up kissing.

When, a few weeks later, she'd told him she was pregnant he'd said, 'God, that's going to be one beautiful baby!'

And she was.

As the appetising smell of sweating garlic filled the kitchen, Robin said, 'Why don't you open another bottle, Coco? I'll need some for the sauce...'

Laura usually held her hand over her glass if it had been refilled, but on this occasion she let Jessica pour.

'It's from a local vineyard. I asked them to stock us up for a week and they've given us so much, I don't think we'll ever get through it. There's a selection of recent and vintage. White and red. This is the new...'

'It tastes a bit like Beaujolais Nouveau,' said Robin. 'Which is barely even alcoholic. Must be almost time for the run...'

Robin's brothers had created a number of obligatory traditions which probably had their origin in a childhood sense of dislocation from their parents, but now felt ritualistic and oppressive. The annual Beaujolais Nouveau party at Crispin's place celebrated the return of a gang of his petrolhead friends racing their Porsches from London to France to be first back with the new vintage. In the orgy of conspicuous consumption and willy-waving that followed, it didn't feel as if the wine was barely alcoholic. Laura put her glass down. The thought of them arriving the following day made her feel suddenly dismal again.

'How do you manage to turn a tin of tomatoes into something totally moreish?' Jessica asked, as she tasted the dish Robin had put down in front of her.

'The secret is a spoonful of sugar, and reduce, reduce, reduce,' said Robin.

Laura was pretty sure it wasn't information either of the women was ever going to use.

'Shall I run through plans for the week?' Jessica asked, when bowls were clean.

'You've worked so hard, Coco,' Robin said, lolling back in his chair. 'Why don't you have an evening off from plans, just relax . . .'

'What a good idea!' said Jessica. 'You're so thoughtful.'

A moment of silence was filled with the restless energy of a child who can't keep a secret.

'I know you're going to love what I've got lined up for this evening . . .' She could finally contain herself no longer.

'What's that then?' Robin asked.

'Fun and frolics!' said Jessica.

They both burst out laughing. It was clearly some private joke.

'Otherwise known as karaoke!'

'Oh my god, Coco, you legend! Karaoke, darling!' He turned to Laura as if she hadn't heard.

'It does sound fun,' she said. 'But I'm really tired...'

'Nonsense! Laura's got a brilliant voice!'

'If she wants to go to bed, Robin...'

'Not allowed! It's my birthday, remember!'

Robin had such a cloth ear at times. It was obvious Jessica had planned the evening for the two of them. Now Laura couldn't see a way of getting out of it. She and Robin loaded the dishwasher while Jessica went to get the party room set up. When they entered, it had been transformed into a surreal disco with a revolving lamp whirling coloured spots of light around the ancient patches of fresco. On the platform beside the piano there was a karaoke machine, the projection of words on the wall overlapping the nose of some unknown saint.

For a moment, Robin stopped in his tracks. 'Are you sure this is allowed?'

He'd been so bullied as a child by his family and his schooling, he was still acutely afraid of doing the wrong thing. Laura thought it was this aura of innocence that made women want to look after him.

'It's deconsecrated, so there's no need to worry,' Jessica assured him.

'You didn't bring all this with you, did you, Coco?' Robin said.

'No, the machine was part of the spec. I just brought the lamp, with an adapter plug obvs, and I made a playlist. All your favourites! Plus costumes and accessories...'

She pointed at the top of the piano where there was a small array of garments and wigs laid out.

Robin leapt onto the platform and picked up two long wigs with headbands.

'Oooh, I know what song these are for!'

'We don't have to go through the decades in order if you don't want to... but I thought it might be fun...'

'Laura! Come on!' Robin said, thrusting a wig in her direction.

'No, really, I've never done karaoke,' said Laura.

'Not even at a hen night?' Jessica asked.

'I haven't been to a hen night,' Laura said. She had never been invited to any of those she'd heard her colleagues excitedly planning. She'd told herself it was because she was their boss but suspected that the truth was they didn't like her.

'All right,' Robin picked up one of the microphones. 'We'll show you how it's done.' Putting on his wig and switching on the microphone so that his voice boomed out, 'Will Coco, or should I say, Cher, please join me on the stage?'

He bobbed to the beat as the unmistakable intro to 'I Got You Babe' flowed through the speaker. Jessica stepped up and hurriedly pulled on a hippy wig just in time to sing the opening line. Her voice was flat, but that didn't hold her back and they were both clearly enjoying themselves so much, it was impossible not to smile and cheer at the end.

'Moving on to the seventies,' Jessica spoke into the microphone, handed Robin a pair of oversized glasses and they segued straight into an enthusiastic rendition of 'Don't Go Breaking My Heart' by Elton John and Kiki Dee.

Robin was in his element, Laura thought, looking younger and happier than she'd seen him in ages. Was this how he and Jessica had been as students? For the first time she began to understand his devotion to her. It wasn't anything to do with her voice, which was terrible, but there was something about the way she totally committed to the song that made her enjoyment almost infectious.

'Coco's the embodiment of a good time in human form,' Laura remembered him saying, when she'd been curious why the only non-negotiable evening of his week was their Friday-night meet. It had made Laura feel like the dullest person on earth.

As the introduction to 'Summer Nights' from *Grease* started playing, and Jessica handed Robin a black wig with a quiff, he beckoned Laura to the stage.

'Come on, darling, you must have a go!'

'I don't know the words...' said Laura, nervously smoothing down her hair.

'Words are on the wall,' Jessica muttered.

There was no way she was going to get out of it.

It was ridiculous to have stage fright when nobody was watching, but she'd always had it when she acted at school and still now when she was called upon to speak publicly. She had found the only way she could manage it was by taking such deep breaths that she descended into an almost catatonic state where the audience became a blur and she was aware of nothing except the words coming out of her mouth. Taking the mic, she managed to get through the whole song, which was much longer than she remembered, with Jessica shouting out the 'Tell me mores' from the side.

At the end, Robin's hug was so fervent, it picked her up off the floor. Looking over his shoulder she saw the despair on Jessica's face. She'd donned a pink satin jacket in readiness to be Sandy and Laura had stolen the moment from her. It took her right back to how she'd felt at school when, however hard she tried to fit in, she'd always realised too late that she'd said or done the wrong thing. Recently, she'd begun to wonder whether, if she were a teenager now, she would have had a diagnosis of autism, like several of the very bright but quiet girls at her school. Then, the only strategy open had been to find ways of removing herself from social situations, which had exacerbated the problem as she'd been labelled snooty.

Laura ostentatiously stifled a yawn.

'I'm so tired,' she said. 'Does anyone mind if I turn in?'

Robin's attempt to protest was superseded by his need to sing the first line of 'You're the One That I Want', which was up next on the playlist, allowing Jessica to murder Sandy's verses. The 'ooh ooh oohs' followed her all the way upstairs.

Closing the door, Laura ran a bath and shook in the contents of a small bottle that foamed and filled the air with the scent of sandalwood, then lay wallowing for a long time in steamy silence.

Slipping between crisp cotton sheets and closing her eyes, she could now hear mournful strains of Jessica's Lady Gaga and Robin's Bradley Cooper belting out an emotional rendition of 'Shallow'.

She allowed herself to wonder what Alex was doing, told herself she absolutely must not call, closed her eyes again, then opened them, grabbed her phone and looked on WhatsApp. He was online.

She typed out a short message, only to let him know that they'd arrived safely, adding, with finality, *It's a beautiful place.*

She turned off the light.

Her phone buzzed.

He'd sent a message back.

*Glad to hear it. How are you?*

She was considering how to respond when she heard footsteps and put her phone down quickly as Robin came in.

'Just setting the alarm. Thought I'd get up and have an early swim.'

'Good idea,' he said, plonking himself down next to her on top of the brocade cover.

His breath had the mouldy smell of red wine, his clothes the sharp reek of garlic.

'Just wanted to say thank you for driving and everything. And the singing. Know you hated it. You're doing so well ...'

'Am I?'

'I need a shower, don't I?' Robin said.

76

Surely he wasn't intending to initiate sex after all this time?

When he went into the bathroom, she switched her bedside light off and turned over, her back to his side, feeling her heart beat faster at the prospect of having to refuse him. When he got into bed, she pretended to be dozing. In the darkness, he reached for her hand and gave it a little squeeze, then turned away from her onto his side and she felt comfortable again. They were both experts at concealing their vulnerability, she thought. It was why they had found a kind of silent refuge in one another.

# Chapter Eight

## Jessica

## Sunday

In London, she always knew what time it was when she woke up from the noises outside. The almost undetectable rumble of the first Piccadilly Line train at five thirty, a crow cawing in a nearby tree at daybreak, the barking of next door's dog when the owner left for work at seven. Here, there was total silence. The edges of the window seemed to be glowing dark pink. Throwing back the starched white sheet and cosy down duvet, she touched a toe on the stone floor, grateful for the incongruous warmth of the underfloor heating, and opened the shutters. The sky was a fuchsia colour she'd never had believed if she'd seen it in a photo, so unexpected it almost scared her. Jessica wriggled into her swimming costume, shoved her feet into the slippers she found in the pocket of the towelling robe provided, then dashed out without even looking in a mirror or pulling a brush through her hair.

The fiery tones were fading by the time she reached the terrace. As her eyes adjusted to the dawn, she began to see the hills awakening as the rising sun picked out distant settlements, turning their stone from pink to gold. Alone with just the sound of her breath, she felt like the only being on earth experiencing the beauty of this moment. Then a bird began to sing.

The pool had a cover on. Vittoria had shown her where the keys to the pump room were. She found the switch to start rolling it back, startled by the efficiency of the mechanism and the sudden whiff of chlorine on the air. There were a few leaves on the surface, but it looked clean, and as she cautiously put her foot on the first step, she could feel that it was warmer than she was anticipating, so she slid straight in, the water enveloping her like silk. In one direction, the paved area round the firepit; in the other, the panorama of hills. The pool was long enough to crawl one way then return with a leisurely breaststroke, looking at the view. Eighteen metres, she seemed to remember from the details. She tried to calculate how many lengths she would need to swim to get to a mile, wishing she didn't have a brain that had to work stuff like that out before it could allow her to relax. A hundred, she thought, should be more than enough. Putting on goggles, with nothing to think about except the counting, her mind began to drift.

How wonderful it would be to have a private pool to swim in every day. Perhaps she should have taken her chance with the American banker whose daughter's wedding she had organised in a manor house in Wiltshire. He'd demanded everything be bigger and more historic than the groom's family home, which was on the fringes of the Cotswold set. It had involved quite a lot of research, all of which had seemed redundant when Robin had commented that in general with the upper classes, the shabbier the home, the older the lineage. Randolph, however, had clearly interpreted the in-laws' awkwardness and early departure as a win for him. He'd insisted Jessica address him as Randy when she'd caught up with him for feedback in the orangery the next morning after the guests had left. There couldn't have been the same double entendre in America. And he didn't appear to be joking when he'd invited her to become his own personal events organiser at his home in Florida. When he'd shown her photos, she'd been tempted. How bad could life be if it began every day in an Olympic-size pool in the sunshine? Fortunately, she'd watched a Netflix documentary on Jeffrey Epstein the same evening.

'OK if I join you?'

Jessica had just turned on seventy-nine lengths when Laura's voice snapped her out of her meditative state.

'Of course,' she said, putting her feet down and pulling up the goggles, telling herself that seventy-nine was nearly eighty, which was almost a hundred and it really didn't matter anyway because she was supposed to be on holiday and not counting every single step or stroke she did.

How was it even possible to look good in a short wetsuit after bearing two children? Laura had the figure of a model. Flat chest, flat stomach, long slim legs with only the merest hint of cellulite. Perhaps the wetsuit held everything in better than the panel in Jessica's costume did. Maybe she should take up wild swimming. Did the coldness of the water tone you up? It was supposed to be good for your mental health. She wondered if there was anywhere local to her other than the reservoir Laura frequented.

'Did you see the sky?' she asked, as Laura stepped into the water.

'Yes. Extraordinary, wasn't it?'

'Red sky in the morning, though,' said Jessica.

'Luckily we're not shepherds,' said Laura.

Was it a joke or a put-down? With Laura's flat delivery, Jessica was never sure.

'Did you sleep well?'

'Very well, thank you. How about you?'

'Very well.'

Jessica imagined they were both lying. The last time she had looked at her watch it was after four. The anxiety of getting them all there, together with the adrenaline of the house being a success, then many glasses of red wine and karaoke had proved difficult to come down from.

Laura was one of those swimmers who knew how to time her inhalation exactly as her head came out of the water, and barely made a splash even though her kicks were propelling her along much faster than Jessica's. Was there anything she wasn't good at? Even karaoke, which she claimed never to have tried, then sang so sweetly it could have been the ghost of Olivia Newton-John in the room. Jessica told herself it was injustice she was feeling, rather than jealousy. Now that she had lost her aerobic speed due to the interruption, there didn't seem much point in continuing, but she thought that getting out straightaway might appear hostile, so she swam up and down a couple of times more before stopping, waiting for Laura and saying, 'I think that's me done.'

In the pool house, there was a lawnmower, a neatly arranged array of other garden tools, and shelves with piles of fluffy striped towels. Jessica was wrapping one around her dripping body when the door opened, which made her shriek as loudly as if the man had caught her naked.

'*Scusi!* I'm sorry,' said Enzo.

'I just wasn't expecting anyone,' Jessica said.

'Also I,' he said, with a shrug. 'Don't worry, I come back.' He pointed at a wheel of hosepipe.

'No, no. I was on my way out.'

She picked up another towel and made to leave as he stepped forward and brushed against her, creating another awkward moment.

'Please!' he said, standing back with a chivalrous flourish.

'Thank you. You start work early.'

'It is always a good time for the garden. Normally, nobody is awake.'

'No rest for the wicked!' said Jessica.

She saw that he didn't understand and realised she'd never actually thought about the meaning of the phrase. Was the idea that wickedness was so compelling you could never stop doing it, or that evildoers weren't allowed to rest, in Hell, presumably? In which case, why did people say it in such a jolly way? Either way, it was inappropriate at this moment.

'Exactly,' she added, nonsensically.

Enzo was attaching the hose to the outside tap so that he could water the planting around the firepit.

'The earth is very dry after the summer,' he said. 'Pay attention if you light a fire.'

'Noted,' said Jessica. 'Any other dangers I should be aware of?'

Enzo gave the question serious consideration.

'You will probably not see snakes at this time of year, but pay attention because they are – how you say – lethal. Do not approach the savage pigs.'

'Pigs?' Did he mean wild boar?

'Mostly they stay in the forest.'

She didn't find that information particularly reassuring.

'What are those things for?' She pointed at some globelike objects hanging from posts around the pool area that seemed too large and ugly to be outdoor lighting.

'To trap the horseflies. Some people have very bad allergy. Not to preoccupy, I think now it's too cold for them.'

Jessica was beginning to wish she hadn't asked. But it was best to be prepared. Fortunately, she always packed a supply of antihistamines.

Laura was getting out of the pool.

'Having a Lady Chatterley moment?' she asked, as Jessica handed her a towel.

'What?'

'In the shed with the gorgeous groundsman!'

The statement made Jessica uncomfortable. After years of women battling not to be judged on their appearance, she didn't find the current vogue for making leery comments about fit men acceptable. And if anyone had been flirting with him it was Laura, yesterday.

'Are you a tea person or a coffee person in the mornings?' Jessica asked.

'Tea. You?'

'Coffee,' said Jessica.

'Bit cold now,' said Laura. 'Think I'll go up and have a shower.'

Alone in the kitchen, Jessica tried to work out how to use the Nespresso machine, wondering what had possessed her to say she drank coffee. It was like that time when Laura had asked her if she was a cat person or a dog person and she'd said a dog person, only because Laura had Bobtail on her lap at the time. It had proved a bit awkward when she'd first met Lammie and screamed when he'd jumped up at her. She had been bitten badly as a child by the dog of a man she always thought of as Bill Sikes, who lurked around the entrance of the flats where she and her mother had lived. She still had the marks on her arm.

Now she faced a week of drinking coffee in the mornings, which would make her more jittery than she already was.

'Do you want a hand with that?' Robin entered the kitchen, looking bleary. He was wearing jeans and a soft raspberry-pink wool jumper she had given him a few Christmases back, that made her want to hug him.

She watched as he slotted a capsule in and pressed the button.

'No thanks,' she said, as he took the espresso. Too hungover to ask for an explanation, he downed it in one and prepared another. The two of them leant on the work surface staring vaguely out of the window. At the far end of the lawn, Enzo was clipping the edges of a flowerbed, regular, audible snips cutting through the silence. The swim had flushed away Jessica's headache, but the tender, slightly time-lapsed sensation of a hangover remained.

'He's very good-looking, isn't he?' Robin remarked.

'If you like that kind of thing,' she said. 'There's yoghurt? Fruit?' She pointed at the bowl in the centre of the kitchen island, noticing for the first time that one of the apples was gnawed.

As she picked it up, a mouse shot across the surface, leapt down to the floor and disappeared behind the wood burner in the fireplace.

'Bloody hell!' Robin pointed at the apple still in her hand. 'Get rid of the evidence! Whatever happens, Coco, my brothers must not know about this . . .' He looked completely panic-stricken.

'You know what?' said Jessica. 'This is not acceptable. Not in five-star accommodation. I'm going to speak to Enzo.'

Marching outside and across the lawn, she realised that she was still in her towelling robe.

Enzo turned round as he heard her approaching and it occurred to her that he looked a bit like someone she knew, but she couldn't think who it was. Was it Rufus Sewell? When he was younger. Or was that just because he'd played an Italian detective? Probably some film star. It had happened the other way round. She'd once said, 'Hi, how are you?' to Ryan Gosling on Bow Street. He had smiled, clearly used to that sort of thing, waiting for the truth to dawn and for her to rush away embarrassed. Instead, she'd taken the opportunity to tell him that *Crazy, Stupid, Love* was her favourite rom com and that she thought he should have won an Oscar for *First Man*.

'How can I help you?' Enzo asked.

What could be the word for mouse? She wished she had her phone with her for Google Translate.

'Er, *scusi, c'e un animale piccolo chi ama formaggio . . .'* Excuse me, there is a small animal that likes cheese . . . She put her hands up to her face like paws and bared her front teeth, making a squeaking sound.

He laughed.

'A mouse?' he said.

'You know?'

'You are in the country. It's getting cold outside now. For sure, the mouses they like to come in . . .'

'Mice,' she corrected.

'Excuse me.'

'No, no, you speak English very well . . .' She didn't want to offend him when she needed his help.

'I used to live in London. Shoreditch . . .'

'Nice!' There was really no time for his life history. Laura would be down shortly and they needed to have a plan in place.

'The thing is, we have a problem. The other woman . . .' She glanced back at the house, hoping Laura wasn't looking out of the bedroom window.

'*La bella bionda?*'

The beautiful blonde.

'Yes, her. She's very frightened, terrified, mad, in fact . . .' The thought that Laura did after all have a weakness was rather cheering. To emphasise her silliness, Jessica started flapping around miming screams.

'She has a phobia?'

'Exactly!'

His English was actually quite good, she realised, which was a relief as she wasn't particularly enjoying this game of charades.

'The rest of the party should be arriving fairly soon, so my plan is to book a restaurant for lunch somewhere interesting enough for us to spend an afternoon. Then you can deal with the problem. Do you have a recommendation?'

He thought for a moment.

'Allow me to call my cousin in Sansepolcro. He has a very good restaurant, and afterwards you can go to see the work of Piero della Francesca.'

God, she loved Italians. How many gardeners in the UK would think of Renaissance paintings as a family pastime?

'I love art,' she said. 'Not sure about the rest of us, but if the restaurant's good . . .'

'Yes, of course . . . how many people?'

She told him, and he pulled out his phone and made the reservation.

'He will be very happy to accommodate you.'

Twelve unexpected covers. I bet he will, Jessica thought, knowing she should have negotiated a discount.

'Can you make absolutely sure the problem is sorted by the time we return?'

'I will do my best,' he said, smiling.

He didn't appear to be taking it nearly seriously enough.

'Discreetly, obviously,' she instructed.

He put a finger to his lips.

'Your secret is safe with me!'

Glancing up at the house again she saw that Laura was watching them from the window, no doubt assuming that Jessica was coming on to him.

She walked briskly back across the lawn with as much

haughty intent as disposable slippers would allow, checking her watch to make herself look busy. One hundred and thirty-three steps, but it already felt as if she'd expended a marathon's worth of nervous energy.

Laura stayed upstairs doing yoga for the rest of the morning while Robin stood guard in the kitchen, staring at the fireplace as if to face down the mouse should it dare to emerge again.

Around midday, a black SUV accelerated up the drive and parked in a swirl of gravel. Robin's brother Crispin jumped out, followed by Piers and, from the back, the two wives Cassandra and Camilla and Camilla's younger son Barty.

'Oh, I didn't think you were bringing . . . ?' said Robin.

'Needed to get him out of the country,' Crispin said darkly, clapping Robin on the back so hard, he winded him. 'We won!' he shouted, as the other SUV, driven by Tim, pulled up. 'Lunch on you, Beast!'

'OMG, don't call him that!' Cassandra tittered. 'He's not even ugly anymore, IMO.'

'Probably had work done,' Piers guffawed. 'I expect he gets mates' rates.'

Jessica noticed the tiny flicker of anxiety in Camilla's eyes and realised that her alabaster complexion and fixed expression were probably due to Botox. Cassandra's cheeks looked as if two small apples had been forced up under the skin. Were they patients of Tim's? He was apparently one of the best cosmetic surgeons in the world, which made it somewhat uncomfortable when he looked at you directly, not that she would ever consider having work done even if she could afford it. Jessica wasn't bad-looking but, as Mandy put it, she was no oil painting. Nothing she could do about that. Sometimes she thought true beauty must actually be a burden because when people had been admiring your face all your life, ageing was so much more noticeable. Although annoyingly, Laura was the only woman she'd ever seen who seemed to become more beautiful with age, as if she'd grown into the seriousness which had been rather forbidding when she was younger.

Ignoring both the brothers, Tim walked towards Robin with outstretched arms and gave him a hug.

'Missed you,' Robin said.

'Sweet!' chorused the brothers.

'Promise me you'll never allow your children inside a car driven by these maniacs,' Tim said.

'You always were a sore loser, Beast,' said Piers.

'You almost killed us all, overtaking like that. It wasn't a race!'

'You were the ones who hotfooted it to the car rental.'

'Only because none of our lot had hold luggage,' said Tim.

'Loser, loser!' Crispin and Piers started chanting, with Barty quickly joining in.

George got out of the front seat and Ellis emerged from the back. They really were stunningly beautiful children, especially next to the thuggish Barty. Gorgeous George with his dark curly hair that suited him in whatever cut was the latest vogue for footballers, currently a Jack Grealish-style short back and sides. Ellis, who had inherited Laura's beauty and white-blonde hair that they now wore cut in a crop, which, with their black clothes, made them look like the gamine star of a French movie from the sixties. They were with a very pretty young woman with long black hair.

'Jessica, this is Jaz,' Ellis said, ostentatiously taking the girl's hand.

It had been 'Jaz' this and 'Jaz' that the last time Jessica had gone to lunch, but she hadn't realised there was a relationship going on. Nor, it seemed, had Laura, who'd emerged from the house and was staring open-mouthed at the linked hands, as were Robin's brothers.

'You two must have one of the doubles,' Jessica said immediately. 'In fact, have mine ... I certainly won't be needing it!'

Ellis smiled infrequently, so it was like receiving a gift when they did.

'You are the coolest godmother ever!' they said.

Jessica's brain was whirling with the new arrangements. She would have to move to the room next to George. Where Barty would sleep wasn't her problem. Thank goodness she'd insisted on the brothers renting the unit separately.

'*Garçon!*' said Crispin, waving the menu at the waiter. 'We are ready.'

As he had plonked himself at the head of the table and was taking command of the ordering for all of them, Jessica assumed that meant he was going to pay, so she didn't point out that they were in Italy, not France, though she doubted that way of addressing the waiter would have gone down well there either.

There was a family resemblance in all the brothers, but similar features arranged with less than Robin's perfect symmetry made Crispin look supercilious and Piers cruel. Mandy had once told her that the essential character of men showed in their faces as they grew older. Even in their youth, either Crispin or Piers could have been cast as a sadistic upper-class bully in any episode of *Endeavour*. Not that they were actors. Robin's vocation had been the object of their derision even during the short time he was successful. Crispin was a hedge fund manager. Piers was a prosecuting barrister. Jessica had never seen him in a wig, but she could imagine exactly what it would be like to face him in court. She'd observed his like when she'd once sat in the public gallery of the Old Bailey. Any working-class person in the dock hadn't a hope because they literally didn't speak the same language. On a recent date with a solicitor she'd learned that the most talented barristers did defence rather than prosecution work. They'd consumed a bottle of rather nice Malbec in the bar of Picturehouse Central, which was a conveniently public place to meet for the first time and meant you could see a film if the date didn't show up. The sex hadn't really worked, but at least she'd gained a little piece of information to comfort herself with privately when Piers was being particularly patronising.

Everyone had sat down at the long table set up for twelve before she had a chance to organise a seating plan, with the children gathering at one end and the adults at the other. She ended up in the middle between Tim and Piers and opposite the brothers' wives. They were both willowy and aristocratic, the sort of women whose idea of work was an hour's session with a personal trainer. She could never remember which was the one with the title.

'How was your flight?' she asked.

'We normally use City airport, tbh,' said Cassandra.

Initialisms were useful in a text, but surely it was just as easy to say the whole words in conversation?

'It's a bit pricier, but by the time you've paid for parking . . .' Camilla remarked. 'And Florence airport is so convenient for the *castello*.'

The brothers jointly owned a holiday home in the Chianti area.

'Although *castello* is rather a grand term for somewhere with only five bedrooms,' Cassandra added.

It was what they always said when their holiday home was mentioned, just so there was no risk of Jessica imagining she would get an invitation, she assumed. She had hoped Robin's brothers would stay there this week, only joining the rest of the party for the evening of Robin's birthday. It didn't look that far on the map. Turned out that the space between was mostly mountains, so it would have been a three-hour journey each way, even for a mad driver like Piers.

'I'm afraid there are only five bedrooms in the main house,' Jessica had relished typing as she'd forwarded Camilla a link to the adjacent converted stable block. At least it meant she didn't have to front up the money for them too as she was already pushing her credit limit. And she didn't trust them to pay her back. It never seemed to occur to rich people that trifling sums to them might be crucial to a poorer person's livelihood. Or perhaps, she sometimes thought, it did occur, and that's how they became rich in the first place.

'Stop it, Barty!' Ellis cried.

All the adults turned to look.

'He keeps kicking George!'

'I do not!'

'George, you and I swap seats. He won't dare kick me,' said Ellis.

There was a moment of prevarication as all the adults wondered about intervening but the problem seemed to be sorted as the kids changed places.

'Thank you, Ellis,' Robin said.

'What a sweet little bag!' Cassandra suddenly pointed at Jessica's cross-body purse.

She was the sort of person who could spot a designer rip-off at a hundred paces, and it was from Primark. Jessica knew that nobody was going to believe that she actually found pleather more practical for travelling. She didn't dare risk a joke about people who bought real Chanel having more money than sense. So she decided to say, 'Thank you!' with a laugh she hoped sounded ironic rather than embarrassed.

Conversation between them had always been limited even though she'd known them almost as long as she'd known Robin. During the first vacation he had invited her back for breakfast after clubbing all night in Shoreditch. At the time, the brothers owned the Hackney house and Robin preferred to stay there than fly to whichever country his father was working in. She'd never met his parents, but they sounded very distant in all senses.

Camilla and Cassandra were sitting beside each other at the kitchen table, the long-established girlfriends of the brothers. Both wisp-thin, they wore their perfectly fitting jeans and oversized cashmere cardigans with casual elegance. Jessica was a size twelve, sometimes a fourteen because of her height. She'd never felt as ungainly in her life.

'How do you know Robin?' one had asked.

'We're at uni together,' she'd replied, disappointed that he hadn't mentioned her.

'Really?'

She never established whether they actually had jobs at *Tatler* and *Vogue* or just hung around with people who did. If *Made in Chelsea* had started ten years earlier, they might well have become reality television stars. Instead, they had lavish weddings in Georgian manor houses in the Cotswolds, to which Jessica was not invited, and bore two sons each, returning to their pre-pregnancy weight in days.

Jessica felt that they regarded her as a curiosity, someone they might occasionally mention to friends to demonstrate that they knew some working-class people. Or perhaps she didn't even hold that significance for them. She saw them as one of the main reasons why she and Robin had never got together. Not necessarily because of anything bitchy they'd said against her, but because beside them she looked like a different species, not someone who would be considered wife material. Being the youngest of the family, Robin was very influenced by his brothers. But perhaps that was just how families were. She'd only ever had her mum. Although Mandy had been like a big sister.

'I don't think they liked me,' she'd said, as Robin walked her to the bus stop.

'That's my family, Coco, it's not me.'

They'd been working their way through the *Godfather* trilogy at Blockbuster.

She'd laughed, before realising, sitting alone on the top deck, that it was a charming way of leaving her assertion un-challenged.

The waiter recommended the porcini mushrooms which were locally picked and in season.

'Are you sure they're not poisonous?' Tim asked.

'I doubt they'd last long if they were in the habit of killing their customers,' said Robin.

Crispin started recounting an anecdote they'd all heard many times before about the macho challenge of eating a potentially lethal blowfish in Japan. Over the years, Jessica noted, it had gone from a tale he had told about business associates, to a deed he had accomplished himself. Did he have to win at every-thing, she wondered? What must he be like in bed? Selfish, insufferable, probably not very well endowed. She glanced at Cassandra's smooth, expressionless face and found herself feeling slightly sorry for her.

Once Jessica had established that Ellis and Jaz's portions could be made with pasta containing only flour with no egg, everyone chose the porcini dish to start. The mushrooms were delicious, the portions enormous, and the general ambience of the group grew warmer and louder as several carafes of white wine were downed like jugs of water.

Jessica kept to just one small glass and she saw that, down at the end of the table, Laura was doing the same. She also noticed the thinness of her smile when Robin, pouring at least his fourth glass, suddenly said, 'Oh, bugger. I said I'd do all the driving, didn't I?'

'Too late now,' said Piers, ordering a carafe of red to go with their main course of sliced rare steak. 'It's your bloody birthday, Robbo!'

'Boyfriend coming later, Beast?' Crispin shouted at Tim.

There was a sharp intake of breath at both ends of the table. The brothers weren't as openly homophobic as they had been twenty years ago, but their prejudice wasn't very well hidden beneath the friendly veneer of the enquiry.

'Not coming at all,' Tim replied equably.

Beside her, Piers sniggered.

'He was a bit younger than me. Week in a remote house in Umbria not really his kind of thing . . .'

'What first attracted this young man to a fabulously rich middle-aged cosmetic surgeon, do you think?' Piers asked.

Tim laughed. 'You're probably right,' he said. 'But it was fun while it lasted.'

'I'm sorry,' Jessica said.

As Robin's best friends, they'd always got on, with just a slight edge of competition for which of them Robin liked most. Jessica generally preferred the company of gay men to straight men, although Tim wasn't outrageously camp like the men she had grown up with. Her mother had shared a dressing room with several drag queens at the club, and it had been like a second home during Jessica's childhood. She'd had a cot there, which became a convenient, off-floor container for the ostrich feather fans when she got too big to sleep in it. As she got older, they'd cleared a bit of dressing table for her to do her homework. Studying had never felt quite the same without a mirror with a frame of lights to gaze into as you pondered the best way of tackling an essay.

'So what's the plan this afternoon?' Crispin demanded.

Jessica automatically defaulted to her professional mode of trying to please the client. Not that the brothers were clients exactly, but she'd taken the opportunity to research Sansepolcro while waiting for them to arrive.

'The town is mainly famous for two things: the Buitoni factory where pasta is made, and a very celebrated work of art by Piero della Francesca. It is said that the painting saved the town during the war . . .' Hoping that a military angle would interest them, she recounted the story of how a British officer in the liberating army had read that the *Resurrection* was considered the greatest painting in the world. He had therefore delayed bombardment of the town hoping that the Germans would withdraw, which they did.

'So the painting saved the town, some thought miraculously,' she added, looking up and down the table. The teenagers were looking at their mobiles. Robin stifled a yawn.

'Anyone interested in art?' Crispin asked.

Nobody spoke.

'This is the trouble with Italy,' said Piers. 'It's all art, art, art. Boring!'

'Boring!' echoed Barty without looking up from his phone.

'There are ancient ruins,' said Cassandra, smiling across the table at Jessica.

'Boring!'

'And fashion, don't forget,' said Camilla.

At least the wives were trying to be supportive.

'No, really, there's so much more to Italy,' Jessica said.

'Like?' Piers challenged.

'Well, there's design, of course, and supercars,' she said. 'I've just booked a stag party to go to this Ferrari festival on Capri. Apparently they bring in about a hundred Ferraris on a boat and drive them in a cavalcade around the island in evening dress.'

'Why didn't you organise that for us?' said Crispin.

'It's in May.'

'I'm not that into cars, and I much prefer Umbria,' Robin chipped in loyally.

'In Emilia Romagna there's a whole region devoted to cars called Motor Valley ... racetracks, car factories ...'

'That's not too far from here, is it?' said Piers.

'If you wanted, I could book for you guys to go to the Lamborghini experience?' Jessica had researched the site in case of exactly this kind of impasse, but she hadn't expected to need it so soon. 'You can test drive ...'

'Now you're talking,' said Piers.

She got out her phone. 'Who's in?'

'Me,' said Piers. 'Cris, Barty ... George?'

'No thanks,' said George.

'Robbo?'

'I think I've got a cookery lesson ...' Robin stuttered.

'Very limited availability,' Jessica said, perusing the site. 'Wait, a slot has just come up for tomorrow. Must be a cancellation. Do you want it? You'll have to be quick ...'

There were in fact quite a few free slots, but it was a well-known law of economics that exclusivity carried a premium.

'Grab it!' said Crispin.

'Credit card?' Jessica held out her hand to Piers, who somewhat reluctantly handed it over.

'There we are! All booked. Bit of an early start, but I'm sure it will be worth it.'

'Early start?'

'Ten o'clock, but it's a two-and-a-half hour drive ... or possibly less for you,' she said, smiling sweetly at Piers.

'Hang on, where is it?' Cassandra asked.

'Near Bologna, which is very good for shopping.'

The restaurant was empty now apart from their table and the waiter was hovering.

'Hands up for the *Resurrection*,' said Jessica. It wasn't a phrase she'd ever thought she'd hear herself saying.

'Why not?' said Laura.

'We'd like to see it, wouldn't we?' said Ellis to Jaz.

'Come on, lads,' said Robin. 'Better give culture a go.'

'We'll head back to the house,' said Crispin. 'Find our way around.'

'Unpack,' said Cassandra.

'Settle in,' said Camilla.

'Early start today, early start tomorrow . . .' Piers glared at Jessica. 'I thought this was supposed to be a holiday!'

'Barty?'

'I'll stay.'

Jessica had been about to congratulate herself on deftly getting rid of the brothers' party. Now she felt guilty for failing to complete the job.

# Chapter Nine

## *Robin*

Too much wine had made his brain slow to come up with a plausible reason why Barty should not stay behind before his brothers and their wives had scraped back their chairs and left.

The waiter handed him the bill, which was in his hand long enough to see it was considerable before being snatched by Tim, who paid it.

Once outside, the group split by gender, with Jessica leading the girls purposefully towards the town's little museum and the boys following reluctantly. As they walked across the main square, George spotted a group of lads kicking a football about and ran over to join in, with Barty lumbering after him.

'Someone needs to keep an eye on that hooligan,' Tim warned.

'Coffee?' said Robin, pointing at some tables outside a café.

Why did you always have to do stuff on holiday when the perfect activity was sitting in warm sunshine sipping espresso and a grappa, with your best friend, in a charming little square? The stone towers and pale ochre plaster of the buildings contrasted harmoniously with the blue sky, and the streets were pedestrianised, so it felt as if nothing much had changed since medieval times. The little arched shopfronts were shuttered so that you couldn't tell whether it was a butcher or a computer shop inside. There was an atmosphere of stillness and contentment interrupted occasionally by locals emerging from the café carrying a tray of tiny pastries, wrapped in fancy paper and tied with narrow gold ribbon, to take to family gatherings.

Staring vaguely at the girls as they walked away down a street, he suddenly noticed that Ellis was holding hands with Jaz. He wondered if it meant anything. Young people were so tactile these days, routinely greeting each other with hugs, even George and his footballing friends.

'Can you imagine the price we would have paid for such a public demonstration of affection at their age?' he said to Tim, pointing. 'Isn't it nice that everything's so much more fluid now?'

'Is it, though?' Tim gave him a hard stare. 'Is it really?'

'Well, yes, it is,' said Robin, a bit surprised by the jarring confrontational tone.

'I wonder whether your liberal credentials are quite as shiny as you think.'

'What on earth do you mean?'

'Well, for instance, is it because I'm gay that you didn't ask me to be godfather to George?'

The question came out of nowhere.

'Of course not! How could you even think that?'

'Apparently, Jessica's godmother to Ellis . . . I heard her say so.'

'Jessica appointed herself almost the moment Eliza was born. You know what she's like . . .'

'She's a person who would love to have kids and saw an opportunity to form a special bond. Didn't it even occur to you that I might like someone to call me godfather?'

Robin put on a gravelly Marlon Brando voice. 'Why do you disrespect me so much? You don't even call me Godfather . . .'

'Very funny.'

Tim seemed in rather a brittle state. Robin hoped he wasn't

going to be like this the whole week. It was his birthday. Everyone was supposed to be nice to him. He took a slug of his digestif, enjoying the mild anaesthetic hit.

It had never occurred to him that Tim might want children. Robin had assumed he was happy with his jet-setting bachelor life. He was at the pinnacle of a successful career, owned an apartment in Belgravia as well as one in Brooklyn Heights and was building a weekend place on Fire Island. Even his looks had improved with age. His face, which had been pockmarked with acne as a teenager and had a permanent five o'clock shadow from the moment he started shaving, was now almost handsome in a Byronic kind of way. Curly hair, left to grow a little and swept back to form a natural quiff, its premature whiteness perversely making him appear younger not older. But he seemed about as successful at sustaining a long-term relationship as Jessica was. He'd always been very kind and generous to the kids, so if it meant something to him to be godfather, why not? Tim didn't really have a family, except for a mother with dementia in a care home, whom Robin dutifully visited every fortnight because she seemed to find comfort in stroking Lammie.

'It's not really up to me, and it's a bit late in the day, but if you wanted to ask George . . .' he offered.

Surely Laura couldn't object to that? She'd been absolutely furious about Jessica, but that was long ago. Perhaps he should have waited to consult his wife, but he didn't want to cause more offence now by withdrawing the offer, so he quickly changed the subject.

'How's the house on Fire Island coming along?' he asked, trying to bring the focus back to Tim's good fortune. The last time he had been in London he'd shown him the architect's plans. It looked like something you'd see in *Succession*. Robin had gazed at the sketches in awe.

100

'We live in different worlds,' he'd said.

'You'll always be in my world,' Tim had replied.

'And you in mine.'

They'd been sitting in a pub in Kew after a leisurely summer evening walk along the Thames, a couple of beers on the table in front of them, the sunshine warm enough not to need a jacket. It had felt rather grown-up, being men having a pint who were metrosexual enough to express their affection for one another.

Now, from the photos on Tim's phone, the house appeared almost finished apart from the garden landscaping, but Tim didn't seem particularly thrilled.

'It's too beautiful a house to be empty most of the time,' he said.

'You're finished with Jonny, are you?' Robin said. It felt a bit strange using the name of someone he'd learned of second-hand.

Tim sighed.

'I was too boring for him,' he said. 'I mean, I like parties as much as anyone else, but not twenty-four seven.'

'Why did you choose Fire Island, then?'

'Being on the ocean. Views, walks. It's companionship I'm after, not orgies.'

'That does sound rather middle-aged.'

'Well, we are, aren't we? We've probably only got twenty more good years, at most . . .'

'Bloody hell, Tim! We're supposed to be celebrating our life beginning, remember!'

Their attention was distracted by shouting from the other side of the square.

Barty had brought down one of the local boys in a dirty tackle. The Italians had picked up the ball and were making it clear that, though George was welcome, they wouldn't play with Barty anymore.

'Football's gay anyway,' Barty said, as he marched past their table.

'Where are you going?' Robin asked.

Barty didn't reply.

'Good riddance,' said Robin.

'Should we follow him and see he doesn't get into any more trouble?'

Not being a parent had made Tim more anxious about these things. 'He'll be back . . .' Robin said, in a *Terminator* voice.

His friend seemed very resistant to being amused today.

'I hope you're not going to allow history to repeat itself?' he said.

'What do you mean?' Robin asked.

'You must not allow Barty to bully George like your brothers bullied you.'

'Oh, come on, Tim! Boys will be boys. It didn't do me any harm!'

'Funny thing is, I think you really believe that.'

# Chapter Ten

## *Laura*

A few metres in front of them, Ellis and Jaz stopped to kiss. With Ellis's pale blond crop and Jaz's long dark hair, they made rather a stunning couple. Yin and yang. Laura wondered why she hadn't realised they were becoming intimate when her daughter had asked if Jaz could join them on the holiday. She'd been happy to accommodate. Jaz was so much better than the last shouty group of Ellis's friends, who talked about nothing but lip fillers and *Love Island*. Jaz was so quiet you almost didn't notice her, although sometimes Laura had the uncomfortable sense she was being observed. Like just now in the restaurant when the others were looking at their social media on their phones, she'd been pretty sure that Jaz was filming proceedings. She tried to work out how she felt about her daughter having a sexual relationship. Was it even correct to assume Jaz was Ellis's first partner? Had they even reached that stage?

Had George known about this development? They used to talk about everything, but recently he seemed to have retreated from her, perhaps because she wasn't at home as much these days. He seemed completely unfazed. Robin hadn't mentioned it either, but that could just mean he was hoping that if he said nothing then other people wouldn't notice. He had been so terrorised by his brothers' accusations of homosexuality ever since he was a small child, and they were bound to relish the opportunity to tease him. Did Jaz's parents know? They were both above the age of consent. So it didn't really matter whether anyone approved or not.

At least Ellis hadn't confided in Jessica before her, Laura thought. From her reaction, the relationship had clearly come as a surprise, but she'd said the perfect thing, always eager to show she was a cool godmother, a title she had awarded herself when Ellis was born. They were not religious people and even if they had been, Laura wasn't sure that Jessica would be the person she would choose to look after her daughter. Typically, Robin hadn't wanted a confrontation. And, to be fair, his prediction that she would give fantastic gifts had been accurate.

As Ellis turned and glared, Laura realised she was staring. Too late to look away, she attempted an easy smile, trying to show she was cool with it too. In a way, she rather envied her daughter the choice, if choice was the right word. The terminology was such a minefield. When she was Ellis's age, lesbianism was still taboo. At least at her school. There had been rumours about two girls in the year above but they'd never come out. In reality, there must have been plenty more if the numbers nowadays represented a truer proportion. Nearly all the year eleven girls at her school seemed to be in relationships with each other. If it had been an unremarkable option when she was a teenager, Laura thought, she would have appreciated the chance to experiment. She'd have found her clitoris much sooner, for sure.

'Have you got a problem?' Ellis demanded.

'Not at all,' said Laura.

'Why are you looking at us like that then?'

'There isn't an instruction manual for what expression your face should make when your child has their first serious relationship!'

Ellis was momentarily pacified by the acknowledgement.

Occasionally, Laura had the terrible thought that she didn't really like her daughter anymore. When Ellis was little, she'd been so proud of their intelligence and all the funny, weirdly sophisticated things they'd said. Now that they were becoming an adult, Laura couldn't seem to get the register right. If she imposed limits, she was a villain; if she allowed more freedom than other parents, she was a joke. She suspected Ellis and their friends were the alphas of their year. They exchanged looks just as the cool girls at her school had done, and Laura found herself struggling with feelings of exclusion she'd had when she was their age.

'You can see it's the Umbrian countryside, because it still looks just like that round here, doesn't it, although technically Sansepolcro is just over the border in Tuscany,' said Jessica as the four of them stood in front of the fresco of the *Resurrection*. 'But did you notice one side of Christ is winter with the trees bare, and the other is summer?'

Laura wouldn't have done if it hadn't been pointed out to her.

'Paintings are like windows on the past, aren't they?' Jessica continued. 'Look at the guards, sleeping in front of the tomb. They were probably portraits of the young men of this town. They're wearing the clothes of the period, and they look as if they're fast asleep after a heavy night out...'

Jaz and Ellis were taking photos.

Jessica's enthusiasm reminded Laura slightly of a clever sixth former who thinks she's the first person to have discovered Sylvia Plath. Art was a passion none of the rest of them shared. When Ellis was little, Jessica had reacted to the nursery daubings Robin had dutifully stuck on their kitchen fridge as if they were a budding Picasso, and taken them to children's activities at the Tate. At their recent Sunday lunch she had banged on about the virtuosity of the Raphael exhibition at the National Gallery, becoming almost tearful about the artist's untimely death.

'We should go, shouldn't we?' Robin had suggested, and they'd all dutifully nodded, knowing that they never would. It was admirable, really, that Jessica continued to believe that one day they would have an epiphany and be able to appreciate what she so clearly saw. The triumph of hope over experience.

'So, the question is, was the artist simply using local people as models, or was there a deeper meaning? Was he making the point that Christ is risen for all of us?' Jessica asked. 'I did a course in lockdown . . .' she added, as if she thought Laura might dock her marks for plagiarism.

Christ's piercing gaze was strangely disconcerting to Laura. He was strong and muscular, quite unlike the usual crumpled figure on the cross. Climbing purposefully out of the tomb, he seemed to be staring directly at her as if he knew her secrets. She turned away.

'It feels like he can see your sins, doesn't it?' Jessica said.

Laura's sense of disquiet slid towards panic. 'I'm sorry?'

'He's confrontational rather than comforting,' Jessica said.

'Yes, I see what you mean,' she stuttered, feeling blood rush to her cheeks.

Outside, the light was fading and there was an autumnal shiver on the air. Ellis and Jaz were deep in murmured conversation, their arms draped over each other's shoulders. Occasionally they stopped to take selfies of their lengthening shadows.

'Where does your interest in art come from?' Laura asked, trying for once to be the one to initiate conversation.

'When I was little I used to go to the National Gallery all the time,' Jessica said. 'It was free and warm and interesting to look at beautiful things. Other little girls wanted to be Disney princesses, I wanted to be one of the angels from the *Wilton Diptych*. The guards knew me, so it was kind of a welcoming place for me, not a big deal like galleries are for most kids.'

'How old were you?' Laura asked.

'About eight or nine, I should think,' Jessica said.

Laura assumed this was another exaggeration.

'Your parents allowed you out alone?'

'It was just Mum, and she worked nights. She was asleep a lot of the day. So it was either the National Gallery or the library just off Leicester Square. I was better off there than the area round our flats.'

Fair enough. It was wrong to assume that home was always the safest place for a child. Robin always said how amazing it was that Jessica had come from nowhere, but she never really knew what that meant and it was hardly something you could press her on without getting too personal.

Remembering the games Jessica and Robin were always playing, which seemed to her like talking without saying anything, she asked, 'If you could have one painting, what would it be?'

Jessica's forehead creased momentarily in surprise at the question, then puckered with concentration as she considered her answer.

'Difficult one. I mean, Monet's water lilies would go with the colour scheme of my flat, but I think it would have to be Raphael's self-portrait. He was so handsome. I have a kind of crush on him!'

Even as a teenager, Laura had never experienced the passions her peers had about boy bands or film stars, let alone artists, let alone dead ones.

'Sounds like the ultimate parasocial relationship,' she said.

'What's that?' Jessica asked.

'It's the psychological term for a one-sided relationship where one party is in love and the other doesn't even know they exist ...'

'Well, that just about sums my life up!' Jessica said with a tight little laugh.

Laura hadn't meant to offend her. Why wasn't she better at small talk?

'OK, here's one for you,' Jessica said. 'You're an English teacher, so if your childhood was a novel, what would it be?'

'I suppose it would have to be something by Jane Austen,' Laura offered. 'I used to spend my holidays with my maiden aunt in Bath.'

'You didn't go home?'

'My mother and I didn't get on.'

Aunt Gillian's elegant flat in one of the less grand Georgian terraces had long sash windows with window seats, where Laura used to sit and read the many hardback books on the shelves lining the walls on either side of the fireplace. Every evening, they ate sliced egg and tomato sandwiches with salad cream. She didn't know if her aunt had a hot lunch. Questions about her work were not permitted. Laura was given a small weekly budget to buy a few basic provisions for the fridge. The only time she ever saw her aunt smile was on Saturday mornings, when she ate cornflakes in her dressing gown and remarked how nice it was not to have to think about going shopping. If it was fine, they would go for a long walk together. Gillian was interested in botany. Their limited conversation revolved around rare fritillaries.

She had never known whether Gillian enjoyed having her there or whether she had simply seen it as her duty to provide a home. Gillian was older than Laura's mother and unlike her, plain, childless and single. She had some kind of important job in the Ministry of Defence which she wasn't allowed to discuss. They also never talked about why Laura had written to ask for her help, but Laura somehow knew that she harboured a low opinion of her stepfather.

'What about your childhood?' she asked Jessica. 'As a novel, I mean . . .'

'First thought, Dickens,' she said. 'More the Artful Dodger than Oliver Twist, although I suppose being in care for a while was a bit like the workhouse.'

'You were in care?'

'Just for a couple of years . . . It was OK because I met my best friend Mandy. If the Harry Potter books had existed then, I would definitely have been Hermione, but there weren't so many relatable children's books for us, were there? The first one I identified with was the story of Tracy Beaker.'

Laura tried to remember the story from Ellis's childhood. She thought Tracy Beaker's mother had abandoned her. Was that what had happened to Jessica? They'd both given glimpses of troubled and lonely childhoods. She knew that the opportunity had opened to understand Jessica better, but she couldn't think of a way of pushing the conversation further that didn't feel intrusive. In another life, she thought, perhaps they would have been friends.

'Was Jane Austen the reason you ended up teaching English?' Jessica asked.

'Among others,' Laura said.

The echoey tap of their footsteps in the silence as they walked back towards the main square made her realise she had inadvertently closed the conversation down again. 'What about you? Didn't you do drama at uni, like Robin?'

'Business studies.'

'I thought Robin said you were treasurer of DramSoc?'

'I was, but only because I knew about money, never having had a lot of it. I wanted to do art history but you couldn't make a living from that.'

They had gone round full circle back to art, which Laura knew nothing about. As they spotted Robin and Tim waving them over, she tried once more.

'Thank you for getting rid of Robin's brothers . . . Well done you!'

Did that sound patronising?

'They're Robin's weak spot, I'm afraid,' she added.

'Well, they are his family!' Jessica immediately retorted in his defence.

George was playing football with a trio of Italian boys a few years older than him. There was no sign of Barty.

'Typical George,' said Jessica. 'He doesn't talk very much, but he can communicate in any language.'

Laura was irritated that Jessica thought she had a right to say what was typical about her son, especially since her observation was spot-on.

The football game stopped as the local boys noticed Ellis and Jaz. They gathered around the table where they sat down. One of them showed Ellis something on his mobile phone.

'Oh my god!' screeched Ellis. 'That's so cool!'

It was a photo of him and his friends dressed in costumes that looked very like the youths in the foreground of the painting they'd just seen.

With her smattering of Italian and gift for mime, Jessica was able to ascertain that the town had a flag-throwing competition with a neighbouring town. It was a tradition handed down from medieval times and the boys were keen for Ellis and Jaz to see them in their team colours. When they returned, clad in brightly coloured velvet doublets and hose, Jaz arranged them around one of the benches in the middle of the square in the exact poses of the guards in the *Resurrection* painting and asked Robin to stand in for Jesus. Always keen to take on a role and not in the least embarrassed by the idea of playing Christ, Robin posed enthusiastically. Then Jaz posted it on her BeReal.

'Wouldn't it be a great idea for an advert?' Jessica said. 'I wonder if we could sell it to Buitoni?'

'Christ coming out of the grave with a fistful of spaghetti?' said Robin.

Both he and Jessica creased up with laughter, like a couple of naughty year eight students sharing a joke at the back of the class. Laura felt like the grown-up keeping a watchful eye on them. And yet what had that attitude achieved? Whenever he was with Jessica he seemed happy. Nobody could say that being with Laura had allowed him to fulfil his potential. Had she diminished him? Would he have been a more successful person without her?

'Did you enjoy seeing the painting, darling?' Robin asked.

'Actually I did,' Laura said. 'Jessica is very good at making art accessible.'

Jessica's smile told her that she had finally landed a compliment.

'There's another Piero della Francesca painting in a town a few miles down the road if you're interested? The *Madonna del Parto*,' Jessica said, overenthusiastic as usual. 'It's one of the few paintings of the pregnant Madonna.'

'I need a coffee,' Laura said. 'Why don't you go with Jessica, Robin? I'll get the kids a gelato.'

'Pregnant virgin or gelato, Tim? Which camp are you in?' Robin asked.

Tim elected to stay and Laura was glad. He was the one adult she felt relaxed with at the moment.

'Jessica can be a bit full-on, can't she?' he said, when Robin and Jessica were out of sight, although they could still hear the distant crescendo of their laughter.

He was very good at reading what people were thinking, Laura thought. Perhaps because he spent his working life looking at faces?

'She's as passionate about an advert as she is about a Renaissance masterpiece,' Laura said. 'It makes me feel very dull in comparison.'

'Someone has to provide security.'

He was also good at saying what you needed to hear. He'd possessed that kind of emotional intelligence from his youth. At school, all the other boys had called her cold. Tim's word, she'd found out later from Robin, was self-contained. Tim understood how her relationship with Robin worked. Was there a subtext of warning in his use of the word *security*?

On the other side of the square, the Italian boys sloped off as Ellis and Jaz started kissing. Once again, Ellis caught her looking at them.

'Where have Dad and Jessica gone?' they called.

'To see another painting.'

'What are we supposed to do now? It's getting a bit cold.'

'We could go back to the house?' Tim suggested.

'Er, I think Robin still has the key to the SUV.'

They'd come in two cars with Jessica driving the smaller one.

'Can't we text him to come back?' Ellis asked.

'They won't be long. It's important to Jessica. You can borrow my jacket if you want . . .' Laura offered.

'God, you're such a martyr!' said Ellis.

'Why don't we all have a gelato?' said Tim.

'How will that help, exactly?' said Ellis.

'I'd like one,' said George.

He and Tim went into the café to choose flavours, leaving Ellis staring at Laura, as if to face her down.

'I'm going to go for a walk...' Laura said, removing herself from any more confrontation.

How could she be reduced to an emotional pulp by her daughter when she dealt perfectly competently with hundreds of teenagers every working day? She had done everything the books about motherhood had told her to do, but somehow there had never been a bond between them. George had always been much easier to like. People said that you were more relaxed with a second child, but she knew it was because he was a boy. In her determination not to repeat the relationship she had had with her own mother, she seemed to have ended up not having a relationship with her daughter at all.

Laura wandered round every street in the centre of the small town, but the only place that appeared to be open was the café in the main square where the others were sitting. She wanted to avoid going back for as long as she could.

Peering round the corner, she watched Tim and George competing with keepy-uppies, Ellis and Jaz deep in conversation. She found herself fighting back tears. She was the outsider of the party, the outsider in her own family. But was it her fault? Did she make herself unlovable to pre-empt rejection? Or to make it easier to leave? Did she really want to leave? Would Alex one day find her unlovable too, once he really knew her?

She got out her mobile phone, opened WhatsApp, saw that Alex was online, tapped the call button, regretted it instantly and tapped end call. She saw that he was typing.

*Are you OK?* he asked.

*Sorry misdialled*, she typed back.

It was her problem and she had to deal with it herself, but it was only day two. How was she ever going to last the week?

# Chapter Eleven

## *Robin*

The painting itself was in a darkened room and even though they were the only people there, Jessica was whispering her commentary respectfully.

Apparently, it was a masterpiece of perspective. Robin couldn't see it. The angels on either side of the Virgin looked far too small to him, although who knew how tall angels actually were? The one with green wings had matching green boots and a brown dress, the one with brown wings had brown boots and a green dress. Who knew angels wore ankle boots?

'It's enigmatic, isn't it?' said Jessica.

'I suppose . . .'

'There's a mystical quality. Local pregnant women come to pray here. They let them in free,' she said.

'Perhaps you should give it a go?' said Robin.

'What do you mean?'

'Pray for conception. Not immaculate in your case, obviously.'

He expected her to laugh, but the words hung in the solemn space. Awkward.

'Take as long as you like,' he said, stumbling into a seat in his haste to get out.

Waiting in the car, he saw her take a deep breath as she came out and force a smile onto her face.

'Without Piero della Francesca, art wouldn't have developed as it did,' she said, as she got into the car.

'Isn't that true of any famous artist?'

'Very few, I'd say. I suppose Velásquez, Cézanne, Picasso of course...'

'Almost everyone then,' he said. 'I think you may be in danger of becoming a serious person, Coco.'

It was about a fifteen-minute drive back to Sansepolcro. For the first ten of them, Jessica was unusually silent and he felt rather nervous but managed to stop himself making a joke, though one about a pregnant pause was almost too good to resist. As they slowed down, approaching the car park outside the pedestrianised centre, she sighed and said, 'I decided it would be unfair to bring up a child alone.'

'But you'd be so good at it,' he said, automatically charming.

'You think?'

Damn! Now he'd have to justify his statement.

'You're so full of imagination. Good at telling stories. Know about art and things. You'd be an absolute natural.'

She smiled and he was pleased to have turned it round.

'It wouldn't be fair on the baby, though, would it? Just to have one parent. I mean, what if something happened to me?' she said.

That was a bit of a downer.

'You managed OK, though, didn't you? More than OK...'

'But... oh, never mind. Sorry, far too gloomy a conversation...'

This time he didn't contradict her.

'Do you think it's our age?' he said, as they pulled into the space next to the SUV. 'We keep thinking about death. Tim's the same.'

'Don't be ridiculous, forty is the new twenty.'

'But when people say sixty is the new forty, don't you find yourself thinking they're a bit sad?'

'Who's the serious person now?' she asked.

As they started walking back to the square, the rest of the party were coming towards them, George carrying one of two large paper carrier bags, Laura the other. Barty had rejoined the party but was being practically frogmarched by Tim, whose face was white with fury.

'You went off with the key to the SUV,' Laura said.

'Why didn't you text?'

'Told you!' said Ellis.

'They caught Barty stealing a box of cantuccini,' Laura said. 'Let's just say we were no longer welcome.'

'I was going to pay!' said Barty.

'With what? You don't have a card or any euros,' Tim said.

'I was going to ask you to pay. That's why I came out . . .'

He was looking to his peers for support. Ellis and Jaz turned their backs to him. George rolled his eyes.

'Tim offered to buy the entire stock of perishables . . .' Laura said.

'Plus some fancy jars of sun-dried tomatoes which were approaching their sell-by date,' said Tim.

'Well, at least we'll have something to eat tonight!' said Robin.

The attempt to lighten things up didn't go down well.

'Jessica, would you mind driving Barty back as we've had enough of him for one day,' Laura asked.

'Would you, Coco?' Robin asked.

'You're going with them, Robin.'

They drove back in close convoy, with Jessica pulling in first. Robin accompanied the now silent Barty to the door of the annexe his brothers were in and knocked.

When Camilla opened it, looking a little the worse for wear, Robin gave the boy a gentle push on the back.

'He's in disgrace. The rest of you are welcome to our place for supper. Not you, I'm afraid, Barty.'

No supper had been one of the punishments meted out by his father when he was a boy. He'd never had to threaten it with his own children. Hopefully, Barty would be chastened enough to behave for the rest of the holiday.

As Jessica switched off the headlights, Robin's eyes took a few moments to adjust to the total darkness, making his other senses sharper. He could smell the mustiness of rotting leaves on the air, feel the chill of altitude on the tip of his nose, hear the scurrying of some nocturnal animal in the bushes, which made him suddenly remember the mouse. Dashing to the door and slamming it behind him as the SUV pulled up the drive, he did a quick check of the kitchen, keeping his ears peeled for squeaking. Satisfied there was no evidence of droppings or mousetraps, he went back to the door and opened it, welcoming the rest of them in as if he'd been there all the time.

# Chapter Twelve

## *Jessica*

'It's like playing Russian roulette with pastries,' said Robin.

He had arranged all the baked goods Tim had bought on a platter. Apart from the *pizzette* and the croissants dusted with icing sugar, a couple of which were oozing their custard filling, there was no way of knowing whether the individual pieces were sweet or savoury. His delight at having invented a new game in which points were awarded for guessing the filling turned what could have been a disappointing supper into an activity that was making them all laugh.

One of the things Jessica most loved about Robin was his almost childlike ability to enjoy himself in any situation. She had books on mindfulness that spent hundreds of pages telling you to practise what just came naturally to him. The only time she'd ever seen him struggle to make the best of things was when he'd thrown up in the zorbing sphere. Even then, as he emerged spattered all over with his own vomit, he'd said, 'Lucky I was wearing old trainers.'

His energy was infectious. Even Ellis and Jaz were joining in the guessing, while eating only pasta with sun-dried tomatoes that Robin had cooked for them. Everyone was so absorbed by the pastries that the knock at the door made them jump. Like a moment in a horror film, they held their breath as they heard the front door creak open and footsteps in the hall. Then Crispin and Piers pushed open the kitchen door.

'Mind if we join you?'

They looked as if they had been drinking all afternoon.

Robin's brothers were like the Dementors from Harry Potter, Jessica thought. They didn't have to be in a room for very long before all the energy was sucked out of it.

'Of course, come in, come in!' said Robin. 'Would you like a pastry? There's plenty to go round.'

Piers helped himself to a doughnut.

'Stop!' said Robin, as his brother went to bite it. 'You have to guess the filling ...'

'Jam?' said Piers.

'Now you can taste.'

'Ugh. It's bloody Nutella,' said Piers. 'Hate the stuff.'

He put the doughnut down and reached for another.

'No, you have to eat it now!' Robin said.

'Why?'

'Rules of the game, I'm afraid.'

Jessica was amazed to see Piers obediently pick it up and eat the remainder.

'So no points for you,' said Robin, creating a column for each of his brothers on the tally sheet.

'Your turn, Cris!'

Crispin picked up a tiny choux bun.

'Crème anglaise?'

It turned out to be pistachio.

'Bloody stupid game,' he said. 'What sort of a supper do you call this anyway, Robbo?'

'Tim bought the whole bakery!'

'Bit excessive, Beast,' said Piers.

'It was a peace offering to get your son out of difficulty ...' Laura pointed out.

'Yes, heard about that. Bloody annoyed with him. It's not the first time either.'

'Does his school have a counselling service that might be helpful?' Laura asked. 'If he has a problem.'

'Barty's only problem's getting caught. I mean, everyone tries a bit of shoplifting at that age, don't they?'

'Do they?' said George.

'We don't,' said Ellis, linking arms with Jaz.

'Cowards!' said Piers.

'I also bought these,' said Tim, producing two bottles from the other carrier bag.

'Vin Santo!' said Robin. 'It's just about my favourite drink ever, especially with a cantuccini dipping biscuit.'

'Ta da!' Out of the carrier bag, Tim produced a fancy box of the almond biscuits. 'One of the bottles is cheap, the other vintage. The proprietor suggested I buy both...'

'This calls for a drinking game,' said Robin.

'I'll just go and get some equipment,' said Jessica.

It was quite convenient now that the bedroom she'd swapped to was on the ground floor. Unfortunately, there wasn't the cupboard space to unpack all her stuff, but she found what she was looking for quickly enough in her large suitcase.

'Vin Santo pong?' she suggested, producing a stack of paper cups and a box of ping-pong balls. 'Like beer pong but...'

'You should excel at anything pong, Robbo,' said Piers.

That bloody advert. One poor choice that had plagued Robin ever since. Not that it had been a choice, because he'd thought his agent was talking about a commercial for a new range of toiletries by Dior. He'd been flattered, got himself a fake tan in case they asked him to get his top off. Turned out it was in fact a new brand called Nodor. And the product was a toilet freshener, not cologne. The shoutline was 'One drop and the pong is gone'. They'd wanted him, they said, because people didn't think about posh people going for a poo. It was funny, subversive. Had he ever done comedy?

'You didn't think to call me?' Jessica had asked him as he recounted the story when they met for their usual Friday-night drinks.

She had crossed his mind, but unfortunately it was her saying that all publicity was good publicity. Turned out it wasn't. It was quite literally flushing what was left of his career down the toilet.

'OK,' said Robin. 'Let's have boys against girls? That's roughly equal.'

'Can you pour a very small quantity please, Jessica?' Laura asked, as Jessica uncorked the first bottle, ready to fill the triangular grid of cups she had placed at either end of the long refectory table.

'Don't worry, darling, Vin Santo is like maple syrup,' said Robin. 'It's actually impossible to have too much . . .'

'Jaz doesn't drink and nor do I,' said Ellis. 'We're going to bed.'

George took a look at the rest of them as if weighing up the alcohol against the company.

'Me too,' he said.

'What snowflakes you and the Ice Queen have produced!' said Piers, rather pleased with the pun.

'At their age, I'd have done anything I could to get wasted,' said Crispin. 'Do you remember climbing in through the house master's window to steal his bottle of Harveys Bristol Cream?'

'Never touched sherry since!'

'Eliza's friend's very attractive,' Crispin remarked.

'She's lesbian,' said Robin.

'And your point is?' said Crispin.

Laura, who'd been containing her fury, wasn't able to let this go.

'Do you have any idea how inappropriate these comments are?' she said.

'Watch out,' said Piers. 'The woke police are on to you, Robin!'

'Teams are uneven now,' Crispin observed. 'So you'd better be a girl, if that's not too much of a stretch, Tim.'

'With pleasure!' said Tim.

Jessica thought it made the three of them even keener to win. Turned out that Laura had both aim and technique. They'd also consumed far less alcohol before starting the game, so they easily beat the boys.

'Stupid game anyway,' said Piers, gulping the contents of yet another cup that Laura had successfully dropped a ball into, then swaying and looking distinctly queasy. Perhaps you could have too much Vin Santo?

'Let's get you home,' Crispin said, quickly. 'Early start tomorrow.'

Robin accompanied his brothers to the front door. When he returned the rest of them burst out laughing and the energy started flowing back into the room until Ellis shouted from upstairs, 'Can you keep it down, some of us are trying to sleep!'

'Let's transfer to the party room,' Jessica whispered and the four of them tiptoed across the hall, trying to stifle their giggles.

'What other games have you got up your sleeve, Coco?'

'How about Truth or Drink?'

'I don't think I can drink any more,' Laura said. 'I'm going to turn in.'

'Nonsense!' said Robin. 'The night is young. The more people, the more fun.'

'If you don't want to drink you can do a forfeit,' Jessica offered. 'One moment.'

She rushed across to her room again and returned with two

123

Tupperware boxes, one of which had Truth written on the lid, the other Dare.

'So, how it works is you pick a question, read it out, and if you aren't willing to tell the truth, you have to drink a shot or take a Dare.'

'You've pre-written the questions?' asked Laura.

'I know from experience what works and what doesn't. They're laminated and sanitised,' Jessica assured her. People generally had no idea of the work involved in organising events. Spontaneous games never worked without a lot of careful preparation.

'I'll kick it off, shall I?' Robin closed his eyes and dipped his hand into the box, picking out one of the tiny rectangles and reading.

'Tell the group something you're glad your family doesn't know about.' He thought about his answer for a moment before declaring, 'No way! Drink!'

Jessica poured him a shot of the vintage Vin Santo which was treacly thick with an aroma of muscatel.

'What is it? You have to tell us now!' said Laura.

'That's the whole point of the game, Laura. If you don't want to tell the truth, you drink,' Jessica reminded her.

'When I was thinking of family, I didn't really mean you and the kids. I meant my parents and brothers . . .' Robin tried to mitigate.

'So why can't you tell us?' Laura demanded.

'I've had my drink!'

It was a bit of an awkward start, Jessica thought, but it would pick up. Usually these things were hilarious.

'Me next,' she said quickly, dipping her hand into the box and reading.

'Have you ever peed in the shower? Of course! Who hasn't?'

'I haven't,' said Laura.

'Your turn,' Jessica held the box out.

'Who was the last person you fancied?' Laura read.

Jessica didn't think she'd ever seen Laura looking embarrassed before. Too much time passed for it to be believable for her to answer Robin. All of them were staring at her.

'I'm going to have to say Enzo,' she finally admitted.

Jessica looked for Robin's reaction. He shrugged and said, 'Can't say I blame you.'

'Who's Enzo?' asked Tim.

'The gardener,' Robin said.

'Oh yes, he's gorgeous,' said Tim. 'I would . . .'

'Would you, Jessica?' Robin asked.

'Definitely not,' she said. 'Not my type at all.'

'That's unusually picky of you, isn't it? Your turn, Tim.'

Robin didn't seem in the least bit bothered about Laura fancying another man, Jessica noticed. Perhaps they were bored with one another?

'What's the best kiss you've ever had?' Tim read. 'No, I'm afraid I am not going to answer that one.'

'Oh, come on!' said Robin.

'No, it's personal.'

'But that's the whole point!'

'Drink or Dare?' Jessica asked.

'I'll take a Dare.' He put his hand into the box and pulled out a laminated card. 'Twerk for a minute. Some music, Maestro!'

The first song on Jessica's party playlist was 'Bamboléo' by the Gipsy Kings. Tim got up on the table and twerked the whole way through. He was surprisingly good at it. The sight of him giving it some in his posh chinos and Ralph Lauren polo shirt was so hilarious, the rest of them started clapping then dancing around the room. This was how it was supposed to work, Jessica thought. The one good thing about public school was it did teach you to stick to the rules of a game. Unless you were born sore losers like Robin's brothers.

'My turn, Coco!' yelled Robin as the track came to an end and they all collapsed, breathless, onto the squashy sofa.

'Who's your best friend?' he read.

Jessica was suddenly aware that she'd had enough alcohol to put her on the verge of tears if he gave the wrong answer.

'Tim, of course!' Robin said, then seeing her face, 'I mean he's my oldest male friend, but obviously you, Coco...'

Now her eyes felt teary with affection.

'My go,' she said. 'What's your biggest regret?'

She didn't want to put another dampener on the vibe. Doing a forfeit might be more fun.

'I'll take a Dare,' she said.

'Seductively eat a banana,' she read.

'Can't wait for this,' said Robin. 'There's one in the kitchen.'

Jessica gave the banana a full blow job before biting it off.

'Ouch!' shouted Tim.

'Bloody hell, Coco! Have you ever thought of working in the porn industry?' Robin asked. 'Laura, you're up next!'

Reluctantly, Laura took a Truth card.

'When was the last time you lied?'

For a few seconds, her face completely drained of colour and there was panic in her eyes. Then she said, 'Oh, I re-member. When I said I liked that Ottolenghi dish you made last Sunday...'

'The candied beetroot with lentils and yuzu?' Robin asked, astonished.

'Yes. Never been a big fan of lentils...'

'You said you loved it!'

'Exactly. I lied. I suppose I was trying to please Ellis. And you, of course. Sorry.'

There was an awkward silence. Robin looked hurt.

126

It seemed such an insignificant lie to remember, and together with the overelaborate explanation, made Jessica slightly wonder whether the lie itself was a lie.

'It sounds delicious to me,' she said. 'Your turn, Tim.'

'Where's the weirdest place you've made love?' Tim read. 'Well, I'm not sure if I'd call it making love...'

'Forfeit!' Robin shouted at him. 'We really don't want to know!'

'Remove four items of clothing.'

Tim obediently took off his chinos, his shirt and both socks, leaving him sitting in boxers.

'Me again!' said Robin. 'What's the drunkest you've ever been? Can't remember... does that mean I have to drink?'

He was already much drunker than the rest of them.

'What's the biggest secret you've never told anyone?' Jessica read. She looked dramatically round the group. 'Obviously, I'm not telling!' she said, knocking back a shot. She offered Laura the Truth box. Laura took a card and read.

'What's your biggest fear?'

The very thought of it made her look so frightened that even Jessica felt a bit sorry for her.

Finally she said, 'Don't want to put that into the Universe... I'll take a Dare.'

Jessica handed her the box.

'Give your phone to the person on your left so they can send a text to the last person you messaged.'

'Hand it over,' said Tim, with as much authority as a man wearing only boxer shorts could display.

Now Laura's fear became total panic.

'I'll take a drink instead,' she said.

'Too late!' shouted Robin.

'No, Robin, I can't possibly, it's someone from work. Tim can't possibly text them. I'll tell the truth...'

Jessica had never seen Laura as anything other than calm and collected. Now she was visibly shaking. Could she be hiding something? Her evasive answers put a whole new complexion on her.

'It's mice,' she said. 'I have a phobia.'

'Told you!' Robin shouted, pointing at Jessica.

'Shall we try another game?' Jessica asked. Over the years she'd developed a sense for when things were about to get out of control.

'No way!' shouted Robin. 'It's my birthday, so I get to choose!'

# Chapter Thirteen

## *Robin*

## Monday

He woke up alone and fully clothed on the chaise longue. The sweetness of the Vin Santo had turned to a sticky liquorice coating on his tongue that tasted sourly toxic to tooth enamel. At least he didn't have a headache, he thought, raising his head slightly, then slumping back as if he'd been hit by a wrecking ball.

One by one, memories as sharp and painful as needles stabbed through his tender brain.

Jessica answering, 'Last night,' to the question, 'When was the last time you cried?'

He had only seen Jessica crying once or twice in all the time he'd known her.

'What about?' he'd asked.

Laura's face when she read out the question, 'What was the biggest mistake you've ever made?'

Her thinking about it for a long time before saying, 'Giving up the piano.'

She'd never even mentioned playing the piano to him. Did he not know her at all?

'What's the worst thing you've ever done at work?'

Was it really accidentally pranging the head teacher's car?

They'd laughed about that. In his view it had been a mistake to own up, but she'd said she was so terrible at lying. Was she, though?

Then, as if she'd sensed he was rumbling her, Laura had gone on the attack, saying, 'Oh, come on!' when Jessica drank instead of answering the question, 'What's your biggest fantasy?'

And Jessica had collapsed into floods of tears, he wasn't sure why. It wasn't supposed to be like this. His wife lying, his friend crying, it felt as if all the foundations of his life were rocking.

He'd accused Laura of not playing the game properly, and she'd stood up and said, 'Am I allowed to go to bed now?'

Surely he couldn't have shouted after her, 'That's right, go all frigid deputy head on us!'

He thought he remembered Tim gently pushing him back down into the cushions when he'd tried to follow her to apologise.

'We've all had far too much to drink. Think you'd probably be better off leaving her alone tonight.'

Robin made to sit up, but the headache was so acute he thought he'd be sick on the antique Persian rug if he didn't lie back down immediately. Equilibrium was going to be difficult enough to restore this morning without vomit on the soft furnishings. Seeing that someone had left a large glass of water and a blister pack of paracetamol just in reach on the coffee table beside him, he gingerly drank a little, swallowed two, then lay back down motionlessly.

The converted-church party room had a small round window above the heavily curtained door. He realised with relief that it was still dark outside. No need to worry about getting up for ages. As the tablets began to numb the pain, he became aware of a regular, rumbling sound distant enough to be more soothing than intrusive. Closing his eyes he drifted off to sleep lulled, as he had been all the way through his teenage years, by the rhythm of Tim's snoring.

# Chapter Fourteen

## *Jessica*

The skin around her eyes was taut and dry from the salt of many tears. She'd slept fitfully, and now, as darkness dissolved into the pale glimmer of dawn, lay motionless staring at the ceiling wondering how it had descended to this.

The stillness was suddenly broken by the crunch of footsteps on gravel and the sound of a car starting as Robin's brothers left for the Lamborghini experience. At least they wouldn't be able to complicate what had become a fraught situation. Why had she ever suggested Truth or Dare? It always worked very well as an icebreaker for groups of people who'd just met, but it turned out to be a disaster for people who'd thought they knew everything about each other.

She couldn't decide what to think about Laura. Jealousy had always blinded Jessica to seeing her as anything but the luckiest woman on earth. Everything fell into her lap, including Robin and their two beautiful children. The drinking game had shown the relationship had all sorts of complexities that she knew nothing about. And the glimpse Laura had given in Sansepolcro of a troubled background was intriguing. Perhaps she wasn't so much stand-offish as insecure? She'd actually felt sorry for her when Robin insisted on them playing on. To be fair, it was pretty decent of her to have gone along with a holiday that clearly wasn't her thing at all.

Jessica sat up. Perhaps one way of making things better would be to organise some me time just for Laura? Picking up her phone from the bedside table, Jessica was googling spas in the area when the air was rent by a blood-curdling scream.

There was a body floating in the pool.

Laura was on the terrace, dripping wet and jumping up and down as if she couldn't bear her feet to be in contact with the paving stones and screaming, 'Oh my god, oh my god!'

When Jessica tried to put a towel around her shaking body, she pushed her away and fled to the lawn at the front of the house, where she stood in the middle, still jumping from foot to foot in her shortie wetsuit.

Robin emerged with a blanket round his shoulders through the door of the church.

'Whatever's happened?' he asked.

'Oh my god!'

Tim came out of the kitchen door wearing a white towelling robe, his bare feet shoved into his untied brown leather brogues. He and Jessica watched as Robin inched closer to Laura, like a scene from a police drama where the specialist officer attempts to disarm a suicide bomber. Eventually, she allowed him to put the blanket around her shoulders and his arm around her trembling body.

'I was swimming. It was floating in the pool. I almost swallowed it!'

Now she was sobbing, almost choking.

'What?'

'A mouse!'

'It's probably just a leaf, darling!'

'I KNOW WHAT A BLOODY LEAF LOOKS LIKE!' she screamed at him.

Robin looked over at the two of them for support.

Jessica turned to check the pool, already knowing it wasn't a leaf, although there were several floating on the surface. There was a moment where she wondered whether to scoop out the small corpse and throw it into the hedge, destroying the evidence. She sensed Tim was thinking the same thing, but she took the executive decision that it wasn't fair or realistic to think of gaslighting Laura any longer.

'It's not a leaf,' she called, causing Laura to emit another horrible primal scream.

'It's only a little mouse,' Tim called.

'I think that might be the worst thing you could say,' Jessica hissed.

Her mother had had a phobia of spiders. Large ones were worse but even the tiniest money spider caused a near-hysterical reaction. The ability Jessica had acquired at a young age to pick up spiders with a tea towel had proved very useful in her work.

'If there's one mouse, there's bound to be more!' Laura's voice was now hollow with dread. She looked questioningly at Robin for reassurance but all he could do was shrug. 'You knew? You've let me stay in a place that's riddled with mice and you bloody knew!' She stamped her foot just like Ellis used to do when she had one of her tantrums, then rounded on Jessica. 'And you knew, too! That's why Robin said "told you" last night!'

'Darling, come inside,' Robin tried to cajole her. 'You're freezing!'

'I'm not going inside. This place is my idea of hell. I'm not the slightest bit interested in playing your stupid games in a house full of vermin...'

'So that's a no, is it?'

For a second, Laura looked as if she was going to hit him or explode with anger. Instead she let out a howl that sounded like giving vent to years of pent-up exasperation.

'You're supposed to save me from mice! That's the only reason I married you!' she wailed.

'Bit harsh,' Tim muttered.

'I want to go home,' Laura wailed.

'Oh dear, that's going to be a problem,' Tim said.

'I'm not interested in problems, I'm interested in solutions,' Jessica heard herself saying which was always the first sentence she used to disarm furious clients. All traces of her own hangover disappeared as she realised someone needed to get a grip on the situation.

'Tim, make coffee,' she instructed. 'Laura, I am going to sort this out.'

'I want to go home!'

'I hear you, Laura. I'm going up to your room now and bringing down some clothes for you. Let me make a few calls.'

The list of local spas was already on her screen.

Jessica managed to get Laura dressed on the lawn, holding a towel up like her mother used to do for her on Brighton beach when they went for a day at the seaside. She'd gone very quiet now. Robin loaded her suitcase into the boot.

Enzo arrived on his motorbike just as they were pulling out of the drive. None of them responded to his cheery wave.

As soon as they were on the main road, Laura visibly relaxed.

'I'm sorry,' she said. 'I know it's mad...'

'Not a problem,' said Jessica. 'My mother had a phobia. Spiders. Ever since I can remember I've been checking the bathroom.'

'I feel like a complete idiot. I'm sorry about losing it...'

'These things happen...' said Robin feebly, from the back seat.

'I'm not excusing you,' said Laura.

'No, of course not, darling...'

Jessica glanced in the rear-view mirror. He still looked very rough. Jessica felt like an umpire stuck in the middle, duty-bound to be fair to each of them, at least while they were both in the car.

Happily the spa she'd chosen a few miles away from Città di Castello looked even better in real life than it did in the photos. The original medieval building had been a convent with a walled herb garden, but the conversion was very recent and high-end. The receptionists wore white uniforms and the room was reassuringly fresh and modern.

'Will you be all right here?' she asked Laura.

'I think so,' said Laura, sitting down on the bed, breathing a long sigh.

'I booked you in for tonight but I checked that they have availability all week...'

'I was set on going home today, but seeing this place, maybe I won't change my flight...' Laura issued a rare smile.

'Shall I move Robin's birthday dinner on Thursday to lunch in a restaurant in Città, so we can all be together?'

'Can I think about it?' said Laura.

'Of course. Are you sure you won't need a car?'

'I'm rather looking forward to doing absolutely nothing except treating myself to some of these...' Laura picked up the menu of massages and treatments.

'Anything you need in the meantime, just call.'

'Thank you, Jessica, you've been exceptionally understanding. I'm sorry I shouted at you. It's entirely Robin's fault.'

Jessica restrained herself from defending him as she usually did. Seeing Laura so vulnerable had made it more difficult to resent her.

'I rather wish I was staying here myself,' she said.

'Oh, I'm sure you don't,' said Laura, adding quickly, 'I mean, you'll have a whale of a time. I'm no good at games-playing . . .'

Nor at pretending, Jessica thought. If she knew about Jessica's feelings for Robin, why wasn't she more concerned about leaving them alone together?

Robin was now sitting in the front passenger seat.

'Everything OK?' he asked.

'She's looking forward to a bit of pampering.'

'Honestly, Coco, you really are brilliant.'

'It's my job. So, what now?'

'Coffee,' said Robin. 'I am in desperate need of coffee.'

# Chapter Fifteen

## *Laura*

The hotel appeared to be deserted. Was she the only guest? The waiter informed her that the season finished the following week but that there was an American woman staying who had gone to Arezzo for the day. After showering and unpacking, Laura sat in the conservatory where he brought her a cappuccino and an almond croissant because she'd arrived too late for the buffet breakfast.

A black cat was sitting in the sunshine on the steps down to the gardens. As if it sensed her watching, it got up, stretched and walked towards her. She bent to stroke it, tickling it under the chin, enjoying the contented rhythm of its purring that was so exactly like Bobtail's, she thought English and Italian cats would have no difficulty communicating. The cat slunk around her legs until the waiter suddenly appeared and shooed it away.

'*Sfortunato!*' he said. '*Il gatto nero.* Not good!'

'Isn't it supposed to be good luck?' Laura said.

The young man looked warily at her.

'In Italy, no,' he said, with a troubled frown.

Laura didn't believe in superstitions but she was still feeling fragile after the morning's events. Her mild sense of foreboding was kneaded away by a deep tissue massage and she almost fell asleep in the cloud of ylang ylang. Emerging from the windowless treatment room with no idea what time it was, she was surprised to find it was still only two o'clock in the afternoon. She decided to explore the gardens. There were a few late-blooming roses, but most of the flowerbeds had been tidied and pruned for winter. She liked the fact that everything was ordered, with neat gravel paths and no undergrowth of straggly shrubs for creatures to lurk in. Each time the breeze shunted a fallen leaf across the peripheries of her vision, her heart rate accelerated with another onset of panic. The pool was turquoise and pristine, as if it had been filled with fresh water only that morning, but she didn't yet feel brave enough to swim again.

People said that phobias were irrational and in a sense they were right. The creature she'd encountered that morning had clearly drowned and was unable to harm her, but coming literally face to face with it had been the actualisation of a nightmare she'd suffered in times of stress ever since she was ten years old and whose origins she could pinpoint exactly. Panama.

'It'll be a fresh start,' her mother had said.

Laura's father was a soldier who had been killed in action just before she was born. Her mother was a beautiful young widow. They had moved into her sister's flat in Bath. With Gillian always available to babysit, her mother was able to pursue an active social life. She'd had several proposals but held out before settling on Grant, a wealthy businessman several years her senior.

'He'll look after us,' she had told Laura.

They'd moved to Panama straight after the wedding when Laura was five. Within a year, her mother was pregnant with twins.

Laura must have been about eight when she'd fallen ill with a fever that made her drift in and out of sleep. She'd been startled to open her eyes and find her stepfather sitting on the bed. She could feel the weight of him dipping the mattress next to her leg. She didn't like him being so close. Usually she tried to avoid him because he was always asking her stupid questions then laughing when she attempted to answer, saying he was only teasing. In the playpark, he pushed her too hard on the swing when she didn't need help. Sometimes, he tried to pick her up and swing her round in a circle like he did with the twins, but they were just toddlers and she felt as if her arms would come out of their sockets. Now, as he leant over her stroking a damp frond of her fringe back from her sweaty forehead, she felt trapped.

'You mustn't sleep with your mouth open, Laura,' he said. 'Because one day a little mouse will come along and pop inside.'

She knew she must not scream or she'd be in trouble with her mother who was always telling her to be nice to him, but swallowing her fear made her gag and choke and she'd started vomiting so much that an ambulance had to be called to take her to hospital. She remembered lying in the back, seeing the lights of their house growing smaller through the back window, finally able to breathe again. But the feeling of safety didn't last long as blood tests all came back negative. They gave her medicine to cool her fever and Grant came to pick her up.

Her mother was standing on the porch with a twin on either side.

'Glad to be home?' she asked.

'Yes.'

It had been the only possible response, but it wasn't true.

She'd never felt comfortable in that house again, although the phobia itself hadn't manifested until many years later. She and Robin were sprawled on the sofa together watching *The Wire*, so absorbed in the story that a mouse had run backwards and forwards along the skirting board under the television a few times before it suddenly occurred to her what she was seeing. Then she'd lost her marbles.

Uncharacteristically, Robin had taken control of the situation, sending her upstairs, then catching the mouse in a newspaper and letting it go in the park at the end of the street. The following day he'd adopted an aggressive ginger rescue cat who'd lost his tail in a fight. At first, Bobtail was so grateful for a home he'd arranged presents of dead mice on their doorstep. Robin was always up first to deal with them before Laura left the house. Either the cat had learned the gifts were unwelcome, or the mice had taken fright, but there hadn't been any further sightings for as long as Laura could remember. The strange thing was that when she'd come home from work and seen Bobtail on Robin's lap, she'd been filled with such an overwhelmingly happy feeling of being looked after, she'd wondered if this was what people meant by love.

So a few weeks later, she'd had no hesitation in saying why not, when Robin had asked her, half joking, whether she thought they should get married.

It wasn't a conventional reason for tying the knot, but it had worked pretty well all this time. They'd loved and honoured one another, shared their worldly goods, looked after each other in sickness and in health. Robin was a great father. The only missing element was passion. And people said that disappeared pretty quickly from any marriage, especially after kids arrived. So why did every single thing he did which she had found only mildly irritating or amusing before, now leave her spitting fury? He wasn't the one who had changed. She had. She didn't want to do him any harm, but she wasn't sure she could live in her own crushing unhappiness for the rest of her life.

Wouldn't it be wonderful if Robin could see how much Jessica loved him? She was exactly what he needed because organising came naturally to her. It was probably why she'd chosen events management as her job. It would have made her a good mother, too, Laura thought, guiltily remembering her own categoric reaction when Robin had raised the question of donating his sperm to Jessica for her IVF. It had been selfish, really, based entirely on her aversion to the idea of Jessica becoming even more entwined in their lives, but the more time Laura spent in her company, the more she saw that Jessica wasn't such an awful person. Would she have made the same decision now that Alex was back in her life? Was it too late to change her mind? At the time, Robin had seemed relieved. Perhaps now . . .

# Chapter Sixteen

## *Jessica*

It was market day in Città di Castello and the car park was almost full. Golden leaves from the avenue of tall deciduous trees swirled around them as they walked towards the *centro storico*. Within the shelter of the town's walls, it felt warmer. The market was bustling with purveyors of clothes and local artefacts jumbled among greengrocers offering fresh produce and baskets of mushrooms. There were washing lines pegged with printed tea towels, vans stinking of cheese, shelves laden with jars of honey, stalls garlanded with dried sausages. The garlicky fragrance of cured meat mingled with the yeasty scent of fresh bread and the bitter aroma of coffee.

Sitting at a table outside a bar, they tilted their faces to the sun, downing espresso, freshly squeezed orange juice and sweet croissants, gently convalescing without feeling the need to speak.

Jessica guessed that the large church on the other side of the square was probably the one where Raphael had painted his first commission. The painting itself had been removed when Napoleon conquered the region. She was interested to see where Raphael had worked as a boy, but she thought she'd probably tested Robin's tolerance of Renaissance art to its limit.

The following day, there was truffle hunting for anyone who wanted to go. She didn't, so she'd come back and investigate.

'What would you like to do now?' she asked.

'Frankly, I could sit here forever watching the world go by.'

'But what about the others?'

'Tim can ogle the gardener. God, he's almost as attractive as I used to be...'

'Still are,' she said.

'Thank you, my loyal friend. I love hanging out with you... except when you insist on educating me, obviously.'

Jessica congratulated herself for making the right call on the Raphael.

'And the others?'

'Oh, the kids won't be up for ages. It's amazing how long teenagers can sleep. If they're hungry, Tim's got the SUV.'

His phone buzzed. Holding it at full stretch of his arm, he read the message.

'He must have heard us!' he said. 'Tim's going to take them to Gubbio where there's a cable car. Brilliant. We're free, Coco!'

'You're supposed to have a cookery lesson at three...'

'Oh, I'm not interested in learning anything today,' Robin said. 'I can't face finding out what a terrible cook I am as well as a terrible person.'

Jessica got out her phone and cancelled the booking. She'd paid in advance, but an afternoon alone with Robin would be worth it.

'You're not a terrible person...' she said, focusing on him again.

'Not a good idea to combine Truth or Dare with alcohol, I fear.'

'Sorry.'

'Not your fault. Please don't look sad. I can't bear you being sad . . .'

Automatically, she smiled.

'Why were you crying, by the way?' Robin suddenly asked.

'When?'

'You said in the game that you'd been crying the night before . . .'

Was now the time to tell him that she cried almost every night about one thing or another, usually the fact that he wasn't in bed beside her? No. She always revealed her complexity too soon in relationships. Sometimes she felt that the men she dated felt defrauded by her, as if they'd been promised non-stop laughter and were now entitled to return her under the Trade Descriptions Act. With Robin, it had taken nearly twenty-five years to get to this point, in which time she didn't think he had ever seen her depressed because to him her unique selling point was that she was fun. To reveal herself now as melancholy, when everything still felt so wobbly, would be risky.

'Oh, you know. Just a bit lonely,' she said.

'But you've got loads of friends . . .'

Did she dare?

'But no one . . . special,' she said.

'You're special to me . . .'

A rush of belief and disbelief all mixed together.

'You're so wonderful,' he continued. 'You will find someone . . .'

He paused, looked intently into her eyes. 'Can I tell you something, Coco?'

It was as if he had pressed a button that put her whole life on pause.

'You're an amazing person, but the problem is you put too

much pressure on. Not that I'm in any position to give anyone advice about their love life, but it's the one thing men can't stand. Parking your tanks on their lawn. With you it's not so much parking your tanks as driving them straight into the house...'

'But...'

She'd never put any pressure on him, but he wasn't talking about him. She was so good about not putting pressure on him he didn't even realise.

'Note to self,' she said, brightly. 'No tanks. So, what shall we do?'

'How about a game?'

'"I went to market..." but in Italian?' she suggested.

'You've got an unfair advantage because you're learning Italian,' said Robin. The competitiveness started immediately.

'It could be useful vocabulary for you, though,' she argued. 'Here's how it goes: *Sono andata*, I went, *al mercato*, to market, *e ho comprato*, and I bought, *una bottiglia di vino*.'

'Typical, wine's the first thing in your basket, Coco!' said Robin. '*Sono andata...*'

Jessica corrected him. 'For a man, it's *sono andato...*'

'I was always useless at Latin. *Sono andato al mercato e ho comprato una bottiglia di vino e un limone*.'

'Brilliant!' said Jessica. '*Sono andato al mercato e ho comprato una bottiglia di vino, un limone* and what would you like to know the word for?'

Robin gave a glance at the pyramids of shiny vegetables on a nearby stall.

'Aubergine. No, wait, I know that, it's *melanzana*.'

'Bravo!'

'And courgettes are *zucchini*! Turns out I can speak Italian!'

Armed with a few words, a chef's appreciation of the produce and a talent for mimicry which made him uninhibited about

146

gesturing with his hands, Robin was an immediate hit with the stallholders.

'I mean, smell that, Coco!' he said, thrusting a tomato under her nose.

She'd never considered sniffing a tomato before. The sharp, grassy smell surprised her.

'That will be great in salad, and now we need some of the riper ones for sauce. I'm thinking a melange of roasted vegetables. Couldn't help noticing some rosemary in the garden which will be good with these lovely potatoes.'

'*Fantastico!*' he said to the woman serving who popped several more in free. 'I'm starving now, Coco.'

'It's almost lunchtime and the market's closing, so why don't we take these back to the car first,' said Jessica.

As they walked towards the gate where they'd entered the city, she was suddenly aware of a child's voice calling her name. Vittoria, Enzo and Gaia were walking towards them.

'*Ciao, bella!*' she said, bending down to the little girl's level and giving her a gentle high five. She was wearing a tiny denim jacket with patch pockets in the shape of strawberries. 'So cute!'

'How is your little problem?' Enzo asked. His smile annoyed her.

'As a matter of fact, you didn't do a very thorough job,' she said. 'There was a mouse in the pool...'

'Perhaps instead we did too good a job, driving him outside?' he winked.

What a nerve! In her head, the star rating she was intending to give the property sank from four to one. Maybe she'd go for a full refund plus compensation for at least one of Laura's nights at the spa.

'We've had to relocate one of our party,' she said, putting

147

on the most serious face she could. 'It has been a very difficult morning for everyone . . .'

'But she is OK now?' Enzo asked.

'She's absolutely fine!' said Robin, before Jessica had a chance to prepare the way for her potential refund.

'Such a big terror for a little creature,' said Vittoria with a smile.

'Elephants are supposed to be scared of mice, aren't they?' Robin said. 'Not that I'm likening my wife to an elephant, obviously!'

Jessica sometimes wished he didn't always feel the need to be amusing.

'Luckily no elephants in Umbria!' Vittoria said.

'*Elefanti?*' Gaia echoed. '*Dove sono gli elefanti?*'

Elephants. Where are the elephants?

Her parents laughed.

Nobody was taking this nearly as seriously as they should be.

'The alternative accommodation is extremely expensive,' Jessica pressed on.

'Nothing but the best for Laura!' said Robin.

'*Papa, ho fame!*' said the little girl.

'Someone is ready for her lunch,' Enzo said. '*Allora*, see you later . . .'

'Is there a trattoria you can recommend in Città?' Jessica asked.

He and Vittoria conferred in Italian, debating a couple of options before deciding.

'There's one on a street on the other side of the main square . . .'

'Near my studio . . .' Enzo delved in his pocket and produced a card with the address on it.

'You're an artist?' Jessica asked.

'A restorer. Maybe you would like to see my work?'

'We probably won't have time, will we, Coco?' Robin said, giving her a little push.

'No. We are in a bit of a rush,' she confirmed.

'*Allora, buon appetito!*' Enzo said.

'Aren't you forgetting something?' Robin said, as soon as they were out of earshot.

'What?' she asked, with a slight feeling of panic. She hated forgetting things.

'You promised me a hot porchetta sandwich!' he said. 'If we don't get a move on, they'll have packed up with the market.'

They chose the van with the longest queue and stood in line, watching the servers carve thick slices of roast pork fragrant with fennel and garlic, shovelling it into hunks of bread with shards of crackling for those who requested it. Then they sat on the steps of a church, out of the way of reversing trucks and the clanking dismantling of the market.

'We should trademark this as a hangover cure,' Robin said, crushing the shiny paper his sandwich had been wrapped in. 'It's the perfect combination of carbs and fat.'

He wiped his mouth with a paper napkin, missing a crumb of crackling that was stuck to his stubbly cheek.

Instinctively, Jessica reached to brush it off. He caught her hand in his and gave it a kiss.

'*Sono andato al mercato e ho comprato un* – don't know the word for sandwich – *di porchetta buonissima!*'

'I think it's *panino*,' she said.

'Possibly the best lunch I have ever eaten, Coco!' he said. 'In the perfect setting and with my favourite person in the world!' He gave her a hug.

There actually was a god.

As the town turned sleepy, with the shops all shuttered up, they wandered around the walls, arm in arm, pausing occasionally to look at the views of the hills surrounding the town, which shimmered with an embroidery of autumn colours. The sunshine was still bright, mellowing as the afternoon went on. She wondered, as she often did in Italy, what it would be like to live in a country of such history and tradition that life seemed to go on as it always had, with an unhurried rhythm that was so different from the constant multitasking pace of London. It was only a two-hour flight, but she felt as if she'd been miraculously transported to a place of timeless calm where, for the first time in ages, she could be totally relaxed and happy.

'What would your ultimate lunch be?' Robin broke the easy silence that had fallen between them.

It was just a way of having a conversation without actually saying anything, which, it suddenly occurred to her, was their normal way of communicating. There was no reason why it should be any different in Italy, but somehow she'd imagined it would be. She couldn't think of a lunch she'd enjoyed more than the one they'd just had, but he'd already bagged the porchetta, so she had to come up with something else which they'd then debate the merits of.

'Sushi, I think,' she said.

'One type of fish or a mixture?'

'A mixture, but not random. I'd like tuna, salmon, those little raw prawns...'

'Scallop?'

'I've never had scallop sushi.'

'Delicious. Surprisingly soft,' he said. 'Side order of chicken yakitori?'

'If I'm allowed! And miso soup.'

'Miso goes without saying.'

She wanted to bring it back to something more Italian.

'How about best pasta dish?' she said.

'Very simple. Some butter and shaved truffle.'

'You're going truffle hunting tomorrow.'

'I know, and I can't wait. What's the plan?'

'You meet up with the farmer and the dogs. Then I suppose you just follow them until they sniff something and start digging.'

'Dogs are so clever,' Robin said. 'I know you don't like them...'

'It's more that dogs don't seem to like me.'

'That's where you're wrong. The thing about dogs is that all they want is for people to like them. So if they sense you don't, they get even more enthusiastic trying to persuade you...'

They'd had this conversation before. Jessica didn't think it was especially clever to jump up at someone who was clearly frightened, but she knew there was no point in saying this to Robin, who would never see her fear as anything other than illogical. Dogs were so important to him, she was going to have to look into dealing with her fear. She wondered if there were aversion therapy courses, like the ones you went on if you were afraid of flying.

'I'm missing Lammie, you know, and I bet he's missing me too...' said Robin with a tragic face. 'I wonder if I could train him to sniff out a truffle?'

The sun was going down now and there was a slight chill on the air. Jessica looked at her watch. One thousand three hundred steps, but who was counting on a day like today?

'Better get back and cook supper,' said Robin. 'Can you guess what I'd most like to do tonight, Coco?'

He took her hand and squeezed it.

She was almost sure that it wasn't what she had in mind.

'Charades!' he said. 'While the cat's away, the mice shall play. Almost literally, in our case!'

# Chapter Seventeen

## Laura

Laura was expecting to see the other guest at dinner but the restaurant was silent and empty as she sat alone eating a grilled fillet of sea bass with a salad of shaved fennel, with the waiter staring at her through the window in the kitchen door.

Back in her room, she looked at her phone. There were ten WhatsApp messages from George. Usually the kids only got in touch when something was wrong. She opened it anxiously and was relieved to find only a rambling account of the day spent in Gubbio with Tim, illustrated with photos of the precipitous views from the flimsy-looking mountain chairlift, a plate of the pasta they'd had for lunch, and one of Tim, Ellis and Jaz brandishing ice cream cones.

*Tim's a legend*, George had written.

She felt stupid for missing a nice day out and a bit embarrassed about her behaviour. She was glad that Ellis hadn't witnessed it, but she was sure George would have been understanding.

*Hope it's OK me having a few days in a spa?* she wrote.

*Enjoy yourself, Mum, you deserve it*, he wrote back.

*You too*, she wrote and put down the phone, then picked it up again, staring at the next listing on her record of calls, Work

2. As if he'd been waiting for her to look at him, Alex suddenly came online and started typing.

*How's it going?*

She was about to tap out a response, then realised that there was no need for subterfuge here, so tapped the voice call icon instead.

'Are you OK?' he asked.

His voice flowed through her body like an aphrodisiac potion. Talking him through the day's events, she found herself able to laugh, even managing to say the word *mouse* a couple of times without a squirm of terror running up and down her legs.

'So here I am,' she said eventually.

'Sounds like a result to me,' he said.

'I didn't plan it,' she said, defensive.

'It would have been really bizarre and Machiavellian if you had.'

'It's all worked out rather well though,' she said. 'Jessica has Robin all to herself. The children are given treats. The party pooper is gone . . .'

'I'm sure they'd rather you were there.'

'I honestly don't think so, Alex. I actually think that Robin might be happier with Jessica than he is with me . . .'

'Hang on, Law,' Alex interrupted. 'If you're going to make this decision you can't tell yourself you're doing it for him. You've got to take responsibility for it, whether it ultimately makes Robin happy or sad.'

He knew her better than she knew herself, she thought, feeling ashamed for entertaining the idea of manipulating the situation to her advantage.

'At least I've got the space to think here. Time seems to pass much more slowly when you're alone,' she said.

'Enjoy,' he said.

She lay back in the drift of pillows, holding the phone against her ear with one hand, the other slipping between her legs.

'I'd enjoy it more if you were here,' she whispered.

'What are you wearing?'

'Just a fluffy white towelling robe.'

'Nothing underneath?'

'Let me check . . .'

'Tell me what you're doing now . . .' he whispered.

'Oh god!' The thought of making love to him here in this oasis of anonymity on fresh white bedding that smelt of ironing was so naughty and so chaste at the same time, she climaxed almost immediately.

Afterwards, they repeated 'I love you, I love you', to each other, neither of them wanting to be the one to say it last, until her phone buzzed with a WhatsApp notification from George, which made her end the call feeling flustered and guilty.

*Dad made roasted vegetables and bought a rotisserie chicken for the meat eaters*, the text said with an accompanying photo of a chicken carcass and the remains of red and yellow peppers on an oily platter.

*What are you up to?* Laura typed.

*Charades. It's dumb. We played bar football with Tim. Ellis and I smashed him and Jaz. He says he'll buy me a football table – a real Italian one. Dad's OK with it. It could go in the hall.*

Laura tried to envisage it. They would have to clear the shelves of shoes and the hooks of a great bulge of winter coats, but that would probably be a good thing.

*That's generous of Tim*, she typed.

*Can Tim be my godfather? Dad said to ask you.*

Bloody hell, Robin!

*Ellis has Jessica*, George added.

*Why not?* she typed. *If it means something to you.*

*I think it would mean a lot to him*, George typed back.

Laura felt a warm wave of pride wash over her. Sometimes she thought that George was her only real success story. A career was one thing, but to produce a kind, well-adjusted, considerate boy felt like real achievement, although she knew it was more down to having Robin as a father that anything to do with her. George had always had the example of a supportive father, unlike the egotistical bully Piers that Barty had learned his behaviour from. The character traits of Robin that infuriated her, like his general idleness, lack of focus and need to be liked, were useful qualities in a father. Robin had always been there for the kids, whether it was helping out with the cake stall at their primary school Christmas Fayre, running in the parents' race on sports day, or standing for many hours on football pitches all over north London. Not that it was all to do with nurture. From the moment he was born, George seemed to have an equable nature which made him popular. Unlike with Ellis, she'd never had to pray for George to find a friend at primary school. He'd been captain of the football team in every year except year seven when he'd moved up to the academy. Even then, when she'd asked him how he felt, he'd said it was probably sensible to give the position to a defender rather than a midfielder because they had a better view of the game.

Temperamentally, her children couldn't have been more different. Academically, too. George was average in his class, whereas Ellis's record of excellence made them prone to perfectionism. It was something Laura blamed herself for. She didn't think she'd put pressure on, but it had been so exciting to have an exceptionally clever child. Perhaps she'd been guilty of hothousing them? She worried about it constantly, as the statistics around eating disorders in high-achieving girls were alarming and the toxic combination of lockdown and social media had led to a proliferation of mental health problems. But her communication skills with her daughter were so poor, she didn't dare talk to them about it, fearing that she would say something wrong, as she always seemed to.

She knew where she was with George.

*Goodnight, sleep well*, she texted.

*Goodnight Mum XXX* his text pinged back.

Usually, she was so exhausted at the end of the day, she fell asleep immediately. Alone in unfamiliar surroundings, the barrage of questions firing inside her head kept her wide awake and restless. How would her son react if she were to leave Robin? It would have to be her as it wouldn't be fair to uproot the lot of them, nor expect Robin to move out of what was more his house than hers, even though she'd been the one who'd been paying the mortgage all these years. Ellis already hated her, but George didn't. He would already have the spots, smells and ungainliness of puberty to cope with without adding more stress. She didn't want her lovely boy to be torn between parents. She saw it all the time at parents' evenings. The child sitting between two people who were at war with each other. Sometimes it turned the child into the grown-up. More frequently, their anger turned inwards. Neither outcome was healthy.

Not that she and Robin would ever be enemies, would they? How was it possible to live with someone for eighteen years and not even know the answer to that question? Was it healthy for children to live with parents who barely communicated, one of whom was in love with someone else?

At two thirty in the morning, Laura got up and made herself a cup of camomile tea, then looked at her phone and typed, *Are you still up?* to Alex.

The two ticks did not go blue.

# Chapter Eighteen

## *Robin*

It was noticeable how much easier the group dynamic was without Laura. Charades was proving a blast despite the fact that Tim had insisted on separating him and Jessica, claiming that the others wouldn't stand a chance if they were in the same team. Robin was with Jaz, who was very intuitive and clever at guessing, making up for their other team member George, who was playing on his phone the whole time.

Robin was finding it more hilarious being in competition with Jessica than being on her team, especially when you knew what it was she was miming because you were the one who'd put the suggestion into the hat. It was a stroke of luck she'd picked out *When Harry Met Sally* for the final round. The teams were currently tied, but this would be the decider. Robin knew from experience that it looked very simple, but was quite hard to do. Film, four words, was straightforward enough, but nothing really sounded like Harry, except marry and her team only got as far as ring. So now she was trying sounds like carry, but they got stuck on suitcase, then Prince Harry, but they couldn't seem to get past Nazi. The more Robin rolled about in fits of laughter, the more frustrated she became. Time was running out. She clearly couldn't think of anything to rhyme with Sally, so now she was deciding to attempt the whole title by enacting the orgasm in the diner scene. Typical Coco, throwing her whole self into it. God, was that really her orgasm face?

'Four words . . . sexy . . . climax . . .' said Tim. 'What's another word for orgasm, Ellis?'

'Come?'

'Wait a minute, come and now she's eating something. I know, *Come Dine with Me*!'

Jessica shook her head furiously as Robin almost wet himself.

'Stop it, Robin!' shouted Tim. 'So it's not *Come Dine with Me*?'

'*Come Dine with Me* isn't even a film!' Jessica screamed at him.

'No speaking!' Robin reminded her.

'Wait a minute . . . it's four words and it's sexy. Ellis, help me!'

Ellis, who was showing only moderate interest, looked up from their phone.

'*Fifty Shades of Grey*?'

'Brilliant!' said Tim, as Jessica furiously shook her head. 'Oh, it's not *Fifty Shades of Grey* . . . ?'

'That's time,' said Jaz, as the stopwatch pinged on her phone.

'We win!' Robin jumped up and punched the air.

Jessica flopped exhausted onto a sofa.

'So what was it?' Tim asked her.

'*When Harry Met Sally*, obviously!'

'What's *When Harry Met Sally*?' Ellis asked, which was a little ironic, Robin thought, seeing as the film had played a major role in their conception.

'So what was all the sex and eating about?' Tim wanted to know.

'The diner scene!' said Jessica.

'I don't think I saw the film,' said Tim.

Robin almost felt sorry for Jessica, but rules were rules and at least she wasn't a bad loser.

The sound of a car drawing up outside made them all freeze. The brothers were back.

'Quick, turn off the light,' said Tim.

They all sat in darkness keeping silent as they listened to the footsteps on the gravel, like resistance fighters hiding from German stormtroopers. Banging on the front door. Everyone held their breath.

Then, Crispin's voice.

'They must have gone to bed.'

And Piers's.

'Wusses!'

The footsteps retreated. And they could all breathe again. But the interruption had blunted everyone's appetite for more charades.

'We're going up,' said Ellis, pulling Jaz to her feet from the sofa.

'Me too,' said George.

'I'm quite tired too,' said Jessica.

'Not surprised after all that exertion,' said Robin.

Nobody bothered to turn the light on again, leaving him in the dark on one sofa with Tim on the other.

'Jessica's great, isn't she?'

'It's amazingly kind of her to organise all this,' said Tim.

'Pity I fucked it up,' said Robin.

'Have we heard from Laura?'

'George texted her. She seems fine.' There was a long pause. 'I wasn't sure whether it would annoy her more if I got in touch or if I didn't...'

'Let me guess. You did nothing.'

'Well, yes...' Sometimes he liked the fact that Tim knew him so well. Others, it made him a little uncomfortable.

'What do you think I should do? I'm really in the doghouse, although I've never understood where that expression comes from. Being in a doghouse quite appeals to me...'

'Isn't it from *Peter Pan*?' Tim said. 'Doesn't the father have to go in Nana's house? I'm not sure why...'

'Should I buy her flowers? Walk barefoot across coals? What do you think?'

'How are you two getting along at the moment?' Tim asked. I mean more generally...'

'Well, it's been a bit tense. Not quite sure why. I mean, Laura's always been sort of separate. But for the past few weeks, since the summer, really, she's been somehow distant, out of reach...'

It was easier talking in the dark. A bit like being back in the dorm. He felt relieved to verbalise the vague disquiet that had been nagging at him for a while. 'It's her first year as deputy head...' It was the reason he always gave himself for not questioning it. Not that he really knew how he would broach the subject with her because it was more of an atmosphere than anything concrete he could put his finger on.

'I did notice things seemed a touch strained,' said Tim.

'Everyone has their secrets, but I've never suspected her of lying before...'

'Lying?'

'In the game last night, she took a drink instead of saying when she last had sex...'

'When did you?'

'I can't remember... Not very recently.' Robin was grateful for the darkness. He could feel himself going red.

'Maybe she couldn't remember either...' Tim suggested.

'I'm beginning to wonder if she's got someone else!' Robin laughed, expecting Tim to tell him immediately not to be so silly.

'This isn't about her fancying the gardener?' Tim asked.

'God, no! Everyone fancies Enzo.'

There was quite a long silence before Tim asked, 'How would you feel if she had? Got someone, I mean.'

Did Tim know something he didn't? Robin was often the last person to hear about things.

'I suppose I couldn't really blame her,' he said eventually.

'Why do you say that?'

Robin thought he'd quite like the lights back on now. The deconsecrated church was beginning to feel like some sort of confessional.

'I suppose I've always expected it to happen,' he said. 'Couldn't ever understand why she married me. I mean, we get on. It just kind of works. But it's never been exactly, you know . . .'

'Passionate?'

'We've had our moments, obviously. I've always thought I was lucky, but I think for a marriage to last you both have to think you're lucky. I mean, I think she did in the beginning. Not so sure now, though. Maybe I let her down?'

'Of course you didn't!'

Tim yawned, then got up, bent down and gave Robin a hug.

'I think she's very lucky to have you. You've always given her everything she needs . . .'

Robin was surprised to feel tears spilling from his eyes into Tim's cashmere roll-neck. He hadn't realised how much he needed the physical affirmation of an affectionate embrace. He clung on for longer than was absolutely necessary, enjoying the feeling of his face on Tim's chest, the smell of some expensive cologne.

'Thanks for saying that, old friend,' he said, finally pulling away and sniffing loudly.

Tim helped him to his feet and they tiptoed upstairs and hugged again briefly outside Tim's bedroom door.

Lying in bed alone, Robin could hear the unmistakable sound of people making love. Ellis and Jaz. He pulled the duvet right over his head. Wasn't this the wrong way round? Weren't teenagers meant to be embarrassed to hear their parents having sex? If Laura were here, they would have giggled about it. Or would they? He wasn't sure about anything anymore.

# Chapter Nineteen

## *Laura*

## Tuesday

Laura was awakened by the phone in her room ringing.

It was only the receptionist reminding her about her facial and manicure.

'What?' Glancing at her phone, she saw that it was almost ten o'clock. She'd slept nearly eight hours.

Alex had read her message, but he hadn't replied. She told herself not to look at the phone again. She had to sort her head out. If she allowed herself enough time, then surely everything would become clear to her.

She sat in the waiting area sipping water that tasted of cucumber until the door to the treatment room opened and a middle-aged woman came out and did a double-take.

'Oh, hello!'

'Hello,' Laura replied uncertainly.

'We were on the same plane.'

Of course. It was the agent whose compliments she now she wished she hadn't dismissed so readily because it felt quite lonely with nobody else around. They could perhaps have eaten meals together, compared notes on the various treatments on offer.

As the woman handed a euro note to the beautician, it

suddenly occurred to Laura that she hadn't tipped the masseuse. She didn't have any cash with her. Perhaps she should get a taxi into town after and find an ATM so that she could tip for the rest of the week?

'Having some me time?' the agent said.

'Exactly. Did you enjoy Arezzo?'

A frown.

'They said the other person staying had gone there...'

Now Laura felt as if she was exposing the staff for indiscretion. Along with the lack of tips, she was not going to be a popular guest.

'It's where they filmed *Life is Beautiful*,' the woman said. 'And there is a famous cycle of paintings by Piero della Francesca.'

'Going anywhere today?'

'I thought I'd check out Città di Castello. Have you been?'

'No, not yet.'

'I don't think there's a lot there, but you can only have so much art!'

'Exactly!'

For a moment she thought the agent was going to ask if she would like to go with her. A distraction would be tempting. The luxury of having space and time to yourself very quickly became too much space and time.

'Don't let me keep you from your treatment!'

'Of course.'

'Nice meeting you again.'

'And you!'

How did she manage to make even the most banal small talk uncomfortable? Fortunately the beautician did not try to chat. Laura found it difficult enough in English. It was one of the reasons she rarely went to the hairdresser, preferring to keep it long and usually wearing it pinned up in a chignon for work.

*

165

The sunshine wasn't really strong enough to lie out by the pool, but she couldn't think of anything else to do. Closing her eyes, she tried to concentrate, then yelped as something soft touched her leg, but it was only the black cat. Not entirely black, she saw. There was a little circle of white fur on its chest, like a medallion. Did that cancel out the bad luck? Or possibly the good luck? She couldn't believe that her brain was wasting time weighing up such nonsense. At least its presence probably ensured no mice. She got up, put a toe into the clear turquoise water. It was colder than she expected, which made it even more tempting.

Whenever she swam in cold water, her mood improved. Putting on her goggles, she dived in, swimming lengths with tumble turns as fast as she could until the point when the temperature of her body equalised with that of the water. She crawled up and down, taking a breath every four strokes, the rhythm as regular as a metronome, allowing all her worries to float away so successfully that when a shadow fell across the water, she thought it was a cloud passing over the sun. It was only when the figure crouched down beside the edge and she realised it was a man that anxiety flooded back. Had something happened to the kids, and they'd sent the waiter to tell her? Ripping off her goggles, she opened her eyes.

'What the fuck?'

'They said I'd find you here,' said Alex.

'But what did you tell reception?'

'I just asked where you were.'

'How did you get here?'

'I hired a car at the airport.'

'Why didn't you tell me you were coming?'

'Would you have said yes?'

'No.'

'But you are happy?'

'Oh my god, come here,' she said, pulling his face towards hers, and kissing him with such wet fervour, he almost toppled into the pool with her.

How was she ever going to make the right decision now?

# Chapter Twenty

## *Robin*

It was going to be a good day, Robin thought, as he waited for the others to get themselves ready. Things always seemed so much better after a sleep, especially if you'd limited your drinking the night before. He'd got up before everyone else and was dealing with the traps, just as he used to in the days before Bobtail became the family's official pest control operative, when Jessica came into the kitchen in her robe.

'Sorry, did I wake you?' he asked.

'No. It's fine. I could have done that . . .' she said.

'Imperative that Ellis does not see we're trying to kill animals,' he said. 'To lose one member of the party could be regarded as a misfortune, to lose two might look like carelessness!'

Jessica always laughed at his jokes, even first thing in the morning, clearly appreciating his adaptation of Miss Prism, whom he'd played in a gender-blind production of *The Importance of Being Earnest* that had toured provincial cities to enthusiastic audiences but proved a bit too niche to transfer to a West End theatre.

'In fact, they're all empty,' he said, tidying them away into a cupboard under the sink and feeling oddly fulfilled.

Jessica made them both a cup of tea and they stood at the kitchen window blowing steam off their scalding mugs, hugging their robes tight around them in the chill of early morning and staring at the mist in the valley that made the distant settlement with its bell tower look like a castle in a fairy story sitting on top of a cloud.

'I'm relying on you for a full report about the truffle hunting,' Jessica said.

'Would you like me to score it?' he asked, delighted by the idea of being welcomed back as her accomplice tester.

'Yes, please. Out of five, please, for interest, value, hospitality. On a scale of one to ten for whether you would recommend it to friends and family.'

It was her job, but maybe she was so good at it just because she was so competent. Even at uni, Jessica had always seemed more grown-up than other students. She excelled at blokes' stuff, like darts and pool. She was the treasurer of DramSoc, made people pay their dues and sought sponsorship for productions. Even then, she'd understood about getting quotes for printed programmes and materials donated by local businesses. A lot of people had thought her pushy, but that could be a good thing. She was the person who had seen the ad for extras for the film which had made him famous and practically forced him to go along, banging on his door the morning of shooting when, left to his own devices, he would probably have stayed in bed.

'Shall I get Piers and Crispin to rate it too?' he asked.

Jessica frowned, then smiled.

'Actually, why not? That's a brilliant idea, as they're the most . . .' she paused for an appropriate adjective, finally coming up with, 'demanding clients.'

'What will you do?' he asked.

'I thought I'd take Ellis and Jaz into Città. Maybe check out the restaurant that Vittoria suggested. See if it's vegan-friendly.'

Jessica thought of everything. No wonder she was the only one of them Ellis tolerated. Laura said that was due to all the bribes, but he knew it wasn't just about supplying them with the latest iPhone. Jessica listened to Ellis and took them seriously. Laura dealt all the time with teenagers who had bigger problems, like hunger, deprivation and abuse. But all young people who had lived through Covid had mental health issues. Bad enough being forty and having two years taken out of your life, but at fifteen, as Ellis had been ... Sometimes he thought Laura should give Ellis a bit more of a break. Yes, they were luckier than most people, but that was a bit like Matron telling him he had to eat his dinner because other people were starving. Guilt didn't help the developing world nor improve the appetite.

'If it's any good, I thought I'd book it for tomorrow ...' Jessica said.

'I was hoping to cook something with the truffles ...'

'You can do that tonight. Laura said she'd like to be at your birthday lunch ...'

'Did she? Oh, well, in that case ...'

Spending more time with Jessica, especially in the rather fraught dynamic of his family, he'd begun to see a more thoughtful, caring side to her. Yesterday, when they were in Città, he'd watched her crouching down and communicating at the level of the caretakers' little girl and found himself thinking that she really would be a good mother, even if she did decide to go it alone. She possessed both the strictness and the softness required. In their family, Laura was the one who set the rules and he brought the tenderness. Jessica embodied both aspects in one person. He must find a way of telling her that.

'Thank god we've got rid of the women at last, eh, Robbo?' said Piers as the SUV containing his brothers and Barty screeched to a halt outside the farm where the truffle hunt was due to begin.

'What have you done with Cass and Cam?' he asked.

'We've dropped them off for a spa day. Place just outside Città.'

Laura wasn't going to be pleased about that. For a moment, Robin wondered whether he should alert her. It was too late now. If she knew that he knew Camilla and Cassandra were going to rock up, she might think he could have prevented it.

Two men with guns slung over their shoulders approached with a pair of excitable dogs on leads. None of them understood the instructions, and the farmer's English was rudimentary. Two out of five for communication, he thought, remembering his promise to score. However, it was pretty obvious how to hold a dog lead. Robin wasn't familiar with the breed. He thought the farmer was saying Lagotto Romagnolo. Their thick curly coats and cute faces weren't unlike Lammie's, except they were a light brown, the colour of a much-loved old teddy bear. He had to curb his immediate instinct to bend down and play. They were working dogs and the farmer, who was now showing them how to hold them back while still allowing them to sniff out the buried treasure, didn't look like a sentimental man.

Before being issued with wellington boots and walking sticks, they had to hand in their mobile phones, which were put in a basket in the outbuilding which served as an office.

'Is this really necessary?' Crispin objected.

'Will you accept liability if the phones are stolen?' Piers demanded.

Robin looked around. The farm was the only building for miles. He thought it unlikely that thieves would drive this distance into the countryside and trespass on a property full of barking dogs.

'You want *tartufi*?' The farmer pointed at the basket with a look that made Crispin meekly obey.

'Why the guns?' Tim whispered to Robin, as they followed the men to the truck.

'*Perche...?*' Robin asked, pointing, then pretending to fire a gun.

'*Cinghiale!*' came the reply.

'Oh, I think I know what that is!' Robin got down on all fours and did a passable impersonation of an aggressive pig oinking and twirling his finger behind his bum to indicate a curly tail.

'*Si, si!*' For the first time, the farmer's face broke into a smile.

'*Salsiccie!*' said Robin, pretending to eat and smacking his lips.

'*Vero!*'

'Wild boar,' he explained to the others, getting to his feet again. 'They make delicious sausages.'

'Are they dangerous?' asked Tim.

'Oh, for god's sake, Beast!' said Piers. 'Man up!'

'But is it dangerous?' asked George.

'Well, I imagine so, otherwise they wouldn't carry guns,' said Robin, suddenly a little nervous. It must be safe, mustn't it? Jessica wouldn't have booked it otherwise and it wouldn't be very good for business if tourists were gored. Should he give a score for health and safety?

'You're so gay,' said Barty, giving George a punch on the arm that Robin suspected was much harder than it looked.

'I'm not gay, but I find your use of the term as an insult offensive.'

'Offending someone isn't a crime,' said Piers. 'You're becoming as politically correct as your mother.'

'If you're saying I'm not a racist or a homophobe, I'll take it,' said George.

It was the most Robin had heard George say all holiday. He felt rather proud of him for standing up for himself in such a grown-up way.

'Mummy's boy,' taunted Barty.

'Shut up,' said Tim.

'Ooh, now we've offended Beast as well.'

'Guys!' said Robin, putting on a gravelly Clint Eastwood voice. 'There are truffles out there and we're gonna hunt them down!'

The party got into the back of a truck with the farmer, his son and the dogs in the front. They rattled along a track between two vineyards. The grapes had been picked and the leaves were turning yellow. There was a tinge of mould on the damp autumnal air. The truck's gears began to grind as they climbed up the hillside into the forest and stopped so suddenly Tim was thrown against Barty, who pushed him off forcefully as if he was making an inappropriate advance.

'What are truffles anyway?' George asked, as they followed the farmers through the trees. 'I thought they were chocolate.'

Crispin laughed.

'Are you sure he's your son, Robin? If he doesn't know what a truffle is.'

'They're a type of fungus,' Robin explained.

'Why are we hunting them then?' George asked.

'No, the dogs find them and we take some home to adorn a dish of pasta,' said Robin. 'It's really an excuse for a walk in the countryside.'

Out loud, it sounded rather a lame activity for four grown men and two teenage boys, but it was beautiful with the sunlight filtering through the golden leaves above their heads, dappling the mulchy forest floor beneath their feet. Feeling the energy of the dog pulling on its lead, eager to sniff out new adventure, reminded him a little of one of his favourite walks along the disused railway line from Finsbury Park to Highgate that was often so quiet during the day you'd never believe it was in a city. Were there undiscovered truffles nestling beneath the roots of the old oak trees? Surely if there were, the chefs of north London would have found them. Perhaps they had and were keeping it secret. It would explain the current enthusiasm for foraging which always seemed disproportionate to the handful of nettles collected.

'Are you missing Lammie, Dad?' George asked, as if he'd tuned into his thoughts.

'Do you know, I really am!' said Robin, giving his son a squeeze around the shoulders.

'If I'd known about the boar, I'd have booked a proper hunt,' said Piers. 'Went hunting for boar in France once. Hip flask of cognac at the ready. Great day out.'

'Isn't hunting illegal?' asked George.

'Only in England, although there are ways of getting round it . . .' said Piers.

'Your brothers haven't improved with age,' Tim said, falling in beside Robin.

'They don't mean any harm . . .' said Robin.

'You are kidding? They've always meant harm. You're so bullied by them you don't even realise it.'

'We're grown up now, Tim.'

'Sometimes I wonder if you ever did.'

'What?'

'Grow up! Honestly, you're like Peter Pan. You have the soul of a child in a middle-aged body.'

'Ouch!'

'Which bit of that statement do you object to?'

'Are we actually middle-aged yet? I mean, that's more fifty or sixty nowadays, isn't it?'

'Well, if my point needed proving . . .'

'What's wrong with wanting to be young?'

For a moment, Tim looked cross with him, then his face relaxed into a smile.

'Nothing's wrong with it,' he said. 'I suppose it's rather endearing. And it makes everyone want to look after you.'

'Except Crispin and Piers!' said Robin. 'Although, in their own way, I think they do.'

Up ahead, the dogs were getting excited.

'Look at them! I honestly think I love dogs more than humans,' Robin said.

'Why is that?'

'They're so uncomplicated.'

Tim smiled at him. 'Come on,' he said, 'we've walked all this way. We have to be there when they unearth the bloody things.'

The haul was underwhelming. Just two small truffles were dug up before the dogs calmed down, the farmer shrugged, looked at his watch, and they all started heading back. Robin couldn't suppress the slight suspicion that they'd been planted there, though he didn't want to introduce the idea if Piers and Crispin hadn't thought of it. He would only award two out of five for interest.

'There's more than enough to shave over buttery ribbons of pasta this evening!' he said, trying to put a positive spin on it. Since the cost of the package had included taking home what the dogs found, it was unlikely that they'd find kilos of the stuff, but still, currently just one out of five for value. A cloud of dissatisfaction had settled on his brothers' shoulders as the truck bumped back down the track.

'They smell like shit,' said Barty.

'They look like shit,' said Piers.

'They taste like shit too,' said Crispin.

'What is actually the point of them?' George asked.

'Ounce per ounce they are worth more than gold,' said Crispin.

'So you want to sell them?'

175

'There are probably rules about importing it to the UK,' said Tim.

'You could swallow them in condoms,' said Barty. 'Like drug mules. Dare you to swallow a condom with a truffle in it, George!'

'Are you for real? Anyway, those police dogs in *Nothing to Declare* would smell them.'

Robin thought it an intelligent point.

'They're only trained to sniff drugs,' said Piers.

'Perhaps it's fortunate then that we don't have enough to orchestrate an international truffle-smuggling operation...' said Tim.

Sitting in the sunshine under an awning outside the farm, Robin had downed two tumblers of rough red wine before their lunch was served and was feeling pleasantly relaxed. It wasn't a high-quality provision, but it was exactly what was needed. Robin wondered if he was allowed halves in the scoring system. If so, he would award three and a half for hospitality.

'Spaghetti bloody bolognese,' said Piers. The wine had done nothing to improve his mood.

'Actually, it's never called that in Italy,' said Robin. 'This is a ragu, I think of wild boar.'

'There's not enough of it,' said Piers.

'That's the authentic way. Italians wouldn't dream of putting all the sauce we do on pasta. It's poor man's food...'

'But rich man's prices,' said Crispin.

'This is why they take away your bloody phone,' Piers muttered. 'To deny you access to Google Translate to complain.'

He suddenly stood up and went looking for the farmer, returning shortly with a grin on his face.

'Result!' he said. 'He's agreed to take us all boar hunting this afternoon for the price for just two people! I'll give it to you for your birthday, Robbo. I forgot to get you anything.'

'Excellent!' said Crispin.

'Boar hunting? With guns?' said Robin.

'Boar hunting! With guns!' Barty screeched in a girly voice. 'You scared, Uncle Robbo?'

'I'm not scared, it's just . . .'

'Well, I am scared. It's a ludicrous idea and I won't be joining you,' said Tim.

'Why am I not surprised?' said Crispin.

'George?' Piers demanded.

'George, would you like to go?' Robin asked.

'You're not serious?' Tim interrupted. 'I'm sorry, but as his godfather, I'm making an executive decision here. George and I are not going boar hunting.'

George looked as relieved as Robin felt at Tim's intervention.

'Sorry!' Robin said to his brothers. 'I mean, it's a terrific present but I can't abandon these two . . .'

'You wussing out, Robbo?'

'Is it wussy not to feel particularly excited about killing a wild animal?' Robin tried a different tactic.

'You eat meat!' said Piers, pointing at Robin's empty plate.

It wasn't the first time Robin had encountered this argument. Ellis had said something similar to him when he'd served up a leg of lamb with a herb crust for the rest of the family. Apparently, if you were prepared to eat meat, you now had to be prepared to kill it too.

'I think of myself as more gatherer than hunter,' he'd said to them, which hadn't gone down well and had cast a shadow over the Easter lunch.

'Look, it won't be a bargain unless you join us,' said Piers. 'Will it?'

Robin could see the logic of that. He didn't have the speed of thought to find a counter-argument.

The farmer was calling from the shed.

George, reunited with his phone, was fully absorbed in the screen. Tim was standing guard beside him.

'What will you two do?' he asked Tim, who simply shook his head in despair as Robin walked over to join his brothers.

# Chapter Twenty-One

## *Laura*

Laura threw back the sheet and gazed at Alex as he lay dozing. He was the only man whose body she had ever felt free to stare at and explore. All her previous encounters had felt somehow furtive. Even Robin, whose body had been so desirable when she first knew him, was nervous unless he had drunk so much that he was usually unable to get an erection. Before him, she had always viewed sex as something she had to put up with, reluctantly obliging the man's needs, never imagining that she was supposed to like it when they sucked a nipple or stuck a finger inside her. With her husband, it had almost seemed like the other way round. They'd always done it in the dark, and after a few months they had mostly given up trying, hugs and kisses becoming more pleasurable and affectionate without the pressure of proceeding to intercourse. It seemed to suit them both.

Before Alex, she had never had an orgasm. The first time they'd done it, she couldn't stop screaming and laughing in happy astonishment that this was what it was supposed to feel like. He taught her to navigate her own body and his. Under his guidance she had learned the geography of pleasure. Now, she gazed at the landmarks she loved. The little mole on his inner thigh, the hollow V at the base of his throat, the tiny tufts of hair around his nipples on an otherwise hairless chest. His penis, softly curled on the cushion of his pubic hair, that stood up so straight and huge it felt like it was filling her completely.

He opened an eye, smiled lazily at her, then pulled her on top of him.

Afterwards she stared down at his lovely face, dropping a kiss on lips that still tasted of her.

'What would you like to do?'

There was no timetable. A whole day stretched ahead of them. He had a car. They could go anywhere. Or they could stay in bed, making love.

'To be honest, I'm starving!' he said. 'Let's go out and get something to eat.'

'How about Arezzo?'

Alex looked on his phone.

'That'll take at least an hour. Is there somewhere nearby?'

'Città di Castello is the nearest place.'

The rest of them were truffle hunting today, she remembered, so the chances of bumping into anyone were minimal. She looked at her watch. It was approaching one o'clock so restaurants should still be serving lunch by the time they got there.

She put on a summer dress she had packed optimistically, pure white and tiered, with a lace detailing at the neck, and teamed it with white trainers and a white denim jacket. She could feel her cheeks blushing with the look he gave her as she came out of the bathroom.

'God, you are beautiful, virginal and wanton at the same time, like a woodland nymph.'

'It works better with a tan,' she said, never knowing what to do with compliments.

She liked the way the floaty fabric made her skin feel naked under his gaze. He'd never seen her wearing anything other than formal dark suits. If she put on a dress for work, it was always a plain navy shift.

The sunshine was blindingly bright after the dim cocoon of their curtained room.

'Wait a minute, I think I left my sunglasses by the pool,' she said, as they approached the red Fiat 500 he had hired.

She ran through reception and out into the garden. There were two women lying on the loungers next to the one where she'd left her towel and sunglasses. Their backs were to her but she heard one of them say, 'I'm stalking Piers's bit on the side on Instagram...'

'WTF?'

'Young, obvs. Blonde, obvs.'

'So sorry, Cam.'

'Frankly, it takes the pressure off. My fanny's like sandpaper these days.'

'TMI, Cam!' Cass shrieked. 'You really have to change your HRT.'

'Menopause is meant to be so cool. But I just don't get it, Cass.'

Laura froze just in time to stop her shadow falling over her sisters-in-law. What could she do if they turned round? She'd have to join them for a chat, minimum.

'At least we've got away from the boys for one day!' said Cam.

'And the LGBTQ!' said Cass.

Peals of laughter.

'I mean, I know Barty's a pain, but at least he's normal...'

Part of Laura wanted to let them know that she'd heard, see how they defended themselves, but it wasn't worth exchanging for a day with Alex. There was no way of warning him about their presence because her phone was in her handbag, which was sitting on the front seat of the hire car. Eventually he would come looking for her. She suddenly realised she had been eavesdropping for too long. As she turned to make her getaway, she heard Cass say, 'Was that Laura?'

'In a dress?'

'OMG, you don't think she heard us, do you?'

Laura walked not too fast, not too slowly back to the conservatory, breathing again only when she reached reception.

'I see that two more guests have arrived!' she said to the receptionist.

'The English? Just for today!'

'When does the day end?' Laura asked.

The receptionist looked perplexed.

'I mean, how long are they allowed to stay here?'

'They can leave when they wish.'

'They're hardly likely to want to be here when it's dark, are they?'

Thinking out loud was making her sound unreasonable and aggressive.

'You wish to cancel your massage?'

She'd forgotten all about the massage.

'Actually, would that be possible? My friend and I . . .'

'Don't worry. Everything is perfect,' said the receptionist, putting one finger to her lips as if she knew. Was it so obvious?

'Where are they?' Alex said, as she got into the car.

'Who?'

'Your sunglasses!'

'Just drive!' she said. 'As fast as you can!'

Inside the city walls, they weren't sure which direction to head. Città di Castello was not a big tourist destination and it didn't seem to have a plethora of restaurants.

'Small world!' someone called out as they walked through the piazza beside the church.

Laura immediately dropped Alex's hand and looked towards the bar where the agent was sitting at an outside table with an espresso. This morning seemed so long ago, when they'd bumped into each other, Laura had forgotten she had mentioned going into Città.

'Looking for somewhere to eat?' the agent called.

'Yes, we are, actually,' said Alex.

'I've just had the most divine pasta at a place on the other side of town.'

She gave them directions, calling, 'Good luck!' as they thanked her and hurried off.

It didn't feel like especially good luck to have had two unexpected encounters in the space of an hour. Laura remembered the black cat squirming and purring around her legs. She told herself not to be so silly.

# Chapter Twenty-Two

## *Robin*

There was an abattoir area at the end of the barn with a stainless-steel counter and half a dozen sides of wild boar suspended from the ceiling that dripped blood with irregular pings and splashes into metal pails beneath. The smell was a bit like walking past a butcher's shop. Robin guessed the animals were recently killed as the flesh hadn't yet taken on the sweetness of rot.

The farmer was on his knees, making pig noises.

'Il cinghiale . . .' said Robin.

The farmer gave him a thumbs up.

'So, the wild boar . . .' Robin translated for the others.

The farmer stood up and walked round the three of them sniffing the air, then pulled a grimace and dashed towards the door.

'We smell bad . . . oh, I get it, the *cinghiale* . . .'

Robin went down on his hands and knees.

'If they smell us . . . ?' Robin stood up quickly and sniffed his pits, then dropped to his knees again, once more becoming the wild boar and moving towards the door as fast as he could on his hands and knees. 'They run away!'

'*Si!*'

The farmer gave him a high five. Who knew how useful an aptitude for charades could be?

'The wild boar run away if they pick up our scent, which is why we have to put on this foul-smelling hunting gear...' Robin explained to his brothers.

The farmer left them to change.

'It really does pong,' said Piers.

'Didn't happen to bring any Nodor with you, did you, Robbo?' added Crispin, just in case Robin hadn't got it.

'Are you really sure it's worth all this effort?' Robin said, tying up a pair of ill-fitting leather boots. 'Are you even allowed to hunt without a licence?'

'Are you even allowed to...' Piers mocked in a sing-song voice. 'No, of course we're not allowed to, but we've paid cash...'

The farmer returned with three pieces of paper that were still warm from the printer. The operation was a peculiar mixture of medieval and modern.

'What's this?' Robin asked, as the farmer indicated they should sign.

The farmer pointed at each of them, then put two fingers to his head like a pretend pistol and rocked sideways.

'I expect it's disclaimer forms. Probably not worth the paper they're printed on,' said Piers, signing his.

Robin followed suit. Piers was a lawyer, after all.

The farmer handed Piers a rifle.

'Only one?' said Crispin.

'You don't have a licence, do you?'

'Nor do you.'

'Not on me. But I do at home, so I could produce it in court.'

Robin breathed a sigh of relief that Piers was going to be the only one shooting.

'Ever handled a gun, Robbo?'

'We used to have those water pistols...'

'Ever wondered what it's like to have the power of life and death in your hands? Here, feel it, Barty...'

'You can't let him...'

'He can hold it, for fuck's sake!'

The deafening force of the explosion made Robin duck and cover his ears, not quite sure what had happened.

# Chapter Twenty-Three

## *Jessica*

Jessica could hear the murmuring of a priest talking to a young couple near the altar. She imagined they were planning a wedding. She had never really believed in God, but she thought that if anyone had proposed to her, she would have chosen an Italian church. She'd been baptised a Catholic but never really practised. Religion seemed to have given her mother all the guilt and not much of the grace, and when she'd died, it had offered no comfort at all. But in Italy the buildings were so beautiful and awe-inspiring, they felt like the perfect setting for solemn vows. If you weren't going to do it in style, why bother to get married at all?

Robin and Laura's wedding in Hackney Town Hall had hardly felt like a ceremony. Laura seemed to have no friends or relatives except for a rather severe-looking woman in a tweed suit, who must have been her aunt. Robin's parents had flown in but their disapproval was written all over their faces. Laura was fairly obviously pregnant and had worn a white trouser suit. Cassandra and Camilla were both in understated Armani. Jessica had bought a black and white checked shift dress in Karen Millen which she'd thought could almost pass as Chanel and teamed it with a bright pink tailored jacket.

'You look absolutely delicious,' Robin had told her, when she congratulated him. 'Like a Liquorice Allsort.'

Afterwards, they'd all gone to a gastropub. There'd been no ribbons on chairs, no speeches, no cake. Of course, it didn't mean they didn't love each other. They must have done.

Did they still? Robin seemed much happier now that Laura wasn't there. But who knew what went on behind closed doors? It was a phrase Jessica's mother often used, although it was pretty obvious what had gone on behind the closed door of the living room in their one-bedroom flat. Jessica never knew who she would find there in the morning when she had to tiptoe through to go to school. Sometimes her mother had brought some of the girls back from the club for a party; other times there would be a man Jessica didn't know.

Jessica had never really experienced how proper couples behave at home. Perhaps the coldness between Robin and Laura was typical? And yet he was being so warm towards Jessica, constantly giving her hugs and telling her she was brilliant. Could she dare to think that he was beginning to see how much better his life could be? It never felt sexual somehow, but she could live with that. She tingled whenever he touched her, but she would be happy with whatever pace he wanted to go at.

A shaft of sunlight through one of the high windows illuminated a beam of dust motes in the musty, incense-scented air. Raphael had painted his first commission here. Sometimes she wondered whether tiny invisible fragments of a person's DNA remained in the places they had been even if they had passed away. In London, she could never go to the late-night Chinese restaurant with the exceptionally brusque waiters without feeling her mother was present somewhere in the noisy, steamy, barbecue duck-flavoured atmosphere of the upstairs dining room. Occasionally, she would go to Brighton for the day just in order to get that same feeling of being flung against the edge of the seat on the ride at the end of the pier, screaming loud enough for both of them as if flew out over the sea.

Were there still microscopic molecules of Raphael here in the fabric of the church? She tried to imagine a living, three-dimensional version of his self-portrait as a young man. It was the first work in the recent exhibition at the National Gallery. He was such a handsome youth, although it wasn't until she had seen the later self-portrait in the final room that she'd felt something akin to falling in love, not just because he was gorgeous. His dark eyes seemed to be looking right at her with a kind of amused recognition, as if he knew that in five hundred years' time they would meet. The weirdness of the sensation had been compounded when she had caught sight of the portrait of his mistress, *La Fornarina*, on the adjacent wall. A scantily clad woman, sexy rather than beautiful, unashamedly touching her bare nipple as she stared back at her observer.

'You look just like her!' A middle-aged man standing next to Jessica had whispered, looking from one to the other as if the painting was a mirror.

Over coffee in the espresso bar, he'd claimed to be an artist himself, though she hadn't really believed it. A few weeks later, she spotted him approaching a curly-haired woman in the Wallace Collection with the exact same line about Fragonard's *Girl on a Swing*. Did it ever work? Were there limits? Did he tell women they looked like the Virgin Mary then suggest going back to his studio? She was relieved that she hadn't been tempted, despite having sex on her mind – not with him, but with Raphael.

If she'd lived in Raphael's time, would she have been his muse? It was a shame people didn't really have muses anymore, because it was a role that came to her naturally. Not sitting for paintings necessarily, although she had modelled for a life drawing class to earn extra cash when she was applying for jobs after uni. What she was good at, she'd learned over the years, was making talented people feel better about themselves. It often had the additional benefit of introducing creatives to sources of money. If she'd lived in the Renaissance she'd have been the person organising parties for rich cardinals and introducing them to struggling artists. Not that Raphael would have needed her help because he'd been a successful entrepreneur, charming his way into all sorts of important jobs. Legend had it that he had died from a 'surfeit of love' at the age of thirty-eight. She'd thought it an incredibly romantic fate until Robin had remarked that it was probably a euphemism for syphilis, but Jessica still preferred to think of the artist being so overcome by passion, he'd suffered a heart attack or something.

Emerging from the dimness of the church, Jessica looked at her watch. Two thousand and seven steps. There was still half an hour until her rendezvous with Ellis and Jaz. In the pocket of her jacket, she found the restaurant card Enzo had given her and remembered him saying his studio was nearby.

There was a whooshing noise and an acrid smell of burning wafting out of the open door. Peering inside, she saw him standing with a blowtorch, burning old paint off a huge panelled door. He was masked and the noise was so loud, he wasn't aware of her until she waved at him for the second time. Turning the burner off, he pushed the mask up.

'*Buon giorno!* Any news of the mouse?'

She found his relaxed attitude slightly easier to tolerate today. Things were so much better at the villa without Laura, she thought she should probably be grateful for the mouse. Although with the question of compensation still on her mind, she wasn't about to tell him that.

'No further sightings,' she said.

'You are alone today?'

'Just for an hour. What are you doing with that door?'

'Stripping away two hundred years of paint . . . maybe more.'

'Won't you burn the wood?'

'Not if I am careful.'

'How did you learn to do restoration?'

'I did a Master's.'

'Oh.' She'd been expecting him to say that it was a craft handed down from father to son. 'I thought you went to uni in London?'

He laughed.

'Yes. The LSE. I was a banker for ten years. Then we decided we wanted a more simple life . . .'

He must be older than he looked, she thought. Although now that his hair was scraped back from his forehead with the mask, she could see a few grey strands. She weighed up whether to ask him if there was any chance of him running a weekend of restoration activity. With a banker background, he'd know how to speak to her clients, unlike Jake the stone cutter from Dorset. She glanced at her watch. Only ten minutes before she was supposed to meet up with Ellis and Jaz, and with the question of compensation for the mouse still outstanding, this probably wasn't the time to discuss it.

'Did you go to see the Piero paintings?' he asked.

'The *Resurrection* and the *Madonna del Parto*,' she said.

'You should also see the *Flagellation*.'

'Where is that?'

'Urbino.'

'Isn't that where Raphael was born?'

'Yes, his father was the court painter. You like Raphael?'

'I love him. I mean his art, obviously . . . is it near? Urbino?'

'Not far as the eagle flies,' he said. 'It's in Le Marche, but there are mountains separating . . .'

191

'Crow,' she corrected his idiom. 'But I mean they're birds, so they can both take the direct route, can't they?'

He looked bewildered.

'To be honest, eagles are probably better at flying at altitude than crows, aren't they?'

He smiled.

'How long by car?' she asked.

'You probably need a day to see everything . . .'

'That's a shame. We've got plans. Chocolate festival tomorrow, then it's Robin's birthday and I don't suppose flagellation would be his idea of a treat. Wine tasting on Friday . . . We need both cars, you see.'

'I could drive you?'

Was he coming on to her? She found his raised eyebrow somewhat disconcerting. Now that Ellis and Jaz were the ones that boys looked at in the street, she'd forgotten how flirty Italian men could be. Even, it seemed, when they had exceptionally beautiful wives.

'Well, I mustn't stop you working,' she said.

'It's been a pleasure,' he said, grasping her hand and looking into her eyes for longer than required by a formal goodbye.

It was probably just Italian charm, she thought as she stepped back out onto the street. Of course he wasn't seriously offering to take her to Urbino. Italians were always saying things to make you feel welcome, like telling you that you were good at speaking the language even though you weren't.

# Chapter Twenty-Four

## *Laura*

Walking through the main square and down a long street that led towards one of the town's gates, they eventually spotted the restaurant the agent had named. There were two empty tables in the sunshine. Inside, several people were still eating, but the owner was just taking in the stand with the menu.

'*Per favore!*' Alex said. '*Mangiare?*'

He gave them a long look, then bowed, saying something in Italian, indicating they could sit where they liked.

'That's a bit of luck,' she said to Alex.

'Not luck. Didn't you understand what he said? It is an honour to serve such a beautiful woman . . .'

'You speak Italian?'

'I've picked up quite a lot from opera.'

'Is it warm enough to sit outside?' she asked him.

'Not for Italians, but plenty warm enough for us.'

He pulled out a chair for her.

'You like opera?' she asked.

'Of course. You?'

'I don't really know much about it.'

'I'll take you to Verona. You'll love it.'

Verona. The city of Romeo and Juliet. A slight chill ran through her bloodstream. Whenever people compared couples who were in love to them, Laura always felt obliged to point out that they had both died within three days of meeting.

Opera. There was still so much to discover about Alex. It felt like visiting a country for the first time, knowing the obvious attractions, but learning about the customs, the culture, all the aspects that formed its unique identity.

The proprietor seemed pleased when Alex waved away the menu and asked him to bring them whatever he recommended, adding that he was very hungry. He brought them a flask of water, and another of wine, a basket of bread, then plates with delicate envelopes of pasta filled with squash and scattered with flowers. For a main course, there was saltimbocca, salty with prosciutto, with fried sage leaves and a contorno of roasted potatoes spiked with crisped rosemary.

The shelter of the buildings on the opposite side of the street made it feel as if they were sitting in a courtyard in warm sunshine. The light white wine was refreshing. It seemed to smooth the frown lines from her face. She had wondered whether their private bubble of intimacy would survive in the oxygen of the outside world, but doing something normal like eating a meal with him felt easy. In his company, nothing seemed like a big deal. Telling him about her escape from the party house became an amusing anecdote rather than a melodrama filled with shame. She gazed across the table, occasionally reaching to touch his hand, as if to prove to herself he was real. Alex's charm came from listening. He was not a man who needed to be the centre of attention.

'So what's this phobia all about?' he asked.

'No idea,' she said, automatically.

'Do you have any other fears I should know about?' he asked.

'There are so many things we don't know about each other,' she said.

'True.'

'I mean, children. Do you want them?'

She tried to make the question sound informal, even though it would be a deal breaker for her. If he said he did want children, the decision would be easy. Better to know, one way or another.

'Do you want more?' he asked.

'No. I'm probably too old. I don't think I could go through it all again anyway. I'm not a very good mother...'

He held up his hand.

'Stop punishing yourself. I don't want kids of my own,' he said.

'But you might change your mind...'

'I'm interested in giving kids the best start in life. I'm fascinated by how young minds develop...'

'I know that,' she said.

'And I would take being a stepfather very seriously, if George and Ellis wanted that relationship.'

Stepfather. She felt touched that he had already thought of how this might affect them.

'But I made the decision not to have my own children a long time ago.'

'Why?' Her heart started accelerating again.

'My dad was bipolar. So was my older brother. He killed himself. It's genetic. I couldn't take the risk.'

The clipped way he stated the facts belied a great well of sadness underneath.

'I'm so sorry,' she said, reaching across the table. 'I had no idea...'

Now, she remembered him going to the funeral of his brother right at the beginning of his probation year. She'd insisted on him taking the maximum compassionate leave, covered all his lessons, worked really hard to catch him up when he got back, because it seemed such a tough break for someone at the start of a career for which he showed so much potential. She'd done everything she could to help him professionally, but she'd never asked for details, because, ironically, that would have felt like overstepping boundaries.

'Why would you?' he said. 'I didn't tell anyone for a while . . . I felt so guilty and ashamed. Not of him. Of myself. You always think there's something you could have done. I tried to obliterate the memory with rock and roll.' He smiled across at her.

'And sex?'

'Some of that, too.'

'And drugs?'

'Never went down that route. I found a good therapist.'

'Is that how you came back to teaching?'

'Ultimately, I suppose it is.'

'Are you still in therapy?'

'No.'

'You're not bipolar?'

'No, I seem to have inherited my mother's more even temperament.'

'Is she still alive?'

He raised an eyebrow and she realised that her staccato questions were beginning to sound like an interrogation.

'Yes. She remarried. Nice guy. They live in Bournemouth now. What about your parents?'

'My father died before I was born. She remarried. Lives abroad. I was mostly brought up by my aunt.'

She reached across the table, laced his fingers in hers.

'I think I understand you more now,' she said, wanting to divert any follow-up questions about her background.

'What do you mean?'

'I always thought that you had an old soul.'

He was eight years her junior, but he was the grown-up.

'God, you're lovely when you smile,' he said. 'It's so rare, but so beautiful when you do. You are my drug. I want to make you smile all the time. I want to see you smiling at me first thing when I wake up and last thing when I go to sleep at night.'

If she could capture a scene in her life and keep it as a treasure forever, it would be this, Laura thought. The clarity of the blue sky; the warmth of the sun that gave all the buildings a slightly pink hue and felt like a blessing on her face; the salty flavours of the lunch still lingering in her mouth; the gentle muzziness of the wine that muffled anxiety; the sincerity that shone in Alex's eyes as he gazed at her, the certainty that in this moment she was loved.

# Chapter Twenty-Five

## Jessica

The streets had become quiet with the somnolence that falls over Italian towns on sunny afternoons. She looked at her watch and stepped up her pace, not wanting to be late. Ellis and Jaz had wanted to wander around taking photos while she visited the museum and the church. She was pretty sure they wouldn't come to any harm on their own, but it was a foreign country and in Laura's absence, she considered herself *in loco parentis*. In her haste, she almost bumped into a woman who looked familiar, but who she couldn't quite place.

'Hey, small world!'

The accent jolted her memory. It was the agent woman who'd sat next to Laura on the plane.

'Looking for your friends?'

'Have you seen them?' Jessica asked.

'I recommended a restaurant with the most divine pasta . . .'

'Where?' she asked.

'Towards the end of that long street with the gate.' She pointed.

Jessica hoped it was the same restaurant. She'd agreed to text the girls when she arrived, but maybe just as well they'd gone ahead to get a table, as almost all the shops were shuttering up.

Even at a distance she could see Ellis's long white-blond hair gleaming in the sunshine. Jessica stopped walking. Ellis had cut their hair, so it couldn't be them. From the back, it looked like Laura, whom she wasn't particularly keen to run into just when she'd managed to get rid of her. Surely it couldn't be Laura? The very feminine white dress wasn't her style. The person facing in her direction was a man she didn't recognise. Perhaps she had a body double? What were the chances of finding two Catherine Deneuve lookalikes in one sleepy Italian town? A waiter came out with two tiny espresso cups and put them down on the table. The man chatted with him. The woman stood up and went inside. It was definitely Laura.

Jessica quickly stepped into a doorway, not wanting to risk being seen. These must be the friends the agent had been referring to, she thought. Ellis and Jaz hadn't even been on the plane.

Why shouldn't Laura eat lunch with a stranger? Perhaps he was staying at the spa? In her own experience, there was nothing more boring than lounging about all day with nothing to do, however much you claimed to want some R & R. Now she felt like an idiot for hiding, with her heart racing as if terrified of being caught. And yet, she thought, peering round the edge of the doorway, there was something about the body language, something about the smile on the man's face as he sat waiting for Laura to return, that made her feel it would be inappropriate to approach. Taking the opportunity to walk quickly past while he was alone, Jessica sneaked into an alleyway where she could get a good look at Laura as she came out.

She was smiling. Laura rarely smiled. Normally she wore an expression that made you feel like you knew exactly how it would feel to be called to her office at school. They were sharing a dessert! Something deliciously creamy like tiramisu that involved a good deal of mmm-ing and suggestive licking of lips. Beneath the table, one of Laura's legs was jammed between his thighs.

It couldn't be more than thirty hours since she'd dropped her at the spa. Fast work for someone so uptight. Except, it turned out, she wasn't uptight after all. In fact she looked totally, flirtily relaxed. Did she do this sort of thing all the time? Was she on Tinder? Was this guy one in a long line of casual lovers?

Jessica jumped as she felt her phone buzz in her pocket. A text from Ellis.

*We'll be there in five.*

Panic. Enough had gone wrong on this holiday already. Everything had calmed down now and people were having a much nicer time. It was supposed to be a treat for Robin, and she couldn't bear to introduce any more complications. There might be a perfectly rational explanation but she wasn't going to take the risk of Ellis seeing what she was seeing and jumping to the same conclusion. Ellis was so volatile.

Jessica texted.

*Restaurant closed. Don't come. See you back at the car.*

And her whole body flooded with relief when Ellis sent a thumbs up emoji.

# Chapter Twenty-Six

## *Robin*

The pain was like nothing he had ever felt before, as if someone was applying such crushing pressure he could barely breathe. He looked down at blossoming pool of liquid enveloping his boot like some sort of ectoplasm. In front of him the sides of wild boar dripped blood into buckets on the floor. The last thought before he dropped was how incredibly red his was in comparison.

Hovering in and out of consciousness, Robin heard Barty saying, 'It wasn't my fault!'

Tim's voice saying: 'We have to cut it off!'

George's: 'What? His leg?'

'There's so much blood!'

'Dad's not going to die, is he?'

'Be careful with that knife!'

'George, can you keep the pressure on, yes, just like that. Good lad.'

'Hang in there, Dad!'

A lot of pulling and wrenching. Swooning pain.

'Robin, don't try to sit up. I need to stem the bleeding. Fuck's sake, someone call an ambulance!'

'OK, keep your hair on, Beast!'

'It's your fucking fault!'

'I didn't actually realise it was loaded . . . Google Translate's taking an age . . .'

'Fuck's sake, the word must be something like ambulance!'

Surely he wasn't going to die because of a weak signal?

# Chapter Twenty-Seven

## *Jessica*

Jessica knew she should leave, but it was like a scene from a horror movie where you put your hands over your eyes, but are still compelled to keep watching through your fingers.

Laura was looking down at the table now, the man reaching across, lifting her chin with the tips of his fingers. Was there a glaze of tears in her eyes as she turned her face into the palm of his hand and kissed it? This wasn't just about sex, Jessica suddenly realised. It was about intimacy. Love was in the air and all around them. How long had it been going on? All that time Laura claimed to be working so hard that she couldn't spend any time with her husband or children, was it not so much the result of the new job, but of an affair that she wasn't prepared to forgo, even for his birthday? Had her lover been on the same plane? Was that why Laura had been so eager to sit a long way from the rest of them at the back? Had Laura engineered her getaway from the house, knowing that he was waiting for her in Città di Castello? So much for her life being like a Jane Austen novel. Jilly Cooper, more like. How greedy to have a perfect husband and a lover too. Sitting there looking like a bride on honeymoon in her floaty white dress.

There was a part of Jessica that burnt to confront her, but she held back, knowing she needed to be smarter. Perhaps this was the opportunity she'd been dreaming of. When Robin's marriage blew up, she would be there to pick up the pieces.

Realising that she couldn't pass the restaurant again without being spotted, Jessica walked along the alleyway until she found a parallel street, then legged it back across town, wondering why she was the one feeling terrified of being rumbled.

Ellis and Jaz were standing beside the car.

Four thousand six hundred and twenty-four steps.

'Where are we going to eat?' Ellis called as she approached.

'I think we'll have to try another town.'

'What about Mum, though?'

For a moment, Jessica thought they had seen her too.

'Isn't she coming to Dad's birthday lunch?'

'We can pick her up . . . I really don't know,' said Jessica.

Ellis looked at her curiously.

'Are you OK?'

'What do you mean?'

'You're very red. Unusually flustered. Is it a flush?'

'A flush?'

'You're allowed to talk about the menopause, Jessica. It's not shameful.'

Damn the self-righteousness of teenagers and all the bloody celebs who'd started banging on about it like it was a great look for the new season.

'I'm not . . .'

She was about to say 'anywhere near the menopause', but she'd read that it crept up on you stealthily and involved anxiety and mood swings, not just your periods stopping. So perhaps . . . ?

Her phone rang, rescuing her from extrapolating that depressing thought.

'Hey, Tim!' she said. 'What can I do for you?'

'Are you with the girls?' he said.

'Yes . . .'

'I'm very sorry, Jessica . . .' His voice sounded strange.

'What about?'

'There's been an accident . . .'

# Chapter Twenty-Eight

## *Laura*

The tiny glass of grappa the restaurateur had given her remained untouched on the table as she watched Alex taking a sip of his. He smiled at her, his hand lightly stroking the inside of her thigh under the table, turning her body to liquid in anticipation of what they would do later. She tried to stay in the perfect moment for as long as she could, until a great wave of panic swept it away. He was so honest. She wasn't. And all the time the stakes were getting higher and the risk of losing him terrified her more.

She jumped as her phone rang.

The screen said it was Jessica calling. What did she want?

'I'd better answer,' she said.

Within two seconds the best day of her life became the worst.

'What sort of accident?' she asked.

'All I know is that he's in an ambulance on his way to hospital. Tim's following in the SUV with George, so he can't talk,' Jessica said, sounding frightened but in control.

'Which hospital?'

Jessica gave her the name.

'OK. I'll be there as soon as I can.'

'Are you at the spa?' Jessica asked.

Laura felt herself reddening as she said, 'Yes.'

'I could pick you up?' Jessica offered.

'No, you need to get there as soon as possible. You're the only one who speaks any Italian ... I can easily get a cab ...'

Alex instinctively understood that she needed him to drive quickly but carefully, saying nothing. The only voice in the car came from Google Maps.

Laura's mind was a whirlwind of fear and guilt. Was Robin going to die? Had she in some way caused this terrible thing to happen by her infidelity? Had the black cat been a warning that she should have heeded, instead of welcoming Alex like a bouquet of flowers that she knew had been delivered to the wrong address, fully aware that her selfishness would have unhappy consequences for other people? Did this overwhelming feeling of dread mean that she really did love her husband? Would it be too late to tell him?

The journey took them from sunlight to darkness. It was dusk when they pulled into the hospital car park. Her flimsy white dress now seemed totally inappropriate. She pulled the jacket round her shoulders but it did nothing to warm her. She felt frozen inside and out.

'I'll wait here,' Alex said. 'Call me when you know what's happening.'

She walked slowly towards the emergency department, trying to remember how she usually behaved. The waiting area was fairly busy, but she couldn't spot anyone she knew there. She kept repeating Robin's name to the reception staff, louder and louder until they finally seemed to understand and pointed at seats, indicating she should wait.

'I'm his WIFE!' she heard herself screaming.

A nurse came and took her through double doors with rubber flaps.

'Hello, Laura,' said Piers solemnly. He was standing with

Barty and Crispin, a little apart from her children and Jaz, who had their arms around each other's shoulders, supporting one another. Next to them was a cubicle with curtains drawn around it. Oh my god. Didn't they draw the curtains when someone had died?

# Chapter Twenty-Nine

## *Robin*

'Blood pressure's normalising.'

He was lying on a bed with a tight band around his arm that released as a machine bleeped. The smell of floor cleaner and antiseptic was a welcome relief from the stench of blood. Tim's eyes smiled down at him above a blue surgical mask. Jessica's frown lifted as she saw him looking at her.

'He's awake!' she said.

'My two favourite people!' he said.

'Thanks a bunch, Dad . . .' said Ellis's voice. He couldn't see them because there were curtains around the bed.

A man in a white coat came in and started talking in Italian, with Jessica translating as best she could,

'So, the doctor says you've been very lucky. You've lost the top of your little toe but a centimetre further in and it would have been . . . a different story. They are going to dress the wound and give you some antibiotics. Is your tetanus jab up to date? No. You'll have a booster then. Anything you're allergic to? They'll keep you in overnight for observation. Tomorrow you should be fine to go home with crutches . . .'

A nurse came to put in a cannula.

'Small prick,' said Tim as the needle went in.

'Not the first time someone's said that to me . . .' Robin joked.

There seemed to be some sort of commotion on the other side of the curtains. Then Laura's voice, unusually shouty.

'I'm his wife!'

Tim squeezed his hand and said, 'Only two visitors allowed around a bed, Robin, but I'll be right outside.'

The curtains parted and Laura was there. For a moment, he thought she was wearing a nightie.

'What are you doing here?' he asked.

'That was going to be my first question to you!' Her face looked hot and red, as if she'd spent too long in the sun.

'I appear to have been shot in the foot!' he said. 'Not by myself on this particular occasion.'

He saw Jessica's worried face breaking into a teary smile, but Laura looked as if she would explode.

'For god's sake, Robin! What were you thinking?'

'It was Piers's idea,' said Tim's disembodied voice from behind the curtain.

'What was?'

'We tried to stop him,' said George.

'Boar hunting.'

'For god's sake, Robin!'

'It honestly serves you right, Dad,' said Ellis. 'I mean, think what that bullet would have done to a boar.'

'Killed it,' said Barty. 'That's the whole point, isn't it?'

'Shut it, Barty. Apologise to Uncle Robbo . . .'

'It wasn't my fault.'

'Barty shot him? What was he even doing with a gun?' Laura screamed, putting a stop to the off-stage chorus. She pulled back the curtain with such force the top of it ripped from its rings, then still holding the fabric in one hand, she pointed at the exit and ordered, 'Get your vile, delinquent son out of here!'

After a moment of stunned silence, Piers said, 'Not sure that's politically correct language to use about a minor, is it, Laura?'

'Just fuck off, will you, Piers.'

Everyone was as shocked by the words that had just come out of Robin's mouth as he was.

'Language, Robbo.'

'I said fuck off and take Barty with you,' Robin repeated firmly.

'All right, all right, keep your hair on!'

'I mean it. And I don't want any of you there when we get back.'

Piers opened his mouth to respond, but Crispin pulled him away. 'Sounds like we'd better pick up the girls and head to the *castello*, old chap.'

The doors with rubber flaps slapped together behind them, leaving everyone staring, fearing their return. After a few moments, Tim said, 'Bloody hell, Robin! Well done. I didn't think you had it in you.'

'Must be the drugs,' Robin said, feeling a wave of unalloyed triumph wash over him.

Laura's face was still ugly with anger.

'You didn't have to come, darling,' he said.

'Of course I did!'

Silence.

'I'll take these guys and see if there's a vending machine,' said Tim. 'Anything you want?'

'More morphine, if that's on offer,' Robin said, as the pain began to bite again. He closed his eyes, beginning to drift.


'Aren't little toes redundant, like a kind of evolutionary left-over?' Laura was asking.

'I think you need them for balance,' said Jessica.

'Never my strong point!' Robin said.

'We didn't realise you were awake, Robin.'

He opened his eyes, looked at the women on either side of the bed. Laura's almost white hair, Jessica's almost black. An image drifted through his consciousness, a curtained tent, two figures holding back the drapery.

'You're angels,' he said. 'Like the *Madonna del Parto* ...'

'Must be the meds,' said Laura.

'How's the spa, darling?' he asked.

'Very nice, thank you. But we'll all go back to London to-morrow, obviously.'

'No need to ruin the holiday,' said Robin. 'Tim's my own private surgeon and there's Nurse Jessica ... I don't know who's going to cook ...'

'Don't worry about that now, Beau. I'll organise something,' said Jessica.

'I'm not sure Deliveroo comes that far up a mountain!'

Gratified to hear her laughter, he dozed off again, waking some time later to the voice of an Italian doctor talking at speed.

'*Capito! Cinque minuti!*' said Jessica. 'OK, I think I understood. They're admitting you for the night, so they'll take you up to a ward now. We're not allowed to come with you and you need to sleep anyway, but we'll sort everything out and come back to collect you in the morning. Now, I'm putting your mobile phone beside you on the bed alongside a toothbrush and mini Colgate kit ...'

'Where did you get that?' Laura asked.

'I always carry a couple, in case.'

'In case of an emergency admission to hospital?'

'Fresh breath improves most situations.'

'Well, that's true.'

Suddenly a whole battalion of masked staff arrived, hooked his IV up to a trolley that looked a bit like a hat stand, lifted the brakes on his bed and pulled back the curtains to push it away.

'Bye, darlings!' he said, as the bed clanked and started rolling. It was a bit like a ghost train at the fair, he thought, entering a dark corridor where you didn't know what would happen next, which was fun, but quite scary at the same time.

'See you tomorrow, Beau!'

As the familiar voices grew more distant, he heard Laura saying, 'I'd better call a cab.'

And Jessica replying, 'Don't be silly, I'll take you.'

'There's really no need, Jessica.'

'It's no problem at all.'

How nice the two of them were getting along so well, Robin thought. He'd always thought they could. Perhaps all it took was a crisis.

# Chapter Thirty

## *Laura*

Tim and the kids were sitting in the now deserted reception area of the emergency department. They all jumped up as she and Jessica pushed through the double doors.

'They've taken him up to the ward,' said Jessica, stretching out her arms for a group embrace. She noticed now that Tim's eyes were bloodshot with tears and his shirt was spattered with blood. It had clearly been very stressful for all of them. Once again, she was the outsider. Catching sight of her over Jessica's shoulder, George broke away, came over and gave her a hug.

'You OK, Mum?' he asked.

'I'm fine. But are you guys OK? Would you like me to come back with you to the house?'

'We're good,' said George. 'Dad's safe now.'

'Nobody wants to deal with your hysteria along with everything else,' said Ellis, who was still standing metres away holding Jaz's hand. They clearly didn't want her to return, but their stare felt like a challenge. What sort of mother are you, leaving us to go back to your spa?

Was this how it was always going to be now? Was this the last time she could choose them before Alex? Had the moment of decision arrived in the dim anonymity of a hospital waiting room on the outskirts of an unfamiliar Italian city?

'I'll run you back, then,' said Jessica.

'Isn't it in the other direction?'

'It's not that far,' said Jessica. 'Tim can take the kids in the SUV. I'll drop you off in the Fiat.'

There was to be no escape.

'I'll get this lot back then,' said Tim, as they all walked out of the building.

Laura had no idea how long it had been since she arrived. Hospital time was different from normal time. Was Alex still out there, waiting? There hadn't been any opportunity to call him.

'I'm actually desperate for a wee,' she said in one last effort to find an escape.

'Me too. See you later!' Jessica waved at the kids.

Together they walked off to find the toilets.

*R OK. Staying overnight. J taking me back*, Laura texted.

'So you got a cab here?' Jessica called from the adjacent stall.

It wasn't possible that she could see through the partition, but it felt as if she could.

'Yes.'

'Pity you didn't think to get a number.'

'I had a lot on my mind.'

That was true at least.

# Chapter Thirty-One

## Jessica

The same guy she'd seen in the restaurant was sitting in the car with the light on, looking at his phone, as she and Laura walked across the car park.

'Another rented Fiat 500!' Jessica said. 'I wonder who he's waiting for? I thought we were the last people here ...'

Jessica started the engine and pulled out of the car park. It felt almost as if she'd kidnapped Laura. It was the first time she'd ever had the upper hand in their relationship and yet her feet were shaking on the pedals, as if she was the one with the secret and it would be her fault if everything blew up.

'Weirdly, he looked familiar,' she continued. 'I'm almost sure I saw him eating lunch at a pavement table in Città earlier ...'

It was such a long silence, she could almost hear the processes inside Laura's brain working. Eventually, she let out a long sigh.

'You were spying on us?'

'I wasn't spying on you!' Jessica protested, although technically she supposed she was. 'I was checking out the restaurant for Robin's birthday.'

'What did you see?'

'I thought I saw a couple in love ... but I don't want to jump to any conclusions, although I have to say you're not exactly making it hard for me . . .'

'He is a colleague of mine . . .'

'A very close colleague?'

'I know what it looks like, but I didn't plan this. I called Alex in distress and he arrived without asking me . . .'

'You didn't invent the mouse phobia as an excuse to be with him?'

'I'm really not that good an actress.'

'Seems to me like you are quite a good actress if you're having an affair.'

Another long pause.

'Are you?' Jessica persisted. 'I mean, having an affair?'

'Yes.' A long sigh. 'Actually, it's quite a relief not to have to pretend anymore. I'm not good at playing games, as you know . . .'

Surely she wasn't looking for sympathy?

'Robin doesn't know?'

'No, of course not!'

'Are you going to leave him?'

'I think so.'

'Jesus,' said Jessica, lifting both her hands from the steering wheel and banging them down hard. The car swerved, but they were on an empty road. 'You're so fucking cold!'

'Just because I'm not incontinent with my emotions, doesn't mean I don't have them!'

'What?' Jessica couldn't believe the nerve of it. Any grain of sympathy she might have had for Laura vanished. 'You're unbelievable!' she said.

'I didn't mean you are emotionally incontinent . . . I just meant that you know what it feels like to be in love . . .'

The belated attempt to appeal to common ground was so inept, Jessica felt nothing but contempt.

217

'I was intending to tell Robin,' Laura offered.

'When?'

'I don't know . . .'

'Well, how about tomorrow, because I'm not prepared to collude in your lies.'

'But it's his birthday on Thursday! He's lost half a toe.'

'They say bad things come in threes.'

'His birthday's not a bad thing, though,' Laura pointed out, pedantic on top of everything else.

'I'd say spending it on crutches probably is!'

Laura didn't have any comeback to that. For a few miles the car felt like a pressurised container. Jessica's body felt charged with hostility, as if any further provocation would make her lash out physically. She tried to concentrate on driving, her knuckles white from gripping the steering wheel.

'I'm not sure he'll even care that much.' Laura broke the silence.

'Of course he will!' Jessica shouted. 'He worships the ground you walk on!'

That was a truth that she'd never quite been able to admit to herself before. For whatever unfathomable reason, Robin loved Laura. She suddenly felt sorry for what he was about to learn.

'I think I know him just as well as you do,' Laura said. 'That is, the reality of him.'

'What's that supposed to mean?'

'Well, if anyone worships anyone . . . Let's face it, I'm not the only one harbouring a secret passion, am I?'

The car swerved alarmingly, skidding perilously close to the concrete barrier in the centre.

'Slow down!' Laura shouted. 'You'll kill us both!'

Fortunately the road was still empty, but Jessica no longer trusted herself to drive. Indicating, although there was nothing behind her, she pulled in to the verge, put on her hazard lights and switched off the engine. They both sat staring through the windscreen at the blackness of the road ahead, occasionally lit by the headlights of a car rushing past.

'You could see it as an opportunity . . .' Laura suggested.

'You're not seriously trying to suggest you're doing me a favour?' Jessica said.

Jessica couldn't work out how Laura had managed to turn this round and make it about her, taking the power back. If they were in a movie this would be the moment when all the resentment she had felt for the past twenty years came out and she'd end up hitting Laura, perhaps even pummelling her to death and dragging her body into a ditch. But she was so exhausted by the fluctuations of the day, she couldn't seem to find the energy even to talk.

'Look, if it helps,' Laura finally said, 'I hate myself just as much as you hate me, and I'm probably condemning myself to the misery of being hated by everyone. I'm honestly not trying to turn it into anything other than the mess it is.'

There was a long silence.

Jessica glanced in the rear-view mirror as another car's headlights approached, then slowed and pulled over.

'Your man has just pulled in behind us,' she said. 'Why don't you get out and go with him? It's too bloody far out of my way.'

# Chapter Thirty-Two

## *Laura*

The road was so dark, it was like a secret spy exchange, with both drivers remaining inside their cars as Laura walked the short distance between them. As her eyes adjusted, she saw that the sky was full of stars. The cold night air cleared her brain. Jessica was right. It wasn't fair to ask her to keep this secret. And she couldn't risk her deciding to tell Robin and the children. Laura had to take control of her narrative. After a couple of paces she turned, walked back and tapped on the passenger window.

'Look, why don't I pick Robin up from the hospital tomorrow and bring him back? I'll find a way of telling him.'

'Fine,' Jessica said, yawning.

The vitriol seemed to have evaporated from both of them.

Jessica started the engine. 'Better get going.'

'Can I ask you something?' Laura asked. 'Why did you offer to drive me when you already knew?'

'I had to be sure I wasn't imagining things as I wanted them to be,' Jessica said. 'I know I do that.'

She wound up the window. It felt almost like a peace offering.

'Pleasant evening?' Alex asked, as Laura got into his car.

She heard herself groaning like an animal in pain as grief and relief spewed out of her.

Eventually, she took the bunch of tissues he handed her, wiped her face and was able to modulate her breathing again.

'Robin's OK. That's the main thing,' she said.

Alex started the car and drove, intuitively understanding that she didn't want to talk as she processed what had happened.

The last few hours had taught her that she did love her husband, but not in a way that was good for either of them. When she'd seen him lying with no visible injury apart from a big bandage on his foot, she had felt a surge of the love you might feel for a mischievous child. Incorrigible, she thought, was a word often found in the children's books she had grown up with that was rarely used nowadays, but that suited Robin perfectly. He so enjoyed being centre stage with an audience, everyone telling him how brave he was. He'd actually made a feeble joke. Was there nothing he wouldn't do to get people to like him?

Back in her room at the spa, Alex ran her a bath, emptying into it the contents of the aromatherapy shower gel, then knelt beside it, gently sponging her back, trickling warm water down her spine as she sat in a cloud of bubbles. He held a towel for her as she stepped out, wrapping her in it, then lifting her onto the bed. She must have been asleep before he joined her. In the middle of the night she woke to find him holding her as she slept, still in his bathrobe, smelling of rose and geranium. The closeness felt exquisitely intimate, as if he had understood she needed his reassurance that it wasn't just about sex. When she was in his arms, her cheek pressed against his chest, she felt as if everything was going to be all right. But would it still be if she were ever brave enough to tell him her secrets? Would he still love her then? A tumble of anxious thoughts made it impossible to get back to sleep again. As soon as six o'clock came, she texted Robin. Hospital mornings started early. He was sure to be awake.

*I'm going to pick you up, so let me know as soon as you have an idea of timing.*

*Sweet of you, darling, but you haven't got a car.*

*I've rented one.*

*OK. I'm hoping to escape as soon as I've seen a doctor.*

'What's happening?' Alex asked, woken by the pinging of the texts.

'I'm going to pick Robin up and take him back to the villa,' she said. 'We can talk in the car. Or stop for lunch. I don't know quite how it's going to work . . .'

'Are you sure you want to do this alone?'

'I have to.'

He was frowning.

'What?' she said.

'It's going to be pretty rough on Robin, isn't it?'

Was he now beginning to see her as cold and ruthless, as everyone else did?

'At least I won't be lying to him,' she said.

'*You wicked little liar!*' she remembered her mother screaming at her, the moment she had decided to tell her the truth.

'*I'm not a liar! I swear!*'

Ever since, whenever she'd lied, she'd wondered if maybe her mother was right and she really was a bad person.

222

# Chapter Thirty-Three

## *Robin*

## Wednesday

He was sure he'd heard Laura saying the day before that she'd come to the hospital in a cab. Maybe the painkillers had confused him? They were certainly strong because in the night he thought he'd seen a giant magpie perched at the end of his bed.

'Good morning, Mr Magpie,' he'd said. 'Where's your lady friend?'

It had continued to stare at him. Perhaps it didn't understand English. When he'd woken again, it had gone, but the throbbing pain was back.

It was sweet of Laura to offer, especially as she hated driving abroad, but the gratitude he knew he should be feeling was slightly tempered by the prospect of a tense journey back. It would have been so much more fun being able to tell Jessica the whole story, rehearsing ways of creating an anecdote he would dine out on forever.

Would Laura come into the house? Surely not after the mouse incident? It was weird how much more harmonious the vibe was without her. He wasn't looking forward to her berating him about the boar hunt that never was either. Laura could be a bit of a drain, but he wasn't really in a position to argue when she'd gone to all the trouble of renting another car. And he wanted to get out of hospital as soon as possible. The man in the next bed had no trouble sleeping at all, emitting a pattern of two snores followed by an extremely loud and smelly fart. First the sound, then the smell. It wasn't ideal accommodation on the holiday of a lifetime.

Robin was sitting in a chair in reception when she arrived. He was still dressed in a hospital gown, with a trainer on the foot that wasn't injured and a pair of crutches propped up beside him.

'What happened to your clothes?' Laura asked.

'So much blood. Not mine, the porker's.'

'The porker's?'

'Sides of boar. I kicked over a bucket of blood. I kicked the bucket! Well, almost. I suppose you had to be there.'

Laura failed to manage a smile.

'They had to cut the boot and my trousers off but my boxers remain unspattered,' he said, hoisting himself to his feet to give her a back view of the open gown and underwear. 'So I'm decent.'

'Are you sure you want to leave like that?'

'I've got my discharge papers,' Robin held up an envelope. 'And I'm getting pretty nifty on these,' he said, pushing himself up to standing with the crutches.

'Well, if you're sure.'

'Once more unto the breach!' he said, brandishing a crutch like a spear.

Even with the front seat pushed as far back as it could go, there wasn't enough space for him to sit next to her.

'Tell you what, why don't I lie along the back seat?' he suggested.

'Comfortable?' Laura asked, once he'd shuffled his way in.

It wasn't particularly.

'Can't think why I've ever travelled any other way...'

His attempt at levity failed to lift her frown in the rear-view mirror as she started the car and concentrated on the road. His wife was never the most chatty person, but he'd known her long enough to recognise that there was something she was holding back. Better get it over with.

'I know I was an idiot...' he said, as she glanced back at him in the mirror.

'Well, yes, you were, but...'

'What's wrong?' he asked.

'I can't talk to you in the rear-view mirror,' she said.

'I could murder a coffee. You'd think all coffee would be brilliant in Italy, but hospital coffee not so much...'

'You can't go into a bar in a hospital gown.'

'No, but I expect you could bring one out to me,' he said. 'Why don't we pull over?'

Through the window of the bar, he saw the barista's face light up as she ordered. He felt a swell of pride. His beautiful wife. The cappuccino she brought out had a heart swirled into the foam, not intended for him, he knew. The cup shook on its saucer as she handed it to him.

'Nothing for you?' Robin asked, as she got into the passenger seat so that she could face him, though it was still a bit awkward with the headrest in between them.

'Robin, I've got something to tell you...' she said. 'I didn't mean for it to happen like this...' She looked on the verge of tears.

'Are you terminally ill, or leaving me?' he laughed, then saw she wasn't smiling.

'I think I am leaving you, Robin.'

'Oh...'

He waited to feel something. Shocked, numb, devastated. Weren't these the feelings people had in such circumstances?

225

But somehow it wasn't really a shock at all, more like an inevitability he had been expecting almost since the day she moved into the house in Hackney, looking like an angel. Over the years he'd seen imperfections and vulnerabilities beneath her serene exterior, and he liked to think he'd found ways of supporting her. But there had never been a time when she hadn't felt slightly unknown to him.

'Is it the person you went to the Globe with?' he finally asked. She'd taken a party of sixth formers a couple of weeks before.

'How did you know?' She looked astonished.

'You came back glowing. I mean, I know Shakespeare can be transformative, but *Lear*?'

He laughed. She didn't.

'Why didn't you say anything?' she asked.

'I suppose I thought it might be a temporary thing,' he said. 'We all have our moments of indiscretion, don't we?'

He hoped she wasn't going to ask him what moments he'd had. Not that he'd technically been unfaithful, but there had been several occasions where it had been a pretty close call.

'I suppose I thought you deserved some...' he paused, not wanting to say sex because it sounded crude, but trying to think of another word; '... excitement.'

'You don't seem angry,' she said.

'I don't really get angry, do I? Doesn't mean I'm not sad.'

'Me too. I'm so sorry.'

'We had a good run at it,' he said. 'Eighteen years! I hope I didn't make you unhappy. Because I couldn't bear that...'

'No, you didn't make me unhappy...'

'Although you always are a bit unhappy, let's face it. But I liked being the one who cheered you up.'

'Yes.'

He hated seeing her looking so sad.

'I never could understand what you saw in me,' he said, trying to lighten things up, but instead she started sobbing. He'd never seen her cry, except when Ellis was born and those were tears of pain and happiness, not at all like this wretchedness. He wanted so much to be able to put his arms around her, tell her it was going to be all right, but he couldn't shift forward without bumping his toe and he was sure she would be cross with him if he did that. Instead, he reached his hand as far as he could, managing to touch the top of her head with the tips of his fingers. When she grasped his hand and held it there on her shiny blonde hair, he felt more connected to her in this strange position than he ever had before, until her sobs subsided and she finally let go, brushing her wet face with the back of her hand.

'Remember that vase my father inherited from his grandfather who was something in the Opium Wars?' Robin asked, although how could she forget since his father droned on about it at every opportunity, speculating how much it might be worth, with China booming, and frustrating Crispin by not selling it when he judged the top of the market.

Laura looked at him curiously.

'I've always sort of seen you as my version of that,' said Robin. 'Like I've been lucky enough to have temporary guardianship of a beautiful thing and should do my utmost to pass it on undamaged . . .'

She stared at him, tears rolling down her cheeks again.

'That's a lovely thing to say.'

He was pleased she liked it.

'I'm sorry,' she said. 'I didn't mean to spoil your holiday. Alex just turned up after I called him from the spa.'

Alex. Wasn't he the teacher at her school who'd been in a band? A lot younger than her. For a moment, he felt slightly anxious on her behalf.

'He's here in Italy?'

'I didn't make up the mouse,' she said.

'You're not that good an actress!' he said, with a laugh.

'That's exactly what I said to Jessica.'

'Jessica knows about this?'

'She happened to see us together in Città yesterday . . . Put two and two together.'

'Coco's always been good at sums!' he said.

'Oh, Robin!'

She smiled at him with that look of affection and exasperation which had recently swung more towards exasperation.

'So, how are we going to go about telling the kids?' she asked.

He'd been rather looking forward to getting back and not having to think about it anymore.

'Do we have to do it now?' he asked. 'I mean, can't it wait until we're back home? I don't want to spoil my birthday for everyone . . .'

# Chapter Thirty-Four

## Jessica

It was the first time she'd used the sewing kit she always brought in case of emergency. She'd packed a bunting banner with the words *Happy Birthday* appliqued on in contrasting gingham, but when she'd woken in the early hours and tried to think of ways of making Robin's return from hospital happier, she'd realised that if you included an exclamation mark there was only one space difference in the words *Welcome Home!* Then, she hadn't been able to get back to sleep, so she'd come down to the kitchen and cut the letters out of a couple of tea towels, which could easily be deducted from the deposit, or thrown in free after negotiations around the mouse issue, and had spent hours stitching them carefully onto the reverse side of the little flags. She was just wondering whether it should in fact say *HOME!* or whether there was enough tea towel left to cut out the letters *BACK!* when Robin called.

His name appearing on her screen made her pause for a moment to compose herself. Laura must surely have picked him up by now. He was going to be distressed. She took a deep breath.

'Robin?'

'Coco, I gather you've heard our news? Look, could you get Tim to take the kids out for the day? I need a bit of time to figure out how to play this, prepare my lines, if you know what I mean. Neither of us feels up to facing interrogation by Ellis . . .'

He sounded fine, almost businesslike.

Jessica switched immediately into planner mode. 'How about we send them off to EuroChocolate in Perugia today instead of tomorrow?'

'But that's my birthday treat!'

'But . . . well, if you still feel you'll be able to do that . . .'

'Miss an international chocolate festival, are you kidding?'

Jessica glanced out of the window. It was a beautiful sunny day. 'How about I suggest they all go to the seaside? I think Rimini is in striking distance . . .'

'Perfect!'

'Shall I say the admin's taking an age, or something?'

'Brilliant!' he said, cutting the call and leaving her staring at the screen.

'*Buon giorno!*' Tim was standing in the kitchen doorframe. 'Was that the patient?'

'Yes. He's fine, but they're taking an age at the hospital. He doesn't want anyone to lose a day, so we were wondering if you could take the kids to the seaside?'

It was a little bit thrilling being the friend Robin had trusted with the secret. Not that it was a competition. And she already knew the secret.

'That's unusually selfless of him . . .'

Tim sounded almost suspicious. Had her explanation been too fulsome? When you were telling a white lie, it was best not to overexplain.

'Could you give me a hand putting this up?' Jessica asked him, finishing off the last letter of the bunting and biting the end of the cotton off.

Both of them were tall, so by standing on tiptoe, they managed to loop the garland from the utensil frame above the kitchen island to a picture hook above the fireplace.

As she waved them down the drive, Jessica made a mental note that villas on top of Umbrian mountains were not the best places for parties that included teenagers, especially not in autumn, when no matter how warm the water in the pool was, the nip in the air made sunbathing unattractive. George would probably be happy enough kicking a football around on the lawn all day, but he could do that at home. Ellis and Jaz were clearly restless, and it wasn't fair to make their going out dependent on someone else driving. If she was organising their next holiday – Jessica crossed her fingers to prevent the thought from jinxing it – maybe she'd organise somewhere with guaranteed sunshine where they could safely do their own thing. A Greek island, perhaps? Or even a cruise. There were cruises catering for all tastes and age groups, and the ships were so huge you wouldn't need to see the kids all day but could still be safe in the knowledge that they were on board. They could skateboard, water slide and flirt with people their own age, while she and Robin ate tasting menus and drank cocktails. Perhaps she could find one with Argentine tango classes? They'd showed a lot of promise on the taster day.

She could hear the rumble of a vehicle coming up the mountain as soon as she'd sent her text that they'd departed.

It was only Enzo's motorbike.

'*Buon giorno!*' he said, taking off his helmet, releasing his shoulder-length dark hair.

Today was her only chance to be alone with Robin. It was warm enough to sit in the garden. He might want to talk or even cry. But if someone else was there clipping edges or mowing, he would feel he had to make jokes to entertain them.

'Actually, there's a bit of a situation, so could you just leave?' she said.

Enzo looked perplexed. He was one of those men who were so handsome they'd got used to having things their own way, she thought.

'Now!' she said.

'OK with you if I come back tomorrow?' he asked, giving her that slightly amused look that was beginning to irritate her. Ultimately, she was the customer and he was the gardener. Anyone would think he bloody owned the place!

'Yes, that will be fine,' she said, curtly. 'We're all going to the chocolate festival in Perugia, so you'll have the place to yourself.'

'The city will be very busy,' he warned, throwing his leg over his bike and fastening his helmet again.

'Yes, well, everyone loves chocolate, don't they?' she said, wishing he would get a move on.

Jessica went back into the kitchen, pleased that the bunting made it look festive. Perhaps too festive, she thought, suddenly nervous as the red Fiat crawled up the drive.

It was always difficult to know what Laura was thinking, which was probably why she was a good teacher. There was something pathetic about teachers who tried to get you to like them. Today, her normally perfect skin looked blotchy, her eyes bloodshot. She said nothing as she opened the back door and took the crutches so that Robin could shuffle his bottom along the seat, coming out feet first. He was still wearing his hospital gown.

'Do you want a hand?' Jessica asked.

'No,' he said, pushing himself up to a balance from the edge of the seat, then taking the other crutch from her.

'Thankfully I've still got core muscles!'

Robin wasn't really someone you'd go to for psychological

insight, but the one observation he often made was that people were either radiators or drains. He was the warmest radiator she'd ever met. Why he had chosen to marry the deepest drain on the planet, she'd never know. However, if it was a case of opposites attracting, she'd consoled herself with the knowledge that while Robin definitely considered her a radiator, because he'd said so on many occasions, Jessica had hidden drainy depths that could be revealed if and when the moment required.

'OK then,' Laura said.

'OK then,' he replied. 'I suppose we'll meet up at the airport.'

'Yes. Fine. Have a lovely birthday.'

They looked at each other for a moment, then both of them looked at Jessica. She stepped forward, offering her arm.

'I can manage on my own, Coco,' he said, adding with a smile, 'I'd better get used to it!'

Was there a slight dig at Laura? She thought probably not. One of the lovely things about Robin was that he didn't really bear grudges.

With none of them quite knowing what to say, Laura got back into the driver's seat, started the engine and reversed down the drive.

Robin waved a crutch at her as she drove out and onto the track, then he turned to Jessica.

'Onwards and upwards!'

Was the morphine still having an effect, she wondered, or could it be a relief? Was he already seeing the benefits of being with someone whose normal facial expression was a smile?

'Shall we sit out in the sun like mad dogs and Englishmen?' Robin suggested, before she had a chance to show him her banner.

'Yes, whatever you want.'

'The air up here is lovely after the hospital.'

233

'Yes, of course.'

She got two plastic chairs out of the pool house and put them on the lawn in the sunshine so that he could sit on one and rest his foot on the other, then she brought one for herself.

'Shall I get you some clothes?'

'Maybe a bathrobe. Might be tricky putting jeans on. That's if I even packed a spare pair...'

She fetched him a robe and put it over him like a blanket as he couldn't be bothered to get up, then sat with him, contemplating the rich panorama of colours that complemented each other so perfectly it was easy to believe that some higher power had created the landscape of Italy. The gold of the oak trees, the almost-black spikes of cypress, the ochre of harvested fields, the terracotta roofs of settlements on distant hills, bathed in light from a sky as pale and blue as a painting by Piero della Francesca.

'How are you feeling?' she asked.

'Well, it's painful, obviously, but then I've lost a part of me, haven't I?' he said.

'It's been a long time,' she said, in a softly sympathetic voice, shifting her chair slightly so that her hand was in grasping reach if he felt like holding it. Instead he looked at his watch.

'Less than twenty-four hours,' he said.

'Oh, you meant your toe.'

'Oh, you meant Laura!'

They said simultaneously.

He threw back his head, laughing, stopping suddenly as if he was being irreverent.

'Bit of a surprise, obviously,' he said.

'Obviously.'

'Actually, not that much of one.'

'Really?'

'It did cross my mind she might be having an affair...'

'You never said...'

'Thought it would blow over. It happened before.'

'When?' Why hadn't he ever told her?

'A while back. To be honest, I don't really blame her. We're not all like you, Coco, at it all the time...'

Was that what he thought of her?

'Actually, I've been trying to work out what difference it will make day-to-day. I think we'll manage. But it's still rather sad...'

Robin finally took the outstretched hand she was offering and gave it a quick squeeze.

'I expect we'll see how it's going to work when we're back.'

'You're not going to tell the kids?'

'No point in spoiling everyone's holiday before, is there? They're out today, chocolate tomorrow, I'm sure you've got something nice planned for Friday. So it's not long to wait, and Laura's in her spa anyway... Look, can we not talk about it anymore?'

'Of course, whatever you want.'

She closed her eyes, trying to relax, letting the sun's warm rays bathe her face and paying mindful attention to all the sounds around her. Long breath in, count to four, breath out, counting to four. She could hear the rustle of leaves in an occasional waft of breeze, sporadic tweeting from a tuneful little bird, the hum of some distant farm machinery, which she thought might be one of those specially adapted tractors for harvesting grapes from vines which she'd seen on *A New Life in the Sun*. It was a daytime programme featuring people who had acquired derelict properties in Europe. She pictured herself lime-washing a wall while Robin picked fresh herbs from the garden, to go on the pizza he'd prepared for the chiminea on the terrace of some cottage they'd just restored. But she had no interest in DIY, and the most Robin had ever done was put together a flat-pack bunk bed for George, which had collapsed, luckily before he or any of his friends tried to climb into it. Perhaps Robin's brothers would let them the *castello* at a discount if they stayed there off season? Once the children were at uni, obviously.

Breathe in again. The trouble with mindfulness was that it always seemed to release cascades of scenarios in her brain rather than stemming the flow. Or maybe she never got far enough in the books to learn how to stop that happening? Relax, deep breath in . . . I am here in the present in a peaceful garden, with the man I love, who is now available, vulnerable even, not that I'm going to take advantage of that, in a house we might now always think of as our place, although possibly not, if we take up the offer of the *castello*. Forgot to count the breath out. There are tons of equally attractive places on Airbnb. In fact, why would anyone choose to buy with all the bureaucracy, which is bad enough in your own language, let alone dealing with connecting up utilities and broadband. Not forgetting all the seismic activity.

'Do you think it's even possible to get buildings and contents insurance in an earthquake zone?' she heard herself saying.

'What?' said Robin, sitting up alarmed. 'Did you feel a tremor?'

'I think it's only a grape-harvesting machine,' she said.

'Talking of grapes,' he said. 'It has to be wine o'clock, doesn't it?'

She was glad to have had the foresight to put a couple of bottles in the fridge that morning. She found a jar of olives and a packet of breadsticks left over from Tim's bakery sweep that first day in Sansepolcro, which seemed like a distant memory now. She shoved a handful of breadsticks into a tumbler, drained and decanted the olives into a little ceramic bowl and took a tray with the opened bottle and two glasses out to the garden.

'*Aperitivi!*' she said, rather proud of herself.

Robin popped an olive in his mouth and pulled a face.

'You couldn't make a little marinade, could you?'

Was she going to fail at the first hurdle? Not that it was a proper hurdle because Robin loved cooking, so there was no need for her to be good at it too. In fact, he would probably prefer it if she wasn't.

'What would you like in it?' she asked.

He laughed. 'Slug of extra virgin, few dried herbs. Don't bother with garlic...'

Could he be anticipating kissing?

She went back in, followed his instructions, even finding a packet of toothpicks while rooting around in a drawer, then brought the dish back out.

He speared one, tasted it, nodded at her appreciatively, took a sip of his wine.

'I could get used to being waited on. Cheers! This is the life, isn't it, Coco?'

'It is,' she agreed, not trusting herself to say anything more.

'So what are we having for lunch? I'm famished!'

'We could go out?' she said, putting down her glass of wine immediately so she'd be able to drive.

'Do we have to?' Robin said. 'It's such a palaver with the crutches and clothes and everything. Can't you rustle something up?'

Another hurdle.

'I'll see what I can do.'

Looking in the fridge, she saw that it was empty apart from some butter and eggs Robin had bought in the market. Omelettes were notoriously difficult to get right. There was no pancetta to attempt a pasta alla carbonara and she vaguely remembered Robin saying that English people always did it wrong anyway. Spotting the half-loaf of stale bread on the breadboard, she had a sudden inspiration. There was a treat her mother used to make that involved dipping bread in beaten egg and milk, frying it in melted butter, then topping it with sugar. It was only allowed when you were ill or sad, because it had special restorative properties. She'd realised when she'd started living on her own that it was really just a way of using leftovers when money was tight, but she still sometimes made it for herself when times were tough, because the magic her mother had created around it lingered in the taste. For her, it was the ultimate comfort food.

'Oh my god! *Pain perdu*! My absolute favourite thing in the world,' said Robin when she presented him with it, hot from the frying pan.

She had always known it by the less romantic name of eggy bread.

'The only possible improvement would be a touch, just a touch, of cinnamon!' said Robin, tasting his first mouthful as if he was one of the critics on *MasterChef*. 'Otherwise, inspired!'

'Mum used to make it for me when I was poorly,' she said.

'Good woman!' he said, then, after a moment's thought, 'Do you know, I think that's the most you've ever told me about her?'

He'd never asked, but to be fair, she had been avoiding the subject when they met because it was still raw and she didn't want people to judge her. Just like all the other students, she used to talk about going home in the vacations, but home to her was an empty housing association flat. She hadn't even realised then what a fantastic location it was because it was where she'd always lived. She'd come up with the phrase 'It was expected' for the rare occasions she'd had to reveal that her single mother had died. Nobody knew how to talk about death anyway, and

238

the last thing people wanted was details. They just needed to know that they didn't have to worry about you. Besides, it was true enough. Nobody expected heroin addicts to live very long.

How to describe her mum? The phrase people who had known her used most often at the funeral was that she'd been so full of life.

A flash of memory: the two of them on the way back from the club in the early hours. Jessica must only have been about eight, not yet old enough to be left in the flat on her own. Still high on adrenaline from performance, her mother had started pressing random bells on the walk up Long Acre, shouting, 'It's the police,' when people in the flats above the shops answered groggily, then singing 'Roxanne' into the speaker and running away to the nearest alleyway, busting herself with laughter so infectious you couldn't not join in, although Jessica hadn't even understood what the joke was then.

She'd only found out that it was a hit by a band called The Police while she was slow-dancing at an Eighties theme party in her third year at uni. She'd had to excuse herself.

'What's the problem?' the bloke had asked, when he'd found her in the street outside looking up at the sky.

'It's my mum's favourite song . . .'

'Is she called Roxanne?'

'No.'

'It's about a whore,' he'd informed her.

'She was fun,' Jessica told Robin now.

'Like mother, like daughter . . .'

'Oh, she was much more fun than me. I have limits. She didn't, really.'

In recent years, now that mental illness was more of a thing, she'd sometimes wondered whether Mum's alcohol and drug abuse had been attempts at self-medicating. Not that she was going to tell Robin that, because after social services had taken Jessica away at the age of ten her mother had got herself clean and remained that way for seven years.

The morning of Jessica's eighteenth birthday, her mother had presented her with a scooter with tiny wheels.

'Should make it easier to get around campus,' she'd said, so proud of her getting to university.

Jessica had been one of the first people to have one in London, and they were still really expensive then. She'd scooted round the courtyard in the middle of their flats with her mum singing 'Born to Be Wild' at the top of her lungs.

Jessica would never know whether her mother had felt free to use again that night because Jessica had reached the age when she knew they couldn't take her away again. More likely, it was because she'd had champagne at the party. Jessica would never forgive herself for letting her, but she hadn't known so much about addiction then, so she'd partied on with her friends, letting Mum go back on her own to their block of flats where Bill Sikes was waiting for her. Maybe Mum had pressed his bell, told him it was the police? She'd been merry enough. Maybe her last words had been the lyrics of 'Roxanne'?

The coroner's verdict had stated the cause of death as incautious use of drugs. The evidence didn't point to a deliberate overdose, because it wasn't enough, unless you'd been a user before. She hadn't left a note.

The fact that Mum made sure that very day that Jessica's name was on the tenancy must have been because she'd always tried to look after her as well as she could. It couldn't have been because she thought she'd be better off without her, could it? Jessica knew she'd never find the definitive answer to the question that had plagued her ever since. Even when Mum appeared in her dreams and Jessica asked her whether she'd meant to kill herself, her mum never answered, telling her not to be so gloomy. She was there now, wasn't she? Then they'd laugh and dance just like they did at her party, and Jessica would wake up feeling happy for just a moment before realising nothing had changed.

At least Jessica had a right-to-buy flat in the middle of Covent Garden, people told her. But even when she'd managed to save the deposit to do that, it didn't ever feel like good fortune. Eventually, she'd sold up and used the money to move to a two-bedroom in leafy Highbury, an area of London which held no memories. But she still missed her mother every single day of her life.

'She was really popular,' Jessica said.

'She was an actress, wasn't she?' Robin said.

'A cabaret dancer, actually.'

Instead of a wreath of flowers on the coffin, they'd had one made of pink feather boas.

'That's amazing. So cool. I wish I'd met her.'

She couldn't quite tell whether Robin was being sincere or just polite.

'You'd have loved her.'

Would Mum have loved Robin though, she wondered, surprised that she'd never asked herself that before. Would she even feel comfortable introducing them if Mum were alive? She'd never dared introduce Robin to Mandy. She suddenly pictured her mother saying, 'If he makes you happy,' which was what she said when she didn't really approve of a boyfriend.

'Come here. Have a hug,' Robin said.

Jessica stretched across and hugged his chest at a slightly awkward angle so as not to disturb the position of his leg, inhaling the newly washed smell of the robe against background notes of sweat, blood and hospital disinfectant. He patted her back gently as you might a sick child, whispering against her neck, 'Tell you what I'd love to do this afternoon...'

'What?' she murmured.

'Guess!'

She lifted her head to try to glean from his facial expression what he was suggesting. There was a naughty sparkle in his eye. Surely he didn't mean . . . ? Not with his toe in a bandage, though there were ways of getting round that. Oddly, she didn't feel at all in the mood, but . . .

'Tell me . . .' she said, her voice still a bit croaky with emotion.

'Board games!' he said.

She got a plastic table from the pool house and brought out a selection of games from the cupboard.

'Hungry Hippos!' he shouted, recognising the box from a distance. 'Let's hope there are enough balls left. They have a habit of disappearing over time. We used to have to fish them out of Bob's litter tray . . . Sorry, too much information!'

The age range on the box was 4+ and the only skill required was feverish hammering on the hippos, but Robin played with his customary competitiveness.

Of course Mum would have loved him, she reassured herself.

'What could be nicer than this?' he said, having beaten her for the fourth time. 'It's so easy being with you, Coco. I love you, you know.'

'I love you too,' she said.

'Scrabble?' he suggested.

It had never been a favourite of hers, and she discovered there was a fine balance she didn't quite understand between being lenient because he was injured and not playing the game properly.

'If you're going to let me win, there's no point in playing,' he said huffily, when she allowed him UNESCO.

Glancing at the level of the second bottle of wine, most of which he had consumed, she realised that he'd got to the point she'd occasionally seen before when his bonhomie suddenly switched to petulance. The sun was dropping in the sky. There was a bit of a chill in the air.

'I need a piss!' he said. 'Can you help me up?'

She had to support him getting to his feet, then took his arm as he hopped across the lawn. As they entered the kitchen through the side door, she realised that he was going to see the wrong side of her banner first.

'Got the flags up already!' he said, not even bothering to look at the message she'd spent so much time on this morning. 'You think of everything, Coco!'

It sounded almost like a criticism.

At the door of the downstairs cloakroom he unlinked her arm. 'I don't need you to hold my willy, thank you very much.'

She waited outside the cloakroom door.

'Think I need a lie-down,' he said, when he emerged.

'Have my bed,' she said. 'I don't want you climbing the stairs without Tim's support.'

She shouldn't have let him drink so much, Jessica thought, as she sat in the kitchen. It was irresponsible given the shock of a serious injury and the breakdown of his marriage. And what had possessed her to talk about her mother? The very moment she had the opportunity to show Robin how much better his life could be with her, and she'd ruined it by revealing her inner demons. Surely one lapse couldn't change the history of over twenty years? He'd said he loved her and that was after she'd talked about Mum. Looking out of the window, she saw that the sun was setting. She must not park her tanks on his lawn, she told herself, as she collected up the plastic chairs that were already a little damp with dew.

A hundred and seventy steps.

She walked round and round the perimeter of the lawn until darkness fell, obliterating all but the string of twinkling lights on the road up to the distant village.

The smell of pizza and the generally happy vibe Tim and the kids brought back seemed to wake Robin up in a much better mood. They'd been invited to play beach volleyball by some local teenagers and then they'd all plunged into the sea, much to the amusement of the Italians. Their hair was still stiff with salt and they smelt slightly of seaweed, but they claimed to be starving, so they sat around the dining table grabbing at triangles of pizza, relaying the high points of the day between mouthfuls.

'What about you, Dad?' George asked, when all the boxes were empty.

'Coco has been a wonderful nurse,' he said, winking down the table at her. 'She even let me win at Scrabble.'

She smiled, acknowledging the unspoken apology for his earlier grumpiness.

He yawned.

'Why don't you get Robin up to bed, Tim?' Jessica suggested. 'It's been a very long day for him. I'll clear up down here...'

'Are you sure?' Robin asked, with automatic politeness.

'Of course! It will be good for you two to have some time together...'

'Thanks, Coco,' he said, smiling at her, as Tim hoisted him to his feet.

'Come on, old man!' said Tim.

'Not so much of the old! I'm a year younger than you until tomorrow, remember!'

She thought it would be good for him to talk to Tim. Perhaps it would enable him to release emotion. She was sure it was Robin's public schooling, as much as his awful family, that had contributed to him being unable to express his feelings, but the one thing it had given him was a dear and loyal ally. Tim probably knew him better than anyone, and he'd had his own break-up recently, so he was uniquely qualified to talk to Robin about what he was going through.

Jessica cleared the table, breaking down all the pizza boxes and putting them in the recycling bin, then wiped down all the surfaces. Stepping out into the hall, she could hear a murmur of male voices in the master suite.

Trusting that the coast was clear, she tiptoed to her single room, pulled her suitcase out from under the bed and unzipped it, feeling underneath the spare nightie for the two boxes of Betty Crocker's cake mix she had brought, along with a tub of frosting and a plastic tube of multicoloured paper cake cases. She always carried the ingredients for a red velvet cake after the time the caterer had let her down for an engagement party. Obviously clients preferred something professionally decorated, but it was amazing how a few cupcakes could assuage disappointment, especially with the addition of dried rose petals or sparklers, depending on the occasion.

The packaging stated the mixture was suitable for vegetarians, but there weren't any ingredients that looked offensive to vegans, so she was going to risk it.

Closing the kitchen door so the clatter and smell of baking would not drift upstairs, Jessica beat up two lots of mixture, one with the remaining eggs in the fridge, the other with water, careful to keep the one for the vegans separate, although the lack of rise was going to be noticeable when they were baked. She doubted they would taste as good either, but not having a slice of birthday cake was bad luck. That's what Mum always said anyway, although a fat lot of good it had done her.

After doing the washing-up while they baked, she left the cupcakes to cool on the kitchen island. Closing the door with a soft click, she was surprised to hear Tim and Robin were still chatting upstairs, even though it was long after midnight. In her single bedroom, she set her alarm for six in the morning, so she could do the frosting before anyone was up, then switched off the light, switching it on again as soon as her head hit the pillow as she remembered the possible presence of mice. Tiptoeing back to the kitchen, she covered the cakes with three saucepans in different sizes.

There was a slight change in the tenor and rhythm of the men's voices now, but she couldn't discern whether they were talking seriously or bantering as usual.

# Chapter Thirty-Five

## *Laura*

## Thursday

Laura was awoken from a deep sleep by a call at six in the morning.

Robin.

'Is everything OK?' she asked, trying to wake herself up at double speed.

'More than OK, I'd say,' he sounded very chirpy.

'It's six in the morning, Robin . . .'

'You're usually up at six. Anyway, you are now, and I wanted you to be the first to know . . .'

'What?'

'I'm in love with someone else too!'

Robin was so competitive.

'That was fast work.'

'Well, we've known each other forever . . .'

'Yes.'

'You knew?'

'I knew it was a possibility. Have you discussed it with Tim?'

'Of course!'

'And he approves?'

'More than approves.'

That surprised her because Tim was usually more circumspect.

At their wedding, Tim had been the only one of the guests who was cautious with his congratulations. Generally people wanted to believe that weddings were about true love, and if nobody who knew them had expected it, the fact that she was clearly pregnant had given an explanation. But Tim had taken her aside.

'You will look after him, won't you?' he'd said, perhaps the only one of them who understood that Robin had remained at the emotional age of the sweet boy who'd been packed off to school in a foreign country.

She had done her best. Sometimes Robin even joked that they had the perfect marriage because neither of them made any demands. If Jessica was going to look after him now, maybe they could have the perfect separation, too?

'So, are you OK with me telling the kids?' Robin asked.

'Are you sure you want to, straightaway? You might find you drive each other mad after a couple of days.'

'When you discover that your best friend is someone you love and want to spend the rest of your life with, then you want to start living as soon as possible ...'

'Robin, that's a line from *When Harry Met Sally*!'

'Oh. I thought it sounded rather too good for me to have invented ...'

'I suppose it's up to you. If you feel you have to ...'

'It is my birthday ...'

'Happy Birthday!'

Laura couldn't get back to sleep. It was typically infuriating of Robin not to be able to wait to tell the children, even though he'd been the one who wanted to put it off. She knew she had given up the right to be part of the birthday celebration, but it felt odd not being there. Although possibly not for the announcement. How could it have taken just a day for him and Jessica to decide? Although it was really twenty years and a day, she thought. Normally Robin didn't respond well to pressure, so Jessica must have handled it with uncharacteristic subtlety. Would the kids be happy? They loved Jessica. She was almost part of the family already.

Beside her, Alex stirred and woke up.

'Did I miss something?' he said, rubbing his eyes.

She climbed on top of him, kissed his lips, wanting to obliterate all her thoughts with sensation.

Afterwards, they flung apart as if scalded by the intensity of their passion. Any whisper of doubt she'd had that sex wouldn't be the same between them if it was no longer a secret was swept away by a heady cocktail of liberation and the responsibility that came from committing to the relationship.

He got them each a bottle of mineral water from the mini-bar.

'I love you,' she told him.

'I love you too,' he said. His lips were cold and prickly from the fizzy water as if they were drinking champagne.

'Robin says that he and Jessica have decided they're in love too, so he's going to tell the kids . . .'

'What? You agreed?'

'It's his birthday. The kids will hate me anyway . . .'

Alex banged his water glass down on the bedside table.

'You can't let him be the one to tell the kids about us. And why do you always expect people to hate you?'

She'd never seen him looking so angry. She wanted to find a way of diverting the conversation, but it was still dark outside so she couldn't suggest a swim, or breakfast. Was there no escape this time? She'd always known that a fork in the road was coming and she didn't know why she kept thinking that she would find a way, if only she had another day, and another day. She took a deep breath. If Alex left her now, it would only be what she deserved. If he stayed, she would know she had made the right decision.

'I will try to explain, but I think you may hate me too...' She tried to keep her voice even.

'Try me.'

She didn't know where to start.

'You're the first person I had an orgasm with...'

He looked confused.

'I know that.'

'How?'

'Could be something to do with you shrieking with wild crazy joy. God, it was so amazing being inside you, feeling you laughing all around me like you were in some kind of ecstasy...'

'I was!' She felt her face blushing. 'Did you think it was because you were so brilliant in bed?'

'Obviously!' He smiled at her.

'Didn't you wonder why I never had with Robin?'

'Not really. I think it's more common than you'd imagine.'

She looked away.

'I hated sex before,' she said quietly. 'But with you, it felt inevitable because I realised I was in love for the first time in my life. You released me.'

'Go on,' he said.

The words were stuck inside her. Not in her throat, nor even in her head, but somehow in her being, and when the sentence came it was somehow from outside of her.

'I was molested as a child.'

She'd talked about the subject many times on safeguarding training days, and whenever she did, she felt dishonest for not being able to admit to her own experience. One of the main reasons she'd wanted to become a teacher was to provide a safe space for children, just as school had for her. She was always on the alert for signs. But however much she understood about the guilt and complicity that victims wrongly felt, it didn't stop her own feelings swamping her with shame.

'Oh my god, Laura,' Alex said quietly. 'Can you tell me who it was?'

'My stepfather.'

The words felt like vomit in her mouth. She wished she hadn't spoken. Inside her head, she could hear her mother screaming.

*'You filthy little liar!'*

It had started when breast buds began to form. She didn't know what was happening. Only that it felt wrong. The almost undetectable brush of his fingers over her chest as he tucked her into bed.

She had been so happy to get away to school in England.

'My goodness, you've grown,' he'd said when he picked her up from the airport for the first summer vacation.

That night his hand went under her nightie.

She protested to her mother the following evening that she didn't need tucking into bed.

'It's nice your father cares so much about you,' her mother said.

She could still feel him breathing his stinking red-wine breath into her ear.

She'd tried to tell her mother. It was so difficult because he kept saying that he loved her and insisting that she loved him. She didn't want her mother to think she was setting herself up as a rival.

'He touches me. Down there.'

*'What a disgusting imagination. You little liar!'*

On the plane back to school after the holidays, Laura vowed never to return.

Her mother wrote to her at school. Flowery notelets with news about the twins, sometimes a photo.

251

'*They miss you. Your stepfather has explained. Girls of your age often get crushes. It's perfectly normal. So don't worry about that. Forgive and forget...*'

'Did you tell anyone?' Alex asked.

'My mother didn't believe me. I didn't dare tell anyone else after that.'

'Not even Robin?'

'No, but I think maybe he understood. I think it might have happened to him too. He was a very pretty little boy. Whenever there were scandals on the news, both of us would find an excuse to go and make tea, pour another drink...'

'Oh my god, Laura!'

She thought for a moment that Alex was going to cry.

'Am I disgusting to you?'

'Darling, of course not.' He gathered her into a firm hug. 'Tell me what you need,' he said.

'I need you to believe me.'

'Of course I believe you!'

'And love me still.'

'Of course I love you still. I'm so sorry that happened to you, Laura. Are you OK? I mean, about telling me. I know that must have been so difficult.'

It now seemed strange that she had feared it so much because Alex was just the same with her. She felt almost silly that the secret had taken up so much space inside her.

'I feel like I've made too big a deal of it,' she said. 'The telling was bigger than the thing itself, like Chicken Licken, who thought the sky was falling down when it was only an acorn.'

'It is a big deal. You know it's big, Laura. You know that victims doubt themselves. Blame themselves. Have you ever talked to someone about it?'

Of course she knew that therapy might help her, but she

252

hadn't ever been able to work out how she would fit in the time each week without telling people what she was doing. And even if she did, she was terrified in case the outing of her shameful secret might cause the whole structure of her life to collapse. It had been such hard work building a home, a family and a career.

'I'm here to give you whatever support you need,' he said.

Perhaps with Alex she would feel secure enough to get help?

She lay in his arms, protected by him. Gradually her muscles began to relax, as if she was letting go of the terror she had held in every cell of her body, like walking into a warm sea then rolling onto her back to float in the sunshine.

# Chapter Thirty-Six

## *Robin*

Sometimes a perfect couple of hours of unconsciousness could refresh you more than a whole night. It was his birthday! His forty-second but really his fortieth, when life was supposed to begin. Suddenly everything made sense to him. It was so obvious now, he couldn't think how he hadn't seen it before, hadn't allowed himself to see it, because, as Tim had put it so perceptively, he had taken his role as husband very seriously. A proper bit of method acting, for once.

Was he imagining it, or was there a distinct smell of cake filtering up from the kitchen?

'Are you sure you should be up?' Jessica was straight out of the kitchen when she heard him on the stairs. She ran up as he took his first step and walked backwards in front of him, which he couldn't help thinking would bring both of them down on top of each other if he slipped. It was quite a relief to reach a level floor and know what to do with the crutches again.

'Happy Birthday!' she said. 'How are you feeling?'

'Like I'm walking on air!'

He loved her for always laughing at his jokes.

'Seriously, Coco, I've had a revelation, but I think you've known for a long time. You clever, clever woman!'

She was standing in front of the kitchen door, reluctant to let him in.

'Can I smell cake?' he asked.

'It was meant to be a surprise at breakfast!' she said.

On the kitchen island, there was a group of frosted cupcakes with letter-shaped candles spelling out the words *Happy Birthday!* They were slightly uneven in height and she had only shaken edible glitter over half of them, but the amateurishness made it somehow more touching. He thought again what a wonderful mother she would make.

'Oh my god! This is perfect. I love you, Coco!' he said.

'OK, if we're doing things in the wrong order, let me get your present!' she said, disappearing from the kitchen for a few seconds before returning with a small, soft parcel.

'Didn't have room in the suitcase for anything big. This holiday was meant to be your main present, so it's just something to open...'

How did she know him so well? He loved opening gifts, but most people didn't bother to wrap things anymore. These days he was lucky if he got a gift bag rather than an envelope with a gift card in it. Now even those were disappearing in favour of emails with links. Ripping off the ribbon and tissue paper, he was bewildered to find a pair of Bart Simpson socks.

'Remember?' she said.

'Remember?' He often found that repeating a word back to the person who'd asked a question he didn't understand prompted them to give the answer they were looking for.

'The first time we met. You were wearing Bart Simpson socks,' said Jessica.

'Of course! Why was that, I wonder? Oh, I remember, Cris and Piers had this thing at Christmas where we'd buy the most tasteless, horrible thing we could find!'

Her face fell.

'Love them!' he said, rather too late to convince.

'I thought you liked *The Simpsons*...'

'I'll tell you who does like *The Simpsons*. George!' he said, as his son came into the room at an opportune moment. 'Bit early for you, isn't it?'

'You were talking right outside my door!' said George.

'Sorry!'

'Happy Birthday, Dad!'

'More gifts!'

He peeked inside the small carrier bag from the O2 shop which contained a pair of the latest edition of AirPods, which Laura must have paid for.

'I chose them,' George said, reading his thoughts. 'And if you don't like them, I can always use them.'

'That's incredibly thoughtful of you,' Robin said.

'So, are we doing this now then?' Jessica said.

Robin put his arm around her.

'Why not? I can't wait to try some of your delicious-looking cake...'

'It's out of a packet...'

'But the decadence... Cake for breakfast! George, wake everyone up!'

On your birthday, you were allowed to say what was going to happen and everyone had to be nice to you. Even Ellis seemed to realise that and play along without too much moaning.

Tim was the last to come down, looking bleary from lack of sleep. He gave him a hug and downed an espresso while Jessica opened a bottle of Prosecco, pouring a small amount into six glasses and passing them down the table. Then she lit the candles and they all sang 'Happy Birthday'.

The cake was absolutely vile, but that wasn't the point.

'Ambrosia of the gods!' he told Jessica.

It was typically efficient of her to have catered for the vegans, although, after one taste, they left most of theirs.

'So, plan for today is everyone get ready and head to the chocolate festival!' said Jessica.

'Cake and bubbly for breakfast, chocolate for lunch and tea and supper,' said Robin, holding her hand and giving it a squeeze. 'That's my idea of a perfect birthday. But first, I have an announcement to make.'

'Are you sure this is the right time?' Tim asked.

'I spoke to Laura, she's fine with it.' Robin cleared his throat. 'So, despite my near-fatal injury, I feel very lucky to be here in this beautiful place surrounded by all my favourite people . . .'

'Except Mum,' said George.

'I'll come to Laura . . . On my fortieth birthday . . .'

'Forty-second,' said Ellis.

'Fortieth postponed,' corrected Jessica.

'Tim and I were up talking most of the night about something he's known for a long time. Maybe you guys have too . . .'

'What?' said George. He seemed unusually arsey this morning. Maybe this wasn't going to be as easy as he thought. But he'd started now.

'Your mother said I should go ahead and tell you. It's all very amicable between us and it doesn't change how much we love you, which we do, beyond anything . . .'

Both his children raised their eyes to the ceiling.

'However, the fact is, Laura is in love with someone else. And so am I.'

There was a sharp intake of breath beside him.

The children were looking at him as they did when he was

telling an anecdote, their expressions tolerant, but not for very much longer.

'There is someone in this room who I've always loved and never been able to admit it, even to myself. Someone who has always loved me and taken care of me. Someone who has grown more and more attractive with age. Perhaps it's unexpected, perhaps not. I know it will take some getting used to. But I think you guys are grown up enough, and I know Jessica realised long before I did . . .'

He smiled at her. Squeezed her hand again. Her eyes were shining with encouragement.

'Maybe we should wait, but I'm telling you now because, as Jessica says, life begins at forty. Forty-two.' He nodded at Ellis. 'So let's start living straightaway . . . if you can help me, Coco . . .'

Pushing down on his crutch and with her hoisting him up, he managed to stand up.

The others pushed back their chairs and stood up too.

'I'd like you all to raise a glass to me and the person I have always loved . . . to Robin and Tim!'

The expected echo of the toast did not happen. Instead, in the shocked silence, Jessica said, 'What the fuck?' Her voice sounded as if she was being strangled. The grip she had on his arm became so tight it was as painful as his foot, and then she suddenly released him and stepped back, so he almost toppled over and had to thump down onto his chair.

Everyone was still looking at him as if waiting for the punch-line.

'This is a joke, right?' Ellis finally said.

'I thought you at least would understand,' Robin said.

'Meaning?'

'Well, you know . . .'

258

'I'm cool with it,' said George. 'As long as Mum is.'

'Tim?' Robin pleaded for help.

'I think it's probably a bit of a shock, Robin.'

'It's not a shock to you, is it, Coco?' Robin turned to her in desperation.

'What the fuck are you talking about?'

Now her eyes had a very different sort of gleam. Quite frightening. He'd often thought how amazing it was that she didn't have a temper. But it appeared she did.

'You must remember, Coco, you asked me soon after we met.'

'Asked you what?'

'If I was gay.'

'But you said no!'

'Exactly! You know me better than I know myself.'

'You're a fucking moron!' she screamed.

'As I said, you know me so well!'

He was quite pleased with that one, but it failed to land with his audience. A very uneasy silence fell around the table, the only audible sound the gardener's motorbike coming up the gravel drive.

'Excuse me.' Jessica left the room.

'Was it something I said?'

'Oh, Dad! Jessica is in love with you . . .' said Ellis. 'She'd do anything for you. She planned this whole thing for you.'

'Don't be ridiculous . . .'

Jessica went for alpha males, usually with a creative side. Artistic types who treated her badly. He didn't claim to have no faults, but misogyny wasn't one of them. Of course he loved her. She was his mate, his best buddy, someone he'd thought he could say anything to.

He heard her clattering about, then the front door banged.

They all remained standing in silence with the echo of Jessica's fury still reverberating around the kitchen.

'Do you think that means she's not coming to EuroChocolate?' he asked.

# Chapter Thirty-Seven

## Jessica

'Get me out of here!'

Enzo did a double-take.

'Please?' she said, remembering her manners. He frowned but didn't ask for an explanation as he opened the box on the back of the bike, took out a spare helmet and gave it to her, turning the bike around and waiting for her to get on before pushing off down the drive.

He steered the bike slowly down the country track, carefully avoiding potholes, then kept at a fairly slow speed down the little road that wound along the valley. Bright morning sunlight was burning off the low-lying mist, occasionally blinding her with its intensity as they swung round corners. The canopy of leaves above was much sparser and yellower than when they'd arrived just a few days ago, but the sky was once again a pure, celestial blue. She could feel the dampness of dew permeating her jeans, the scent of fallen leaves in her freezing cold nose. On a bike, you were more connected to the landscape. She felt calmer, as if she could breathe again.

As they turned out onto the main road, Enzo opened the throttle, throwing her backwards, forcing her to grab his waist, her chest squashing against his leather-clad back. With the wind full in her face, the cold air making her eyes water and numbing her fingers, the roar of the engine obliterated everything from her mind except the need to hold on. She shouted at the top of her lungs.

'Born to Be Wild!'

She hadn't ridden pillion on a bike since she'd got a lift home with a Hell's Angel she'd been sitting next to at a performance of *Bat Out of Hell* in Milton Keynes, ahead of making a group booking for a City stag party when the musical arrived in London later in the year. She was meant to be staying over at Mandy's that night, but he had nice eyes under all the hair. As they'd roared down the M40, she'd wondered if the life of a biker girl might suit her. He said he worked as a computer games designer, so she wouldn't have to support him, and went to biker meets on the south coast every Tuesday. It might be fun and she rocked a leather jacket.

Now, drinking that same exhilarating cocktail of speed, freedom and danger, she found herself thinking that if they crashed she wouldn't care, because there was no future to look forward to.

Just outside the walls of Città di Castello, Enzo pulled into a petrol station. She stayed with the bike at the pumps while he went in to pay, feeling rather cool with people staring at her, wondering who the biker girl was, until the reality suddenly dawned that they were local and knew he was married. She didn't want to get him into trouble.

'Thanks for the lift. You can leave me here.' She handed back his spare helmet when he returned.

'Do you have plans?' he asked.

'Just need a bit of time to regroup,' she said.

'Regroup?'

'Not the right word in the circumstances,' she said. 'De-group would probably be more accurate.'

He didn't understand.

'Are you OK?'

'I'm fine,' she said automatically, although now that the exhilaration of the ride was over, she felt completely numb both in her body and her soul.

'Can I buy you a coffee?' he offered.

'I don't actually drink coffee.'

'*Una spremuta d'arancia?*'

The thought of freshly squeezed orange to wash away the cloying taste of packet red velvet cake was tempting.

'Only if you have time,' she said.

'I was supposed to be gardening this morning . . .'

'Sorry.' Now, on top of everything else, she felt guilty for keeping him from work.

They rode to a nearby bar and stood at the counter staring at the machine that cut, flipped and squeezed the oranges, occasionally exchanging brief, slightly embarrassed smiles. She wished she had chosen a drink that was quicker to prepare because she couldn't seem to summon any small talk.

The waiter put down an espresso cup in front him and pushed the glass with a slice of orange and a striped straw in her direction with a wink.

'Do you come here often?' she asked Enzo, unintentionally stabbing the straw quite near her eye as she picked up her drink.

'Every day.'

'So, is gardening a passion of yours?'

'I like gardening, so I'm fortunate. Vittoria does most of the housework now that we have finished the restoration.'

'You two restored it?'

'Of course! What did you think?'

'But it's owned by a British couple!'

'We sold it to them, but they asked us to take care of it when they are not here. It makes sense because we know it well...'

'So how long did it take?'

She ran through their previous conversations in her head, hoping that she hadn't sounded too entitled in her dealings with him, but knowing she probably had. He didn't seem to hold it against her.

'A long time. Four years. We sold only earlier this year. But of course, work on a building like this is never finished...'

'Goodness! I had no idea. You have done it beautifully. Very high spec...'

'Thank you!'

He downed his espresso in one. She stared into her still half-full glass.

'Can I ask what is the problem?' he said.

'Everything's gone tits up,' she said, adding quickly, 'I mean, wrong.'

'I lived in England for many years. I know what is tits up.'

He said the phrase with such seriousness she started laughing, then straightaway found herself in tears.

'Sorry,' she said.

'What has happened?'

She sighed. What was there to lose by telling him? Perhaps saying it out loud to a neutral person might even help sort it out in her head. She'd often had helpful conversations with old ladies on train journeys. It enabled you to see yourself objectively somehow, when you were just stating the facts, not trying to present an image.

'It's my fault, really. I convinced myself everything was going so right, and it was going so wrong... not for Robin, obviously, or Laura, or Tim for that matter. I don't quite know what they all did to deserve their happy ever after. I mean, all that work, but I suppose it's a result of sorts.'

He was frowning with concentration as he tried to follow her rambling stream of consciousness.

'Long story short, I've been in love with Robin all my life.'

'Robin is the good-looking guy?'

How he'd love that description, she thought.

'Yes. But turns out he's gay.'

'You did not know this?'

'Of course not.'

Enzo shrugged.

'Did you?'

'A man looks at you in a certain way, you know.'

'But you've seen him for a total of less than five minutes...'

'But you know,' he said.

There was no point in arguing, because he was right.

Whatever had happened to Robin to put him in denial his whole life? How was it even possible that someone of their age wouldn't feel able to come out? Shame was surely a thing of the past. Then she thought of his brothers and imagined a whole school of braying, bullying boys like them. Robin wasn't that good an actor, but he had done pretty well playing the role of a straight man. Thinking about it logically, the reason she loved him was because he was so much sweeter and funnier than any straight man she'd ever met. So all this time Robin hadn't been the only one in denial. She had been too.

There was still orange juice left but she couldn't stomach any more. All she really wanted was to be alone and howl silently, like Al Pacino at the end of *The Godfather Part III*, although in this case no one had actually died.

# Chapter Thirty-Eight

## *Robin*

'Sorry about my dysfunctional family, Jaz,' said Ellis.

'Each unhappy family is unhappy in its own way,' said Jaz.

'Thing is, we're not an unhappy family, are we?' Robin said.
'And it's my birthday! So let's go eat chocolate. Eh?'

'You smell a bit, Dad,' said George.

'Oh!' It was nice to have an honest relationship with your
children, but on his birthday . . .

'Showers, everyone,' said Tim.

'You don't think it's gangrene, do you?' Robin asked Tim,
when they were alone.

'No, I think it's because you haven't washed for several days,'
said Tim. 'Let's clingfilm your foot and get you fresh again.'

Tim got one of the plastic chairs from the pool house and
put it in the shower, then carefully removed the boxer shorts
Robin was still wearing.

It was the first time he'd been completely naked in front of
his friend since school. As Tim gently sponged him under the
waterfall shower, he felt vulnerable and cared for at the same
time, giving him a feeling of safety that he didn't even realise
he'd been missing for a long time.

It was only when he'd talked to Tim in the night that he'd

been able to express how frightened he was by the idea of coping without Laura.

'What are you scared of?' Tim had asked.

'That I won't be grown up enough,' Robin had said.

'Of course you will,' Tim said.

'But you're always saying I'm childish.'

'Not childish. Child*like*. It's actually one of your more lovable qualities.'

'What do you mean?'

'You have this sense of wonder at things other people take for granted . . .'

'Do I?'

'As if proof were needed,' Tim said, laughing.

'Laura does everything . . .' Robin said.

'Laura brings in the money, but you're the homemaker, the peacemaker, the one who holds it all together. You do more than you think.'

'Do I?'

'Yes, you do.'

'I'm not very brave.'

'You can be. You saw off your brothers at the hospital. I was proud of you!'

'I was actually quite proud of myself . . .'

'I can move to London for a while, if it helps,' Tim said.

'Would you really do that for me?'

'You've never really got it, have you?' Tim said.

'Got what?'

'I love you, Robin.'

He'd reached across the bed and given him a hug which started off friendly and then, without either of them moving, began to feel like something more.

'I love you too, but I think I'm going to need time . . .' Robin had told him.

'We've got all the time in the world,' Tim said.

Time was something they'd never had before. At school, they'd always had to be quick in case of being discovered. He thought Tim might have found the risk an added turn-on, but he hadn't. Tim didn't have a brother at the school, and the double fear of bringing down disgrace on his family as well as himself. Afterwards, Robin had told himself it was just adolescents experimenting. It didn't mean anything. Everyone at school tried it. If it meant anything then most of the Cabinet would be gay. So he'd pretended it hadn't happened, which might have been why at uni he'd never experienced the sexual awakening that most students seemed to. He'd found it difficult to perform unless he'd consumed exactly the right amount of alcohol to loosen his inhibitions but not enough to obliterate his senses, and that was usually the moment he ordered another bottle. He'd kept his distance from Tim, which was easy enough, being in different cities. Tim had come out flamboyantly at med school, had a different partner every week, sometimes more than one. The truth was that Tim had always been braver about all of life's challenges and Robin had always been a bit of a coward. Tim had worked towards a responsible career. People's lives depended on him. He'd earned money. Lots of it. He'd left home and become an adult, whereas Robin never really had, even though his parents lived thousands of miles away and he rarely saw them.

'Do you really think we could work together?' Robin asked.

'We always have, haven't we?' Tim said.

Robin thought of the days they'd spent together in recent years when Tim had been in London. Bluebell walks with Lammie trotting along beside them, warm evenings in pubs on the river, relaxed times filled with laughter or talking or the restful easy silence between old friends. Days that were only marred by his haste to get away before anything became too intimate, because on the few occasions he had stayed for that second bottle, he'd been tempted to go back to Tim's apartment, then been tormented by a terrible guilt that he didn't have anywhere to hide in the lovely home he had made with his family.

It didn't have to be like that anymore.

'It can't be this simple, can it?' he asked.

'I doubt it will be simple,' Tim said. 'But it might be fun to give it a go, might it not?'

Robin had felt as if his whole life had suddenly shunted onto the track it was supposed to be on. And then they were hugging, which turned into kissing. Long, unhurried, luxuriant kisses filled with the longing of years.

'That's lovely,' he said, as Tim soaped his shoulders, then squirted a cold dollop of shampoo on his head and began massaging that too. Since his hairline had begun to recede, Robin had hated anyone touching his head in case it encouraged the hair loss, but Tim's fingers were so firm and expert, he felt helpless in his hands, like a kitten going suddenly still when its mother picks it up in her mouth.

As Tim rinsed his chest, then gently nudged his legs apart so that he could soap in all the creases, he felt himself stirring.

'Still got it,' Tim said, smiling at him as he rinsed all the soap off. 'There you are, good as new.'

'Not quite as good, I fear,' said Robin. 'I feel old, you know, compared to your other boyfriends . . . Do you think you could give me my young face, back to how it was when I got acting jobs?'

'Certainly not,' said Tim. 'Anyway, your face isn't the problem. It's this air of innocence around you. Doesn't work for more grown-up acting roles. But in real life, it makes everyone around you feel happy. And furious, obviously. But mainly happy.'

There were a lot of compliments in there but also some not very kind observations. Robin struggled to untangle them.

'But what about Ibiza?' he asked. 'Would I fit into that scene?'

'We don't have to go to Ibiza.'

'Actually, I quite fancy Ibiza,' he said.

Tim laughed.

'Then we'll go to Ibiza!'

The thing about their relationship was that they could say things to each other and nothing ever got too mysterious.

'OK, that's you done,' Tim said. He put the still-running shower hose on the floor while he turned to get a big fluffy towel.

In the split second he had his back to him, Robin stretched down, picked it up and started spraying him.

'Jesus, Robin!'

'Sorry, very childlike of me!' he said.

# Chapter Thirty-Nine

## *Laura*

They were eating breakfast in bed. She was still getting used to the excitement of having the timetable for the day set by their desire. She didn't think she'd ever get used to the luxury of physical sensation Alex gave her. Even he seemed surprised by her ardour.

'I'm making up for lost time,' she told him, licking a flake of croissant from his chest.

Her phone buzzed, the name *George* on the screen returning her instantly to mortifying guilt.

Alex was right. She should never have allowed Robin to tell the children without her there. It was selfish of her to take the easy route. She was sure that George would have understood if she'd explained what had happened but she'd let the opportunity go, behaving completely irresponsibly, as if she was a teenager in love for the first time, blind to everyone else's feelings. Her son deserved better.

His WhatsApp message said, *Are you OK?*

Her heart melted that he was concerned about her when she was meant to be the one thinking about him.

She tapped back.

*I'm OK. How are you?*

*You've heard from Dad?*

*Yes. Do you want to talk about it?*

*Can't really. In car on the way to some chocolate festival. Feels a bit weird.*

*I'm sorry.*

*Can we talk later?*

*Sure. I really want to.*

She saw the ticks on her message go blue, waited, then put the phone down.

'George,' she said to Alex.

'He's OK?'

'He says so but I feel really bad about not telling him. I'm so angry with myself...'

'There's nothing to be gained by punishing yourself,' Alex said. 'Now you've got to put your energy into working out how you can make it better...'

She liked the fact that he didn't soft-soap her. It had the astringent effect of making her tackle problems instead of trying to ignore them. But she couldn't work out how she was going make things better without introducing even more unnecessary drama into the holiday.

Her phone buzzed.

George again.

*Can we meet?*

*Yes, of course,* she texted back. *Where?*

272

*Bit of a mix-up. Turns out main chocolate festival is
somewhere else. Dad determined to go anyway. So they're
going to drop us in Perugia. Ellis and Jaz want to check out
international university, so I'll be alone...*

'How long does it take to drive to Perugia?' Laura asked
Alex.

He looked it up on his phone.

'About an hour,' he said.

*I can be there in 90 minutes*, she typed. *Will you be OK?*

*I'll send you a pin drop.* George added a smiley face.

'What's happening?' Alex asked, as she jumped up and
started rifling through her suitcase for clean underwear.

'George wants to see me,' she shouted from the shower. 'I'm
going to drive to Perugia. OK if I take the car?'

'I'll drive you!'

'No need,' she said, stepping out into the towel he was
holding for her. 'I need to talk to him alone...'

'I realise that, but I can still drive you. Parking can be a
nightmare. It will save you time.'

'You really don't need to.'

'But I want to,' he said.

'But I must see him alone!'

It was the nearest they'd come to an argument.

'Whatever you want,' Alex remained calm. 'I promise to stay
out of your way.'

She chose a denim skirt and a navy T-shirt.

'Does this look all right?'

'For a repentant mother?' he smiled.

She swiped her wet towel in his direction.

'Pretty much perfect, I'd say.' He ducked away, laughing.

'Thank you,' she said.

'I'm going to have to meet your kids some time,' he said.

'Yes, of course,' she said. 'But just for today. You'll lurk?'

'I'll lurk,' he said, amiably.

She'd told him the worst thing about her, she thought, sitting in the car, listening to Google Maps telling them the way, and it had been OK. But maybe it wouldn't be the worst thing as far as he was concerned. Because there was something else she hadn't told him, and she wasn't sure he would ever be able to forgive her for that.

# Chapter Forty

## *Jessica*

Jessica was sitting on the steps of the church in Città di Castello, in the same piazza where she had sat with Robin just two days before. It had been such a lovely day. Had she been completely deluded to think it might be the beginning of something? Not really, she thought, trying to console herself. It turned out he was prepared to split up with Laura, so it hadn't been entirely mad to believe that there was the possibility. In her worst moments she had even speculated about what would happen if Laura were to die, which was so awful that maybe she deserved her humiliation. But it felt so unfair that just as the door of opportunity had opened a glimmer, it had immediately slammed right back in her face. Searching for a positive lesson to take from it, she told herself that at least now she knew for certain that there was no hope. That must be better than constantly thinking there might be a chance.

'You don't get a fairy-tale ending by dreaming about it,' Mandy always said when they were watching *Married at First Sight UK*, begging the question of how you did get it, if it was even possible. What was the word Laura had used? Parasocial relationship. In future, Jessica decided, she would be better off sticking to crushes on dead artists, knowing her love could never be reciprocated, so she'd never be hurt.

'*Ciao!*'

She looked up to see Enzo walking towards her. How much clearer did she have to be that she wanted to be left alone? She'd asked him to drop her outside the city gate only ten minutes ago, assuming he would go back to do his gardening. She just wanted time to wander and adjust to the new reality.

'Maybe you would like to go to Urbino today?' he said.

'Thanks, but no,' she replied.

Although, after a moment's thought, it certainly was a tempting offer. There wasn't much to do in Città. It was a pleasant enough town but she'd seen most of it now except for the painting by Raphael in the museum. How much more fascinating would it be to visit the place where he'd spent his childhood? What was actually the point in wallowing in self-recrimination all day?

'Did you mean on the bike?' she asked.

'Yes, Vittoria has the car today. Gaia has a playdate with the daughter of one of her friends. Urbino is not so far . . . as the eagle flies.' He winked at her.

It was a bit of a cliché, but nevertheless flattering, to engage in a bit of harmless flirting with a handsome Italian, especially when there was absolutely no danger of a relationship, parasocial or otherwise. She had a strict rule not to sleep with men who were married. She told herself it was a matter of female solidarity, but in truth it was knowing from experience that they would never leave their wives for her. And even if they did, she would already know that they were capable of lying to a woman, so she'd never really have the security she dreamt of. In any case, Enzo was way out of her league.

Unable to summon a valid reason for denying herself the chance to have a nice day out when everyone else was, she said, 'Why not, then?'

It was simply impossible to be depressed while riding on a motorbike.

Enzo ran his eyes up and down her body. In her haste to leave she'd only had time to throw on her down jacket over her T-shirt and jeans.

'I do not think Vittoria's leathers will fit, but we will find you something.'

They walked back to the studio and through a door that led to a staircase to the apartment upstairs. The wooden steps were used as shelves for wellington boots in various sizes along with a pair of children's trainers with soles that lit up when you walked that Jessica had always wished they'd make in adult sizes. From the coat hooks at the top of the staircase he chose a Berghaus cagoule, then ran up another flight of stairs and returned with a soft grey jumper that smelt of his light, fresh cologne as she pulled it over her head.

'Ready?'

The mountainous terrain of Umbria gradually softened into the gentler landscape of Le Marche with fields of pale gold stubble left after the harvest. They sped along a flat road through some fairly unremarkable-looking small towns on the plain, then started climbing into the hills again.

After rounding a series of steep corners, their knees almost in contact with the tarmac, Enzo slowed down.

'Urbino,' he shouted.

The photograph she had seen of the town when she'd googled it gave no impression of the scale of its huge turreted palace, almost pink in the sunshine and looking so completely untouched by time that it was difficult to believe it was real.

After negotiating several hairpins, they arrived outside the walled fortifications. Enzo parked the bike and took off his helmet. With his long black hair damped down, dark, soulful eyes and perfectly arched eyebrows, Jessica suddenly realised that the face his reminded her of was Raphael himself.

'You OK?' he asked.

'Fine,' she said, hoping her cheeks were pink enough from the wind to disguise her blush.

It wasn't so extraordinary, she told herself, because they both came from the same region, so it was even possible they were distantly related.

'Hurry,' Enzo said. 'I want to show you one of my favourite places.'

Entering the town through a stone arch, they walked down a narrow, cobbled street that sloped towards the centre. There was no one about, the only indication they were still in the twenty-first century a blackboard displaying the day's flavours outside an artisan gelateria. After walking a hundred metres or so, Enzo showed her through an ancient wooden door into a dark lobby that opened out on to a verdant botanical garden with gravel paths and raised beds shaded by old trees. They were the only people there. As she looked up at the light that filtered through the branches dappling the ground with drops of sunshine, she became aware of birdsong, the trickle of water, a faint scent of mint on a waft of breeze that rustled the papery leaves above. Had this been here in Raphael's time, she wondered? Monks made potions from herbs. Perhaps it had originally been the physic garden of a monastery.

'It's beautiful, yes?' Enzo asked, reaching forward and plucking a small yellow leaf that had fallen into her hair.

'Catching a leaf is lucky!' she said, wondering whether a leaf landing on your head technically counted as catching. 'Much better than bird poo anyway!'

Enzo frowned at her, perplexed.

'Lunch?' he said.

The restaurant had tables and chairs outside on the piazza but no one was sitting there. Inside, the cavelike space was packed with locals. Enzo ordered a dish called *vincisgrassi* which was a bit like a very rich and meaty lasagne. She didn't realise how hungry she was until she tasted it.

'You like?' he asked.

'*Buonissimo!*' she said, kissing the tips of her fingers, like a chef on an advert for pasta sauce.

His stare was so quizzical she wondered if she had sauce round her mouth and quickly gave it a good scrub with her linen napkin.

'You are unusual, I think,' he said. 'English people are not usually so . . . what is the word . . . *emozionata* . . .'

'Emotional?'

'Excited is more the word I was searching. You are always excited,' he said. 'And you have appetite . . .'

Was he trying to say that she was silly and fat? What had Laura called her? Incontinent with her emotions.

'I think you are a little bit more Italian than English,' he said.

'I'll take that,' she said. 'It's the nicest thing anyone has said to me all week!'

'You have not enjoyed your holiday?'

'No,' she sighed. 'I'm usually much better at planning because it's my job. I'm an events organiser, you know, weddings, birthday parties, corporate dos, all of that . . .'

It occurred to her that now might be the perfect opportunity to investigate whether he'd be interested in providing a restoration-themed activity, so the week wouldn't be a total waste of her time.

'You like this work?' he asked.

She thought she detected a slightly dismissive sneer, which wasn't a good start.

'Well, I mean, it's not necessarily what I wanted to do with my life,' she said, hoping to prove her creative credentials. 'I wanted to work in the arts, but I wasn't the right sort of person, you see ...'

'How do you mean?' he asked.

He'd lived in London, but as a foreigner did you ever really get the English class system? Did they even have one in Italy?

'Well, I didn't talk the right way, didn't know how to dress even when I tried to copy what the women who ran the galleries around Bond Street were wearing. Then one afternoon, I was browsing in a gallery in Cork Street and the owner was in a flap. There was a private view that evening and the caterer had let her down. So there I was, pretending to be studying the paintings while all the time eavesdropping on the phone call ...'

She imitated the woman's tone that descended from haughty astonishment to desperate pleading and ended with her shouting, 'Well, what am I going to do? But it *is* your problem! Hello? Hello? Unbelievable!'

Enzo laughed. He seemed to be enjoying the story.

'So I asked if I could be of any help,' Jessica went on.

' "Not unless you can conjure up champagne and canapés for fifty people in the next hour and a half ..." she says. Well, I can't resist a challenge.'

It was only a couple of hundred metres from her mum's old club. Tony and the girls had always said if there was ever anything they could do to help. Fortnum & Mason's Food Hall was just down the road in the other direction.

'So I asked her, what's your budget, and kept my cool when she gave me a figure, said I'd do it for double.'

Tony had put the champagne on tick and he and the girls had marched over with crates of it and ice buckets.

'I maxed out my credit card on canapés from Fortnum's.

Luckily I was wearing a black suit and white shirt from Next, my attempt at posh, but also worked as waitress. I ended the day a couple of hundred pounds richer. It gave me a taste for it. So I applied for jobs in catering companies. Learned my trade and rose to the top of an events company.'

'Bravo!' said Enzo, clapping.

'Should have stayed there really,' she told him. 'But everyone kept telling me I was so brilliant, I should set up my own company. I finally took the plunge in October 2019. A new beginning. I rented an office. Got a website designed. Launched with a party in Soho House, Shoreditch. My first Christmas was great. And then Covid. One thing you can't do online? Parties, weddings, you name it. I'd invested everything I had in the business. So it's been tough. I'm only just beginning to recover.'

It wasn't just the anxiety about money. It was the loneliness that had almost destroyed her, but she didn't want her only slightly exaggerated anecdote to turn into a sob story.

'This job makes you happy?' he asked.

Funny how a question from a stranger could make you stop and wonder about what you were doing.

'It does,' she said, eventually. 'But I'm not sure it's enough anymore . . .'

'What do you want?' he asked.

They seemed to have strayed a long way from her original intention to ask him about his business and the possibility of a joint venture.

'Oh, you know, the usual, live happily ever after, a baby, if it's not too late . . .' she confided with a self-mocking laugh.

'Perhaps some local cheese?' he asked.

She'd been so absorbed in her reflections, she hadn't noticed that he'd picked up the dessert menu. For a moment, she didn't know whether he was taking the piss, and then she realised he was, and they were both laughing.

'I suppose the local cheese will have to do for now,' she said.

# Chapter Forty-One

## *Robin*

EuroChocolate was like the Chelsea Flower Show of chocolate. There were displays in every colour and form. Chocolate animals, chocolate jewellery, chocolate phones, chocolate discs the size of pizzas scattered with pistachio nuts and rose petals. There were chocolate fountains and chocolate drinks, various chocolate spreads in jars, stalls piled high with macarons in rainbow colours and pyramids of truffles in every conceivable flavour. The exhibition hall was crowded to the point that it was difficult to make progress with crutches and his toe was still flinchingly painful when touched.

The emphasis on artisan bean to bar chocolate was welcome after the giant Baci and the banners of the big commercial producers welcoming them to the festival, but good chocolate had a similar effect to Vin Santo, Robin thought. The first few tastes gave you a hit of pleasure almost better than a drug, suffusing your mouth with sweet deliciousness and your blood with stimulant, but if you were greedy you ended up with palpitations and a terrible headache.

'Love yuzu and chilli in savoury dishes,' Robin said, his mouth puckering with the sourness of a filling inside a bitter seventy per cent single-bean cocoa shell. 'But the reason milk chocolate with smashed hazelnut is so popular is because it's one of those perfect combinations, like lemon and sugar with pancakes. Chocolate with citrus, not so good. The lemon cream was always the last one left in the tray at Christmas because it tastes like washing-up liquid...'

'What about a chocolate orange? That's citrus.'

Being more scientific, Tim never let him get away with easy assertions as other people did, which was probably good for him. At least it meant he was listening, which Robin sometimes thought his family had stopped doing long ago.

'How did salt become a thing?' Tim asked, looking at a range of chocolate buttons flecked with sea salt crystals. 'Nobody put salt on sweet things when we were young, did they? Now there's no such thing as caramel that isn't salted, but nobody seems to question how it suddenly became de rigueur.'

'It does taste better though,' said Robin, who'd never questioned it.

'Strangely irresponsible to take something that consists solely of fat and sugar and decide to make it even worse for your cardiovascular system by adding salt,' said Tim.

'It's like apps.' Robin tried to sound intelligent. 'You know it's bad to accept all the cookies, no pun intended, but you just go along with it because everyone does.'

'Do you accept all the cookies?'

'Er...'

Tim was much cleverer and more rigorous than he was. Always had been. Being with him was a bit like having a personal trainer for his brain. It kept him on his toes.

'Weird that the only people in our group interested in chocolate are the grown-ups,' said Robin.

'Is that how you'd describe yourself?' said Tim.

Robin gave him a soft punch on the arm.

'Had enough?'

'I'd had enough before we got in the hall,' said Tim.

They walked away from the exhibition hall down an avenue lined with giant Lindt bears.

'What's your favourite chocolate?' Robin asked.

'Never really thought about it,' said Tim.

For a moment, Robin wished it was Jessica with him. She would have immediately insisted on defining the parameters of the discussion. 'Do you mean the type of chocolate I'd like to eat every day for the rest of time if I could only choose one, or do you mean the best chocolate-related experience I've ever had?'

'Come on, what's the best taste of chocolate you've ever had?'

'Maltesers,' said Tim immediately.

'Maltesers? Are you mad?'

'You don't remember?' Tim stopped walking and stared at him as a long-forgotten memory began to rush back.

For one of his birthdays at prep school, he'd been given a box of Maltesers by Piers. The brothers could surprise you like that. You'd be braced for a vicious attack and instead you'd get a welcome gift, making you question whether you'd been imagining their cruelty, as they always told the parents you were. He had wasted a couple of the sweets by smashing them to assure himself they weren't rabbit turds. A couple of the boys in his dorm, whom Tim referred to as the Gauleiters, had spotted him carrying the gift. He'd told them it was a book, trying to keep the box completely level so they wouldn't hear the rattling inside. His brother had wrapped it in maps of Africa and the Antarctic. Robin had consequently had to serve several detentions for the defacing of an atlas in the school library, but the nightly hit of sugar made up for it. The only person he'd shared his secret with was Tim, the two of them occasionally sneaking up to the dorm while the others were playing sport. They each had their way of making the sweet treat last. Robin nibbling little bits of chocolate off while leaving the tiny sphere of honeycomb intact for later, Tim popping the whole sweet in his mouth but sucking it really gently so that it slowly dissolved.

'My way makes it last longer,' Robin had claimed.

'But my way tastes nicer.'

When it had come to the final Malteser in the box, Robin had politely offered it to Tim, who'd popped it into his mouth for a few seconds before taking it out and handing it back to Robin, the remaining film of chocolate diluted by his saliva.

Robin could remember exactly the feel of it in his mouth, the way the honeycomb gradually collapsed. How he'd smiled at Tim, acknowledging his was indeed the best way, and how Tim's mouth had dipped towards his, their first kiss tasting of malted chocolate.

Maltesers hadn't come into his life much after that. He wasn't aware of seeing them in a shop, let alone eating one, until Laura had started buying fun-size packs to put in the children's party bags, or dole out on Halloween when neighbourhood kids came trick-or-treating. They contained fewer calories than other sweets and the milky, malty flavour made them seem an almost nourishing and wholesome alternative to the highly coloured confections that Ellis used to demand. To Robin, who'd often sneaked a bag into his pocket for when he was out walking Lammie, popping one occasionally into his mouth and letting it melt, the taste was almost sinfully pleasurable, but he'd never realised why until this moment.

'Of course I remember,' he said, looking up at Tim.

Now his friend's mouth tasted of a different sort of chocolate, dark, sophisticated and so moreish, it made him tremble as he gripped his crutches. When they pulled apart and he opened his eyes, Tim was grinning at him, just as he had thirty years ago, but without the acne that had earned him the soubriquet

Pizza Face. And Robin felt the same simple happiness as he had done then, before he'd had to deny their love.

'Our first public kiss!' said Tim.

Robin looked around, almost expecting his brothers to be advancing on them with faces contorted by apoplectic rage. They'd promised they'd murder him. He can't have been more than ten. Young enough to find comfort in a Malteser. Young enough to believe them.

# Chapter Forty-Two

## *Jessica*

Jessica had never been inside a Renaissance palace that wasn't crowded with tourists. Experience had taught her to book the earliest possible entry time for the galleries in Florence. Even then, it was a bit like queuing all night for the Next sale and making a mad dash for the bargain you wanted. You only got a few moments alone with the famous works before a frantic tide of people rolled in behind you.

The Ducal Palace of Urbino was listed as a World Heritage Site but it was almost completely deserted. As they walked into the main quadrangle, the scale of it was breathtaking. There were four storeys, including an attic floor, all perfectly symmetrical and proportioned. Above the lofty colonnade, the pediments were inscribed with praise for its creator, the Duke of Urbino. She'd seen Piero's famous painting of him in the Uffizi, wearing a red hat and with a chunk gouged out of the bridge of his nose.

'The duke made his money from providing a mercenary army to Firenze,' Enzo said.

'And used it to buy art?'

She was thinking that it sounded rather a philanthropic pursuit for a soldier, until Enzo said, 'It's what powerful people always do, isn't it? They are the ones with the money.'

As they wandered through huge halls with vaulted ceilings and ornate fireplaces that echoed with emptiness, she kept spotting the duke's distinctive hat and profile depicted in scenes by less accomplished artists.

'In the Renaissance, Urbino was one of the most important and rich cities of Italy, but most of the great paintings were taken by Napoleon when he conquered this part of Italy. They are now in the Louvre,' Enzo explained.

'And the National Gallery,' she said.

Had Piero della Francesca's *Baptism of Christ* once hung here? It was one of her favourites. The only work of his left in Urbino was the *Flagellation of Christ*, which was much smaller and stranger than she had envisaged and was hardly worth making a special trip for, although she was very glad they had. The other famous painting in the collection was a portrait by Raphael called *La Muta*, but it was only a reproduction because the original was on tour. She'd seen it in London only weeks before. How strange that the powerful connection she had felt with the artist then had somehow brought her to his birthplace.

'Did Raphael live in this palace?' she asked.

'His house is on the other side of town. Later we will visit, but first, there is something I want you to see.' Enzo pointed at a door, which led to a staircase, then a smaller circular staircase that became narrower and steeper the higher they climbed. At the top, they stepped out onto a small balcony encircling the top of one of the turrets where there was a 360-degree view of the town's terracotta rooftops. Beyond, rolling hills and fields in a subtle palette of natural hues stretched as far as the eye could see, the blue of the sky so pure, it looked almost two-dimensional, like the background of a painting of the Madonna. Far below, the little streets had emptied for the afternoon, and there were no cars on the road that zigzagged up a neighbouring hill. It felt as if they were the only people in the world.

Jessica could imagine Raphael as a small boy running all the way up the tower, the clatter of his excited footsteps stopping as he stood on tiptoe to look over the balustrade, pretending to be king of the castle with the world laid out below like a rich tapestry. There was a strong breeze that sliced through Jessica's clothes to her skin but the golden glow of the dropping sun seemed to bathe her face in smiles. Almost reluctantly, she handed her phone to Enzo, wanting to record the moment, but knowing no image could ever capture the exhilarating sense of privilege she felt being there to witness such beauty.

He took several photos, then handed the camera back to her.

'Selfie?' she asked.

They stood with their backs to the view, hair blowing over their faces, eyes almost closed against the wind. He held the phone at arm's length with one hand, the other slipping gently round her waist. Suddenly, all the glorious sensations she was feeling seemed to focus at the exquisite square inch where the tips of his fingers were in contact with the small of her back. She sidestepped away from him, discombobulated by the attraction she felt like a static shock on her skin.

'Enough?' he asked.

'I could never get enough of this place.' She didn't trust herself to look at him. 'Thank you for bringing me here.'

'It is my pleasure. Let's go to the house of Raffaello,' he said.

As they walked back down past the cathedral and across the main piazza, the vibe between them had slightly shifted. She heard herself filling the silence with silly inconsequential observations like, 'Pretty church! What a dear little cinema. It's actually so peaceful here!'

Raphael's house was situated halfway up a steeply inclined street. Outside, there was nothing to distinguish it from any of the terraced stone buildings. Inside, it felt like a humble home after the vastness of the palace they'd just visited. There were stone window seats on the first floor where she sat down and stared out at exactly the same view of the street the young artist must have looked at every day.

When she visited old bits of London, Jessica always tried to imagine herself back in time, but London had been so changed by the fires and war and developers that you never could quite lose yourself as you could in Italy, where the past seemed so much more present.

In one of the bedrooms, there was a fresco on the wall of the *Madonna and Child*. Apparently it was a matter of debate as to whether it was by Raphael. His family had left the town when he was nine, so it could have been his earliest work still in existence.

'What do you think?' Enzo asked.

She studied the painting. The baby was asleep on his mother's lap, sweetly resting its head on its own chubby arm. The Madonna appeared to be reading a text propped up on a wooden rest. The robes were crudely painted, but the faces were tenderly drawn and realistic. Jessica imagined the little boy who'd run up to the top of the palace standing on a wooden stool, giving his full concentration to his work.

'Definitely!' she said.

'It's a very accomplished work for a nine-year-old,' Enzo argued.

'But it's Raphael we're talking about, not just any nine-year-old!'

Enzo smiled at her with his slightly amused look.

'What?'

'You believe that if you wish for something enough it will be true,' he said.

'You mean I'm a fantasist?' she said.

'Perhaps. For me, it is a quality that is very unusual and attractive.'

'Really?'

Back in the entrance hall, she bought a postcard of the *Madonna and Child*. There was a reproduction of the artist's self-portrait as a young man on the wall.

'Has anyone ever told you that you look like him?' she told Enzo.

He threw back his head and laughed.

'OK, this, I think, is fantasy.'

What had possessed her? She no longer dared to ask whether he'd mind standing next to it for a photo to show Mandy, because even though he clearly did look like the artist, it was a definite case of tanks and lawns. Although he was the one who had started the flirting, she reminded herself –, if it actually qualified as flirting, rather than him just being nice to a client who'd had such a rotten holiday, they'd never give a five-star review.

They were both silent as they retraced their steps back up to the gate where they'd entered the town.

'Would you like a gelato?' she asked, as they approached the artisan gelateria. It was the least she could offer, since he had paid for lunch.

Without even looking at the array of tubs in front of them, Enzo ordered *crema* and chocolate. She wondered if ice cream for Italians was a bit like drinking in pubs was for English people. You had your usual and rarely chose anything else. She opted for pistachio, then saw that there was stracciatella, then wondered if a sorbet would be more refreshing. Her vacillation between the delicious-looking flavours was probably as irritating to him as it would be for her if he stood at the bar, going, 'A gin and tonic, no actually, half of lager, no, make that an orange juice, with vodka, or do I fancy a pint of Guinness?'

'You're like Gaia,' he said. 'She never knows which ones she would like. She usually end up swapping with me.'

Was that the reason for his slightly boring combo?

'Don't worry, I'll stick with my decision,' she said, finally deciding on a lemon sorbet and a flavour called zabaione.

The first lick hit her with an unexpected memory of the Christmas cocktail her mother used to make called a Snowball. She made them every year with advocaat, lemonade and a maraschino cherry. Jessica was always allowed a tiny glass because Mum said it was more like an ice cream soda than an alcoholic beverage. Turned out it wasn't. The first time Jessica had been left alone at ten years old, she made herself a large glass of it, then another, then another because it was so delicious. Mum had found her passed out on the sofa and called an ambulance. Social services had got involved after the hospital found toxic levels of alcohol in her blood. Jessica had tried to tell them it was her fault not her mum's, but they'd still taken her into care.

Enzo's phone suddenly rang, wrenching her back from the complex hit of déjà vu.

He spoke for a few moments and ended the call with, 'Ciao, tesoro!' so she assumed he was speaking to his wife or daughter.

'Everything OK?' she asked.

'Everything is good. They will stay with Vittoria's friend. So there is no reason for us to hurry.'

# Chapter Forty-Three

## *Robin*

Robin's body felt light, almost inflated, with the excitement of the kiss. Now, it really did feel like his life was beginning. What he wanted to suggest was checking into a hotel for the afternoon, but they had all the time in the world, he reminded himself.

'Let's go and find the kids,' he said.

Ellis and Jaz had wanted to investigate the international university. When he'd asked if they would be OK, they'd told him scornfully that they took the tube every day in London, so they were hardly likely to come to any harm on a mini metro in broad daylight, were they? He'd given them twenty euros each for lunch, hoping they'd find the same pleasure he did in choosing a picnic lunch in a foreign country, standing at the counter of a deli, asking for tastes of the local salami, buying a hundred grams of cheese. Although thinking about it now, it wouldn't be that easy for vegans. George would certainly find a way of eating. He'd said he wanted to check out the football stadium. Now, googling AC Perugia, Robin discovered the team was only in Serie B and the ground was nowhere near the *centro storico*.

'Why don't you text and offer for us to pick him up,' Tim suggested.

George's response read, *No thanks. I'll text you later.*

The ancient city of Perugia was built at the top of a mountain. They left the car near the station where they'd dropped the kids, because like so many Italian towns, the *centro storico* was closed to traffic. The mini metro was much more exciting than Robin had imagined, with little self-driven units like a cable car on rails. The construction felt as recent as the Elizabeth Line but had been in operation for more than ten years. He sat at the front as the pod glided soundlessly up the mountain, stopping automatically at a couple of stations on the incline, before entering a steep stretch of tunnel up to the cavernous terminus carved out of the rock. Three long, steep escalators carried them up to the exit. Stepping out from the cavelike interior into the mellow afternoon sunlight, they found themselves looking out at a vast, hazy panorama of mountains. The sun was low in the sky. There was a chill shiver of altitude on the air.

'This has to be the most beautiful metro station in the world!' said Robin. He couldn't imagine anyone not being in a good mood after travelling on it. Part of him would have much preferred to skip all the ancient buildings and museums in favour of trundling up and down pretending he was a train driver for the rest of the day.

'Such an imaginative public transportation solution,' Tim said. 'Makes you remember that Italians today are the same people as the ancient Romans, who were such masters of engineering and conquered the world.'

Robin sometimes wondered whether other people did a lot more thinking than he did.

'And it's so green,' he said. 'Even Ellis will approve.'

A flight of steep steps led to a small alleyway that acted as a portal, magically transporting them back to medieval times. Apart from the shopfronts, the streets of the *centro storico* had remained unaltered for hundreds of years. Everything was on a smaller, less intimidating scale than the grand squares and elegant symmetry of other Italian cities he had visited. There were plenty of shops selling chocolate, so there was really no need for them to have gone to the trade fair out of town. Here, you could purchase novelty items all year round, although heaven knows how you'd transport it in summer. There were bars of chocolate with wrappers for all the names of the alphabet, but in Italian, so he was only able to purchase a Giorgio. He chose two vegan chocolate bars on selfie sticks for Ellis and Jaz, then pondered over bags of dried spaghetti and rigatoni flavoured with chocolate. Were you supposed to use them for sweet or savoury dishes? A chocolate macaroni cheese with a vanilla crème anglaise instead of bechamel and no cheese, perhaps? Or maybe he could team the pasta with arrabiata sauce, as chocolate and chilli always went together. Eventually he decided against it. Turned out you could have too much chocolate on your birthday. He'd completely lost his appetite for it.

The uneven cobblestones weren't the easiest footing to negotiate with crutches, and so they sat down at a café on the Corso Vannucci, the main thoroughfare, which was bustling with bars and restaurants.

'Would you like a gelato, on your birthday?' Tim asked, perusing a menu offering all sorts of extravagant sundaes.

'Just a coffee, thanks,' Robin said.

It was the perfect spot to sit and watch the world go by.

'Do you think I should text George again?'

He hadn't said a lot in the car this morning and it got dark quickly in the afternoons. He was beginning to get a little concerned.

'I think we need to be sensitive to his needs, give him time and space to process,' said Tim. 'It's a lot for him. His mum leaves, he finds out that his dad's gay . . .'

'He seemed fine with it, though.'

'Oh, Robin!'

George would be OK, wouldn't he? The last thing he wanted to do was traumatise his son. He'd managed to get George to this age with none of the dread he'd had of his own father, who had made it clear for as long as he could remember that Robin was a disappointment. Crispin and Piers had never wanted to put on their mother's lipstick and earrings, or at least had never been caught in the act. That was the first of many times his father had threatened him.

'What's disown?' Robin remembered asking, aged seven.

'Cut you off!'

'Which bit?' he'd asked, terrified.

'Throw you out on the street, you moron!' Crispin had clarified.

At school, Robin was frightened of playing rugby and hopeless at cricket. He wouldn't have made it through the Duke of Edinburgh Award if Tim hadn't given him a piggyback most of the way across Dartmoor. He wasn't particularly strong academically and had never been made prefect or given any other position of responsibility. His parents hadn't come to see any of the plays he was in, and when he'd told them he wanted to be an actor, his father had shouted, 'Sometimes I wonder if you're even my son!'

Robin had never allowed himself to extrapolate the thought towards the hideous idea of his mother having sex with anyone else, or indeed anyone at all.

But he and George had a great relationship, didn't they? It had been such a relief when George had wanted to dress up as a fireman when he was a little boy and had been naturally good at sport. Robin had done his best to encourage it. He'd always taken him to football practice, spending Saturday mornings in freezing parks around London, the cold seeping up through his calves like some sort of cryogenic agent as he and Lammie bounced up and down on the touchline trying to keep warm.

'Is there anywhere colder in the world than the edge of a football field in winter?' he'd once asked his wife.

'I imagine parts of Siberia,' Laura had replied, never one for rhetorical questions.

Now that George was a teenager, Robin wasn't as useful for help with homework as Laura was, but he made sure he washed George's football kit, even if he didn't always remember to take it out of the machine, and cooked him plentiful carb-laden meals. They watched *Taskmaster* together and he was always there for a chat or a game of Fifa. He pretended to show an interest in George's team, Arsenal, although it was a mystery to him why you would continue to support if the club lost or sold all the players you liked. Nevertheless, he tried to remember to ask George the score on Saturdays and watch *Match of the Day* without falling asleep. He'd even taken him to a couple of matches at the Emirates before George was old enough to go with his mates.

Surely his announcement this morning wouldn't destroy all that? Now he wished he'd heeded Tim's warning glances over the inedible cupcakes. Jessica's reaction had been shocking enough, but he couldn't bear it if George decided to reject him too.

A sudden crescendo of appreciative whistles alerted them to Ellis and Jaz approaching the café. Robin beckoned them over and Tim ordered them the fresh fruit salads they requested.

They were full of the things they had discovered about the university, where there were courses in Italian culture and cinema as well as a degree involving the study of human rights, environmental policy and international relations, which sounded as if it might be perfect for Ellis.

He'd never seen them looking so animated about their future.

Since the isolation of lockdown, Ellis had retreated behind a wall of resentment and introversion. In their own head, was the expression he knew they used these days, which he thought was a good way of describing it. Just one afternoon of being alone in a foreign city had opened them up to the outside world again.

'So we were thinking, maybe next summer we could come and learn Italian. There's a jazz festival here which sounds really cool. Then we could go backpacking around Italy . . .' Ellis said, grasping Jaz's hand, their eyes shining with excitement. He looked at the two beautiful young people across the table from him, on the cusp of adulthood and yet still innocent in so many ways, and feared for them being so pretty, yet unaware of the power of beauty to make or destroy. They were in love for the first time in their life and proud to declare it.

How would his life have gone if he'd followed his heart at Ellis's age?

Probably to no better place than here, Robin thought, because he hadn't realised until just now that you didn't really know what fulfilment was until you saw your children achieve it for themselves. It felt like such a precious moment, he wished he could suspend time and stay in it just a while longer.

'Have you heard from George?' asked Tim.

'No. He was being very secretive about his plans,' said Ellis.

# Chapter Forty-Four

## *Laura*

They were sitting in a small park at the southern end of the Corso Vannucci between two grand hotels of the Edwardian era, a pot of tea and a plate of delicate pastries on the table in front of them. A string quartet was playing a medley of popular classics. The vibe felt rather staid, like a Sunday afternoon in the Pump Room in Bath, but the view of distant mountains, their contours softened by the pale rays of late afternoon sun, was breathtaking.

'Why did you choose this place?' Laura asked George.

'I wandered round a bit and picked the furthest place from the metro. Dad isn't going to want to walk all the way up here on crutches, is he? I wanted to talk to you.'

The slight rise in his voice loaded the simple sentence with a cry of hurt disbelief that she had betrayed their bond. She had always told her children that they could tell her anything, promising to believe them and never judge them. Even when they were five years old, Ellis had looked scornful at the suggestion, but George had always told her everything. He had clearly assumed that it worked both ways. Seeing his disappointment in her, Laura knew she'd failed him.

'I'm so sorry. Didn't mean for it to all happen like this,' she said.

'How did you mean for it to happen?' The clipped tone of the challenge sounded more like Ellis.

'I don't know,' she said, hoping he would believe that at least. 'Yes, I have been having an affair. I was going to use this holiday to sort my head out and work out what to do, but everything got out of control, I'm not even sure how. You have every right to be annoyed with us...'

'I'm not annoyed with Dad,' said George. 'He's being nice saying it was both of you, but really it was you, wasn't it? Because Dad would never have left you.'

She sighed.

'You're probably right.'

He said nothing. It felt as if a gulf had opened between them. Finally, he broke the silence.

'Don't you want to be with me?' His newly broken voice still had some of the squeaky notes of a child, making his anguish even more painful to her.

'Oh, darling George, of course I want to be with you...'

She wanted very much to enfold him in a hug, but she didn't want to risk embarrassing him in this public place and she didn't think she would be able to bear it if he pushed her away. She stretched her hand tentatively across the table. He stared at it, but did not move his own hand to meet it.

'So how is it going to work?' he asked, his voice now cold.

Damn Robin! They should have planned it all out before telling the children.

'I honestly don't know,' she said.

'Can I still be with you? I mean, until I've done my GCSEs?'

She suppressed a smile at the hint that George's difficulty might possibly be more practical than emotional, once again filled with such love for his candour.

'We will work it out,' she said.

Of course she would find a way of George being with her if

that is what he wanted. She couldn't reject him. Didn't want to reject him. She'd live with him alone if necessary. The image of an ordered life in Alex's pristine flat at the top of a glass tower in Docklands vanished as instantly as the dream that it had always been.

'I'm sure Dad will want to share you though,' she said.

'I know how it works, Mum. You're about the only parents I know who aren't divorced. Only he'll be in America a lot, won't he?'

'America? Why?'

'Because that's where Tim lives!' George sounded exasperated.

'But why . . . ?'

George was looking at her as if she'd lost her mind.

'Oh . . . I see,' she said, as her bewilderment suddenly turned to understanding. Tim and Robin. She thought she should probably feel more shocked than she did, but it made far more sense than Robin and Jessica. Bloody hell, Robin! Had he been living a double life all this time?

'How do you feel about that?' she asked George, trying to play for time so her brain could adjust to the new reality.

'I like Tim,' George said. 'Not sure how I feel about having two dads, though. What do you feel?'

'I like Tim too. It's a bit of a surprise, obviously . . .'

She hoped she'd managed to look as if she'd known but she couldn't think of anything to say. How were you supposed to react when you discovered after eighteen years of marriage that your husband was gay?

George reached for a pastry.

'So what's your guy called?' He was trying to sound more grown up after his outburst and she found it so endearing she wanted to give him a cuddle.

'His name is Alex. He's a teacher at my school.'

'Makes sense,' said George. 'Is he married too?'

'No.'

'Is he here?' he asked.

'He flew to Italy after I called him from the spa. I didn't ask him to...'

'And today, is he here in Perugia?'

She felt herself colouring. Knew she wasn't capable of any more pretending.

'Yes.'

'Can I meet him?' George took another pastry. Having got his worries off his chest, he seemed to have his usual appetite back.

'Do you think that's a good idea?' she asked. 'Don't you think we've all had enough emotional upheaval for one day?'

George thought about it, then, deaf to the attempt to put him off, said, 'No, I'd like to meet him.'

She couldn't refuse now, not after getting back on a more level footing. She took out her phone and sent a WhatsApp, hoping that Alex wouldn't respond, but he texted back immediately.

'I'm in the Piazza IV Novembre reading a book. Come and find me when you're ready.'

'That's the main square at the other end of town,' George said, when she told him.

Laura took her time paying the bill inside the hotel, trying but failing to think of another way out.

When she returned to the table, George was on the phone. He mouthed 'Dad' silently at her.

'No, I'm not at the stadium,' he said. 'I'm in the old bit... just having a wander. OK. Fine. See you there!'

He looked at her.

'I didn't tell him I was with you. We're meeting at the metro station in half an hour.'

Bless you, Robin, she thought.

'Come on, then,' George said, pushing his chair back.

'But . . .'

'Piazza's only five minutes' walk,' George said. 'Ten at most.'

# Chapter Forty-Five

## *Robin*

The girls wanted to see a photographic exhibition before leaving which was in a gallery down one of the steeply sloping streets that led off the Corso Vannucci. Robin and Tim walked the short distance to have a look at the main square before making their way back to the station.

Perugia's most famous landmark was a circular fountain with tiers decorated with friezes carved out of the pale pink and white stone. Like icing on a giant wedding cake, he thought, although the images were hardly romantic, ranging from the usual array of classical figures from mythology and the Bible to more lowly country pursuits on the lower tier, including a particularly animated depiction of a boar hunt. There was only a thin stream of water emerging from the spout at the top. It was nothing like any of the gushing Baroque fountains he had seen in Rome. He and Tim walked around a larger circumference than the rest of the crowd, trying to avoid colliding with tourists intent on getting the best selfie. After they'd done a full circle and were facing back down the Corso Vannucci again, Robin suddenly spotted Laura and George fifty metres or so away, walking in their direction.

'Of all the towns in all the world, George has bumped into Laura!' he said, nudging Tim.

He started waving one of his crutches at them and was about to call out when Tim grabbed his arm.

'Hold on, Robin. George obviously wanted to talk to his mother without us knowing . . .'

'Do you think he arranged to meet her? I did wonder about the football stadium. They're not even Serie A. What do we do? Ought we to say hello, do you think?'

'I think maybe best to keep out of their way, don't you?'

That was going to be impossible on the Corso Vannucci, so they about-turned and walked back past the fountain, positioning themselves in the shadow of the colonnade behind. As he watched mother and son walking along together, Robin saw that George was now taller than Laura. The way their bodies leant towards each other, not touching but somehow connected, produced a great welling of affection in his chest. Laura and George had always been so close. A vague sense of anxiety that had been nagging him all day began to crystallise into fear as it dawned on him that things were going to be very different when they returned to London. He'd been thinking that his life wouldn't be that much affected, but it hadn't occurred to him that George would want to be with his mother. Would his son be leaving the family home? Or would Robin? What would be the point of him if Ellis was at uni and George was no longer there to cook for?

Laura and George didn't appear to be interested in the fountain. They were clearly looking for someone, Laura standing on tiptoe, scanning the crowd. For a second, her gaze landed on Robin before he had a chance to turn away, and he saw exactly the same strange flicker of panic that he'd noticed when she'd had to say what her biggest fear was during the Truth or Dare game. Her forehead puckered to a frown, then, still looking at him, she inclined her head just a fraction, her eyes opening wide. He recognised it as a plea for him not to approach her.

He gave her a tiny nod of acknowledgement, and she returned the slightest twitch of a grateful smile before moving on with her search. The entire fleeting exchange must have taken less than a second, but a whole lifetime of knowing each other. Stepping further back into the shadow of the colonnade, Robin kept watching as she suddenly raised her arm, her face lifting with excited anticipation. He followed her line of sight.

On the other side of the square there was an ancient civic building that looked like a fortress. Built of the same rose-tinted stone as the fountain and topped with battlements, the entrance was guarded by an imposing metal eagle and lion on either side. A steep semicircular pyramid of steps led up to it from the piazza where small groups of tourists were lounging, chatting, eating ice creams. Sitting at the top was a man on his own reading a book. As Laura waved, he stood up and waved back. She and George picked their way up to him.

The introduction looked awkward, neither of the guys quite sure what to do. Then George offered his hand and Robin had to gulp back tears of pride for his son's good manners. The man shook it enthusiastically, said something that made George laugh. Robin watched, unable to tear his eyes away, transfixed by a terrible sense of dread.

He felt Tim's arm go round his shoulder as he saw what Robin was seeing.

'Oh dear!' said Tim.

# Chapter Forty-Six

## *Jessica*

The sun was low in the sky, the forested hills now black silhouettes against a vast orange sky that deepened to crimson before darkness absorbed all the colour and the warmth from the air. As they paused at a junction, Enzo turned to ask if she was OK, telling her to hold closer and put her freezing hands into the pockets of his jacket.

'Better?' he asked, before opening the throttle, jerking her back so that she had no option but to cling on tighter as the bike hurtled through the dusk.

'Shall I take you back now?' he turned to ask as they stopped at traffic lights outside town. 'Or would you like to get supper?'

'That's very kind, but I've imposed on you enough.'

A day out on a motorbike had been exactly what she needed. The exhilarating mix of danger and speed was addictive. In fact, if her business picked up when she returned to London, she might invest in a bike herself, or at least start using electric scooters.

As he indicated to turn right towards the hills rather than the town, she suddenly couldn't stomach the idea of returning to the house. All day, her mind had been so occupied with art, history and the simple act of survival on the back of a motorbike, there hadn't been time to revisit the draining humiliation of this morning. None of the rest of them would believe she had been liberated by the trip to Urbino because they knew nothing about the redemptive power of art. They would think she was putting on a brave face and pity her. She couldn't face that.

Jessica tapped Enzo on the shoulder.

'*Si?*'

'Is there somewhere I could stay in Città?' she shouted, over the noise of traffic.

'*Certo!*' he flicked the indicator to left.

They rode slowly through the pedestrianised streets and stopped outside his studio.

'Welcome!' he said, unlocking and winding up the shutter.

'But this is your place. I can't stay here!'

'You can sleep in Gaia's room.'

'I couldn't possibly . . .'

'She's staying with Vittoria's friend near Perugia. They are going to the last day of the chocolate festival tomorrow.'

'But I mean . . . shouldn't you ask her?'

He laughed, then looked at his watch.

'She's probably asleep by now.'

Was he being deliberately obtuse? She meant ask Vittoria. Or was he just being hospitable in a perfectly normal way? Was she being rude? Since the revelations of this morning, she seemed to have lost confidence in her judgement.

Her hand accidentally brushed his as she handed back the Berghaus cagoule.

'You are so cold! Do you want to get warm with a bath?' he asked, opening a cupboard and handing her a towel. 'I will make us supper?'

It felt somehow wrong, but she was freezing. After a week of showering quickly in the Jack and Jill she shared with George, the prospect of a long soak was too good to refuse.

The bathroom was painted with a trompe l'oeil mural of a

309

window looking out to a garden, where a pergola dripping with wisteria framed a sea view with the white sail of a yacht on the horizon.

'I love the painting,' she called.

'We don't have a garden outside, so I made one inside,' he shouted back.

'You did this?'

'Who else?'

'You are an artist!'

'More a decorator, I think,' he said.

She thought about all the property programmes she watched featuring dull young couples who talked about putting their own stamp on their home, which usually meant a few scatter cushions from IKEA. Was fresco painting in the Italian blood?

Jessica turned off the taps. Taking off her watch, she realised that she hadn't looked at her step count all day. Sliding down so the warm water enveloped her right up to her chin, she picked up a bar of soap and worked it into a lather. It had a light citrus scent with background notes of spice, like the smell of his jumper.

When she finally emerged from the comfort of the steamy bathroom, with the towel held tightly around her, Enzo was standing at the stove with a checked tea towel over his shoulder, similar to the one she'd been cutting up for bunting. Could it be that only a day had passed since then? She recalled the satisfaction that making the *Welcome Home* banner had given her and how it hadn't had the effect on Robin she had hoped. The searing sting of rejection felt more like disappointment now; not at Robin, because he couldn't really help it, but with herself. How could she have been so stupid all these years?

'Smells good,' she said. Garlic was sweating in a glug of oil in a deep frying pan and Enzo was cutting a piece of pancetta into small strips.

'You are ready to eat?' he asked, looking her up and down, reminding her she only had a towel round her body and a turban on her head.

'I'll just get dressed.'

'Gaia's room is there,' he pointed.

The child's bedroom was painted too, with a pale blue sky and a frieze of realistic-looking poppies and grasses growing up from the floor all around the walls. Jessica sat down on the bed, which wasn't any smaller than the one she'd been sleeping in all week, thinking how much happier her childhood would have been if she'd woken up each morning next to a wall that blossomed with flowers instead of black mould, looking up at the sky rather than a single light bulb hanging from a cracked ceiling.

In the kitchen, Enzo had set two places with proper cloth napkins, a wine glass and a tumbler for water.

'*Buon appetito!*' He put a bowl of pasta down in front of her.

The penne were cooked perfectly al dente, the tomato sauce simple, but tasty and sweet, with satisfying nuggets of fatty bacon. He took a tub of grated Parmesan from the fridge and put it on the table between them with a teaspoon, which was a relief because she never got on with the wedge of Parmesan and grate-your-own scenario, always ending up with flecks of cheese all over her clothes. Tipping out a small sick-smelling drift from the cuff of a silk shirt had definitely contributed to the early exit of the interior designer on their first date after zooming during lockdown. She'd dreamt of forming a bubble, but that had been another fantasy.

'This is delicious,' she said.

'Penne all'amatriciana,' he said.

'Do you like cooking?'

'Not specially. When you have a child, you have to learn.'

'You have made your daughter's room so beautiful,' she said.

'One day, it is our dream to move to a house in the country we renovate. But just now Gaia demands a lot of attention, more than a baby who sleeps a lot, and she is so interesting, I don't want to miss the opportunity to talk with her.'

How Italians loved children. English people mostly seemed to consider them a burden. She thought of the impatient mothers who dragged their kids away from the gates of the local primary school, and Mandy constantly moaning about being a taxi service for taekwondo classes. Her kids never said a word in the car because they were either on their phones or told to shut it. Sometimes she wondered why Mandy had kids at all, because she seemed so fed up with them. If Jessica had had kids, she knew she'd want to talk to them and do craft things with them all the time. Or perhaps that was just a fantasy too?

What was it Enzo had said?

'You believe that if you wish for something enough it will be true.'

He'd summed her up. And he'd known her for less than a day.

Perhaps the one thing she could take away from the week's debacle was self-awareness. Perhaps she should even try making a gratitude list each evening for the things she did have, instead of yearning for things she couldn't.

I'm grateful to be given a bed for the night, although, to be honest, it doesn't seem like much to ask after arranging a luxury holiday for six. And, I might add, paying for it too, although I'm going to insist on getting Laura and Tim's share, and with any luck he might now pay for Robin too.

Let superfluous thoughts go. Stay in the moment!

I am grateful to be sitting opposite an Italian who definitely does look like Raphael, whatever he says.

Keep it simple.

I am grateful for a plate of warm pasta.

'What's it like living in an earthquake zone?' she said.

Enzo looked perplexed.

'Isn't Amatrice where the pasta gets its name?'

'Of course,' he said. 'Yes. It is terrible what happened to Amatrice. To answer your question, people who live here have grown up with it. I think perhaps we enjoy our lives each day, not thinking so much about the future ...'

'I've never been in an earthquake.'

'Here, we say the mountains are dancing.'

God, she loved Italians. They could even make natural disasters sound romantic. Perhaps she should come and live in Italy after all. It would make sense since so many of the events she organised were here. Once she could speak proper Italian, she would be able to negotiate better rates.

'Does it affect your work? I mean, can you even get buildings insurance?' she asked.

'It's difficult, of course,' he said. 'But there is always restoration work to be done here.'

That was a positive way of looking at it.

'I was actually thinking of asking whether you'd be interested in participating in one of my events,' she said. 'These days I have to offer more than a venue with a pool for most parties. People like to have a go at something. I was thinking "Restoring Art in Umbria". It's not so much about the craft, of course, more, you know, team-building? You must know the sort of thing when you worked in the City?'

'I came back to Italy because I wasn't interested in living that kind of life anymore. It felt, how you say, superficial ...'

'Oh. Yes. Well. It is, I suppose.'

She felt completely deflated. He'd just dismissed the only thing in her life she had made a success of. It was more than she could stand on a day when she'd already lost so much.

'Do you have the number for a cab?' she asked, folding her napkin carefully.

'You want to leave now?' He sounded surprised.

'Yes, please.'

'Have I offended you?'

'Don't worry about it.'

'I have offended you?'

'I'm really not interested in your critique of my life.'

'I only wonder if this job makes you happy?'

'Well, it does, not that it's any of your business, so there!'

Jessica stood up decisively, then sat down again abruptly as she crumpled into tears.

# Chapter Forty-Seven

## *Laura*

The silence in the car was as thick and sticky as treacle.

Eventually, Alex said, 'You don't seem particularly surprised that Robin is with Tim?'

'I suppose I was less surprised than if he'd fallen instantly for Jessica after all this time.'

'Did you think he was gay?'

'He's always been very camp, but then a lot of straight actors are . . .'

'George seems pretty cool about it,' he said.

'Gen Z are much less bothered, aren't they? But it's still confusing for him.'

'He seems like a good kid,' Alex said.

'He really is. He's so considerate and empathetic, I was going to say for a boy. But I shouldn't, should I?'

'Not really.'

'Ellis is quite different. Very highly strung. I sometimes wonder if it was my fault. They say that you're always more anxious with the first child.'

She realised she was blathering on, trying to get Alex's reassurance, but he wasn't going to grant it this time. She wished he would take his eyes off the road just for a second.

'Can't believe he's a Gooner!' he said, with a little laugh.

She had been delighted when George had started a conversation about football after their slightly awkward introduction, even joshing him about his team's performance in that good-natured way that men who didn't know each other found to communicate.

'Why do you even support Man United when you're not from Manchester?' she asked Alex now.

'Everyone did when I was a kid. They were the team.'

'Arsenal's local, at least,' she said.

'And they're doing pretty well this season.'

'Yes . . .'

She'd exhausted all her football talk. They were only using it as a way of not speaking about the real issue.

'George and I were discussing how it's going to work,' she began.

'How is it going to work?'

'I just don't know yet . . .'

What was the future going to look like now? Would Robin move into Tim's flat in London, or New York? Would she stay in the house? She'd never even considered that as a possibility. Her life felt like a Jenga tower. She had expected it to collapse when she had removed her brick, but it had only wobbled. Then Robin had taken his and the entire structure had toppled, its pieces scattered.

Alex breathed a long sigh. 'Are you really going to make me ask, Law?'

'What?'

'Does Robin have brown eyes and dark curly hair just like mine?'

'He doesn't have that much hair at all anymore.'

'For god's sake, Law. I'm not an idiot.'

'I know. Look, I can't talk to the side of your face . . .'

They were only a few miles away from the spa hotel now.

Hurtling through the darkness towards her lonely future, Laura couldn't rid herself of the thought that her mother had been right all along. She was a liar. She had lied to every single person who loved her. She did not deserve to be loved.

'Why didn't you tell me?' Alex demanded as soon as the bedroom door closed behind them.

'We promised not to contact each other.'

His leaving party after the NQT year was in the beer garden of a pub near the school. She'd only gone along because it would have looked strange as his mentor not to have been there. It was the last day of the summer term and the weather was hot. Most of the staff were pink and sweaty from drinking and the sun.

Everyone seemed much more excited than Alex was about his upcoming tour, making jokes about his new life of sex and drugs and rock and roll, promising they'd buy tickets when the band played the O2.

'Will you still speak to us when you're famous?' Kirsty, the headmaster's secretary, screeched.

'Of course I'll keep in touch. I'll miss you,' he'd said, glancing across at Laura.

She'd looked away quickly, sure that Kirsty had seen the exchange of looks, so she'd stayed longer than she intended so as not to raise suspicion for being the first to leave. When she'd finally got away, she'd managed to hold her poker face until she was out of the car park, but as she'd joined the rush hour traffic all the emotion had convulsed through her body and she'd had to pull into a housing estate.

She shouldn't have allowed herself to open his text. She shouldn't have told him where she was. She shouldn't have driven them to a dingy suburban Premier Inn. It was desperate and tawdry, but the sex had taken her to a place that felt like paradise. For one evening, she had known what love felt like. Beautiful, ecstatic, impossible.

And then they'd parted forever.

By the time she did the test a few weeks later, his band was playing Berlin. The two blue lines weren't a surprise because the sex had felt miraculous. Why else would such deliciously imperative sensations have evolved except to compel human beings to create new lives?

'You didn't think this might constitute exceptional circumstances?' His voice was very flat. Every time she tried to look at him he seemed to find a way of avoiding her gaze.

'What would you have done?' she asked. 'Insisted on an abortion? I considered it, but I couldn't do it. How was I to know about your decision not to have children?'

Still he wouldn't look at her.

'George is a good person!' she cried. 'The world's a better place with him in it. You can't make me regret it!' In sheer frustration she threw herself onto the bed, pummelling the pillows with her fists.

'For god's sake, Laura!' He grabbed her hands, sat her up, looked into her eyes. 'I'm not trying to make you regret it. Regret doesn't come into it.'

She could read in his face the struggle he was having to rewrite the history of his life.

'He's generally very happy and equable. He plays football all the time,' she said, trying to help him. 'He takes after you!'

For a moment, she didn't know if he was going to laugh or cry, then he sort of did both at once, his face lit up with astonishment, as if he'd only just realised that he was a father.

'I'm sorry I didn't tell you . . .' she said. 'It never felt like the right time. But it was wrong.'

'Didn't Robin suspect?' he asked.

'He once made a joke about immaculate conception, but

Robin hates confrontation, so he avoids it. He loves being a father, cooking for everyone and making a nice home, because he never had that himself... and he is a good father. He and George really love each other...'

'I realise that,' he said.

She found it impossible to know what he was thinking.

'I have no idea what to do now,' she said.

'Isn't it up to George?'

'What do you mean?'

'Don't you think he needs to know who his biological father is, especially now that you and I...'

A flicker of hope. Was he saying they would still be together?

'And Robin needs to know,' he said.

'I think Robin already does,' she confessed. 'He and Tim were in the square. They saw you and George. He does look so much like you...'

She'd glanced across the square, seen that Robin was still there under the colonnade with Tim. They were both staring open-mouthed. Then Tim had helped Robin hobble away.

'It's a bit weird that the only person who seems unaware is George,' she said.

'This time, you have to be the one to tell him,' Alex said.

'But he's already dealing with his parents separating and his dad being gay. We just got through one very tricky conversation...'

'Laura, you are going to have to start facing your demons.'

The statement was categoric. She knew from his tone that it wasn't advice. It was a condition of them remaining together.

# Chapter Forty-Eight

## *Jessica*

'I have upset you and this was not my intention,' said Enzo, handing her a sheet of kitchen towel to wipe her eyes.

'Really, it's fine,' she said, blowing her nose, trying to pull herself together.

'I think I understand you now,' he said.

She braced herself for more criticism, biting her tongue hard. No more emotional incontinence.

'You spend your life making other people's wishes come true,' he said. 'But who makes lovely things happen for you?'

More tears.

He pushed his chair back and came round to her side of the table. She felt his arms around her, a hand patting her back, the sort of comfort you would give a child.

'I have enjoyed our day together more than any day for a long time...'

'Really?' she asked, looking up at him.

'Really,' he assured her with a smile that didn't look nearly as innocent as his gentle embrace. She allowed herself a second of looking deep into his eyes. It felt a bit like staring at a diamond-encrusted necklace in a window on Old Bond Street, knowing you will never be able to afford it, but imagining it around your neck anyway for just a few precious moments.

'Well, I must get going,' she said.

'Why don't you stay? It's a long way back and it's dark.'

Raphael's eyes, staring into her soul.

Could this be viewed as an exception to her rule about married men, she wondered? On the grounds that she was never going to see him again? He'd made it clear that participation in one of her professional events was a non-starter. And she wouldn't be returning to this part of Italy because of the memories, and there was really too much seismic activity to properly relax.

With such a smooth approach to seduction, it couldn't be the first time Enzo had betrayed Vittoria. And she'd had a shit week, so why deny herself one night of wild sex with no strings attached?

'You are lovely,' he said, dropping a tentative little kiss on one tear-stained cheek, then on the other, then on her forehead and the backs of each hand, as he murmured, '*Bellissima* Jessica, *simpaticcissima* Jessica . . .'

Her name had never sounded so pretty.

And so she allowed him to lead her up to his attic bedroom where the mural was of forested hills with a tiny town in the distance, pink in the setting sun, with domes and turrets, that could have been Urbino, or some other fairy-tale palace.

# Chapter Forty-Nine

## *Robin*

Robin stared out of the kitchen window at the total darkness outside. In space, no one could hear you scream, he thought. Halfway up a mountain, miles from anywhere, there was nothing to do but think.

'All this time! I mean, all this time,' he said, turning from the window to the dining table where Tim was nursing a glass of red wine.

'But you just said you'd always suspected George wasn't yours,' Tim said, wearily. They'd been over and over it ever since the kids had gone to bed and were still no closer to finding the answers he needed.

'You're missing the point! I assumed she'd had a fling and it was over. You can forgive one lie. But if you've been lied to constantly for thirteen years, it puts a different complexion on things. You thought you were living a life that you weren't. I just don't get why she would keep up the pretence all this time.'

'You were colluding in keeping up the pretence too,' Tim said.

'Why didn't she just leave me? What's so different now that she suddenly decides she has to be with George's father? Was it something I did?'

'You are George's father,' Tim said with a yawn.

'You don't understand!' Robin could hear his own voice rising. Keep it down, he told himself. The last thing he wanted to do was wake George up. 'Being a good dad is the one thing I'm proud of and I'm terrified I'll lose him!'

He'd pretended to be jolly all the way back in the car, even managed to cook spaghetti aglio e olio because they'd forgotten to shop. But the last few hours since the kids had gone to bed had been almost constant distress. He wondered how long Tim would put up with it. Perhaps he'd lose him, too.

'Do you think George knows?' he whispered. 'I mean, it must have been like looking in a mirror . . .'

'I honestly don't think he does,' said Tim. 'Maybe it isn't so obvious to him. Anyone our age just looks old.'

'But that guy isn't our age, is he?' Robin pointed out. 'I'd say early thirties, wouldn't you, with a head of hair like that?'

Tim drained his glass.

'Come to bed, Robin. There's no point in speculating about it any longer. You're driving yourself mad and you need to get some sleep. First thing tomorrow we'll go down to Laura's hotel and get some answers.'

'Good plan,' said Robin, adding almost immediately, 'What if she doesn't want to, though?'

'We won't tell her we're coming, so she won't have a choice,' said Tim.

'That sounds like an ambush. Perhaps we should wait until we get back to London.'

'How will that help? You really have to stop being afraid of confrontation, Robin.'

There was clearly going to be no getting out of it.

Feeling slightly calmer with a plan, Robin hobbled round the kitchen putting the dishwasher on and switching off the light.

'What did I ever do without you?' he whispered, as Tim helped him up the stairs.

'You never were without me,' Tim told him.

# Chapter Fifty

## *Jessica*

## Friday

When she woke up, her bare skin illuminated by sunshine flooding in through the skylight, every single cell in her body seemed to be dancing with joy, apart from her right leg where the blood supply had been cut off by the weight of Enzo's thigh on hers. She eased her leg out gently, not wanting to wake him. Looking up at the cloudless azure sky, the phrase 'died and gone to heaven' crossed her mind.

How could you die of a surfeit when passion made you feel so alive? Sex with Enzo felt as if their bodies were engineered to fit together perfectly. Bizarrely, she found herself thinking of those steam engines you sometimes saw at the beginning of black-and-white movies, starting slowly, pistons sliding in and out, picking up speed until puff puff, puff puff, the energy generated found its only escape in the scream of the whistle. She'd never recognised the subliminal messaging before. No wonder *Brief Encounter* had been such a hit in the forties.

In her experience, very few men were concerned about a woman's pleasure on one-night stands, except the older ones who billed themselves as feminists, spent ages feeling around for your clitoris, then expected you to work magic on their erectile dysfunction. Not that you always wanted the intimacy that came with orgasm. There'd been times where she'd lain thinking, let's just get it over with; occasionally she'd heard herself saying it out loud. There was always a place for a quick, honest fuck, someone saying you were dirty and meaning it as a compliment. She'd had to be more careful since the pandemic, especially with younger men who spent lockdown watching porn. Did any woman really get off on being choked? The one time it had happened to her, she didn't think he'd have heard the safe word anyway, because he hadn't heard *no*. Fortunately, there'd been a pair of nail scissors within reach.

'I thought you said pain was a turn-on?' she'd said, as he'd hopped around the room clutching his punctured buttock.

Nothing like that with Enzo, who seemed to know exactly when to be gentle and when to be forceful. Now gazing down at his long lashes, she remembered him saying, 'You are beautiful, Jessica, inside and out.'

It was such a nice compliment, it didn't matter if he'd said it a thousand times before. Even if he was the Casanova of Città di Castello, he'd given her such intense pleasure she'd only just managed to stop herself yelling out. Perhaps that was why they called it 'making love', she suddenly thought; short for 'making you say I love you'. She'd always found the term at bit coy before.

'What's the best sex you've ever had?' wasn't one of the conversations Robin had ever wanted to engage with. She and Mandy used to, before Mandy married Keith and became a loyal wife.

From now on, Jessica's answer would forever be October 2022, Umbria, Italy. Guy who looked like Raphael and turned sex into an art form.

Or perhaps she'd just keep it to herself, like a gift of expensive chocolates she didn't want to share with anyone else.

A lock of his shiny black hair had fallen over his mouth.

It blew up and down every time he exhaled. She smoothed it back, not wanting him accidentally to take a mouthful. His face puckered into a frown, and his hand automatically brushed her finger away as if a fly had landed on him, then he opened his eyes. There was the slightest change in the dilation of his pupils as he questioned, then remembered, who she was.

'*Buon giorno*,' he said, then kissed her.

God, he was gorgeous! Tanned muscles so perfectly sculpted they looked as if they'd feel firm to the touch but instead were pliant and warm and smelt of the light citrus fragrance of his soap, overlaid with the heady musk of sex. During the night, just before orgasm obliterated every other sensation, she had forced herself to acknowledge the sight of his beautiful face smiling up at her, the slick, rhythmical sound of their bodies, the smell of his skin, the feeling of him inside her, hoping to imprint all the glorious sensations of that moment, like the sexual version of mindfulness.

She thought she'd never go there again, but why not just one more time? There was no logic in denying herself at this point.

Afterwards, he got up, made her tea as requested. A properly amber cup of English Breakfast instead of the usual Italian offering of lukewarm water and a tea bag that never got past beige.

'You can tell you've lived in England!' she said, appreciatively, sitting up to drink it. As he stared at her breasts, she felt herself blushing with odd modesty given everything they'd just done. She pulled up the white cotton sheet to cover herself.

'Do you know you look a lot like *La Fornarina*?' he said.

'You're the second person who's said that,' she said, adding quickly when he looked surprised, 'He hadn't seen my tits, though.'

'I would like to try to paint you,' said Enzo.

Turns out I am an oil painting, she might tell Mandy.

'I bet you say that to all the girls!'

'What girls?' he said, all innocence.

On the floor beside the bed, his mobile phone buzzed. He leant over to pick it up. Smiled. Showed her the photo of Gaia next to a giant golden Lindt bear.

'They are on their way home now,' he said.

'Is there time to give me a lift back?' she said, getting up immediately and wrapping the sheet around her.

'Do you have to go so soon?'

'Look, Enzo, you don't have to do all this romantic Latin lover stuff. Despite all indications to the contrary, I am a grown-up. I know how this works.'

'I don't understand.'

'Listen, we had a great shag. Now I have to get back to pack.'

'It means nothing when I say yesterday made me happier than I am for a long time?'

'It's really sweet, and don't get me wrong, I feel like I won the lottery, to be honest, but I need to get going . . .'

'Are you sure?'

This was getting a bit silly now.

'Enzo, your wife is on her way home!'

He frowned. Looked away.

'Unfortunately not.'

'Vittoria?'

'You thought Vittoria was my wife?' he laughed. 'Vittoria is my sister. This is the reason Gaia and I came back to Italy. For family . . . and to mend our hearts. My wife died. It's four years now. Gaia had just one year with her.'

'Oh my god, I am so sorry.'

'A brain aneurysm.'

'Oh my god! I had no idea.'

The silence felt interminable as she searched for things to say, rejecting all of them as crass or overfamiliar.

'You are the first woman . . . since four years.'

'Really?'

She didn't know what to do with that information. Was it true? Was he testing out whether it still worked? Was it because he knew there was no danger of seeing her again?

'So you thought I was married, eh?' He gave her a mischievous smile. 'You thought I was the sort of man who . . . ?'

He didn't need to add, 'And you're the sort of woman who . . . ?'

Because it was apparent in the gleam of his eyes.

'I've had a shit week,' she said.

Strangely, putting clothes on in front of him felt more wanton than taking them off, so she fled downstairs to the bathroom and stared at herself in the mirror, her face framed by an arch of a wisteria-covered pergola on the wall behind her. The one time in her whole life she hadn't even started to dream of a fantasy future, because she'd been sure he was married. He wasn't, yet she'd still managed to ruin everything by breaking her own rule.

# Chapter Fifty-One

## *Laura*

A frost had fallen over the hills, making the fields and forests look as if they'd been dusted with icing sugar. The leafless skeletons of the trees overhanging the road were laced with droplets of dew that sparkled in the bright morning sunshine like tiny jewels. As the car climbed up through the valley, her ears began to pop. She wondered if it snowed here in winter. It was difficult to imagine the landscape with all its contrasts of green and gold hidden beneath a blanket of whiteness. Goodness knows how you'd ever get up to the house on these roads in icy conditions.

As they turned into the driveway, their red Fiat almost smashed head-on into the SUV. Both vehicles just managed to stop in time and for a moment, it felt like a stand-off, until Tim put the SUV into reverse and backed up the drive and they followed.

Laura got out, took a deep breath of the thin, chill morning air.

'Robin, this is Alex. Alex, Robin and Tim.'

All the men shook hands politely.

'Shall we talk outside?' Robin asked. 'It's a bit nippy, but we can get some blankets?'

He knew how much it had taken for her to come back to a house with a mouse.

'We could light a fire in the firepit,' said Tim.

'I'll help you,' said Alex, immediately, leaving them alone.

'So, where do we begin?' Robin asked, as they walked round the perimeter of the lawn.

No gardener today. She was glad not to have any distractions as Robin listened, allowing her the space to explain without interrupting or trying to make jokes. She felt such shame, the only way she could do it was by looking straight ahead, giving the facts in strict chronological order.

'I never expected to see him again,' she said. 'But then he applied for a job. If it had been up to me, I wouldn't have employed him. You have to believe that.'

Finally, she turned to face Robin. He was smiling.

'Well, that's a relief! It's sort of what I thought all along.'

'You never said anything . . .'

'Would you have preferred it if I had?'

The question took her by surprise, but the answer was immediately clear to her.

'No, I wouldn't,' she said.

'Isn't that how good marriages work?' Robin said. 'You're prepared to overlook the occasional thing, make a few sacrifices, because on the whole it's much nicer to be a family than on your own?'

There was something so beautifully innocent about him. She didn't think she'd ever loved her husband more than she did at that moment.

'But I couldn't bear to think you'd been leading a secret double life all those years,' he said.

'Nor I you,' she said.

'I'm not that good an actor.'

'I'm not that good an actress.'

They spoke simultaneously, then laughed. You developed a private language with someone you'd known for so long, with little references to a shared past and catchphrases that no one else really understood. She didn't have that with Alex. Not yet. She thought it was one of the many things she would miss.

'So now we have to talk about how we're going to approach this with George,' Robin said. 'Have we got to tell him today? I mean, it's the last day of the holiday.'

'I think we do,' she said reluctantly. 'Because if it is so apparent to all of us, it will be to Ellis, and it just wouldn't be fair for him to find out from anyone else . . .'

'I'm scared,' Robin blurted.

'What do you have to be scared of? I'm the one he'll hate.'

'Why wouldn't George want a younger father who plays keyboards in the world's biggest stadiums?'

'Oh Robin . . . because he loves you. You're his dad.'

'Yesterday I was. Now he's got three!'

She was absolutely certain that George wouldn't reject Robin, but the only proof was going to be by showing him.

'Let's go and wake him up together.'

Her legs were wobbly with fear as she stepped through the front door into the hall. She wasn't sure whether her terror was more about seeing a mouse, or Ellis, or George, but she knew she had to overcome it. Robin reached for her hand, she thought to reassure himself as much as her.

'It's George,' he said, with a nervous laugh. 'What's the worst that can happen?'

The room had a slight whiff of adolescence and there were a few moustache-y hairs sprouting around George's top lip. Thankfully, no spots yet. They stood on either side of the single bed, reluctant to wake him. Why did people look younger when they were asleep, Laura wondered? Probably because unconsciousness made them so vulnerable. As she touched him gently on the shoulder, it was heartbreaking to see the innocently delighted smile he gave them both on waking.

'Mum? Dad?'

'We need to talk to you.'

'What are you even doing here, Mum?' George asked, rubbing his eyes.

'There's something important we need to discuss. Just the three of us.'

It felt very similar to the day they'd decided it was time to tell him the facts of life.

George drew his knees up so they could both sit at the end of the bed. 'Discuss away,' he said.

'First of all, you need to know that we both love you very, very much . . .' she said.

'Now you're worrying me.' The alarm on her son's face almost made her lose her nerve. She felt Robin tense up beside her.

'George, you remember Alex, from yesterday?' Laura began.

'Obviously.'

Her heart was racing as she rattled through once more the facts of his conception, with no elaboration nor excuses. When she was done, the silence seemed interminable, until George finally looked at Robin.

'But you're still my real dad, right?'

Robin couldn't stop the emotion rushing out of him in a joyful scream. 'YESSS!' He practically smothered George in a hug.

'Jesus, Dad!'

How had the two of them ever managed to raise such a sensible person?

'So can the two of you clear off so I can get dressed?' George said.

It was only a month or two since George had suddenly stopped allowing anyone into the bathroom when he was

333

showering. She assumed it was because he'd started growing pubic hair. Her boy was growing up. It was unrealistic to think that they would get through his teenage years without a lot of angst. But it was a good start, and that was so much better than she had dared to hope for.

Robin gave her hand another quick squeeze before letting go as they rounded the side of the house, where Alex and Tim had managed to get a fire blazing in the firepit. They had been joined by Ellis and Jaz. As usual, Jaz was looking at her mobile phone while Ellis was talking to Alex.

'So how did you guys meet?' Ellis sounded friendly and relaxed. Perhaps they had grown up more than Laura had given them credit for. Perhaps everything wasn't as precarious as she had imagined. Was it possible that they could become a blended family, which was the preferred term now for a broken home?

'We teach at the same school,' Alex replied.

Ellis raised their eyebrows, turned to stare at Laura.

'Wow, Mum, doesn't that constitute workplace sexual harassment?'

The annoying thing was that they were probably right, if Alex had wanted to make a case, although of course he didn't. Laura had no response.

'Give your mother a break, Ellis,' Robin said, sitting down next to Tim, leaving Laura the only one standing. Always the outsider, she thought.

Ellis, momentarily silenced by his unexpected intervention, regrouped and took the opportunity to deliver their coup de grace.

'Just so you all know, Jaz is making a film about this week...'

'Really?' said Robin, instantly sitting up straight, showing his best profile to Jaz, as if he was only now aware of her constant filming.

'There are numerous data protection laws against that,' Laura said.

'This is research to write a script. We'll get real actors, for fuck's sake,' said Ellis.

'I'm going to call it *The Birthday Party*,' Jaz announced. It was the first thing Laura could remember her saying all week.

'I believe Pinter got there before you,' said Robin, clearly slighted by the implication he wasn't a real actor. 'From what I remember, it's rather a surreal piece with extremely unpleasant characters...'

'And your point is?' said Ellis.

They were only doing it to annoy her, Laura thought. And the more she failed to engage, the more Ellis would up the stakes. Maybe one day it would be possible for them to be a blended family, but not yet.

She glanced at her watch as if she had an appointment to go to. It was only eleven o'clock in the morning, but she felt exhausted, as if she'd already lived a whole life in a day.

'We'd better be going,' she said.

As they walked to the car she could hear Robin saying, 'Pity we haven't got any marshmallows, or chestnuts for the vegans...'

And everyone laughing.

For a moment, she wanted to go back and be with them. They were the only security she had ever known, but it was too late.

'Sorry about Ellis,' she said to Alex, as he started the car.

'If they were one of your sixth formers, you'd think them smart and funny,' Alex said. 'They certainly know how to push your buttons.'

Laura stared out of the window at the beautiful view for the last time, with no better idea of how her life was going to be now than she'd had a week ago.

# Chapter Fifty-Two

## Jessica

'Born to be wild!' Jessica said, as the little girl scooted off down the street. Vittoria had dropped her back early, leaving no time for Enzo to run Jessica back up to the house. They walked to a little patch of park just inside the city walls where there was a swing and took it in turns to push. Then Jessica scratched out a hopscotch grid as best she could in the dry earth, selected two stones from the gravel and taught Gaia how to play. With each gust of breeze, there was a fall of golden leaves from the big trees above, which she couldn't resist leaping to try to catch. Gaia followed suit, both of them grabbing and jumping, as Enzo sat on a stone bench laughing at them before reaching up himself to calmly remove one that had fallen onto his head and present it to his daughter.

'She'll be lucky now,' Jessica told him.

He explained to the little girl. She asked a question. He laughed, shook his head.

'She asks if that means she can have a dog,' he said, as they ambled back. 'But we have to wait until we have a real garden.'

As he made lunch, Gaia introduced Jessica to all her soft toys, most of which were dogs in all shapes and sizes. The black one on the bed, who looked a little bit like Lammie, was cuddled so much that the weave of the fabric was showing through the worn fur.

The sauce he made for their pasta was just a few fried courgettes with a squeeze of lemon, tossed with some al dente spaghetti and sprinkled with ready-grated Parmesan from the tub. It had taken approximately ten minutes, which was less than the time involved in getting a sandwich from Waitrose on the Holloway Road, Jessica thought. And a good deal cheaper. She was going to be more Italian when she got back, she promised herself. Make wholesome lunches, whizz around London on a motorbike, live each day well, because even though London wasn't an earthquake zone, you never knew what was round the corner. A brain aneurysm, for heaven's sake.

After clearing the table, she helped him wash up, finding it curiously intimate standing beside him at the deep rectangular sink with Gaia behind them, drawing a picture of the chocolate festival with the jar of crayons kept permanently on the table.

'She's inherited your talent,' Jessica said, as Gaia showed them the picture that was recognisably a market stall with oversize chocolates piled one on top of the other and three adults standing in a row beside a little girl.

'*Chi sono?*' he asked. 'Who are they?'

'*Io,*' she pointed at the child then put her finger on each of the bigger people in turn. 'Vittoria, Papa *e* Jessica.'

Jessica was so touched she was unable to look up, not knowing whether to be flattered or embarrassed at being included in his family.

'Let's get you back,' he said. 'Gaia can have her afternoon nap in the car.'

They walked through the now empty streets to where the battered old Fiat Panda he shared with Vittoria was parked.

The route they were taking wasn't the one she was familiar with. When the car started climbing up a steep, winding road, she suddenly realised that they were going up the mountain on the other side of the valley, to the tiny hilltop town with the bell tower you could see from the lawn of the party house. Gaia had fallen asleep in her child's seat. Just outside the town, Enzo pulled over next to a dilapidated-looking farmhouse.

'Come! I want to show you something,' he said, producing an ancient key from the pocket of his jeans.

The interior was much bigger than it looked from the outside. Due to the slope of the hillside, there were two further levels below the single storey you could see from the road. In the high-ceilinged hall at road level there was an old fireplace, and another one in what must have been the kitchen below. The rooms had been gutted and stripped back to bare stone walls and floor. Enzo helped her down a ladder to the cellar, where the outside wall had been opened up and the structure was currently supported by scaffolding.

'This is where the animals lived, but we will put in glass doors before winter . . .'

The view was spectacular.

'You are going to live here?'

'This is the plan.'

He took her hand as they picked their way along a broken path edged with straggly lavender and rose bushes speckled with bright red hips. The plot gave on to steeply sloping terraces, so it felt almost like an infinity garden stretching into the breathtaking panorama. Far away on a distant hill, she thought she could just make out the party house.

There was a terrace with fruit trees, the remains of a crop of pears still hanging from gnarled, twisting branches and beneath that a patch of scrubby grass and a stone barn with no roof.

'The land is suitable only for goats, I think,' Enzo smiled.

'Perhaps a dog,' she said, remembering his promise to Gaia.

He smiled at her.

'What do you think?'

'*Bellissima!*' she said.

'It will be a lot of work,' he said.

'It certainly will,' she said.

'But I think we will be happy here. For the outbuilding,' he waved at the barn. 'You have given me an idea. Maybe a studio. For events?'

'It would be perfect,' she said, thinking painting, or maybe ceramics. Who didn't want to get messy with clay after *The Great Pottery Throw Down*? Maybe she would be coming back to Umbria, after all. Maybe one day in the future she might return to Umbria after all?

'Maybe you could help with the design, so I know exactly what is required?' he asked.

'Definitely. I'll give you my email.'

'Do you have to leave so soon?'

She peeled her eyes from the view and stared at him as he took both her hands, then brought one to his lips and kissed it.

'You've had a shit week,' he said.

She loved how he listened to her, repeating her phrases with his Italian accent that made the words somehow softer and funnier.

'I have to get back for work.'

'Do you have events you have to be at?'

'Not right this minute, but . . .'

'We have Wi-Fi in Italy.'

'But I have loans to pay off, a mortgage.'

'Jessica,' he said, kissing the palm of her other hand. 'You are the first woman I have been attracted to since my wife, and you make me feel good and I think I make you feel good too? This is rare . . .'

'But I hardly know you! And you hardly know me.'

'So we can discover each other.'

She sighed.

'Thing is, all you'd discover is that I'm not just a good time. I've got hidden drainy depths of neurosis. Honestly, I'm crazy, desperate, just too much.' She reeled off some of the excuses past dates had given her. 'There are times when I'm a total fun sponge.'

He shrugged. 'I know this.'

Fair enough, she'd been in tears at least half the time they'd spent together.

Renovate an authentic Italian farmhouse with a bloke who looks like Raphael and knows how to install an RSJ and bifold doors? It sounded like an episode of *A New Life in the Sun*, which had been a bit of a lockdown addiction. She looked at the view again.

How different her life would be here. The simple pleasures of fresh air and sunshine, wafts of lavender on the breeze, the constantly blue sky. She'd never been to Italy when it rained. It must do, but she thought probably brief, intense showers, not the endless rainy days in London where you looked through the water flooding down your window and felt you couldn't go out because you weren't an amphibian. Delicious pasta lunches. A dear little child to do crafting with. Evenings sitting beside an open fireplace. Wondrous fucking followed by deep sleep after all the manual labour. No traffic noise to wake you up.

She didn't think it would really suit her. She'd always been a city girl. And from her experience of taking Mandy's kids to petting farms, goats stank and you had to be really careful about E. coli. In real life, Enzo was way out of her league. You couldn't base a relationship entirely on sex, and she wasn't sure she'd ever feel comfortable around a dog.

She heard herself saying, 'Sorry, Enzo, I'm not that much of a fantasist.'

# Chapter Fifty-Three

## *Robin*

'I'm hungry,' said George.

They'd eaten all the food in the house, including an entire tin of amaretti biscuits. Robin had shown them how to make tubes from the paper wrappers and light them so that they floated up into the sky like miniature Chinese lanterns. The sun had dropped beyond the mountain on the other side of the valley, and the light was now almost gone.

There was nothing left on the shelves apart from some pasta, but spaghetti aglio e olio seemed like a dull option for the second evening in a row, especially on their last night.

'Whatever happened to the truffles?' Robin asked.

'I think Crispin and Piers made off with them,' said Tim.

'They'll be swallowing their condoms round about now then,' said George.

'What?' Ellis asked.

'You had to be there,' said George, winking at Robin.

If anything, he felt closer to his son than before, as if George had made a choice, rather than just putting up with him. Although who knew how long that would last?

Alex seemed like a decent enough chap. He believed passionately in the power of education to change people's lives, so really he and Laura were ideally suited. Robin couldn't picture him in a band, although it did explain his hair. Mick Jagger, Keith Richards, Jon Bon Jovi, they all had exceptional hair for their age, despite all the drugs and alcohol. George wouldn't be inheriting male pattern baldness from him anyway, which was a good thing because it could really blight your life, whatever anyone said about it being sexy. Alex seemed a bit worthy and woke to have been a rock star, but not when you remembered Brian May's obsession with badgers.

'Why don't I drive down and get us a takeaway?' Tim suggested.

There was a general chorus of approval.

'What would you most like on your final evening?' Robin asked.

'McDonald's,' George said.

'We're in Italy!'

'You asked.'

'I doubt there even is one,' Robin said.

'There is. Tim took us there on the way back from the hospital. There's plant-based for Ellis . . .'

'OK with you, Ellis?'

'Fine by us.'

'Well, if that's really what you want . . .' He was going to have to speak to Tim about getting five a day but now wasn't the time. 'I'll have a Big Mac with large fries and whatever McFlurry they've got . . .'

It seemed almost sacrilegious in the land of gelato, but there was something about a McFlurry.

Robin watched them all piling into the SUV, enjoying the good-humoured way Ellis and George fought for the front seat as they'd always done. George won and turned on the sound system at top volume. There was a definite aura of happiness around them, he thought. Perhaps relief that they were going back home. It hadn't been an especially fun holiday for anyone, although in years to come, there would be such good anecdotes to entertain dinner parties with if anyone suggested the worst holidays they'd ever had, they might eventually look back on it with affection.

As the SUV rolled down the drive with everyone waving, the vibe felt so different from when Laura had left a few hours before, staring straight ahead, not once looking back. People thought her cold, but they hadn't seen her in the throes of labour, or that time they'd had to rush Eliza to the hospital when she was two because she'd started fitting with a high temperature, or all the nights she had held Robin silently in her arms after encounters with his parents had left him an emotional wreck. Laura was incredibly good at keeping her own emotions out of things, Robin thought, but it didn't mean she didn't suffer. Probably more than any of them, in fact. He hoped Alex could make her happier than he had been able to.

The light had faded so rapidly that all he could now see was the little chain of lights leading up to the settlement with the bell tower in the far distance. Robin turned to hop back inside.

Some people enjoyed a sense of isolation, but he'd never seen the attraction of being away from it all. He much preferred being right at the centre of things. Parkland Walk from Finsbury Park to Highgate in the uncomplicated company of a dog was rural enough for him. He couldn't wait to see Lammie again.

# Chapter Fifty-Four

## *Jessica*

It was dark by the time they drew up at the bottom of the drive.

'Will you be OK?' Enzo asked.

'Of course,' she said.

'Got your keys?'

She pulled them out of the front pocket of her jeans.

'Leave them on the kitchen island when you go.'

'Yes.'

She was glad he wasn't coming to tend to the garden in the morning. Not before they'd left anyway. It was tricky enough knowing how to say goodbye now. She didn't want an audience watching them.

She glanced towards the back seat where Gaia was still asleep, then looked at him one last time. Raphael's face, staring out of the darkness as if he knew they would meet in five hundred years' time. Not such a parasocial relationship after all, she thought.

'It's been real,' she said, opening the door.

He smiled, clutched her hand and brought it to his lips for one last brief kiss.

She watched him turn the car round, salute and drive away.

The red blur of the back lights remained in her vision long after the sound of the car's engine had faded.

Turning towards the house, she noticed that there were no lights on in the windows and yet there was a peculiar orange glow around the outline, like the last embers of a sunset.

As she approached, she could hear laughter coming from the back of the building. A moment of satisfaction that they were getting some use out of the firepit snapped to high alert as she sensed that the crackle of the blaze and excited screeching were somehow too loud. And the sun usually set in exactly the opposite direction.

Running round the side of the building, the air was thick with smoke from the burning bushes around the seating area. She could hear Tim shouting.

'Get some water!'

'Where from?'

'The bloody pool!'

'The cover's on!'

'The pool house is locked!'

With the keys still in one hand and covering her face with the other, Jessica dashed to open the pool house door, switched on the outside light, shoved the wheel of hosepipe at Ellis and pointed to the tap on the side of the building. As Jessica tried to lift the fire extinguisher, George was there to take it from her, running it towards the blaze and letting it off like a trained professional. He'd always wanted to be a fireman when he was little, she remembered. In just a few seconds, the fire was out, but the air was still thick with smoke.

The others piled in on her like footballers after a match-winning penalty, except Jaz, whom Jessica noticed had been coolly filming throughout.

Under the bright white light, and with the smoke dispersing, the firepit now looked like a crater where a small bomb had landed, the shrubs around it blackened skeletons. Everyone retreated inside, leaving her to check there were no embers lurking beneath the mess of fire extinguisher foam. She got a black bin liner from the kitchen and collected up the debris. Did they just not care about leaving the place like this, or were they all so entitled they expected someone else would take care of it? Perhaps Tim and Robin were drunk, she thought, picking up a second empty wine bottle and the litter of McDonald's boxes and amaretti wrappers, some charred, others chucked in the vague direction of the firepit ready to catch and float towards the tinder-dry vegetation.

'Coco!' Robin shouted, as she came back into the kitchen. 'What would we do without you?'

'Where have you been?' Ellis asked.

'We were worried about you,' Robin said.

'Were you?'

She hadn't received a text or call from any of them. They had all been so involved in their own dramas, including almost burning the house down. Presumably the owners had insurance for fire? What would have happened if she hadn't turned up when she did?

'Who's up for charades?' said Robin.

'I'm going to leave you to it,' she heard herself saying. 'Early start...'

# Chapter Fifty-Five

## Jessica

## Saturday

For just a moment, waking up in a single bed, Jessica mistook it for her childhood bedroom, where she could always tell what time it was at night from the noises outside. The shouts and laughter of drunken clubbers in the early hours; the grind and bump of the bin lorry at dawn, as she lay perfectly still until the rhythm of traffic on Aldwych at the bottom of the road was loud enough for her to know that rush hour was beginning. Only then would she tiptoe into the other room, not knowing how many people she would find sleeping there. The day always got off to a good start when it was just Mum, especially if she woke up with a happy face, wanting to share the tea and toast that Jessica made for their breakfast and asking, 'So what's the story for today?'

Jessica lay with the covers pulled right up to her chin, exposing only the tip of her nose to the chill of dawn. What would Mum think of the life she had made for herself? She'd always told her to work hard at school because with a good education she'd never have to rely on anyone. She thought Mum would be proud of the career she'd built. She was good at her job. She was independent. Covid had made things difficult, but business was coming back and she was paying off the loans she'd had to take out. It was a struggle, but she was confident now that she'd cope. Her watch said six o'clock. Time to get up. Jessica drew back the curtains, but could see absolutely nothing. For a moment, she wondered if there had been some sort of natural disaster obliterating the world during the night, then realised that they were in a cloud. At this altitude it wasn't surprising. It showed how lucky they'd been with the weather. Would things have rolled out differently if there had been rain instead of sunshine, or fog blotting out the view? It was a useful reminder that a beautiful house on top of a mountain could be less than idyllic.

She decided to have a last swim in the pool. The water was already colder because she'd turned the heater off last night as requested by Enzo. It was probably good practice for the wild swimming in the reservoir she was definitely going to investigate when she got back, although possibly autumn going into winter might not be the best time of year to start.

The sun was beginning to burn off the mist as she got out, but the outline of the little village with the bell tower was still so ghostly, she wasn't sure whether she was imagining it.

Enzo's face waking up. That was the image she would treasure because it was just hers, imprinted in her mind and unshareable. He was just so gorgeous. Of all the lessons learned this week, the most important would not go in her feedback list. You could enjoy a fantasy fuck without worrying whether it was happily ever after.

She was quite looking forward to telling Mandy.

'Doesn't sound like you,' she could almost hear her friend saying.

'Maybe it's the new me? Maybe I've got a future as a lab rat after all!'

Now she wished she had taken a photo of him asleep, because Mandy would only think she was exaggerating.

In the pump room, she pushed the button to roll the cover back over the water, checked to see that the wheel of hose was tidily wound and the fire extinguisher back in its place. It might need replacing. She would text Vittoria, or possibly leave a note on the kitchen island. She didn't want a health and safety concern to be her last communication with Enzo. About to switch off the light, she imagined him arriving at the property later in the day. The first thing he would touch was the lawnmower. Kissing the tip of her forefinger, she pressed it against the handle.

Then she went inside to make sure they were all up and getting ready to leave.

Fortunately, despite all the potholes, both of the rental cars had survived undamaged, so there was no longer a stop on her credit card. Before walking the short distance to the terminal, Jessica paused to breathe in the atmosphere of Italy one last time. When they arrived, the air had still carried the gentle warmth of late summer. Now, the lingering catch of frost signalled winter was fast approaching. A slight haze still softened the outline of the distant mountains. On the other side of the valley, the sunshine was beginning to fall on a hill town she thought was Assisi, turning grey stone buildings to radiant white. No wonder this was a country where people believed in miracles.

As they waited for the flight to be called, all the original members of the party were spread out in little groups like passengers in a tube compartment during Covid, keeping as far away as geometrically possible from each other. She noticed that Jaz was filming them with Ellis's arm draped around her shoulder, the only couple who were prepared to touch in public.

There was often a scene like this at the beginning of a movie,

Jessica thought. A collection of disparate people about to go on a journey that would seal their fates together. Or in this case, returning from one that had blown them apart.

Camilla and Cassandra had clearly overindulged on their last night, their make-up hastily applied over blotchy skin, lipstick bleeding a little.

'Fourth negroni never a good idea,' said Camilla.

'YOLO,' replied Cassandra dismally.

Crispin and Piers were creating a scene in the line for the small bar serving coffee. The brothers did not like queuing.

'Bloody ridiculous!' shouted Crispin.

'You'd think they'd want to make money!' said Piers.

'I'd like my cappuccino hot, if you don't mind.'

'Nothing worse than a lukewarm cappuccino!'

Barty was standing on his own watching George and Tim doing keepy-uppies with a tennis ball. For a moment, Jessica was minded to pity him. What chance did he have with a father like Piers? But any compassion she might have been about to feel vanished as the tennis ball ran past his foot and he kicked it away so viciously he could have blinded the toddler playing nearby if his aim hadn't been off.

Laura and her man were sitting next to one another but nobody would have known they were together. Alex had headphones on and his eyes were closed. Laura had a book open in front of her but Jessica was almost sure she wasn't reading the page she was staring at, only using it as a shield to ward off any approach.

Robin was sitting alone, crutches beside him. When he spotted her, his face lit up and he beckoned her over, but there were no seats near him, so she sat down on the floor where she was.

At the end of an event, she always did feedback to herself,

enumerating the pros and cons of the venue. On the whole, it was definitely somewhere she would recommend for an intimate house party, so she could justify putting her share of the trip against her business expenses. She started writing a list of things to remember for the future.

'You look busy!'

Robin was looking down at her.

'I am,' she said, quickly turning over her notebook because she didn't want him to see that she had written:

- *You are beautiful inside and out!*
- *Try to enjoy each day as if you live in an earthquake zone*

Normally, it was things like:

- *Washing-up sponges*
- *Adaptor plugs both ways*

'Darling Coco!' he said. 'Thanks for all the fun and frolics.'

'It didn't exactly go as planned,' she said.

The secret to a successful event was being able to adapt to problems and find solutions. So in that sense, the party with the theme Life Begins had been a triumph for almost everyone involved. She had her doubts about whether the current status quo would survive once they all returned to real life, but that wasn't her issue now.

'At least no one died!' Robin said.

A week ago, she would have laughed.

The slightly awkward impasse was interrupted by a tannoy announcement advising that Passport Control was now open, and everyone merged to start forming a line.

At the front, Crispin spluttered out a mouthful of coffee.

'Bloody hell, I didn't mean scorching! They bloody did that deliberately!'

'And I bet they won't let us take these through security now!' said Piers.

If he was looking for sympathy, it was in scant supply among their yawning fellow passengers.

'Tossers!' said the man in front of Jessica.

Jessica had spent twenty years trying to impress Robin's awful brothers because she knew how important they were to him. Yet a complete stranger could see in one second exactly what they were. Tossers.

The others in the party fell in behind her.

'Have you all got your passports?' she asked.

A quick search showed that Robin hadn't forgotten his as he feared, because Laura still had it in her handbag. Everyone dutifully held out their documents for Jessica to check as if she were a preliminary border control.

As she handed them back, she heard herself saying, 'Do you think you guys can manage to get on the plane on your own?'

'What do you mean?' Robin asked.

'I've decided to stay a while longer.'

'How long?'

'I don't know.'

'But what about our Friday nights?'

Did they really do that every week? Same food, same wine, same jokes? It was as much her fault as his.

'I've no idea how long I'll be here.'

Once you got the hang of not trying to please with every response, it became easier.

They were all staring at her as if she was about to deliver a punchline.

'It's a great idea, Jessica,' Ellis finally said. 'Jaz and I both think you should get a life.'

'Ellis!' Laura reprimanded.

Jessica laughed. 'It's fine, because it's true. Ellis and Jaz are the only ones who've been honest all along.'

'And me,' said George.

What did he think about it all, Jessica wondered? He was a lovely boy, but wasn't it a bit much to expect him to develop a relationship with two additional fathers at an age when most teenagers started resenting the parents they already had?

'And you, George!'

Jessica gathered both of them into a tight hug, then, aware of impatience building in the queue behind them, kissed their cheeks and walked away without looking back.

The bus to Perugia was leaving in half an hour. Hopefully it would be easy enough to find somewhere to stay now that the chocolate festival was over. It was a shame to have missed it – not that she had a particularly sweet tooth. She thought it might be a city she could fall in love with. A medieval fortress on the top of a mountain, a fascinating history dating all the way back to Etruscan times. The main street was named after its most famous artist, Vannucci, more commonly known as Perugino, who had been a major influence on Raphael. As well as the famous fountain with all its unique bas-reliefs, there was a recently restored gallery with a comprehensive collection of local art and window seats with views all over Umbria.

Sitting down on a bench, Jessica took out her notebook and started adding to her list.

- *Find someone who listens to you and isn't afraid to have a serious conversation about art. Or anything, really*
- *Don't always start planning a future*
- *Take things one day at a time*

Her phone buzzed with a message as the engines started up and the plane began to taxi to the runway. A text from Robin.

*Guess what, Coco? The agent who approached Laura has just given me her card! Apparently there's a demand for middle-aged men with hints of a misspent youth but who look comfortable in their skin. Crutches could actually work to my advantage. Who knew? Maybe life really does begin at 40 (42)?*

She found herself automatically typing *That's brilliant, congratulations!*, then deleted it, sending instead just a smiley face emoji.

A blast of horn. The ancient white Fiat Panda rolled up in front of her.

'That was quick!' she said, as Enzo leant across to open the passenger door for her.

'We were already here in the car park. Gaia wanted to wave goodbye to the plane.'

'I forgot to put the keys on the island,' Jessica said, handing them to him.

'You missed your flight for this?'

'There's one every morning,' she said. 'Anyway, I was thinking about staying another day. Or maybe two . . .'

Enzo waited until she had fastened her seat belt before turning out onto the main road. The sky was now as lucid a blue as the backdrop to the altarpiece Raphael had created for the church of San Domenico in Città di Castello, which she had gazed at in the National Gallery throughout her life. A single golden leaf fluttered across the windscreen, catching for just a moment, before dancing away.

Glancing sideways, she saw that Enzo was smiling.

'*Jessica sta tornando a casa?*' Gaia's voice chimed through the contented silence.

'She asks if you are coming home with us,' Enzo's shining dark eyes held hers for just a second as she turned to clasp the little girl's outstretched hand.

'*Si!*'

# Acknowledgements

Thank you, Sam Eades, for your insight, skill and enthusiasm. Thank you, Mark, Benedict and everyone at The Soho Agency as well as Nicki, Jenny, Katherine, Jack and everyone at ILA for supporting and promoting my writing.

Thank you, Connor and Becky, for making my life happy.

# Credits

Kate Eberlen and Orion Fiction would like to thank everyone at Orion who worked on the publication of *Life Begins* in the UK.

**Editorial**
Sam Eades

**Copy editor**
Jenny Page

**Proof reader**
Alex Davis

**Audio**
Paul Stark
Louise Richardson

**Editorial Management**
Anshuman Yadav
Charlie Panayiotou
Jane Hughes
Bartley Shaw
Lucy Bilton

**Contracts**
Dan Herron
Ellie Bowker
Oliver Chacón

**Design**
Charlotte Abrams-Simpson
Nick Shah
Deborah Francois
Helen Ewing

**Finance**
Jasdip Nandra
Nick Gibson
Sue Baker
Tom Costello

**Publicity**
Sarah Lundy

**Marketing**
Louis Patel
Katie Moss

**Production**
Ruth Sharvell
Fiona McIntosh

**Rights**
Rebecca Folland
Tara Hiatt
Ben Fowler
Alice Cottrell
Ruth Blakemore
Marie Henckel

**Sales**
Catherine Worsley
Dave Murphy
Esther Waters
Victoria Laws
Group Sales teams across
Digital, Field, International
and Non-Trade

**Operations**
Group Sales Operations team